DRUID MAGIC

Dunskey Castle 1-3

JANE STAIN

janestain.com

Also published in separate volumes:

Tavish
A time Travel Romance
Dunskey Castle 1

Seumas
A time Travel Romance
Dunskey Castle 2

Tomas
A time Travel Romance
Dunskey Castle 3

To Mom

Thank you for sending me Outlander in 1997.

It made an impression!

TAVISH

꧁ I ꧂

AON (1 IN GAELIC)

Kelsey examined a beaten silver necklace, holding her phone close so Sasha could see. "Yes, this interlace pattern is at least a thousand years old, probably older, judging by these animal designs woven in along here. Sec, let me zoom in. See?"

"Wow. It does look like it. Have you done the chem bath yet?"

"No, I'm just about to. Here, you can watch."

Kelsey could barely contain her excitement, even as her nose stung from the acrid smell of the chemical tests that would give the necklace's age within a hundred years. Her foot bounced impatiently while she let the university's automatic computerized microscope do its thing and she admired her surroundings outside the canvas flap door of the work tent.

The ruined tower house sat on one of Scotland's high craggy sea cliffs, with a view over the ocean of the distant green hills of Ireland. The fifteenth century stone house called Dunskey Castle had been built over the ruins of a much older fortification, rumored to be an underground palace chipped out of the very rock, with secret passageways right down to the sea. Her grey-haired client had recently won a court battle to come into ownership of it all, after his family had all but abandoned it five hundred years ago.

Even as much as the work excited her, she itched to get done so the client could take her on the tour he had promised. He had flown her all the way from the U.S. to examine some artifacts he had found in chests in one of the three previously sealed and secret cellars.

Well, now she would tell him he had a trove of antiques—and he would give her a big payment!

Her eyes drifted back to her laptop, and she paused them there, analyzing what she saw and searching for an explanation. Her training kicked in, telling her to collaborate with the trained colleague that protocol had caused her to invite along, if only by phone.

"Are you sure you can't come by, Sasha? This necklace is odd. The patterns aren't matching up with any in the computer. It's still searching, but it's going slower and slower."

Sasha's redheaded face appeared in the corner of Kelsey's screen.

"No, I have to lecture this afternoon, sorry. But tomorrow's the weekend, maybe then. I just logged in so I could see. Fascinating. Maybe you'll catalogue an entire newfound strain of Celtic expression."

"Wouldn't that be something?"

Kelsey wanted to say more, but the boyfriend she

had loved and lost came bustling into the work tent, completely distracting her. And not only because he was bare chested.

Bronze haired and brown eyed like Kelsey, Tavish MacGregor had been a nosy construction worker at every last one of her Scottish clients' ruins these three months—after completely dropping out of her life seven years ago. No contact for seven years, no explanation, he was acting like nothing was wrong, and he always stubbornly wore that red and green plaid great kilt that made him so darn sexy she could just...

Oh no.

Kelsey sat up straight and smiled at her client, whom Tavish seemed to be dragging in on the hem of his kilt.

"I have to go, Sasha."

"Business?"

"Yeah, call you back tonight."

Typical. Tavish had wandered away from his own work and was looking at hers.

"'Tis na 'Celtic jewelry,'" he said to Mr. Blair. "Nay, it be not auld warld."

And he said this in his sexy accent that had drawn her to him in the first place. Not to mention those twinkling brown eyes that could see into her soul whenever they wanted. And those strong arms that had made her feel so loved and cherished, all those years ago. And his fighting prowess that had protected her a time or two...

Kelsey blinked herself back into the present and

turned to her client, to gauge his reaction to what Tavish had told him.

Mr. Blair looked skeptical, but patient.

"Hold on, nae. Let the doctor finish her appraisal, lad."

Ha, Lad. Good thing someone was around who could put Tavish in his place. She didn't trust herself to try—and besides, she was a professional woman now, not the teen she'd been when she and Tavish had been together.

She gave her client a patient conspiratorial smile, which he returned. This made her feel warm inside. He respected her expertise, unlike some people.

With the young virile man and the grey stooped man both watching, she finished her complicated high-tech tests on the necklace. Unwilling to believe what she saw and trying not to scowl, she tested a silver goblet next, and then an ornate bronze breastplate.

Finally, she had to admit that Tavish was right.

The items weren't old world at all.

How did the kilted fool know this stuff better than she did? He hadn't even gone to college, let alone researched a doctoral thesis on the meanings of ancient Celtic runes—like she and Sasha had.

"I'm sad to say Tavish is right, Mr. Blair. This is indeed imitation Celtic art from the twentieth century. It's well done and will probably bring five thousand pounds from fans of historical cosplay, but not the hundreds of thousands the Royal Museums would have given you for true antiques. I'm sorry."

Mr. Blair gave her a sad smile and his digital signature for her usual fee, not the huge bonus she had heard you could get from an overjoyed patron who had struck it big. As he handed her phone back to her and headed out of the tent, his eyes fell reverently on the ring Kelsey wore on her right hand.

Her ring from Celtic University.

Crafted in the same style as the items she appraised—and oddly shaped—this silver ring represented seven years of study in a highly niche discipline at the most prestigious university in that discipline—which only awarded three doctoral degrees every five years.

And she held one of them.

Had for three months now.

And Tavish had... what? That stupid kilt he wore all the time? His stupid Scots accent—which by the way he could drop anytime he wanted to and speak like a normal American? No, she knew exactly what he had.

"You've got some nerve, Tavish."

He raised an eyebrow.

"What nae?"

"Who do you think you are, coming in here and butting in on my business?"

As soon as she said it, she knew she sounded childish and wanted to take the words back, but it was too late for that, so she rocked back on one of her legs and crossed her arms, figuring she might as well entrench her position.

Infuriatingly, Tavish puffed out his chest, crossed his own arms, and gave her that smugly coy look which used to always make her kiss the smugness off of him.

"Yer business? I hae the duty of seeing this place restored correctly."

Ooh. He had so much nerve, she was going to—

But Tavish nodded to himself, and his gesture took in all of her equipment as well as the trinkets she was examining.

"It is ye, lass, who are in the way."

Seeing red, she closed her eyes so she wouldn't have to look at him and opened her mouth to tell him how rude he was being, how Mr. Blair himself had invited her here, and wasn't it up to the landowner to say who needed to be on his property or not?

But when she opened her eyes again, Tavish was halfway through the tent flap already. Once more, he'd just waltzed in on her doing business and made her look foolish. Had made what she did look so easy that even an uneducated construction worker could do it. She had to tell him he couldn't do that to her. She wouldn't take it.

But not in front of the client. Not where he could hear her. She looked around for Mr. Blair and found him on his phone out of earshot, outside. She could see him walking along the cliffs by the sea in the sunshine that had just broken through a small hole in the roiling Scottish storm clouds.

She turned to Tavish's disappearing form and yelled after the flapping hem of his kilt.

"It's not like I planted those trinkets in the man's basement for him to find, you know."

And then she blew her nose to hide the tears in her

eyes, in case someone came into the tent. While she stowed her handkerchief in the pocket of her blazer, she admired the soft light gray wool of her skirted suit, proud of how professional it was. She remembered fondly how her mother had tailor-made it and five more just for her —dark gray, dark brown, camel, navy blue, and olive green. She cheered herself up by recalling how much fun the two of them had, shopping for matching blouses and shoes. Professional, but still feminine and pretty.

How on Earth did Tavish know so much about Scottish artifacts? Why did he have to always show off like this whenever she was in Scotland? It was like he made it a point to be there, just to make her look bad.

Apparently, their relationship had meant more to her than it had to him.

Obviously.

Taking a deep breath and blinking her eyes while fanning them with her hands in order to dry them without smearing her makeup, she tried to look on the bright side.

Her career was solid outside of Scotland, away from Tavish. She had proven her parents wrong. They hadn't taken it well when she told them what major she was declaring—which was ironic, seeing how they were the ones who had gotten her involved with the Renaissance faire when she was little.

The faire had interested her in all things Celtic.

And the faire had introduced her to Tavish.

And then she'd chosen to major in Celtic Studies way back in her freshman year at college because of all the Celtic fun she and Tavish had made for themselves at the faire.

She fought to maintain her composure so as not to look a fool in front of her client when he came back into the tent, but she was getting lost in a sea of memories, triggered by his presence.

For her first few months at Celtic University, she had texted Tavish whenever something cool or unexpected happened. Had emailed him photos of her dorm room. Had kept calling him and leaving messages.

But then someone else had answered and told her she had the wrong number.

The same thing had happened when she called his parents.

Finally, she had taken the hint, given up, and thrown herself into her studies.

And now after seven years he had shown up at her job sites three times in three months—apparently just to make her clients doubt her abilities. Why? Why couldn't he just stay out of her life completely?

She smoothed imaginary wrinkles out of her skirt. She needed to have a word with him. In private. No one needed to know their business, least of all her client. But how—

Oh good, it looked like Mr. Blair was preparing to leave. Yep.

He came back into the tent and picked up his briefcase, then shook her hand and gave her a grateful smile.

"Doctor Ferguson, it's an honor to be doing business with you. It's a shame about those... supposed artifacts, but we have found a passageway to the sea through the old cellars. I yet hold out hope that we will find the underground Alba castle. If we find anything at all, I'll be calling you back here to help us look into it. You can count on that."

She gave him as firm a handshake as she could manage, and she returned his warm smile.

Mr. Blair turned his head toward where Tavish could be seen talking and laughing with the other construction workers and then turned back to her with a knowing look.

"Please tak yer time packing up all yer things, Doctor, and enjoy a look aroond if ye like. I've been called into toon for the rest o' the afternoon."

She stood up and opened her mouth to tell him it was okay, she would leave when he did.

But the elderly gentleman closed his eyes and gently shook his head no while holding up his hand and also waving no.

"There's a washroom that functions ower thare in my trailer, which is unlocked. Please sleep there this evening if it gets tae dark tae drive back into town. Nay trouble at all, and help yourself tae any o' the canned food. The men all hae their own trailers up the road."

This was just too much kindness. It made a tear escape and slide down her cheek. She brushed it away with the back of her index finger.

"Thank you so much, Mr. Blair. I may take you up on that offer. Thank you for the opportunity to see your lands and all that has come with them, and have a safe trip into town."

Mr. Blair nodded toward the outside.

Kelsey grabbed her purse and got up to follow him out.

She saw him to his car and waved as he drove off, and then she ran to his trailer to get ahold of herself.

It was tough at first, because this trailer reminded her of Tavish's family trailer at the faire, where among other things she had giggled over pancakes on Saturday and Sunday mornings with them.

She was really glad to have her purse and a functioning washroom. She washed her face and reapplied her makeup, then went back into the work tent by the castle to repack her equipment, glad to have something simple and easy to do while she figured out what to say to Tavish when she caught up to him.

Because she was going to ask him what the hell he was up to. And tell him to quit it. To either be nice, or leave her alone and stay out of her business.

But Tavish was already there when she got back to her stuff. And he had already repacked it for her. Her stuff. Her expensive professional instruments that he had no idea how to use or probably even what they were for.

Her mind whorled and a torrent of insults came to the tip of her tongue. But she bit it. She was a dignified professional appraiser, not some shrew who shrieked at a construction worker. Not where anyone could hear her.

"Well thank you, Tavish, for cleaning up. Now I have time to see the rest of the estate before it gets dark. Do you want to show me around?"

Good. This was a surprise to him, and he looked a

little off balance. But it was just for a moment, and then he recovered.

"Okay. Yeah. I'll just carry this stuff out to your car first so you'll be all ready to go, and then I'll give you a quick tour."

Why was he in such a hurry to get her out of here? Oh well. Let him think it would be a quick tour and then she'd be leaving.

"Thanks. If you can get those two heavy ones, I can get these other two."

The svelte muscles in his arms moved in fascinating ways as he scooped up her two heavy equipment boxes in no time at all and then stood off to the side to let her pass.

Darn. He still had manners.

"After you," he said.

"Thanks."

As she led him out to her rental car, she used her pretty gray high-heeled shoe to kick some loose stones out of the way—and was satisfied to see them fly.

Why was she thanking him as if *he* would be the one staying in the owner's trailer tonight? She was the senior level contractor on site, the one with the most training and the biggest credentials. How did he manage to always be in charge?

She opened her trunk, and he packed her equipment away. She stowed her high heels, got out her boots and socks, sat down in the passenger seat, and was putting them on over her pantyhose when Tavish came right up to her and decided to make small talk.

"Oh, good. I was afraid you were going to break

your ankle on our little tour, in those impractical shoes."

So that was how they were going to play it, huh? Act nonchalant. She took a deep breath and then came up with a genuine smile at the prospect of the tour.

"No way. I came prepared to find out just exactly how extensive the secret passageways are."

At the mention of secret passageways, a little of the young Tavish, her Tavish, came back in the twinkle of his eyes.

"You wouldn't believe how extensive!"

They grinned at each other for a moment, just like old times.

But then his smile fell.

"Oh, but you don't have time even to go down one of the secret passageways."

Her face must have looked puzzled, because he gave her a pitying look.

"You really don't wanna be driving back to town after it gets dark. There aren't any streetlights, and the roads twist and turn every which way."

She decided it was time to set him straight about just how much time she was going to be here with him.

"It's okay. Mr. Blair gave me the use of his trailer." She looked up at where the sun could barely be seen through the thick Scottish clouds. "We have at least 4 hours of daylight left. Even I can hike down to the water and back in that amount of time."

He gave her the thinnest of smiles, but then he put his hands on his hips and turned toward the castle.

Preparing for him to tell her she had to leave, she sat

up straighter in her rental car. If it came down to it, she would call Mr. Blair and have him tell Tavish what was what.

But that giddy smile came back on Tavish's face.

"Do you have a heavier coat along? Because it can get pretty cold down there, even in September."

Smiling, she grabbed her parka and leather daypack out of the back seat.

2

DHÀ

The tower house was mostly just three stories of crumbling stone walls. It was large, about a hundred feet by fifty feet, but had no roof. The true attraction was the rumored underground castle inside the cliffs the house sat upon.

Kelsey pointed to where the castle yard dropped off the cliffs into the sea and started walking over there quickly, doing her best to be the dignified appraiser and not show too much excitement.

"Let's go down into the caves."

Tavish fell in step beside her and gave her a wistful smile.

"We haven't found the way into most of them, but we have been able to get down to the sea through one, and there was that room with the trinkets you examined today." He stopped suddenly and grabbed her hand, lending calm support just when she felt herself tripping. "Watch your step. The foundation of an older structure sticks up just enough to trip over, like right there."

A thrill went through her at the touch of his hand. She held onto it for a moment, in order to catch her balance as she looked down and saw the half-inch which remained of a stone wall, sticking up out of the grass, and then she let go as casually as she could, still tingling from his touch.

"Thanks, I think I will watch my step."

He smiled with just a pleasant amount of teasing and started walking again.

"Good idea."

She followed his flapping kilt through a tour of the teetering tower house. It had a surprisingly open floor plan for a structure that was a few hundred years old. It must have been a party house. She didn't think she would have enjoyed living in it. She preferred a network of small rooms with doors she could close so that she would have quiet to read while people in the other rooms visited or sang or played games and did other loud things.

Ooh, just as she had suspected, there was a cellar in each of the three smaller rooms on the ground floor.

With a ceremonial flourish, Tavish pulled up a modern plastic covering to reveal the first dark hole in the ground.

"When the estate came into Mr. Blair's hands, these three cellars were hidden. The only reason we found them was because of the rumors of their existence. It took quite a lot of experimentation with fancy acoustic equipment that could detect hollow areas underground."

Kelsey could see where this first cellar had been opened with brute force by the construction workers. It didn't have stairs, but Tavish and his crew had installed modern metal ladders, which looked really odd against the stone. Without being asked, he let her go down first, in her skirt. Knowing he had nothing on underneath his kilt, she made herself look away and resisted fanning herself as he came down the ladder next. Everything interesting had already been taken out of the cellar, of course, but exploring was fun. The cellars were irregular, and carved out of the rock cliff.

She and Tavish had climbed out of the second of these three cellars when they heard dogs snarling nearby.

The sound made Kelsey's knees weak, and she leaned against the outer stone wall of the castle. She didn't realize Tavish had run off until she turned to where he had been a moment ago and heard him yelling from the nearby bushes.

"Ha! Ha! Git! Ha!"

She then heard a dog crying and another one barking, and she yelled out to Tavish.

"Are you okay?"

"Yeah. I'll be back in a minute, soon as Tuffy runs off. Go on, Tuffy! Go home! Go home!"

Kelsey's feet were running over there before she knew it. She rounded the corner and saw something she never would have believed if she hadn't seen it with her own eyes.

Tavish was holding a largish dog in his arms almost like a baby, except he had its legs trapped off to his sides and he was hugging it close so that its snarling mouth couldn't get to his throat. His face was all business, with no hint of fear for himself.

On the ground, a smaller dog was barking at the largish dog while running around in circles and jumping up as if he could attack the bigger dog.

Tavish was talking to the smaller dog, visibly concerned about its welfare.

"Go home, Tuffy!"

Kelsey gasped. Her voice sounded really high when it came out.

"Did you grab that dog while it was snarling at the other one? Are you okay? Did it bite you?"

He turned so that he could see her behind the dog he was hugging.

"Yeah, I'm fine. Will you take Tuffy back where the guys can protect him, Kel?"

She laughed at the little dog, who was still maneuvering around to try and get to the larger dog somehow, he thought he was so tough. She kneeled down.

"Okay, yeah. I will if I can catch him. Come here, Tuffy!"

The little dog ran right into her arms, and she laughed her way back toward the work tent, at how he never stopped telling the bigger dog off or trying to get to him.

One of the construction workers saw her coming and cupped his hands around his mouth, calling out behind him, "Gus, the woman's got your dog."

Gus turned out to be a huge older guy. He held out his arms as soon as he saw his dog, and Kelsey had to bite her tongue to keep from laughing at how he spoke to his pet.

"There ye are, Tuffy wuffy. Why'd ye hae ta go and run away, eh?" Once he had the dog in his arms, he raised his head up and spoke to her while petting Tuffy.

"I thank ye, lass, from the bottom of my heart. If ever there be aught I can do for ye, let me know right quick, ye ken?"

She'd observed Gus in the group of construction workers with Tavish earlier, good-naturedly laughing and talking with him. Her gut told her she could trust this old highlander, and that he was capable. She smiled at Gus and lingered for a moment to speak with him about how Tavish treated her.

"Well, there is one thing you can do for me..."

When she got back to Tavish, she felt a little guilty for taking so long, because he was still holding the bigger dog. He didn't look any worse for wear though, and his only concern seemed to be for the little dog.

"Is Tuffy safe?"

"Yeah. Gus has him."

Tavish let the bigger dog go, and it ran off past the ruins into some bushes.

She ran her eyes up and down Tavish. His previously bare chest and arms were covered with a linen shirt and a plaid woolen cloak now, but his hands and face were still bare. There wasn't a scratch nor a mark on any of it.

But just as she relaxed in the knowledge that he hadn't been harmed, a weird feeling of unfamiliarity took hold of her. Now that she looked at him in the sunlight that peeked through the clouds, he looked about five years older than her. Wrinkles were forming around his eyes and mouth. Not smile lines, either.

"Wow, Tav. Construction work must have you out in the sun a lot, huh?"

Ignoring her question, he just smiled and rushed back toward the third cellar, calling to her over his shoulder.

"Come on!"

Once they were down inside this last cellar—which was more elaborately lined with stonework and had clearly been used as a root cellar—Kelsey saw the secret door right away. It was in the corner, clearly labeled with intricate lacy Celtic runes carved into the stone. She went over to get a better look.

Tavish frowned at her oddly.

"Yeah," he said, "that's right where the secret doorway is, to the sea passage. How did you know?"

Oh, so the man did *not* know everything after all. Feeling a little guilty about how much that pleased her, she refrained from gloating when she pointed out the runes. They were gorgeous, and their style suggested they were at least a thousand years old, maybe even two thousand.

"These right here give it away."

He wrinkled his brow at her in a question.

"They're like a door sign that says 'Passage to the sea.'"

Good. He looked impressed. He raised his brows

then and turned to look at them and follow one of the curlicues with his finger.

"Do they tell you how to open it? Because it took four of us a good month to figure that out, after it taking another month just for us to notice it."

She looked all around the old stone portal. Yep. There were arrows carved into the pattern, and a kind of series of movements...

Stone against stone made for a really odd sliding sound, but once she had the correct direction—at a weird angle indicated by the arrows—the section of stone in front of her slid a few feet easily with her push, revealing a dark passageway that opened to her right, bringing with it a cold breeze that made her shiver a little and zip up her parka.

She turned to Tavish with a triumphant smile.

He gave her a congratulatory one in return, and they stood there grinning at each other for a moment as if they were fifteen again, about to sneak off on another adventure away from their parents.

On the verge of going into the darkness with Tavish, it occurred to her there might be a very logical reason for him to basically ignore her whenever he saw her—when he wasn't finding fault with her, anyway. On impulse, she asked about it.

"Tavish?"

"Yeah?"

"I only see a ring on your right hand, but um, that doesn't mean anything for guys these days. Um, are you married?"

And there he was again, the old Tavish. His eyes got

that twinkle in them. It was an amused look, but not one that was laughing at her. He was laughing with her as they used to do, laughing at the strange but wonderful circumstances they found themselves in.

"No. No, I'm still single."

On hearing this, a dizzy dancing feeling filled her. It started at her heart and radiated out to her extremities —and she grew warm. Her body was telling her to grab him and kissed him and hold tight to him and never let go.

But just in time, her brain served up a memory of how rude he'd been not an hour ago. She took a deep breath and let it out audibly, blocking those irrational desires from her mind.

But the fact that he was single was good news. There wouldn't be some wife getting upset if rumors started about the two of them being alone down here. That would be terrible for business, especially if it made it into the paper or something. Yeah, it was really good news. For that reason.

No time at all had passed. Tavish was just now getting over the laugh they had shared.

She was liking this lighter mood.

"Oh," was all she said before turning into the passage and opening up her leather daypack to rummage around for her flashlight.

He took his own flashlight out of a loop on his construction-worker's utility belt, and they were ready to go.

"After you," he said again, gesturing gallantly but with a sincere look on his face. "Later, it gets a little rough, but right at first here you don't need to watch your step yet."

She wasn't going to argue. She took him up on his offer and rushed through the doorway, for once not worrying about how eager she looked or how it would let him know this was her first big adventure as a professional Celtic ruins appraiser.

"Thanks."

She was impressed at first that it didn't smell musty down here, but she remembered that the passageways opened up to the sea. And then she shined her flashlight down the cave and gasped.

Down here, the walls were carved out of solid stone. Ancient carvings. But it wasn't ugly at all. It was wondrous. This wasn't a cave. It was an underground palace.

After every few feet she walked, she couldn't help looking over at Tavish and pointing out to him how smooth the stone was, how gracefully the ceiling arched, how beautiful the Celtic interlace carvings were that graced the walls here and there.

He smiled back at her and nodded each time, and then she went back to exploring.

They came to a three-way fork, and Tavish indicated the right branch.

"Down that way is the dead end we think has hidden doorways to the underground castle. Do you want to go down there and check it out, or go to the left down toward the sea?"

"You know me," she reminded him. "Which way would I find more interesting?"

He pointedly looked at her Celtic University ring.

"I'm not really sure I *do* know you well anymore, but the Kelsey I remember, the adventurous one, she would have insisted on checking out the passage down to the secret doors."

"I'll make you a deal," she said to him.

Wow. He gave her a soft look that she never thought she'd see again. It made her want to hug him...

"I'm listening," he said.

Right. They were just talking. What was she saying, again? Oh yeah. The deal.

"I'll be the Kelsey you remember, if you'll be the Tavish I remember."

Oops. What had made her say that?

The soft look left his eyes, replaced by wariness.

"You know what—" he started.

But she cut him off.

"Not for always, Tavish, just for this tour of the passageways, okay?"

He sighed heavily, and sadness filled his face while his posture relaxed as if he'd been ready for a big something and then just given up.

"Okay, but Kelsey, when this tour is done, promise me you'll go into Mr. Blair's trailer and stay in there until the sun comes up. Please, promise me."

Taken aback by just how desperately worried for her he seemed, she agreed to his terms without any negotiation.

"I promise."

He visibly relaxed.

"Thanks, Kelsey."

And then his eyes were looking far away, and he started to reach out to her, and then let his hands drop.

She stomped her foot to get his attention, to make him look her in the eye. Okay, and maybe she was trying to get him to laugh a little, too. She'd always found foot stomping ridiculous.

"What's wrong, Tavish?"

But it didn't work. He looked away.

"I can't tell you."

Now it was she who relaxed her posture and sighed heavily and kind of gave up.

"So that's how it's going to be?"

For a moment, his eyes met hers and his mouth opened and he was standing up straight again, and she thought he would say no. That he would change back into the Tavish she had known and loved. The one she knew had loved her. But it didn't last. She saw the exact moment when he closed down and shut her out.

"Yeah, that's how it has to be."

Tears tried to come again, but she marched on down the right corridor, put on her professional demeanor, and let the wonder of the old stonework push aside her hurt feelings.

She'd come to see the ruins, not Tavish.

And these worn underground stone hallways were amazing. The Celts had obviously occupied this site before 'civilized' people had built the stone tower house up above—no, much longer ago than that. Even before whoever it was had built the older structure up above, the one that was just a half-inch of stone above the grass now.

She rushed on ahead of Tavish, following a path the interlace carvings promised would lead to a storage room. Dimly aware of him following her but no longer pointing out her discoveries to him, she pushed through two more secret doors and went down a narrow cut-stone stairway.

3

TRÌ

Tavish trailed his hand along the rough stone wall to slow himself as he followed Kelsey down the narrow stone staircase.

On the one hand, he had to get her out of here. They had expressly told him to keep her away from the ruins at night. They were ruthlessly territorial, and despite what a court had said about this being Mr. Blair's property, they claimed first dibs on any artifacts. They were always looking for certain ones, and now was no different. He'd been told to keep his eye out for one item in particular.

On the other hand, it was a few hours until sunset, and whoa. He and the crew had spent months digging out this first passageway, and then Kelsey wanders in and finds another two secret doors after just a few hours? Part of him didn't want to stop her until she'd discovered all the other secret entrances hidden in these ruins. This second part of him was winning, so far.

He would just quietly follow her, observe—and make sure she didn't do anything that would make them too mad.

Kelsey had reached the bottom of the stairs and was inside a small room that had been cut out of the natural rock, gazing all around with wide eyes.

"Oh, look at this place."

When he caught up to her and leaned into the tiny room, he saw what made her marvel so.

"I expected everything to be covered in dust," he told her, taking in all the odd shapes in the room almost as much as the pretty sight of her.

"I did too," she said without looking away from all the items carefully stored here, "but look how advanced the ancient architecture is." She pointed while she spoke. "See how these tiny windows are cut precisely opposite one another?"

"I wondered where the wind was coming from." He nudged away from the wall with his shoulder and leaned forward slightly, toward where she was pointing.

"Come stand here," she said, impatiently gesturing for him to join her in the middle.

He balked, because it was really close quarters.

She reached out and grabbed his arm and pulled him in, as if he were a disobedient child.

He felt himself smiling despite his need to keep her safe from them—which meant uninvolved with him—and he fought to make his face serious.

"There," she said, "now don't you feel the wind hitting you from all sides?"

Mostly, he just felt the bottom of her long soft skirt

rubbing against his bare calves and the tug of his kilt against the front of him, where it had caught against her parka. But he couldn't say that.

He concentrated on making his voice businesslike.

"So you think the wind is clearing the dust away?"

"Yep," she said. "Cool, huh?"

"Not as cool as how you just waltzed right down here as if someone had drawn you a map. How did you know where those secret doors were, let alone how to open them?"

That did it. Kelsey finally looked him in the eye. She was scowling, but it didn't ruin her pretty features. And then she rolled her eyes, held up her hand with the Celtic University ring on it, and pointed at the ring with her other hand.

His throat was suddenly dry, and he swallowed. Other than that, he just stood there waiting for her to answer him. It was weird, seeing this mature businesswoman in front of him, wearing a suit and speaking of architecture. In his mind, Kelsey was still the one friend he'd had in his teen years, the only one who kept in touch with him between the times his parents' traveling Renaissance faire came to her town.

Of course he was glad she'd grown up, but seeing her cultivated mannerisms always caught him off balance. Well, if he was honest with himself, then he would have to admit that what bothered him was how much more educated she was than him. He felt intimidated by her, and his manliness didn't know what to do with that feeling, let alone the envy he felt. She had attended school like a normal child, while he and his twin brother and their two cousins had taken lame online classes, with no one to hang out with between weekends except the kids of the few other traveling Renaissance faire workers.

She tilted her head to the side, crossed her arms, and stood there waiting in return. Maybe she was even tapping her foot, but he didn't dare look. If she was, that would make him laugh, and he knew she wouldn't appreciate that right now.

Gradually, it dawned on him, what she wanted him to say.

"Okay. I guess there is something to your doctorate degree."

She sighed.

"About time you realized that."

But then she turned and looked at the room again, then back at him. She grinned from ear to ear, and her whole body jiggled a little bit. She pulled two fists toward her with a sudden jerky movement.

"Yes! Look what we found! It was so fun Tav, studying for real all the stuff you and I could only dabble in at the faire."

Pride in her accomplishment surged through him, and he did his best to show it in his smile.

"It shows on your face whenever you talk about it. I'm glad you've found work you love, Kel."

At the word 'work', the smile left her face and she started to meticulously check all of the artifacts and garments and tools in the room. He didn't know what she was checking them for, but she sure seemed to know what she was doing.

And this was Kelsey.

Her prim tailored suit, warm parka, and hiking boots covered most of her, but he was still transfixed by the way she moved and by how absorbed she was in what she was doing. And then she started digging in her bag, and he knew she was after her phone. To take pictures.

He held the wrist of her hand that was digging in the bag.

"Kelsey."

She tried to pull her wrist away.

"I have to document this, Tavish."

"I can't let you do that, Kelsey."

"What?"

"I just—"

"You know what?" She was huffing, and the two of them struggled, both of them talking at the same time.

"I know you really want to take pictures of this stuff, Kelsey, but you can't just go—"

"Tavish, I'm not just some stupid girl who wants to take pictures of this stuff—"

"—barging into places you don't know are safe and—"

"—I'm an appraiser who Mr. Blair hired to go over anything discovered here—"

Oh yeah, Mr. Blair.

Tavish eased off his hold on her wrists, and she pulled away, caught herself before she fell against a large standing figurine, and took what must have been her professional lecturing stance, because she started lecturing him.

"—and taking pictures of how artifacts are found is

part of the process. I need to post them to Celtic University's site to document the way they were stored. It might give us insight into Celtic beliefs and technology. I don't expect a construction foreman to understand, but I do expect him to show me the professional courtesy of getting out of my way."

"Kel, I'll get out of your way, but you need to call Mr. Blair and get his permission before you post any of those pictures online. Can we agree on that much? This is his property. He has rights."

She took a deep breath as if to argue with him, but then let it out and kind of deflated.

"Yeah, you're right."

She dug some more and finally got out her phone.

"Kel, that's not gonna work down here."

But she held it up for him to see, pointing at three bars.

"Wanna bet?"

Huh. That was one extensive set of windows down here. They weren't letting any light in, just wind, so how were they letting the phone work? Oh well, it was working.

She put her phone to her ear. A huge grin broke out on her face just before she started speaking.

"Mr. Blair? It's Dr. Ferguson. I am so sorry I got your voice mail. Guess what. Tavish and I found an entrance to the underground castle!"

Tavish smiled back at her when her eyes found his, and he pointed at her and nodded and then pointed at himself and shook his head no.

She wrinkled her forehead at him and held her hand

out to the side, as if to say, "I give you credit and then you don't want it? What's wrong with you?"

He whirled his finger around in a circle to indicate all the stuff in the room and then pointed at the phone.

She nodded quickly.

"We're down in it right now, and you won't believe how much stuff, I mean how many artifacts, are preserved just in this one small room. I'm taking pictures to document the find in its pristine condition. We won't disturb anything until you give us the okay, but I'm itching to post these photos to Celtic University's password-protected site so that my colleagues can see them. Please call me back about that as soon as you can. Thank you so much for letting me look around without you here, but I am so sorry we actually found this in your absence. I'll stay here tonight in your trailer, and hopefully you can come by in the morning. I'm so eager to show you this. Bye for now."

She hung up and proceeded to take her pictures.

Good, she wouldn't disturb anything, and that would have to do. He hoped it would be enough to pacify them. But as usual, they wanted him to find something for them here at this site. This room seemed as likely a place for it to be found as any, so he came back into the room with her and joined in her examination.

He asked her what he knew must be annoying questions, but he needed to keep her engaged so that she didn't do anything he'd regret.

"What are all these little tools for?"

She didn't get annoyed, though, just answered as a teacher would, reveling in sharing knowledge.

"I'm pretty sure they're to carve designs into the stonework."

"Like the designs you showed me in the root cellar?"

"Yeah, just like that. They're all over the tunnels. That's how I found my way down here."

He looked at the old iron tools neatly lined up in their case, wondering why they hadn't rusted away.

"So with these tools, you could make some more of those designs?"

A look of wonder came onto her face, and she stooped to look at the tools longingly.

"Yeah, I think I could. They wouldn't be as good as the ones that are already there, though, and of course they wouldn't be as old, so they wouldn't fool someone who knew what to look for."

"Someone like you?"

"Yeah!" she said with joy, "Someone like me."

He scanned the room for their precious item, throwing out comments as they occurred to him, to keep her from noticing.

"What's all of this white cloth over here?"

"Those are ceremonial druidic robes. The druids are the Celts' priests, you know."

"The druids are Celtic?"

"Yeah."

"No, I didn't know that."

She gave him a smug look and continued photographing everything. She kept her word to the client and didn't disturb anything, but she went over everything very closely, so he was 99% sure that what they wanted wasn't in this room. Well, you couldn't expect it to be that easy, or those who sent him wouldn't need him.

Every once in a while as the two of them looked at the stuff, they would brush against each other, and the old passion would threaten to flare up in him. Aw heck, it did more than threaten. He would need a cold shower tonight.

Finally, she was finished with the room and turned toward the doorway, lit up from head to toe with excitement.

"This room is great, but it's a dead-end. Let's go on back up the stairs and look closer at that old laundry room. I'm positive there are more secret passageways that go out of it."

"Naw," he said, looking at his own phone, "it'll be dark soon, and this area is full of wild animals like that dog you saw earlier. We really don't wanna be outside once it gets dark. And while it's really cool down here," he said, "the part we've found so far doesn't look very comfortable, and I doubt there's running water in any case, let alone flushing toilets."

She groaned.

"You're right. Okay, walk me back to Blair's trailer?"

"You got it."

They started up the stone staircase. He stayed behind her so that he would block her if she fell, but to his relief, she looked quite nimble.

"Tavish."

"Yeah?"

"When Mr. Blair comes tomorrow, let me take him up to that room."

"I'll let ya, but I'm coming with."

"No."

"No?" He tried to keep the amusement out of his voice when she turned around to look at him sternly.

"No."

He reached toward her at the same time as she started walking down toward him. He'd meant to tap her leg to get her attention so that she turned around, but now she was falling toward him.

Her breasts collided with his face.

That wasn't the worst of it though. Suddenly, he was holding her in his arms. She felt so good there, just like old times. He cleared his throat and looked into her soft brown eyes with regret as he slowly steadied her on her feet again.

"Sorry. I just meant to stop you so we could talk."

"I know."

Darn it. He could see the old passion stirring within her, too. This was the last thing he'd meant to do, make her want him again. He couldn't be with her. She didn't know how dangerous that would be for her, and he couldn't tell her. He wished his parents had told him sooner, so that he hadn't let her get close to him in the first place.

Oh well. Done was done, but he wasn't going to let her get trapped in this life. Besides, she had changed. He didn't trust the professional appraiser she had become. She seemed like someone who would sell off the seven wonders of the world to the highest bidder, rather than make them museums for everyone to enjoy.

She wasn't the Kelsey he used to know, and he needed to remember that.

He released her and took a step down, which was awkward because he was talking to her breasts, which were clearly outlined by her form-fitting parka. He did his best to look into her eyes.

"Kelsey, I know you think I'm just a construction worker, and officially, that is all I am. But I have a duty here to... to protect the Scottish national heritage. I have to be along with you wherever you go in Scotland."

She gave him a look of incredulity, and then she crossed her arms over her breasts—thank God.

"Wherever I go in Scotland? Like, even in the cities? You think there's ancient items of Scotland's national heritage in the cities, too? Oh, and then hadn't you better meet me at the airport next time I come to Scotland? We wouldn't want me to disturb any precious national heritage items in the terminals, now would we?"

He sighed.

"You know there aren't. You know I mean just out in the countryside, at castles and other ruins."

Her face cracked into the slightest grin.

"In other words, about ninety percent of the country."

Despite himself, he chuckled a little at that. At least she still knew how to have fun and wasn't always this stuck-up, hoity toity, 'doctor' person.

"Come on, Tavish. You aren't really out to protect the Scottish national heritage. What's this really about?"

"Like I said before, I can't tell you."

She sighed.

"So we're back to that, huh?"

"Afraid so."

"Really?"

"Yeah."

"I can walk myself to the trailer."

She stiffly turned around and marched up the stairs. He waited until she was five steps ahead and then followed her as quietly as he could.

There really were animals about. And worse.

4

CEITHIR

Kelsey knew Tavish was following her, but she pretended not to notice. Let him be the ignored one for a while. Too bad she didn't have seven years to ignore him and not answer his calls or emails to even let him know she was alive. That would be payback.

She continued to ignore him even as she got to the door of the trailer, then went inside and set her backpack down and closed and locked the door behind her. If he wasn't going to be friends with her and tell her what was going on, then why should she talk to him at all? No reason, that was why.

So she took a quick shower, and then while she microwaved some canned ravioli, she called Sasha instead.

"Hi Kelsey. So are you away from Tavish and free to talk yet?"

"Yeah."

"Oh Kelsey. You let him get to you again, didn't you."

"Well he was different this time, Sasha."

"Not different enough, or you wouldn't sound so sad."

"True."

"You didn't—"

"No, of course not. I didn't even let him in the trailer, even though he followed me all the way back here right after telling me he couldn't explain what was going on."

"He was probably just being a gentleman, Kelsey. And I'm glad he was. You're basically in the wilderness out there and really shouldn't be outside alone after dark."

"You're probably right. I mean, about him being a gentleman. But it's so confusing. One second we're staring intently into each other's eyes and I'm sure he's gonna kiss me, and the next second he's not wanting to explain to me what's going on with him."

"Kelsey, if I've told you once, I've told you a thousand times: you can't go by what a man does. If you think a man cares about you and wants to be with you in a meaningful way, wait for him to actually say so."

"Uh... yeah. Well, now that we've gotten that over with, let's talk about you for a while."

"Ha! Fair enough. Well, it's time I admitted it: I envy you, getting to do field work. A professorship sounded so prestigious when I accepted the job, but you're on the verge of a real discovery there, I just know it."

"Oh Sasha, I'm so stupid. I should've told you right away."

"What?"

"We do have a find. Here, let me show you the pictures." She fiddled with the files in her phone, working to bring up the pictures she'd taken with Tavish earlier.

"Hurry up and tell me already, don't make me wait for the pictures. I'm dying of curiosity."

"Here they are. I took tons, so I'm just gonna flip through them slowly and let you look. Stop me if you need to." She flipped through the pictures for several minutes, and all the while, Sasha ooh'd and ah'd. And then when they were done, her friend groaned.

"Oh, why did I take this professorship? All I do is lecture and read papers. Boring! I'm the wild and crazy one and you're the calm cool collected one. We should switch places."

"No way, but if you want, come on over tomorrow and check it out."

They talked for an hour, and then Kelsey fell into bed exhausted, but feeling a lot less alone and frustrated.

But Tavish was waiting for her in her dreams.

She dreamed of his parents' Renaissance faire, where she and Tavish used to dance folk dances together, run around the field in games of rounders and relay races—which was difficult in her long skirts and his kilt—act in plays, walk arm-in-arm in parades, and cuddle in his family's trailer while his parents were busy elsewhere.

Tavish had been so nice back then, the perfect

boyfriend for four years, even though he didn't go to her high school and she only saw him during the summers. During the school year the two of them would text constantly.

So it had been all the more hurtful when he'd stopped responding to her texts that first fall she was at college.

Fast-forward to three months ago, when she'd gotten her first field assignment here in Scotland. There he'd been, acting like a stranger. And here he was now, not acting much better than a stranger. And sometimes it looked like he thought she was his enemy.

But in her dream, the two of them were snuggling in a trailer much like Mr. Blair's. They were seventeen again, but somehow they were talking about what had happened today, when they were twenty-five. Well, it was a dream...

Kelsey broke off their hot french kiss and sat up away from Tavish, giving him a serious face.

"What the heck is going on, Tavish?"

He looked confused.

"What do you mean?"

She mimicked him.

"What do you mean?"

He looked just a tiny bit annoyed, but mostly amused, and he gave her his best and sexiest smile.

"Come on, quit acting like a kid."

She pointed at her heart with her finger.

"Me act like a kid?"

He shrugged, apparently resigned to keep playing her game.

"Uh, yeah."

She took a deep breath and tried to be twenty-five, but she stayed seventeen. Darn this dream. She let the air out of her lungs and felt sort of deflated. But then she got an idea. She gave Tavish her sweetest smile and caressed his face the way that used to drive him crazy.

"You're the one who's keeping secrets."

Something weird was going on now though, even for a dream. She could see it in his eyes. He was twenty-five inside too, and he knew what she was talking about.

"Aw, come on Kel. I can't tell you."

She let the hurt show on her face, which was something she would never do with the real twenty-five-year-old Tavish. No way. She wasn't going to play the fool to someone who couldn't be bothered to tell her what was going on.

"You can't tell even me? It's me, Tavish. We used to tell each other everything, or at least I thought so. I told you everything. I kept on telling you everything for months, even when you never answered my texts or my emails."

And then, for just a moment, she saw pain in Tavish's face. Heart wrenching pain just like her own.

"They took my phone away, Kel. I..."

"You what?"

"You have to know I still love you."

"I still love you too, Tavish."

"So why are we fighting?"

"Because like I said, you're keeping secrets."

But then the moment was over. Twenty-five-year-old Tavish was gone. Her seventeen-year-old boyfriend was sitting in front of her again. The knowledge and the pain had left his face, and he just looked mystified.

"I'm not keeping any secrets from you, Kel."

"You're not?"

"Nope."

"Promise?"

"Promise."

The dream got private after that, and she really enjoyed it.

❧

AT THE CRACK OF DAWN THE NEXT MORNING, SHE awoke with a pleasant sense that something had been resolved, but she also had this nagging feeling she'd found out something important, but couldn't remember what it was.

When she opened the trailer door, Scotland greeted her in all its glory. The pink sky cast its light over the fields of heather and the craggy mountains and the rocky shoreline so that for a moment all she could do was stand there and stare. Truly, only the ruins of an age-old castle could promise more delight, and it just so happened there was one right here. She took off running in her hiking boots.

She only got halfway to the third cellar's trap door before Tavish was with her. And of course he couldn't just wear jeans and a hoodie, like she was today.

"Do you always have to wear that kilt?"

Oh great. That was the wrong thing to say. He

struck a pose, teasing her with it. He knew she thought he looked hot in a kilt.

"Aye lass. That I do."

She put as much annoyance in her voice as she could.

"Why? That has got to be the most impractical thing a construction worker could wear."

At first he was smiling, clearly enjoying her grudging admiration. But then a shadow of the pain she had seen in her dream crossed his face, and he relaxed out of his pose.

"Never mind. When is Mr. Blair getting here?"

She held up her phone.

"He hasn't called back yet, but I'll be ready when he does."

She started moving toward the root cellar again.

He fell into step beside her.

"So where are you going?"

"I don't need to have Mr. Blair with me to go check out the rest of those secret doors, Tavish."

"But—"

"But nothing. My client told me to go ahead and look around at the rest of the property, and that's what I'm doing."

"Well I'm coming with you."

She made sure he could see her roll her eyes.

"I can see that."

"Kel—"

"Don't Kel me. That's a name my friends use."

There it was again. Pain showed in his face, and for a brief moment he looked at her pleadingly. And then that hardness came back into his eyes. He held out his hand toward the root cellar door rather formally.

"You're right, Dr. Ferguson. Please allow me to escort you."

"Fine. After you, Mr. MacGregor."

He let her open the secret door inside the root cellar. She blocked his view with her body and tried not to smile at how smug she felt, knowing that he probably didn't know how to do it her easy way. She went straight back to that old fashioned laundry room where Mr. Blair had found the trinkets, because she was sure she'd seen the outlines of a few more secret doors in there.

When she saw them, she forgot she wasn't talking to Tavish anymore, she was so excited.

"I knew it."

"There are more secret doors?"

"Yep, three of them."

He looked around, but it was obvious he had no idea where they were. He looked right past them. It was on the tip of her tongue to tell him what to look for, but then she remembered he wasn't her friend anymore.

This time she let the smugness show on her face.

"Here, the first one's this way."

"You know, Dr. Ferguson, when Mr. Blair gets here, he's not going to want to go down to the sea. Don't you think we should go down there and check it out now, before he gets here?"

He was right. How considerate.

She narrowed her eyes at him, mostly playfully. He knew darn well she wanted to go down to the sea. And of course this was something he could take the lead in, having been down there before.

"I suppose you're right, Mr. MacGregor." She graciously gestured toward the doorway, the same way he had gestured toward the root cellar door earlier. "Lead the way."

Her subtle attempt to regain control of the situation had not escaped him. He raised his chin and flounced as only a kilted man can flounce.

"I dinna mind if I do."

She forced herself into professional demeanor, stuffing her irritation. Unfortunately, she wasn't able to stuff her attraction toward him. Her only consolation was that he seemed to be having the same trouble, cold one moment and warm the next. Would he just make up his mind? Wait a minute, no. She'd already made up her mind. It was like Sasha said: don't pay attention to what a man does. Wait for him to actually say you mean something to him. Never assume you have his commitment, no matter what he does. Wait until he actually says he's yours.

The trip was worth the aggravation, though. The farther down they went, the less finished the passageway became, until they were walking through a natural rugged cave. She greatly enjoyed the contrast. She could tell they were almost down to the opening because of the freshness of the air when she saw a large section of dozens of strange vertical grooves carved into the raw cave wall and stopped to ponder what they might be.

"Do you know what those are?" Tavish asked.

"No, but I get the distinct impression you're about to tell me."

She looked at him then, and he looked smug.

"They held bows, and quivers full of arrows, for guarding the docks down there."

Now that he said so, it made sense. She could see where the bows would go, and the quivers.

"How do you know all this, Tavish?"

He shrugged and then smiled at her over his shoulder, taking off at a run.

"Come on. The cave mouth's just a little farther."

She followed him, and then of course there was the Irish Sea.

Ireland herself greeted them from across the sea—far enough away that they couldn't make out any details, but close enough to be within reach, to make Kelsey curious what lay over there in those lush green hills.

Tavish sounded as excited here as she'd been up in the rock-hewn storage room full of artifacts.

"They've docked boats here in the past. See the tie spots?"

Sure enough, long ago someone had pounded crude iron rings into the cave wall near the water's edge next to natural stone docks where you could climb aboard a boat. The boat would be sheltered from the waves by the cave, but there wouldn't be far to go at all before you would be out at sea. You could probably motorboat over to Ireland in less than an hour.

Unable to help herself, she smiled up at him in pure delight.

"Don't you wish we had a boat now?"

"I really do. I've been trying to get Mr. Blair to bring one so he could, you know, check out his portion of the coastline—and maybe motor on over to Ireland."

They laughed.

"You mean so you could."

He nodded with a smile.

She looked over at Ireland, along the coastline, and then back at the tie spot.

"This is the most awesome dock I ever saw."

"I knew you'd like it."

She looked back across the water at the Irish shore where she could see two distinct cities complete with ports, one of them very large.

"Yeah, we need a boat here."

"We?"

"Yeah, we."

"Kel—"

"Mr. MacGregor, now that there is so much more to the estate, so many artifacts to document and catalog, my client will ask me to stay on for at least a month, probably three."

Tavish took in a deep breath like he was going to lecture her—but then he grabbed her hand and ran for the passageway up.

"Let go of me."

"They're coming, Kel."

"Huh?"

She looked over her shoulder and then tugged on his arm and dug her feet into crevices in the rock, trying to stop him from dragging her back up.

"Tavish, that's the most gorgeous old Celtic boat I could ever have imagined. Let me go."

"That's danger, Kel."

He grabbed her and threw her over his shoulder in a fireman's carry, and ran back up.

Unable to act on her anger and indignation, she let the professional part of her calmly note how odd the cave looked from the perspective of someone whose head was bobbing upside down. And in that frame of mind, she had a surprisingly calm discussion with the man who was manhandling her.

"Where are you taking me?"

"Back to the trailer."

"But I want to check out those other secret doors."

"Never mind those Kel, at least until Mr. Blair gets here."

"Mr. Blair doesn't seem the type who could protect me from the kind of danger that would make a MacGregor run."

At that, he chuckled the tiniest bit.

"It's complicated, Kel. Just trust me."

"It appears I have to."

"You'll be safe in the trailer, Kel."

But when they got to the old fashioned laundry room, they could both hear harsh voices coming down the corridor toward them from the root cellar.

"Her presence here is a problem."

"We'll deal with it."

"She'll distract him."

"He'll find it."

"He'd better."

"He will. He's one of our better workers."

She barely heard Tavish uncharacteristically swear while changing direction and going down the middle corridor, the one they had never discussed. How weird. She'd kind of forgotten all about that middle corridor.

But those voices. They were familiar. She couldn't quite place where she'd heard them before, but she knew she had. Her mind kept showing her images of who it might be, and she kept rejecting them, one by one, like watching an old movie and being sure you'd seen one of the actors in something before, but not knowing what...

He kept her in the fireman's carry hold the whole way down to where the middle corridor ended in a nondescript dead-end. And then the walls whirled and blurred in front of her eyes as if she were seeing them from the bottom of a whirlpool.

5

CÒIG

They wouldn't follow him and Kelsey to the old time. They never did go there with him, even though they were the ones who had given him the ring and shown him how to use it. She would be safe there—at least from them.

He would find what they wanted from this underground castle in the old time. It would pacify them. It had to.

There were so many things he wished he could grab before he took her to the old time, but he could tell by the sound of the approaching voices that he had less than a minute, and he needed to use as little of that time as possible.

He took Kelsey down the guarded hallway and turned the ring on his finger.

The blurring came. He'd learned that if he focused on one thing during the blurring, he was less likely to get dizzy from it. At least he knew there would be no one around when they arrived. He was always careful to time travel only when there was no one in the travel spot.

At last, the whirling stopped.

They were in the old time.

"Here, let me put you down," he said to her as he did so.

Kelsey spluttered and stumbled a bit when he turned her back over and set her down on her feet.

"Finally. I thought my head was going to pop, it was getting so full of blood. I bet I was just about to pass out. I was getting so dizzy, the walls looked like they were spinning around." She stood still for a second with a far-off look in her eyes. "Well, whoever was saying it was bad that I was in here must have left, because I don't hear them anymore. Who was that, Tavish? And what did they mean about you being one of their best workers?"

He sighed and gave her the most sincere bracing smile he could manage.

"Don't get mad, okay? Please don't raise your voice, and especially, don't go down the hall yet."

Her eyes went down to the opening of the hall and back to him.

"Tavish, you're kind of scaring me."

He looked in her nervous brown eyes and tried to project concern and caring. And he took a giant step to put himself between her and the way out of the hallway.

She scrunched up her delicate brown eyebrows and narrowed her now angry brown eyes at him, then reached up to push him in the chest. She barely moved him.

"What are you doing? If this is some sort of game, it isn't any fun."

He took a deep breath and let it out, then walked about 10 feet up the hallway toward the opening, turning to encourage her to follow him and then waiting until she had caught up.

"Do you see anything different about the runes on the walls now, Kel?"

She blinked, turned to look where he pointed, briefly looked back at him again with a question in her eyes, and then turned to intently study the runes, running her finger along them and gasping every so often.

"Wow! I didn't even notice these when we came in. Of course, that's not too surprising, seeing how I was upside down and bobbing around. But wow. Judging by the relative lack of stone erosion, these runes are at least a five hundred years newer than all the others, probably more like seven hundred years newer."

Great. She wasn't getting it. Best to let her figure it out for herself. She wouldn't believe him if he told her, and that would be dangerous.

"Where are the nearest runes you remember seeing before?"

Wrinkling her brow at him, she raised her hand up and tipped her pointing finger over, which struck him as a quite feminine way of pointing behind him.

"Uh, I looked at some just outside the three-way fork in the passageway when we first came in yesterday, remember? You were looking at everything with me, and then we got to the three-way fork and you asked me which way I wanted to go."

He swallowed.

"Okay, I'm going to take you out there to look at them again now, to see if you notice any changes. But Kelsey, please don't go wandering off. Promise me you'll stay with me."

She started to say something.

But he held up his hand.

Miraculously, she stopped.

"I'll explain why soon," he said. "That, I promise you. Oh, and one more thing. If we hear anyone coming, we need to run back down this hallway. We're sort of safe down here."

She smiled conspiratorially at him and narrowed her eyes.

"I knew there was something weird about this center hallway. I mean I knew it was here, but I sort of forgot about it until you took us down here just now." She looked anxiously down the hall again. "But won't they be immune to it just like you are?"

She had grown up into such a confident, competent woman. A wonderful woman. He wished he could just take her back to their time before this happened and somehow make her forget all about him so that she would be safe and happy.

But he didn't have that much control over his time traveling. He controlled when he traveled, but that was it. They controlled where he had to go in order to be able to travel—and they controlled how far back in time he traveled. Still, controlling when he traveled was a much better deal than his father had, and Tavish was grateful for that.

He sighed. He wished she weren't, but in reality Kelsey was here, and he intended to keep her as safe and happy as he could while she was here.

But they controlled what he was able to tell her.

"The 'they' I'm worried about right now are a different 'they' than the ones you heard talking a few minutes ago. But the now 'they' are mostly not immune to this hallway's influence, if that makes any sense."

She pursed her lips and nodded three times quickly, then smiled at him.

"Actually, yeah, I think I understood what you meant."

"Good. Alright, let's go."

He took her hand so that he could control how fast she walked and keep her behind him as he crept down the hallway—making as little noise as possible, especially when he got close to the opening. He was debating with himself whether he should actually take her out there where the old time people might see her.

He had barely just concluded that she really needed to understand their situation or she wouldn't stay in this safe hallway anyway, when she gasped.

"I can see the runes from here. Tavish, did somebody... Oh. Did 'they' do restoration work on the runes last night?"

He shook his head no.

"You know that's not it, Kel."

Her whole body jerked forward as if she meant to

run over to the runes across the hallway and put her fingers in the grooves of them and feel how jagged the newer cuts were, compared to how smooth they'd been just yesterday.

But he held her hand tight, stopping her from going out there into danger.

She met his eyes then, and he could see the wheels turning in her mind. Her expression was only a tiny bit fearful, though. Mostly, she just looked really, really smart.

It was all he could do not to grab her in his arms and hold her close and tell her he loved her and that he would never, ever let her go, he admired her so much. And she was so much fun to be with.

"Tavish, I think I know what's going on, but humor me. I need to see some more stuff. You know, just to rule out the possibility that you're messing with me." She held up her hand to stop him from saying anything. "Normally, I would be sure you wouldn't mess with me about something this... big. But you have to admit," she gestured all around them, "that this... this is anything but normal."

"Yeah, you're right. The thing is..." He couldn't make himself say it and risk sounding stupid, so he just pointedly studied her jeans for a moment and then looked back up into her eyes.

She looked off into the corridors as if perhaps she could see a way out if she just looked hard enough.

"Well, you're in period clothing. What if you just go... find me something to wear? Heh, and that can double as showing me some more stuff. After all," she looked him in the eye again, "I know that during our time, there aren't any period women's clothes hanging around out there."

"Okay, I'll go see what I can find." He put his hand on her elbow and beseeched her with his eyes. "But Kel, you have to stay here in this hallway." Nothing else he could say would tell her any better how serious this was, so he just put all his concern for her in his eyes and prayed that she would see it.

"I will," she said, pursing her lips a little and nodding gently.

HE HAD TO CALL IN A FAVOR AND TELL A TALL TALE, but he got Kelsey some clothes that would fit and look appropriate on her during the old time. As he walked back through the underground corridors to meet up with her again, he looked around for a place for her to change.

But when he rounded the corner and entered the center pathway in the three-way fork, there was no sign of her.

6

SIA

After Tavish left to go find her some clothes, Kelsey leaned against the cold stone wall for a while, trying to get comfortable. But the cold got to her, so she stood back up. Casting about for a way to pass the time, she looked at the runes carved into the walls and had started tracing them with her fingers, feeling the rougher edges, when she felt a chill and then heard an unfamiliar old male voice behind her.

He was speaking a Gaelic slightly more old-fashioned than what Tavish's parents had taught her and everyone else in their faire clan—and he almost made her jump out of her skin.

"Ye are na of this time."

A jolt of adrenaline rushed through Kelsey, urging her to run. When she didn't, goosebumps rushed up her neck into her scalp and down the backs of her arms and the fronts of her legs.

She took a deep breath to calm herself and kept her

back to him, tracing the runes with her fingers while she spoke to him as nonchalantly as she could in her slightly more modern Gaelic, in which she knew she could be grammatical.

"Why no, I am na. And ye are na fooled by the trick of this hallway."

He chuckled then, the way her uncle used to chuckle when she accused him of cheating at cards after his poker games, while he counted his copious winnings.

"Nay, neither of us is. Sae, can ye read then, or are ye just tracing the pretty lines?"

Loath to admit the fact that she had been just tracing the pretty lines and eager to prove that she could read them, Kelsey turned her left side toward the wall and raised her right hand to the top of the runes to point to her place as she read. This allowed her to sneak a glimpse of him.

The man's long white hair and beard cascaded down over his long white homespun linen robes. His wrinkled face was darkened by the sun, and he held in one hand a gnarled old oak walking staff. He gasped when she raised her right hand.

She looked up toward her hand to make sure there wasn't a snake up there in a crack in the wall, ready to bite her, but all she saw was her hand—oh, and her ring from Celtic University. Wow, was the shape of it something he recognized?

Just in time, her gut urged her to appear unaffected by time travel or his presence. To appear more sure of herself then she was. In short, to hide her helplessness. Still fighting the shiver she felt at the goosebumps, she went ahead and started reading the runes:

"Be happy while ye yet live, for yer time to be dead is long—"

But in a strong booming voice that caused her bones to hum, he interrupted.

"Pardon me, Priestess. I didna see yer ring afore. What hae ye come to study?"

Priestess?

But Kelsey flashed back to a line in the movie Ghostbusters—the original, not the one that came out in 2016: "If someone asks if you are a god, you always say yes." And she figured probably the same thing applies if a creepy old Druid assumes you're a Druidic priestess.

Very carefully, she didn't pause in her tracing of the runes with her fingers. Quite deliberately, she made herself not turn around and look at the man. Nonchalance was what her gut told her she needed to put on right now.

However, she was so busy putting it on that she didn't take time to consider what she would say—so she blurted out the truth.

"In my time, this place is abandonit. I've come tae see it in its former glory."

"Och, well nae, ye have come at least a thousand years ower late for that—"

Yikes, better to cut him off before he gave voice to his expectation that she just flit back in time another thousand years on her own.

"Aye. Howsoever, the castle is in use during yer time,

and it should prove interesting, seeing what type o' use it is being put tae, a thousand years after its prime."

"Ah. Sae that is why you've brought Tavish, then. Tae be yer mundane guide during this time."

It now occurred to her that, as much as possible, she had better stick to the truth. It would be the easiest thing for her to remember, should she be questioned under duress. And duress seemed likely in this time. She was holding her own at the moment, just barely, but... some instinct told her to let this particular truth out.

"Forsooth, Tavish did bring me. I dinna hae the ability, myself."

The man chuckled.

"Aye, isna that a darned inconvenient limitation on us? 'Tisn't fair, that the mundanes get to do most of the time traveling."

Nonchalance. Keep up the nonchalance.

She just gave him the slightest nod in acknowledgment of what he'd said.

His footsteps went up the hallway toward the fork.

"Tavish returns, and talking tae him would be... inconvenient for me. Sae I shall leave ye tae it. Be well until we meet again, Kelsey. And when we dae, ye may call me Brian."

She felt the chill again, and then she could neither see nor hear Brian.

A few seconds later, Tavish bumped into her and dropped onto the smooth carved stone floor a lovely red wine and black tea dyed plaid overdress and a coordinating black tea linea blouse with Scottish thistles embroidered round the neckline, and a matching embroidered red wine linen snood.

"Kelsey! How did you do that?"

"Do what?"

"You know what!"

"Um, no I don't."

"You were invisible!"

"I was?"

"Come on, you know you were."

"Tavish, to me, you're the one who was invisible. I had no idea you were coming until you bumped into me just now."

They stared at each other for a few moments, apparently both waiting for the other to speak up and explain what was going on. He obviously knew something he wasn't telling her. Well, she was done telling him everything, too.

7

SEACHD

Tavish picked up the old time clothes and rather helplessly looked around the empty corridor again, for a place for Kelsey to change. Maybe he should go out to the stables and get some hay bales to stack in the corner so she could go behind them?

But she was already taking off her leather backpack and her sweatshirt, which she stuffed inside the pack before donning the old time clothes and then putting her leather backpack on once more.

"I'll just wear it over my real clothes," she said. "That way if anybody comes, at least they won't see me naked."

"That's... surprisingly practical. I have to admit, I was seventy percent sure you would freak out when we got here to the old time."

She shrugged.

"University taught me to keep calm in strange situations. And by the way, I believe you now, about us having... gone back in time."

"Well good, because we're probably going to be here in the old time a while."

Her eyes got really big.

He rushed to explain before she panicked.

"My ring can take us back to our time, but only in this hallway. We'll arrive right back where and when we left our time. There was no one around—I'm always careful about that—but they were coming. If we go back to our time without the artifact they want, I'm afraid of what might happen to you. The artifact is probably here in this underground castle, which as you've seen is quite extensive. So we're in for a search that will certainly take a few days, if not weeks—or even months."

"What is it they want?" Her stomach growled loudly. "And I hope the people of this time have something to eat around here, because I was so excited about exploring these underground passages that I ran outside without eating breakfast first."

He looked her over to make sure her tank top and jeans weren't showing, but she'd done a good job covering them with the old time clothes. He sighed and looked up toward the fork in the corridor, then met her eyes and pointedly switched to Gaelic and went into the old time persona he put on here, while he took her by the hand and gingerly led her out.

"Well enough. There won't be anything to eat down here. The underground castle is only used in this time to fortify the docks below, and the current laird forbids the guards to eat on duty, and as you can see there's no place to sleep either. There is an upper castle where he resides, and around it there's a substantial castle town, or castleton." He patted his sporran. "I'm employed here as a mercenary guard, so I have coinage of the time. We can buy a meal there and see about a place for you to stay. I have a bunk in the barracks."

As soon as they left the underground castle, they were inside the castleton. Kelsey turned her head every which way, and he supposed he couldn't blame her.

The buildings were close together, which meant that the streets were narrow, so all the action was close. Countless men in leather armor and carrying weapons swaggered up and down the streets along with the housewives on errands, some on their way to guard duty and others going to break for a drink at one of the many taverns. Dozens of vendors called out their wares from carts set up in the street. These were mostly edible wares, and the scent of roasting meat and baking bread and cheap wine filled the air.

Grinning a little at how preoccupied she was, Tavish bought her a 'toad in a hole' at a vendor. He didn't tell her what it was, just handed it to her.

"Here. These are good, by fegs."

His amusement grew when she took it from him and ate it without really stopping to look at it, still taking in all the sights and sounds. He let her enjoy herself, surreptitiously steering her by her elbow so that she didn't bump into anyone, and handing her his water skin when she was obviously thirsty. Watching the joy spread on her face brought him his own kind of delight.

But this wasn't a vacation.

Once she was done eating, he dug out of his sporran the drawing they had given him of the artifact they wanted and showed it to her. Couldn't hurt for her to keep an eye out. She obviously had a way of seeing things he didn't.

Her face grew concerned as she looked at the drawing.

"Forsooth Tavish, I'm in the thick o' it now, sae ye must needs tell me who 'they' are."

But he couldn't do that.

So relief coursed through him when his sparring partner in the old time—a large red-haired highlander—picked this moment to arrive and greet them, also in Gaelic. He clasped forearms with Tavish, but all the while he was smiling at Kelsey.

"Och, there ye are, Tavish. Wait, who is this?"

Tavish took advantage of the large man's distraction and grabbed the drawing from Kelsey and stuffed it back into his sporran.

"Seumas! (Pronounced Shaymus) Och, ye've found me. This is—"

"Pleased to meet ye, Seumas. I'm Kelsey." She held out her hand like the businesswoman she had become. He hoped it was obvious only to him that she meant to shake the man's hand. If anyone of the old time saw it that way, they would be scandalized.

But Seumas sparkled his green eyes and took Kelsey's proffered hand. Like one of those ridiculous portrayals of old-time men in the movies, the fool looked likely to raise it to his lips. He gave Tavish a look that dared him to stop the action, all while being apparently a complete gentleman in Kelsey's eyes, the brute.

"It is glad to know you I am, Kelsey..."

Tavish put a stop to that line of reasoning by throwing his arm around Kelsey's waist and pulling her close to him.

"Aye, Kelsey is clan, and I will thank ye to keep yer hands off her, Seumas."

He expected Kelsey to put up a fight at his protectiveness, being a modern woman and all, but she surprised him by melting into his side. Apparently she still had some sense in her.

"Tavish wis juist showing me around."

He was sure Kelsey didn't see it, but Seumas narrowed his eyes at Tavish and grinned ever so slightly before he turned to Kelsey with an open face and asked what she probably thought was an innocent question, but to him it seemed loaded.

"Do ye mean to stay here awhile, then?"

"Aye," Tavish said, "I mean to apprentice her with the weavers."

Kelsey's eyebrows wrinkled in the cutest way and her mouth hung open for a second before she recovered and got that uppity look on her face again, the look that went with her new business suits.

"The weavers?"

"Hae ye skill at the weaving?" Seumas asked her respectfully.

"I hae seen how the weaving is done," she said to Seumas while staring daggers at Tavish, "but I hae nay desire tae do it myself."

Tavish gave her a significant look.

"Och lass, did ye think Laird Malcomb would take ye on here and let ye stay for naught?"

She had to understand the old time was different, that men would be in charge of her here. He couldn't let some other man grab charge of her, and she needed to realize that and help him keep her under his protection. The way she clung to him was reassuring, along these lines, but he spelled it out a bit, just to be sure she understood.

"Ye must work if ye are tae bide here at the castle while I dae ma part. Else ye must gae home to the glen with the marketing this very day."

Kelsey looked like she'd swallowed a fly.

"But couldna I do aught other than weaving? I would much rather apprentice to someone more learned."

Seumas gave Kelsey an all too charming smile and then laughed in his jolly way. Too bad there was no potbelly to go with it. The darn brute was all muscles.

"There are nae learned people here but the laird himself and his family, lass."

She pressed her lips together and then licked them, all the while wrinkling her forehead in that adorable vulnerable way that made him want to throw his arms around her and tell her everything would be fine.

"What about the laird's sons? Who teaches them?"

But Seumas beat him to it, putting his hand on her shoulder and tilting his head to the side in a way that made his long red hair tickle her cheek, so that she brushed it aside, and in so doing, touched his arm.

"Well nae, the priest does that, and ye canna mean to apprentice with him."

She went a bit limp at that, and Tavish took advantage of his arm around her waist and pulled her away from Seumas and toward the door, turning them around in the process.

"The weavers will suit ye just fine, Kel. Ye shall see."

Seumas quickly caught up and joined them, smiling at Kelsey while he spoke to Tavish.

"And I will be seeing ye out to the sparring yard."

Now that the man was safely on the other side of him and away from Kelsey, Tavish warmly slapped his other arm around his sparring partner.

"I dinna doubt it."

But Seumas leaned forward so he could talk to Kelsey.

"So did yer husband come here to market, lass?"

Tavish tried to nip this line of enquiry in the bud. He would give her an imaginary husband, and that would keep Seumas from coming on to her. Because... Because she clearly was in over her head with an old time man. Yes, yes she was.

"Nay," said Tavish, "her husband stayed at home."

But Kelsey spoke at the same time.

"Nay, he's passed on."

Tavish couldn't help but respond with irritation to that, even though a part of him realized it would look irrational to Seumas. Why couldn't she just let him handle this? Didn't she know he was familiar with this time and knew better than her what would be acceptable now, what would be safest for her?

"And when were ye gon to tell me this?"

She put on a fake sad face for Seumas, but her finger jabbed into Tavish's rib.

"It happened but a month ago. Poor Duncan expired when a horse fell upon him."

Tavish crossed himself, as did Seumas, and Kelsey had the sense to imitate them as she prattled on about her imaginary husband's death for five minutes. Finally, she got to why she was here.

"I was after a bit o' distraction when they did say would I come along to market—"

Here, she put her hand on Tavish's face in that way she had that always melted his heart.

"—and perhaps to visit with any clan at the castle."

Hold on, he could make her crazy story serve his purpose. His eyes held Seumas's while he spoke to Kelsey.

"It's as well. Only *clan* ought to console you during this time."

This brought them to the weaver's shop up top in the castle town, which was bustling with people who had come from far and wide—mostly by boat at nearby Port Patrick—to buy and sell goods before winter set in.

Tavish rapped on the door.

"Hey ho, the weaver shop."

The door banged open and four well-dressed blond children greeted them with laughter while they chided and tickled and poked each other, all the while running about in circles and finally down the lane.

Tavish, Seumas, and Kelsey went inside the shop, where they saw a grey haired woman weaver at her loom, a blonde woman about their age working wet strands of the flax plant into threads, and two men who were probably the women's husbands, one gray-haired and one blond, pounding on soaking flax plants to separate them into strands. They were all weavers, so of course all their clothes were finely made and new. Verra respectable, Tavish noted with satisfaction.

The blond woman working the wet strands set them down and came to the door with a question in her brown eyes.

"What can I dae to help ye?"

"It is we who will be helping ye. Kelsey has come to apprentice."

The woman looked Kelsey up and down.

"A bit old for an apprentice, be ye not?"

Tavish gave Kelsey a grudging nod, because her story made more sense now. To support it, he put his arm around her in comfort.

"My clanswoman has lost her husband and seeks some distraction these weeks while she is here tae visit me."

The woman gave Kelsey a comforting smile and reached for her hand, which Kelsey slowly gave her while looking back at Tavish with near panic in her eyes. The woman led Kelsey over to her work.

"We could use the help. I'll show ye how tae separate the strands."

"See ye at supper, Kel."

And with that, Tavish quickly walked off, before Kelsey could introduce anymore awkward conversation.

Seumas was still there, though.

"Your clanswoman is a pretty one."

"Aye."

"Mind if I—"

Tavish turned toward his sparring partner.

"Ye had better not."

The kilted warrior grinned at him.

"If yer wanting tae mak some time with her, then whyever did ye put her in with the weavers?"

"I am na wanting tae mak time with her."

The huge red-haired highlander laughed and clapped him on the back, hard.

"Ye can fool yerself, MacGregor, but ye will na fool me."

"I am na fooling myself. I did na want her tae come here, but now that she's here, 'tis my duty to protect her. She'll be safe with the weavers. And they'll keep her busit."

But Seumas kept laughing and patting Tavish's back.

"Ye mark my words, MacGregor. Ye will be sorry they keep her sae busit."

8

OCHD

"Glad tae know ye, Kelsey. I'm Eileen."

Kelsey tried not to have a sour face. It wasn't Eileen's fault Tavish had dumped her in this fourteenth century sweatshop. Maybe if she just left this room, she could catch up with him, and... No, the stubborn arse would just bring her back here.

"Hello," she said to Eileen as brightly as she could. "It looks like ye need a lot of help."

The blonde woman's brown eyes lit up with a smile, and she bent over a bit in laughter.

"Aye, and this weaving is na the half of it. Ye saw my wild ones just now, running oot."

Eileen had a warm manner, and soon Kelsey was doing her best to help the woman.

The work didn't demand very much mental activity at all though, so while she worked, Kelsey considered her options. Chasing after Tavish was out, but just leaving and going back into the underground castle? No, if Seumas was down there, then other people might be down there, and while they might know Tavish, she was a stranger. Who knew what they might do to her.

But Eileen was understandably curious and asked questions as the two of them combed flax into thread.

"I'm sorry about yer husband. Were ye married long, and hae ye wee ones?"

Kelsey pretended it was Tavish she was being asked about, and answered with details of their prior relationship. She'd had other boyfriends, but if she was honest with herself, he was the only one who... She didn't let herself think about that.

"We were together four verra good years filled with love and laughter, and nay, no children."

"Aw, sad I am for ye on both counts, from the loss of yer husband to the lack of children."

Lack of children was the least of it. Now that she knew why Tavish had disappeared, her feelings were even more hurt than they had been freshman year at college.

A lump formed in Kelsey's throat as she looked around at the intact stone walls of their castleyard stall, the chinks freshly reinforced against the wind with wet straw, the amazing loom busy weaving a plaid.

If she had been the one to time travel instead of Tavish, she would have shared this with him. He'd known how fascinated she was with the past and how much she would've loved to be involved with this sooner. Obviously he didn't... no, obviously he hadn't felt the same way about her.

But she gave Eileen her bravest face.

"Dinna fash for me."

Eileen gave her a kind smile, and then her eyes grew full of mischief.

"I see that yer clan man is fond of ye."

Huh? Kelsey searched Eileen's eyes for sties, or glaucoma, or cataracts. Hm. They seemed to be clear and unimpeded.

"Ye think Tavish is interestit in me? It does na seem sae tae me. After all, he dumpit me here and ran off tae hae fun with his friend."

Eileen laughed hard at that.

"He did na run off tae hae fun."

"Aye, he did. He and Seumas were talking aboot sparring with their swords."

"Ye haven't spent any time at a castle, have ye?"

"Nay, does it show, then?"

The weaver bit her knuckle, apparently to keep from laughing anymore at Kelsey's expense.

"Aye, it does, for this whole place is naught but a fancy barracks for soldiers, ye ken. They spar most of ivery day sae that they can fight when they're needed, or else the laird does na feed them."

"I thank ye for the explanation. I sort of wonderit about all the shapely men wandering aboot with swords."

Eileen must have been disposed toward laughing, for she did it some more, and it didn't seem to take much effort. Kelsey also noticed that one of the male weavers kept eyeing Eileen and talking about her to the other.

But Eileen's brown eyes were still full of mischief.

"Nay, I dae think Tavish is sweet on ye. Protective. I

did see the way he lookit aboot the shop in an attempt tae suss oot any trouble that might be lingering, before he left ye here. He is na a relative, is he."

It wasn't a question, but Kelsey answered it anyway. Semi honestly.

"Nah, he is na, and we playit kissing games when we were children. But even if he's not off having fun, he's off me, and has been for years." She'd had enough of this line of questioning, and she remembered something about how the best defense is a strong offense, so Kelsey lowered her voice and leaned in toward Eileen, squinting her eyes conspiratorially. "So I guess that's yer husband ower thare?"

Eileen leaned in too, but her jaw dropped, and she quickly dipped her chin so that she was looking at Kelsey almost through her own forehead.

"Fergus? Nay, my own husband did pass six months ago."

"Oh. I'm sorry for yer loss an all. I just thought from the way he was looking at ye that the twa o' ye were marriit. I'd say he thinks ye are headit that way."

Good, Eileen blushed. Now to keep her on the defense so she would quit making Kelsey think of things that she could only regret thinking about. Expensive notions, when it came to getting her feelings hurt. Again.

Kelsey gave the weaver woman an appraising look. Eileen's clothes were modest, of course. Everyone knew that was just the way things were back in this time. Women couldn't seem too forward or they would be mistaken for whores, much more so than in modern times. But Eileen was attractive, an eight without trying, who could be a nine if she put in some effort.

"Yer een are still free o' wrinkles, Eileen. Ye can dae better than Fergus. Don't ye think ye should try?"

Eileen's attractive face scrunched up. Yeah, Eileen was way better looking than Kelsey herself. If she scrunched her face up like that, she would just look ugly. On Eileen it was cute and made Kelsey want to help her. The woman didn't appreciate her own beauty.

"Better?" said the weaver, "How dae ye mean?"

"I mean, you're a craftswoman, and there's no shame in that, but isn't there a single man who has more status than a weaver does, and who you have a chance with?"

Eileen discreetly looked over at Fergus and then back at Kelsey. She still kept her voice low.

"Aye, there is."

"A man who ye like and who might like ye?"

Eileen not only stopped working, but also took a strand of her blonde hair and started twirling it around her finger.

"Hmmmmm."

The way the woman hummed made Kelsey's cheeks ache with a smile. She made a conscious effort not to laugh and attract the attention of the men.

"I thought sae. Now when's the neist time ye are gaun'ae see him?"

"This evening at supper, I suppose."

"How aboot if ye pinch yer cheeks an crush some berries tae put on yer lips, put on yer finest clothes, an make some conversation with him?"

Eileen quit twirling her hair and got back to combing the flax into thread.

"I don't really have anything in common with him, Kelsey."

"Of course ye dae."

Eileen stopped working again and put her hands on her hips.

"Verra well, if ye know sae much, what could we possibly hae in common?"

Kelsey met Eileen's eyes and very pointedly looked at Fergus and then at their flax work and started working again, waiting for Eileen to start again too. And giving her time to think of an answer.

The weaver paused only a few moments before she nodded and started work again, but it was enough. Inspiration struck Kelsey.

"Ye both live here in this marvelous castle town, do ye not?"

Eileen nodded at her, putting more effort into the work as she spoke.

"Aye, we do, but everyone here does, sae that doesn't give us any special connection."

Kelsey met Eileen's eyes and tsked.

"But it does give ye things tae talk aboot: the weather, if naught else, but ye also know all the same people and see all the same merchants and ships, eat the same foods, have heard the same stories growing up, and the same rumors. Ye have all things in common, really. I envy you. My parents and I movit tae a new town when I was fourteen, and I had tae start all ower again with people who did na hae a thing in common with me at all, not even the weather. If it had na been for Tavish…" Ugh. She had done it to herself this time. She needed to get off that topic posthaste. "Sae aye, ye can speak with this more successful man." There. She'd made a good case for Eileen to step out and make something of herself.

But the weaver seemed to know a bit herself, about a good offense.

"Ye movit tae a new place ootside o' a castle with juist yer parents and no yer whole clan? Thare has tae be a tale in that."

Now Kelsey had done it. Put her foot squarely in her mouth. For a moment, she considered toppling something so the men would come over. But it was going to be a long day, and there was no way Eileen would let this go.

"It is na much of a tale, for sooth. Da took work with a… merchant. He's good at… selling things. Soon, everyone in our clan's area had the merchant's goods, but Da enjoyit the money he made doing this work. When the merchant offerit him the same work in another place—and also offerit tae pay sae Da and his family could move there—Da acceptit."

Eileen smiled at her sympathetically.

"So ye left all that ye knew. And ye were fourteen? And then ye met Tavish?"

Kelsey gave her new friend an exasperated smile.

"Aye, now can we stop making all things be aboot Tavish?"

Eileen's smile turned mischievous again.

"I daresay that for ye, all things already are aboot him."

And round and round they went, but it passed the time. Meanwhile, for the first half of her workday, Kelsey meant to kill Tavish when he came to see her for supper. He had dragged her out of an underground castle—incredible, marvelous, and secret—in order to dump her in the weaver shop and make her work all day? And it was hard, boring work. She'd had no idea linen was so difficult to make in pre-industrial times.

But after a late morning break for bangers and mash, the scholar in Kelsey started to appreciate what an opportunity this was.

By the decorative patterns Eileen's coworker was weaving into the linen, Kelsey knew this was the 13th century. Her eyes began to drink in all the details of the weaver shop, from the construction of the loom to the way the people dressed and even the game the children played in the corner during their short breaks from helping with the work—one sort of like jacks but with little stones.

Kelsey asked and was told where to go relieve herself, and once she had privacy, she put her phone in the hanging cradle of one of her huge linen sleeves and cut a hole in the linen next to it, just big enough for the camera lens. By crossing her arms just so, she could look natural while using it.

She carefully snapped about a hundred photos on her short walk from the privy back to the weaver's shop —mostly of the intact castle and its courtyard, but also of the way people were dressed and their various weapons. She could blow the pictures up on her computer once she got home, and hopefully see all the fine details of craftsmanship.

When she got back inside the shop, she snapped one of the loom and the way the woman who worked it was sitting at it. And then she turned her phone off to save the battery and got back to her hard, boring work.

After an early afternoon break—for more bangers and mash—she started to worry. What if something happened to Tavish? Would she be stuck here for the rest of her life?

Her mind went back to Brian. Could he help her? He'd implied that he wasn't able to time travel himself, but that he knew others who could...

But Brian was an unknown. She didn't know if she could trust him. Tavish was a safer bet, and it sounded like his time traveling ability was dependent on whoever 'they' were. And 'they' wanted that artifact. So shouldn't she be looking for it, not wasting time here in this shop?

IT WAS GETTING DARK WHEN TAVISH FINALLY CAME IN the door to get her for supper. Anxious to have a word with him, she dropped her work, jumped up, and rushed to meet him at the door. But she was puzzled when he wouldn't lock arms with her when she offered. He just scooped up her leather backpack and headed out the door.

She rushed to keep up with him.

"So do we eat dinner in the castle? Where am I going to sleep? Will I get my own room, or do I have to bunk with others?"

He kept quiet until he had walked them the long way out of the castle wall and up a barren hill, where no one was around. When he stopped and turned to look at her, there was fear in his eyes.

"What do you mean to do with all the pictures you took today?"

She couldn't ever remember seeing him afraid before.

"No one noticed I was taking them, Tavish. I mean, I guess you saw me, but no one else knows what a phone is, so they don't know I did it."

He grimaced and looked away for a moment. When he turned back to her, the fear was gone, replaced by... determination. He spoke softly, so that she had to strain to hear.

"Let's assume for right now that they didn't notice."

"They didn't."

He put his hand out in front of him palm down and lowered it toward the ground.

"Fine. Given the best scenario where no one here knows anything is amiss, you do understand that once we get home, you can't post those photos online for your university colleagues to see, don't you?"

Really? Here they were back in the fourteenth century, and he was worried about her posting photos online when they got back home?

"Come on, Tavish. I know that."

He looked her in the eye then, beseeching her with his deep brown eyes.

"Are you sure?"

She let herself get lost in his eyes for so long, he finally raised an eyebrow in inquiry. Oh yeah, their conversation.

"Of course I'm sure. Come on, why do you think I'm so stupid?"

He pursed his perfectly shaped, manly lips.

"Because you were awfully insistent about posting the photos you took of the client's property back in our time, and I doubt very much he wants that."

She nodded to the side and threw her hand up a little bit.

"Okay. You have a point."

He grabbed both of her upper arms and drew her toward him, causing a different kind of goosebumps to run all the way down to her toes.

"This isn't the debate team, Kelsey. This could be the death of us. Do you see that now?"

"Tavish, yes, I do, okay?"

"So what are you going to do with these pictures?"

"I just want to have them for my own knowledge."

"Do you promise?"

"Yes, I promise."

"And isn't your phone one of those android phones that automatically upload to Google Pictures?"

"Yeah, but no one can see my Google Pictures unless I share them."

"Are you sure about that?"

"Pretty sure."

"Kel, make darn sure, okay?"

"Right now?"

He looked around.

"No, not here out in the open. Let's go sit on the grass between those rocks."

Once they were seated side by side, he took out another drawing he had in his sporran and held it in his lap where they could both look at it. She used their tableaux as lookers at a drawing as a cover for playing with her phone.

"Okay. Now I'm 100% sure that my camera won't upload these to Google Pictures."

"Good. Now let's just pray that no one did notice you taking them."

No one here could possibly understand what it would mean for her to be aiming her elbow subtly and casually at things and pausing for a second, right? But Tavish acted so worried about it that his paranoia was rubbing off on her. Add to that her keen awareness that she was dependent on him to get home, and now her body was once again urging her to run somewhere, blood pumping and heart racing.

"Let's go to dinner," he said, getting up and giving her a hand to help her up.

"All right," she agreed, taking his hand.

But when she got up, she was trembling, and she clung to his hand in real need of support for a few seconds longer.

His support was unhesitating, firm, and sure. He patiently stood there waiting for her to steady herself.

Before she realized it, she was looking up into his eyes, searching for reassurance.

And it was there, right there on his face: loyalty, devotion even—the promise that he would never leave her behind—

"Och, there ye are, Tavish. Laird Malcomb sent me oot after ye, says ye best come quick if ye want tae gae tae Bangor with us on the morrow."

Seumas bent over a bit and put his hands on his knees, gulping air.

"Aye?" said Tavish. "Well then, see gin ye can keep up wi us."

He kept hold of her hand and started running in the direction where Seumas had come from, laughing the whole way. She knew he wasn't running his fastest, because she kept up with him easily. At first.

But when Seumas passed him, Tavish dropped her hand and tossed her leather backpack to her, then went running to try and catch up to Seumas, but he didn't. Panting a bit, the two men stopped at the castle town gate and turned to look at her.

"I'm coming, I'm coming," she assured them as she walked more sedately, with the pack on her back, because she was approaching the castle and didn't want to trip over her long skirts where anyone could see. Her slow approach allowed her to appreciate the beauty of the sunset behind them, off the cliff and over the sparkling sea next to Ireland.

They both offered their arms to her, and she took both, so that the three of them were walking through the town in a linked chain with her in the middle.

"Another merchant ship wanting a guard tae Bangor?" said Tavish.

"Aye, and no juist any merchant ship, but Donnell's again."

Kelsey pulled on both of their arms in order to get them to quit talking over her head. "Sae ye hae guarded merchant ships?"

"Sure, thon is most of the work we dae here," Tavish told her.

"Well, whit dae ye guard from, pirates?"

She'd been grinning a silly grin because she'd said that in fun, but Tavish and Seumas turned serious faces to her. This time it was Seumas who spoke.

"Aye, there are pirates aboot betimes. 'Tis no a laughing matter, lass."

She smirked at him.

"Nay, that canna be true."

"Aye, lass, it is."

Kelsey looked to Tavish for an admission that they were having fun with her, pulling her leg. What she saw in his eyes surprised her. He was serious. But more than that, he looked worried again. And determined.

"They've never yet gotten the best of us, mostly because we know what we're doing. Donnell runs a tight ship, aye Seumas?"

The red haired giant pursed his lips and nodded yes to Kelsey.

"Aye, that he does, indeed. We hae only been boarded twice, and both times we killed every one of those sorry MacDonalds. The world would be a far better place if they would all die out, ye ken. Why, we ought tae…"

What? Kelsey put a hand up in front of Seumas's face and waved it to get his attention.

"Wait a minute. Ye mean tae tell me the pirates are other Scots?"

Seumas and Tavish exchanged a look over her head.

For a moment, it was all she could do not to stomp on their feet, but she forced herself to be polite. Only because she was walking through a medieval town—in a backward time when women had to be even more careful than in the twenty first century.

This brought them to the oak plank door of the aboveground castle that in her time had been long destroyed, only lines of different colored stone in the ground, not even sticking up an inch above the wild grass. The castle was huge.

Seumas dropped her arm to hold the door, and Tavish put his hand on her lower back and escorted her inside.

The three of them entered directly into a huge dining hall with vaulted ceilings complete with iron candelabras hanging from the eaves. A hundred planked wooden tables stood in three large concentric squares, and the head table where Laird Malcomb sat with his lady and his sons was on the far side of the room.

Laird Malcomb saw them.

"Ah, there ye are, Tavish. Dae come sup at my table, and bring yer lovely clanswoman."

Tavish raised his other arm in greeting and then left his hand on her lower back the whole way across the great hall. His casual touch was reassuring. There were many single men in the room, judging by the lack of women by their sides, and she could imagine them all leering at her. Instead, they were measuring up Tavish.

Oh, there was Eileen across the room, sitting with a very handsome blond man who wasn't Fergus. Kelsey waited until she looked up, and then waved a little. When Eileen smiled at her, she gave the weaver a thumbs up. At the last second, she worried a bit. Would a thumbs up send the same message now as it did in her time?

But yeah. Whew, Eileen smiled back and raised her eyebrows a little before turning back to her handsome dinner partner.

Seumas must've seen Kelsey wave, because he spoke to her then while he gave the couple his own wave, which was much more enthusiastic than hers.

"Aha. The bonnie weaver ye are apprenticed tae is eating with my brother Alfred."

Alfred raised his cup in a toast to Seumas then, with a smile and a wink that Kelsey figured must be about some in-joke between them.

Tavish took her on across the dining hall, and when they drew near the head table, Laird Malcomb gestured at three seats down the head table from him. Some servants pulled out velvet upholstered chairs for them as he talked.

Tavish steered Kelsey into the chair closest to Lord Malcomb and sat down between her and Seumas. He rested his arm on the top of her chair, and she was acutely aware of how near he was, without quite touching her.

A woman sat at Kelsey's other hand, clearly the wife or relative of the man next to her, because their plaids matched.

But Laird Malcomb was addressing her.

"It is well thon we hae all met ye, Kelsey MacGregor."

She nodded her head at him.

"I thank ye, Laird Malcomb."

The laird turned his eyes.

"Tavish."

"Aye, Laird?"

"On the morn, ye are tae join Seumas's crew agin aboard Donnell's ship doon in Port Patrick, for tae sail ower Bangor way."

Tavish bowed his head the slightest.

"Aye, Laird. I wish tae bring Kelsey along, Laird."

At the mention of her going along with Tavish and Seumas to Ireland and not being left behind here, Kelsey relaxed from a stiffness she hadn't realized was in her body. Her head nudged Tavish's arm, and it dropped down and wrapped around her shoulders, making her whole body hum with the thrill of his touch.

Laird Malcomb fixed his stern eyes on her.

"Is there some aught your clanswoman can add tae the trip, Tavish?"

"Aye, Laird, there is. Kelsey can dae sums."

There was a general tittering. The woman next to Kelsey looked at her with interest.

Laird Malcomb raised an eyebrow, clearly enjoying the theatrical aspect of this announcement.

"Can she, now?"

Kelsey stood up, feeling Tavish's arm ever so slowly release her, then linger on her hand and give a reassuring squeeze.

"Aye, Laird Malcomb. If I can hae some aught to write on, I'll then show ye."

Laird Malcomb turned to some servants.

"There, lad, bring us the writing desk from my study."

A boy of about ten rushed off out the door.

Kelsey squeezed Tavish's hand back, then let go and made her way up to the head of the table and stood behind Laird Malcomb, waiting.

The laird continued speaking, loudly enough so that everyone at their table could hear, and he continued to speak to Tavish about Kelsey, even though she was standing right next to him.

"How can the MacGregors afford tae teach a woman her sums, then?"

Tavish laughed.

"She's very clever, Laird Malcomb. She taught herself by watching. None of us fashit. Quite handy it is, having another soul aboot who can run the numbers."

Tavish winked at her.

She just shrugged with an odd little grin on her face, unsure if it was nerves or smugness, and trying not to gush in front of all these people at how proud he looked of her. She happened to glance over at

Eileen right then, and the weaver shook her head with a big smile on her face before turning back to converse with Alfred. Okay, smugness it was. May as well have fun with this. It would be much easier than the demonstrations her professors had assigned. Piece of cake.

Meanwhile, the boy ran in with the writing desk, looking all around for someplace to set it down.

Laird Malcomb got up and walked over to a side table.

"Set it up here, lad."

He stood aside and watched the boy set down and open a large worn wooden box on top of the table so that it resembled one of those old-fashioned desks with the shelves in front. It was obviously old, but it was also lovingly used—well oiled, without any signs of splintering, drying out, or rot. Inside were folded pieces of what must've been vellum, as well as several quills and an inkwell.

But what caught Kelsey's eye were the decorations on the outside of the writing desk. The Celtic runes were lovely of course, but even more alarmingly, they declared it the property of the king of Alba. There was more, but she could no longer see it now that the writing desk was open. The inside was just as well cared for, but sadly free of runes.

"There we are, my dear. Now dae come sit doon and shew us."

Kelsey tore her eyes away from the desk just in time to see the laird gesture at the chair someone had kindly pulled over, and all she could do was hope she hadn't missed a beat as she sat down, opened the inkwell, and dipped one of the quills in it.

Laird Malcomb's hand hovered near hers the whole time she handled the quill.

But these quills were simple, compared with the fancy art ones she had used in her studies. She looked up at him expectantly.

The laird cleared his throat.

"Verra well. Let us try this sum."

Kelsey pulled out one of the sheets of vellum. It was a rougher piece of deer hide than those she'd used at university, but just as fine and pliable, while at the same time sturdy. She poised the quill over the top of the vellum and turned to look at the laird.

He posed dramatically for a moment as The Thinker, with his fist to his forehead, and everyone in the hall laughed. He smiled—probably at the pleasure of all their attention—and then boomed out in a voice big enough to reach the farthest corner, pacing with a sway of his great kilt as he spoke, quite the orator.

"A laird went tae battle with a hundrit men. Half o' them were marrit, and their wives did come along, tae cook for the men, an tae stitch up their wounds. Along the way, first five men joinit them, and then six more, and then seven more beside, half o' all these with their wives. Well enough, how many mouths did the laird have tae feed?"

Kelsey felt the laird bending over her shoulder as she did the math. She glanced over at the laird's wife and wrinkled her brow in apology, and then went back to work.

"He had one hundred and seventy seven mouths tae feed, Laird Malcomb."

He bent down to check her math, and she scooted her chair back, again looking over at his lady. This time she ventured a smile at the woman.

The woman nodded, and Kelsey breathed easier.

"Verra good," said Laird Malcomb, "I am impressit."

Kelsey started to get up. Everyone else was eating and drinking, and she saw that there was food on her plate. Roasted duck, if her nose was right.

"But stay a while. This is the only show we hae this evening, sae let us see if yer ability with numbers goes beyond sums, an if sae, how far."

Kelsey only dared look at her plate a moment more, where Tavish gave her a soft look of encouragement, and then she scooted back up to the desk, inked the quill once more, and poised it over the vellum.

Laird Malcomb paced while he spoke.

"Two thirds o' the laird's men were woundit in battle. o' the wounded, ivery tenth died. In addition, a fever overtook the camp at night on the way back tae their castle an took ivery fifth person remaining. How many returnit tae the castle?"

Kelsey paused with her quill over the vellum.

"That depends, Laird Malcomb."

"Aye?"

"Aye, Laird Malcomb."

"Upon what, my dear?"

"The eighteen men and nine wives who joinit the laird along the way, did they who survivit among them gae back tae their homes, or did they gae tae the castle?

I'm thinking they went back tae their homes, because they really wouldn't be returning tae the castle, now would they?"

Laird Malcomb threw his head back and laughed.

"Tavish, ye hae the right of it. Your clan's Kelsey is far too clever."

"Begging yer pardon, Laird Malcomb," said Seumas, standing behind his empty plate at the table and wiping his mouth with a large linen napkin, "but should na we give her some merchant items tae sum? After all, while these battle sums are entertaining, it is hoped that she will only need tae dae merchant sums in Bangor on the morrow."

Still chuckling, Laird Malcomb held his palm out toward Seumas.

"Nay, my guid man. Sums are the least o' what she just did. She has the gift o' knowing when someone is leading another astray, as I tryit tae dae with the men who joinit the laird along the way tae battle." He looked over at a man at the table. "She has a good head for business, Donnell. She will be a good asset for ye in Ireland upon the morrow." And then to Kelsey, he said, "Gae on and eat yer food now, lass. Ye've earned it."

"I thank ye, Laird."

Kelsey hurried over to her seat to do as she'd been told.

Tavish and Seumas both stood when she got there, but a servant pulled out her chair and seated her.

Still standing, Tavish patted her on the shoulder.

"Please stay here. I'll be back straight away."

"All right."

The spot where he had tapped her shoulder still glowed with his warmth all the while Seumas made small talk in Tavish's absence. She did her best to keep up with it and be polite while she ate.

"I truly admire yer cleverness, Kelsey. I couldna hae done those sums better myself. But ye are not only clever. Ye make a fine figure of a woman as well."

"Why thank ye, Seumas. I admired the way ye gave Tavish a run for his money earlier."

"It was a good race, was na it?"

"Aye, verra close, but you did come oot the victor."

The big red-haired man was quiet for a moment, and Kelsey thought the conversation was over, but then he continued it, and she kept being polite.

"I have na seen the MacGregor holdings, but dare I say ye could hae as good a life here, in Laird Malcomb's Castle."

She appreciatively took in the grand hall in its present well-maintained state, all the wood polished, all the stonework scrubbed, and fresh candles everywhere, their smoke escaping through artfully placed holes in the roof while fires roared in two huge fireplaces.

"'Tis verra safe here, lass. With all of us aboot, no one is going to set upon ye. And even when we are oot to battle, these walls will protect ye, the walls and yer women's arrows."

She lifted her pewter goblet and sipped her wine, using the gesture to look discreetly and see if Tavish was on his way back to her.

"I can see that is true."

Seumas sipped his wine as well and started to relax

into his seat, but when she set her goblet down, he set his down and looked at her earnestly.

"Laird Malcomb does give us some aught each evening—be times someone of talent such as yerself, but more often than not we get music, and dancing."

His earnestness made her giggle a little.

"Och, it could be fun to live here, that is sure."

Kelsey shared a little smile with Seumas.

General conversation had picked up in the hall, so she was no longer the center of attention. Tavish had made sure she was going along to Bangor tomorrow, and her food wasn't too cold.

Things were looking up.

9

NAOI

Things were looking down.

The longer Kelsey was here in the old time, the higher the chance of her modern sensibilities coming out. She was doing a great job so far, but it was only a matter of time before some man said something—or did something—and she went off on him. And then all hell would break loose.

He had to prevent that, and the only way was to keep her close to him. And she needed to be with him during waking hours anyway so that he could take her with him if some Druid ran into him and sent him to some other time. Or place. He couldn't imagine them patiently waiting for him to get her.

He had to find the artifact they wanted as soon as possible so that he could get her back home where she'd be safe. And now there would be a trip to Bangor tomorrow. The whole day would be wasted.

Good, the weaver lady was still at supper.

"Pray pardon an interruption?" said Tavish to the table at large.

The big kilted warrior she was sitting with looked up first and then smiled and stood.

"Not at all. Ye are sitting at the laird's table with my brother Seumas, so ye must be important." He reached out with his sword arm, and Tavish clasped forearms with him. "I'm Alfred. Tae what dae we owe the honor?"

Tavish smiled at the weaver woman when she caught his eye, but she was obviously under Alfred's protection, so he addressed his comments to the warrior.

"My clanswoman apprenticed with yer lovely supper partner today, and I've come tae see if she can share her accommodation with her, or find her an appropriate place to sleep."

Alfred deferred to the weaver, who smiled at Tavish again.

"I dae thank ye for bringing Kelsey tae us. She is a lot of help. My children and I still hae my husband's house in Castleton, and I would be happy tae make a home for her while she's here visiting ye, Tavish MacGregor. And please, dae call me Eileen."

"Och. I thank ye sae much," he said to Eileen, and then he spoke mostly to Alfred. "Once ye hae finished eating, will ye please come and get us? o' course I will see Kelsey tae Eileen's house safely, and I will pick her up at dawn for our trip to Bangor."

"Aye," said Alfred, "'twill be my pleasure."

"Eileen," said Tavish, "I am sorry for the loss of Kelsey's help on the morrow. If there ever be aught I can dae for ye, I would be pleased if ye made it known to me."

Eileen was looking across the room when she answered him.

"Sure and I will."

Tavish locked forearms again with Alfred.

"We will be at our table."

"We will see ye soon."

Tavish was almost back to the head table when he saw Kelsey and Seumas talking with their heads close together, smiling and laughing over his empty chair. The couple on the other side of Kelsey had left, so Tavish pulled out the woman's chair by Kelsey's side.

At the movement, she turned her head, and when she saw it was him, she turned her whole body.

"I was starting to think ye fell— I mean, that something was amiss."

He laughed.

"Nothing so dramatic, just arranging yer sleeping quarters with Eileen. It appears I've missed a bunch o' fun here, though."

She smiled and glanced at Seumas.

"Yer sparring partner was just filling me in aboot the standard of entertainment in this hall. He says there is something tae see or hear or dae ivery night. Right, Seumas?"

Seumas nodded to her and then met Tavish's eyes over her head, looking more like a doctor or a preacher than a warrior, his eyes had such softness in them.

"Aye, I did tell the lass what a fine life she might hae here, did she wish tae stay."

Uh oh. Here it came. Tavish searched Kelsey's face for any sign of fear at the idea of remaining here—or anger at the idea of a stranger suggesting it, but he didn't see any. She seemed content, relaxed, and enjoying herself. How weird. He opened his mouth to ask her about that, discreetly, but she spoke first.

"Sae what sort o' sums will I need tae dae for Donnell tomorrow?"

"Och," said Tavish, "Donnell is Laird Malcomb's steward of ships. We will take a boatload o' cow leather and vellum ower, and then we will bring all manner o' goods back here from the huge port in Bangor, Ireland."

She winked at him, and smiled in amusement.

"All manner o' goods, eh?"

He raised his eyebrows at her. For someone with a degree in Celtic artwork, she didn't know much about the Celts and the extent of their trading.

"Aye, spices from India, tea from China, rugs from Persia, cedar chests from Lebanon, ye name it, he imports it. Yer task will be tae make sure everything is present after the loaders get finished."

She wrinkled her brow and lowered her chin and dropped her mouth open in the cutest gesture he'd ever seen. She put her hand on his knee and pushed. Hard.

"Tavish. That's a huge task ye hae signed me up for. How am I going tae get all that done?"

He tried to stop himself, but he chuckled a little at her expression. But at the touch of her hand on his knee through his kilt, he took a napkin off the table and put it in his lap, gesturing for Seumas to give him his wine.

"Thank ye, Seumas." He drank it all down, grateful

for its instant calming effect. "Kelsey, ye won't hae tae dae it all yerself. We'll help ye. But ye see it was a long stretch, getting Laird Malcomb tae let ye come along." And then he stared into her eyes, willing her to understand what he meant, despite what he had to say in front of others. "And I know how ye hae always wanted tae see Ireland, aye?"

She sighed, but she popped her eyes wide open for a moment, just for Tavish to see, then slumped in her chair.

"Aye."

Seumas spoke to her, but he met Tavish's eyes over her head again.

"There, there, lass. Ye don't hae tae dae it. We men can manage on our own. There will be other trips to Ireland, many of them, if ye dae stay here. Ye can go another time, when ye are more accustomed tae this place, and tae our ways."

Tavish locked eyes with Seumas to show he meant business.

"Nay, she's going."

Seumas raised his eyebrows at Tavish.

"Aye? Is that the way of it, then?"

Kelsey scooted her chair back, and the wooden legs made a loud scraping noise on the stone floor. When the two of them turned to look at her, she had a twinkle in her eye and she was smiling.

"It's all right Seumas. I dae want tae go. I'm looking forward tae it."

Seumas kept looking at Tavish.

"Well then, things are set. For the morrow."

Tavish nodded at Seumas, then turned to smile at Kelsey.

She gave him a hopeful smile, then followed his gaze over toward Alfred and Eileen's table.

He was relieved to see them walking toward him.

10

DEICH

Kelsey went to meet Eileen when she saw her coming, and she threw her arms around the woman and gave her a big hug.

"Thank ye, thank ye, thank ye!"

Eileen laughed, but she hugged Kelsey back while Alfred went over to speak with his brother and Tavish.

"Och, wait till ye see the place before ye thank me sae much. Thare are four children livin thare, ye know."

Kelsey broke out of the hug and made a dismissive gesture with her hand, looking over to make sure the men were out of earshot and lowering her voice against those still seated nearby overhearing.

"Ay, thank ye for the place tae stay an aw, but I meant thank ye for comin along juist now."

Eileen cast a worried glance over at the men.

"Och? What's the matter?"

Kelsey smirked to let Eileen know it wasn't danger she had fled, but annoyance.

"As if it wasn't enough that Tavish was always butting intae my business, now Seumas is finding the need tae dae sae as well."

But instead of commiserating with her, Eileen got a big grin on her face. What was up with that? Kelsey looked over at the men again.

"Canna ye dae better than Seumas's brother? I mean, he's handsome, but gin he's anythin like Seumas, that's a bit owerbearing, ye ken?"

Eileen bit her knuckle again, and only spoke once she'd contained her laughter.

"Kelsey, Alfred and Seumas are Laird Malcomb's nephews, and the laird's sons are marriit now. Sae thare really is na much better we could dae."

"We?"

Kelsey looked over at the men yet again. Now that Eileen mentioned it, the brothers' linen shirts were a little finer than those of the other warriors in the hall. Their kilted plaids were similar to the laird's. They wore fine brooches that might even be signets of some kind. When she turned back, Eileen was smirking.

"Well, ye are in need of a husband."

"I did na say I needed one, just that I did lose one."

"'Tis the same difference."

Kelsey crossed her arms to show that she wouldn't be persuaded.

"Perchance around here it is, but not where I hail from."

Eileen was giving her a puzzled look, but Kelsey nodded sideways, where the men were coming over.

Alfred found his way to Eileen's side instantly and offered his arm.

"Let us gae an get yer children, and then ma brother and I and Tavish will see ye home."

She smiled up at him and took his arm.

Tavish and Seumas were both looking at Kelsey intently and moving forward as if they meant to come over and take charge and tell her what to do once more.

She headed them off at the pass, stepping between them and grabbing both of their arms again, just like when they came in. Acting like the three of them had been playmates since they were little, she kept her voice cheerful and light, like this was all in fun.

"Come on. I'm dyin tae see where Alfred put Eileen's children."

In front of them, Alfred laughed.

"Na place thon interesting, juist in the nursery with Maw. Howsoever, now I wish I had stuffit them intae one o' the old castle's dungeons."

Everyone laughed, including some of the diners at nearby tables.

Kelsey looked into Tavish's deep brown eyes, and they were aglow with at least as much excitement as she felt. He dropped her arm, raised his eyebrows at her, and gave her a 'Go on' nod toward Alfred with his chin.

Kelsey dropped Seumas's arm, made her way to Eileen's other side, and looked back-and-forth from Eileen to Alfred with all the wonder she could put into her expression.

"The old castle hae dungeons, Alfred? How fascinating! Will ye shew us?"

Alfred looked to Eileen.

Kelsey looked at her new friend too.

Eileen grinned at Kelsey with a look that clearly said "Thank ye" before she turned her huge charming smile back onto Alfred.

"Och, would ye?"

Alfred looked at the other men.

Tavish shrugged at him.

Seumas looked at Kelsey with a question in his eyes much like the one Alfred had asked Eileen.

Kelsey made herself maintain eye contact with Seumas and not look over at Tavish. The red-haired man was good-looking enough that it wasn't difficult. He seemed nice enough. But she'd only just met him. Still, she and Tavish needed to get into the underground castle. She felt the lie in her smile even as she gave it to him.

Seumas clapped his brother on the back.

"Aye, let us gae and tell Maw we shall be a while longer."

Eileen elbowed Kelsey in the ribs just then.

Kelsey broke into laughter when she saw the look Eileen gave her, which bordered between "Woo woo!" and "I thought so!" And then Kelsey did look at Tavish to see his reaction to this whole little exchange.

He moved up to the front of the group, opened a door, and went inside without looking back at her.

Alfred took the rest of them through the same door.

"Maw!"

"Maw!"

"Maw!"

"Maw!"

Eileen's four children ran over and all found a way to hug her at the same time.

Thus encumbered, Eileen still found a way to sort of curtsy at Alfred and Seumas's mother, a woman of about 50 who looked kind but clever.

"I thank ye sae much, ma'am. I hope they were na tae much trouble."

Alfred stepped over.

"Maw, I'm verra happy for ye tae meet Eileen. Eileen, this is my maw, Isabel."

Isabel looked back-and-forth between Alfred and Eileen with a calmly controlled joy. And then she put her hands on the children and patted them gently and smiled at them when their little eyes looked up at hers.

"It was nay trouble at all, dear."

Alfred held out his arm for Eileen.

"Och good. Then ye will na mind at all watching them for a little while longer while Tavish, Seumas, and I give Eileen and her new apprentice Kelsey a tour o' the dungeons."

On hearing this, Eileen's children piped up.

"The dungeons!"

"We want to go to the dungeons tae!"

"Och!"

"Maw, can we?"

Eileen opened her mouth to say something, but Isabel knelt down and held out her arms.

"Nah nah, the dungeons aren't any place for children. Come on ower tae auntie Isabel. I'll tak ye doon tae the kitchen and see if Sorcha has anything sweet we can make for ye."

The children rushed over to Isabel and let her hug them while Eileen walked over and took Alfred's arm, and then the two led the rest of them out of the nursery, down the corridor, down the stairs, and out through the kitchen. Just before they left the Castle, they picked up torches from a bin and lighted them in the fireplace.

There were lamps burning in all the taverns, but the vendor carts were gone for the night, and only a few people wandered the streets—most of them obviously drunk, walking arm in arm.

The whole way to the underground castle entrance, Seumas walked by Kelsey's side. He was a perfect gentleman, never taking any liberties, but he did catch her by the arm once when she stumbled, preventing her from a nasty fall.

His attention made her self-conscious about wanting to stare at the starry sky. She did catch glimpses of the stars now and then, and there were far more than she ever knew existed. She could even see galaxies, and of course the Milky Way.

She did her best not to sigh, not to give away that she was in no way interested. Encouraging Seumas had seemed a good idea at the time, so now she needed to sleep in the bed she had made—hopefully just figuratively.

Every so often, she tried to catch Tavish's eye. If she was honest with herself, she would admit she wanted reassurance that she was not alone here, that someone else understood how it felt to be 700 years outside one's own time. But he was walking on the other side of Seumas and was never looking at her at the same time she was looking at him.

And then they were at this different underground castle entrance, where an elaborate trap door stood open, revealing a narrow stone staircase going down into blackness. It was much farther back from the cliffs than the ruined tower house which covered those three trapdoors in her time. She cast about for some landmarks, thinking to try and dig up this new trap door in her time.

Once she thought she had it triangulated so that she could find it again, she tried again to make eye contact with Tavish. But again he was looking instead somewhere else. She kept looking at him as long as seemed possible without it getting awkward, but he still didn't happen to look at her.

Two kilted guards armed with claymores stood there on watch, but they nodded to Alfred as he approached.

"Evening, Sir."

"Evening Dubh, Luthais," he said to them, "Seumas and Tavish and I wull be taking these ladies doon tae the docks for a quick look."

Dubh and Luthais bowed their heads toward him.

"Verra well, Sir."

Alfred and Eileen went down the stairs first single file, holding the wall with one hand and their torches high with the other. At the same time, Seumas and Tavish both gestured in front of them for Kelsey to follow so that they could take up the rear.

Kelsey held up her torch and followed Eileen down the stairs.

It had been dark when she and Tavish left here this morning, but their eyes had been adjusted to the darkness, and they had been coming out toward the light of the sun. Now they were going down into the darkness—and it seemed foreboding indeed. Thankfully, she wasn't the only one who thought so, or she would've felt really alone.

Eileen brought it up first, smiling at Alfred in the torchlight.

"Are ye sure 'tis safe down here? 'Tis dreadfully dark."

Alfred chuckled.

"Do ye hae second thoughts on coming doon to the dungeons, lass?"

Oh no. Before he had a chance to talk Eileen out of exploring the dungeons, Kelsey butted in.

"I know I'm havin second an e'en third thoughts aboot comin doon here, but with three strong warriors tae protect us, I know we will be fine. Aye, Eileen?"

Eileen gave Kelsey that same impish grin. And she leaned into Alfred as they all started to walk side-by-side along the corridor—which meant Seumas came up beside Kelsey and Tavish stayed by himself in the back. And Eileen winked at her before she turned to Alfred and all but batted her eyelashes.

"Dinna leave my side, and all my thoughts will stay in order."

Alfred put his arm around Eileen's waist and turned to address everyone.

"This is where the odd parts o' the corridor start." He turned toward the wall and pointed to some Celtic runes that Kelsey could see announced a secret door. "Ivry sae often along the corridor, ye wull see these same runes. We dinna know what they mean. Several o' us hae theories." He raised his eyebrow and invited speculation.

Here, at last, Tavish met eyes with Kelsey. He raised his own eyebrow, and she knew without a shadow of a doubt what he was asking: "Is it another secret door?"

Kelsey nodded the ever slightest to him.

He pressed his lips together and looked around, and again she knew exactly what he was saying to her, they'd known each other so well: "Be ready to come back here and explore it. I'm going to cause a distraction at the first opportunity I see."

She made the tiniest nod to him again.

Meanwhile, Eileen was gushing with enthusiasm at Alfred.

"Och, I hae heard stories aboot the things doon in these caves! The ancient druids used tae dae ritual sacrifices doon here they say! There's supposit tae be aw kinds o' secret passageways gang deep intae the cliffs! An aw sorts o' secret rooms with treasure inside! Och, and dungeons as well—ye know, where they did thaes sacrifices!"

Alfred gave her an amused smile and humored her a bit.

"Forsooth, all I hae seen are these strange Celtic markings. I dinna doubt the Celts livit in these caves long ago. As for the rest, yer guess is as guid as mine."

He bowed his head to Eileen a bit, and she caressed his cheek. "Come, we must get on with the tour doon tae the dungeons if we are tae get tae bed afore the cock crows."

Instead of letting Seumas accompany Kelsey as he had before, Tavish fell in next to Seumas and clapped a hand on his back and spoke to him uproariously, demanding all the man's attention as they walked down the corridor.

"I'll wager we find altars in the dungeons gin we look well enough. Whit say ye?"

Seumas was taken in.

"Och I'll willingly take yer money! We hae been doon thare hundrits o' times on the watches, and hae seen nay sign o' an altar..."

Kelsey knew this was Tavish giving her an opportunity to explore the secret door, so she wasted no time slipping away to go back and get it open.

It opened to a stairway going down. She held her torch down as far she could in front of her, but when that only revealed more stairs and more darkness, she went ahead and started going down, although not as fast as she might have were there light in the room. Praying that she wouldn't stumble and fall and break her nose on the hard stone floor, she at last came to the bottom of the stairs and into a room. It was full of stuff, but rather than take the time to notice just what it was, she quickly powered up her camera and took several photos, then put it on screensaver and stuck it back in the pouch in the side of her leather backpack so she could rush back up the stairs, close the door, and run to hopefully catch up with the others before they noticed she was gone.

No such luck.

But to her amusement, it was Tavish who called out to her. She hoped only she could tell he was faking his anger.

"Where did ye go, Kelsey? Ye shouldn't go away from the group like thon!"

Inspiration struck, and Kelsey put her hand on her abdomen.

"Och, I have na gone anywhere, it's just that I have a wee stitch in my side. I canna gae as fast as ye can. Gae on ahead o' me. I'll make ma way at ma own pace. Surely thare canna be any danger in here, with the guards at both ends o' the corridor."

Seumas moved forward as if to help her, but Tavish held him back, still speaking as if he were angry, but unseen, he was smiling at her.

"Nay, Kelsey. Gae back and wait for us with the guards at the entrance, if ye canna keep up."

Seumas took in a breath as if to make a case for Kelsey to come along with them.

But Tavish turned a genuinely angry look on him, and Seumas backed down.

Kelsey waved at them all and turned back to go the way she had come, saying farewell to them over her shoulder.

"Verra well. See ye at the top."

Just before she turned around, she caught an apologetic look from Seumas and shook her head no, hoping he would let it drop.

He seemed to, because she heard them all going off the other way down the corridor behind her.

She kept on going a little ways, until she only heard them faintly and knew they'd gone around the corner. And then she went back and opened the second secret doorway. She took pictures in there with two fingers showing on her hand, so that later on when she looked at the pictures, she would know where this stuff was.

She catalogued a dozen more rooms this way. Unlike the second door room, most of them were very old bedrooms. None had any dust, because of the sophisticated yet simple air circulation system which permeated the place.

The whole time, she kept her eye out for any sign of Brian, but the only thing she noticed was that one of the beds looked slept in. She made a mental note of which room that was before she moved on.

But then the thirteenth door she came to led to a passageway that went down several flights of stairs and around corners and down long hallways—until the last secret door she opened dropped her off in the rough cave near the docks.

Sure enough, bows and quivers of arrows hung from the grooves in the walls. Tavish had been right about those grooves, and no wonder. But that didn't bother her nearly as much as the fact that she had noisily emerged out of the wall on her hands and knees, right behind Seumas.

❧ 11 ❧

AON DEUG

Kelsey met Tavish's eyes, and in just a moment, with only the slightest facial expressions, they held a lengthy silent conversation.

"Hm! I'm impressed that you found your way back to us through the walls!"

"Believe me, I am too."

"Did you find the artifact?"

"No, and I really looked hard, covering as much ground as I could."

"It's okay, I'll just keep giving you opportunities to look."

"Understood. And anyway, I'm having fun looking."

"This is serious business, Kelsey—"

"Of course it is. Quick, do something about Seumas!"

She saw Tavish cast his glance about then, but it was too late.

Seumas turned around and made his way to her side

protectively, narrowing his eyes at Tavish, who wrinkled his brow a little and playfully smirked at Kelsey while the large redheaded man lingered between them and extended his hand to her, offering to help her up.

"Kelsey! Verra glad I am to see ye made it back tae us." He gave Tavish a sidelong glance. "Did ye stumble, Kelsey? Please, allow me tae help ye up."

But she looked to Tavish.

Seumas got out of his way.

And Tavish came forward and tenderly helped her up. After he did, it was clear that he got just as much of a thrill holding her hand and she did his, because he lingered there, looking into her eyes and giving the back of her hand the barest caress with his fingers.

Alfred was standing there in the group with them, holding Eileen by the waist, and he cleared his throat.

"The dungeons we promisit tae show ye are around this last bend, on the other side o' the docks."

Kelsey caught an 'I told you so' raise of Eileen's eyebrows, along with a warm smile of congratulations. She returned the look in kind, and Eileen's smile changed to one of joy.

Tavish hung back with Kelsey a bit and gestured for the others to go in front of them.

"You go on ahead. We wull be there shortly."

Seumas and Alfred took the hint and started off, but Eileen looked over her shoulder as they left and winked at Kelsey.

But just when they started walking that way, they heard shouts from the docks.

"Boats!"

"They're coming!"

"Get the bows!"

"The MacDonalds are attacking!"

Tavish and Seumas and Alfred didn't hesitate to grab bows and quivers from the wall and rush down to the docks, putting the quivers on their backs and drawing an arrow each while they ran.

Kelsey and Eileen stood there staring at each other, blinking.

Eileen swallowed.

"Dae ye think we shoud tak bows ower an gae help them?"

Kelsey grimaced.

"Dae ye know how tae use a bow? Because I don't."

Eileen shook her head.

"Nay, I dinna either."

Meanwhile, they could hear the shouts of battle coming from the end of the hallway around the corner.

Alfred was giving orders.

"Warwick, tak the boat on the left. Seumas, tak the neist boat tae the richt o' Warwick's. Ian, the boat tae the richt o' Seumas's..."

The other men were saying "Aye," accompanied by a lot of scuffling about, and in the distance, the MacDonalds were shouting their own orders, which the women could hear, but not really understand because of the general noise of the sea between them.

Kelsey quietly took a bow and a quiver down anyway, put the quiver on over her leather backpack, then crept over to the wall between her and the battle.

She looked back to see if Eileen was going to do the same, and then waited for her.

When Eileen caught up to her, the sounds of the battle were lower and the waves breaking against the rocks seemed louder.

Eileen whispered, “Ye are na charging in there, are ye?”

Kelsey crept forward along the wall till she was almost at the bend, then turned her head back toward Eileen and waited again for her to catch up before she whispered back.

“Nay, but I am no gaun'ae juist stand around here without knowing what’s gang on ower thare.”

Eileen nodded vigorously and urged Kelsey on with a tap on the waist with the back of her hand.

Kelsey crept along the wall until she could peek around the bend, holding her torch behind her so that its light didn’t give away her location.

Tavish, Alfred, Seumas, and the other dock defenders had thrown their torches down on the smooth stone floor of the dock area and found cover behind various rocks, where they were busy shooting one arrow after another into the dozens of men who were approaching on half a dozen lantern lit boats. Most of these men were rowing, but a few had bows out and were shooting back.

Eileen started to come around the corner by Kelsey’s side with her torch held high, but Kelsey frantically grabbed her skirt and held her back.

Tavish met Kelsey’s eyes full of fear for her, nodding

urgently back toward the secret door she had just come from, silently pleading for her to please go to safety.

The moment she had waited seven years for had finally come. She saw such deep love and caring in his eyes that her heart commanded her to run to him and fall into his arms and never let go. But her head knew he had to pay attention to the battle and would only worry needlessly about her if she stuck around.

She struggled with this choice for a moment, but then another enemy arrow whizzed by and she came to her senses. Putting as much love and caring as she possibly could in her own eyes, she nodded at Tavish, then turned around and gently took Eileen by the elbows to keep her from going into the battle scene.

"There are arrows flying all places, Eileen. We canna gae oot thare."

Eileen struggled with her.

"But we canna make it back tae the top before the invaders reach us. I'd rather dee oot thare shootin at them than feel them at ma back as I run away!"

Kelsey shook her head quickly.

"We can gae up unseen. I found a way. Come on!"

Eileen looked doubtful, but she quit struggling and followed Kelsey over to the secret door, which was down low to the floor.

Kelsey put her bow down on top of Eileen's, handed Eileen her torch, and then wasted no time opening the secret door. With the invader's cries getting louder and the sound of feet scrambling on the rocks ringing through the cave, the two of them got themselves, the torches, and the bows inside, and then Kelsey hurried to close the secret door again.

She and Eileen held each other for a moment and cringed, listening, but determination overtook Kelsey, and she withdrew from Eileen, slung her bow over her shoulder, picked up her torch, and started to climb the stairs—careful to hold up her long skirts with her other hand.

"Come on, let's go get help!"

Hope bloomed on Eileen's face then, and the weaver eagerly climbed the stairs as well.

The two women ran all the way up, went through the other secret door, and then ran up the passageway and the final stairs to the entrance guards before they all but fell on the ground, exhausted and gasping for breath while they explained.

"Dubh! Luthais! We're under attack!"

"Please! Send more men down there!"

"Dozens o' invaders are coming by boat!"

"The guards are holding them off with arrows for now, but hurry!"

Dubh and Luthais blew on the ram's horns they had around their necks, and a runner came over and left.

A few moments later, Laird Malcomb led over dozens of kilted warriors who Kelsey recognized from supper in the castle a few hours before. They all went running down the stairs single file with their claymores strapped to their backs. Up on the sea-facing battlements, dozens more guards were rolling huge stones into the water below. Some yielded distant splashes, and others scored the satisfying sound of a boat's floor cracking and enemy voices calling out in alarm.

Kelsey tried to get up to follow Laird Malcomb downstairs, but she had used up all her adrenaline. Her shaking legs wouldn't cooperate. She looked over at Eileen, who wasn't doing any better.

She'd sat there gasping for breath for a minute, trying to get her legs under her, when she felt a gentle hand on her back and turned to see the sympathetic face of Isabel, Alfred and Seumas's mother.

"I am indebtit tae ye, Kelsey and Eileen, for coming in such earnest tae get help for my sons—even if, God forbid, they should perish." She stood and extended a hand to each of them. "Come inside and let us await them together."

Eileen's children ran to greet their mother before she got halfway down the hallway to the nursery.

"Maw!"

"Maw!"

"Maw!"

"Maw!"

Once more, the small blonde woman was enveloped by her four small blond children, who hugged her various arms and legs and waist.

Kelsey and Isabel stayed back and enjoyed this scene, which while chaotic in itself was calming in contrast to the battle outside. But the battle soon intruded. Even within the thick walls of the castle fortress, they could hear the muffled voice of Alfred's lieutenant shouting orders outside.

Isabel took Kelsey's hand and made her way over to Eileen and the children.

"Let us crowd around the small windae i the nursery an see whit we can see, eh?"

Eileen nodded and led the way.

"Come, children."

Kelsey and Eileen put their bows down on the table and took off their quivers and set them beside the bows.

They all crowded into the narrow arrow-slit window. Unable to move around, Kelsey's view was limited to one section of the battlement, but it was satisfying to watch the kilted warriors there pushing their stones over the edge at the enemy boats. Eileen had a view of the soldiers rolling the stones up a ramp onto the battlement, and from time to time she would comment on that. Isabel had commanded the view of the exit from the downstairs, and she watched it silently, her face a mixture of fear and hope for her sons. All the children could see was the night sky full of billions of stars, and the women took turns picking the children up now and again so they could see what the women were talking about.

Kelsey's breath caught.

"They're all rushing tae ma section o' the battlement!"

She was jostled as everyone tried to see what she was talking about. One of the kids managed to get in there and take her place.

"Look! They are! Everyone's running ower thare."

Kelsey looked at Eileen who gently pulled the child

out of the way—but then Eileen herself pushed into that spot so she could see.

"This has tae mean all the boats are tryin tae dock! Get them! Get them!"

All the children joined in with their mother, yelling and screaming as if the people out there across the courtyard could hear them, and as if they would work more frantically if they did.

"Get them! Get them!"

It reminded Kelsey of the football games her parents used to attend with her at her high school. She nosed in there, pushing Eileen's face away so she could see.

12

DÀ DHEUG

The boats were coming in to land now, and Tavish's fellow guards were rushing them, so he could no longer use his bow. He set it aside and drew his Claymore off his back.

The Rocky dock area echoed with the metal on metal ringing sounds of sword fighting—and then the stones started to fall from the cliffs above. Whoosh! Foom! Crack!

Tavish and Seumas and all their fellow guards cheered.

An answering cheer came from above—along with more of those blessed stones which were tearing the boats to shreds and even hitting a few of the attackers directly.

But there were so many enemies. They abandoned their boats and swam for the rocky shoreline, climbing over each other in their enthusiasm to raid this ancient castle.

Tavish rushed in with the other defending guards, and then he was fighting for his life—hacking and slashing his way through the bodies that scrambled up on the rocks, dodging and ducking the swords that came at him.

It went on and on and on, until he could feel himself tiring.

But all he could think about the whole time he fought the intruders was surviving long enough to get back to Kelsey so he could get her home. Why had he brought her here? The old time was far more dangerous that anything they would do to her in the new time! Yes, he'd known she'd love it here in the old time, and he'd been wishing for years that he could share this with her, but it had been selfish and stupid of him to bring her here. What was he thinking?

Well, done was done. All he could do now was survive this so that he could get back to her—and get her home safely.

They had the high ground, up on the rocks while the enemy tried to climb up from the sea. But they were outnumbered six to one, and Tavish was just about too tired to go on fighting when he heard the battle cry of more fellow guards coming down the inner hallway through the castle toward him. His fellow guards out here on the dock heard it too, and they all let out a cheer.

This reenergized him just enough—he hoped—so that the reinforcements would get here and he wouldn't die and leave Kelsey abandoned.

His fellow guards were almost at the docks, and he

was getting ready to retreat and let them take over, when he felt a blow to the back of his head and the world went dark and quiet.

13

TRÌ DEUG

Kelsey, Eileen, Isabel, and all the children were cheering. All the men on the battlements had come down to the entrance to the underground castle, and the men were running out, slapping the hands of their fellow guards, not unlike sports teams did the beginning of games. They cheered even louder when they saw Seumas come out, and then again when they saw Alfred come out.

A few moments after that, Eileen and Isabel ran out the door together, presumably to go greet Isabel's victorious sons together.

The children stayed with Kelsey.

"Where's yer friend?"

"Did he gae doon thare with Alfred and Seumas?"

Kelsey didn't look at them, just kept staring out the window, telling herself he would come out in any moment. He would be the next one. No, the next one. No, the one after that. The next one now.

"Aye, he shall be coming oot any moment now," she said.

The eldest child scolded her younger brothers and sister.

"Hush, ye dafties! She's afraid he's dead and wull na be able tae come oot!"

Kelsey winced at that, but she didn't dare look the little girl in the eye or say anything to her. Kelsey knew that would break the dam and let out the tears of despair that she was only barely holding in. She took a deep calming breath, telling herself there was no way she was going to be crying when Tavish came up, all triumphant after his battle.

And then she heard everyone else's voices from far down the hallway and knew the awful truth. Alfred's voice was the loudest.

"We thought he came up here before we did. Are ye sure he isna up here with Kelsey?"

Eileen spoke in hushed tones when she answered him.

"Aye, we are sure. We left her alone up here with the children when we came down tae greet ye."

Seumas spoke up.

"Och, there are several ways tae come up. Mayhap he came up another way and is sitting with Kelsey even now. The two o' them seemed very friendly with each other just before the battle started."

Isabel spoke to them softly.

"Hush nae. Let us pray we find him with her, but if we dae na, she will be verra distraught, sae dinna vex her."

The children once more ran to their mother when the group came in, but this time she hadn't been gone long enough for them to cling to her and yell out. It was late, and the excitement was over, and they were starting to show their sleepiness.

"Can we go home now, Maw?"

"I'm tired."

"Aye, isna it after our bedtime?"

Eileen laughed softly at the children's precociousness, but she ended it quickly, glancing over at her new friend.

"Aye, that it is. Alfred, can we take ye up now on that offer tae see us home? Kelsey, as I said before, ye are more than welcome tae come along."

Kelsey looked over at Isabel.

"If it doesna fash ye ower much, I wish tae stay here till..."

Isabel came over quickly and put her arms around Kelsey.

"Nay, it doesna fash me at all. Ye are welcome tae stay. Come, let us gae doon tae the kitchen an hae some tea an scones while we wait for young Tavish tae come up." She nodded her head toward the door while looking at the others. "Alfred, gae on and see Eileen and the children home. Seamus, gae see if ye can find yer friend Tavish. Mayhap he's hit his head or some such and needs yer help."

The others all took the hint and shuffled out of the room. Not even the children said anything.

Kelsey didn't dare look up at them, though. The looks of pity she knew she would see on their faces would be just too unbearable. She sniffed and blinked the tears away as Isabel rocked her gently back and forth in her arms. And then she looked at Isabel with all the pleading she could will into her eyes and spoke to her through her sobs as she stood up, bringing the older woman up with her.

"Please, let us gae doon thare an speak tae some o' the guard. What if Seamus misses Tavish lyin injurit and needing some men tae carry him up!"

Isabel nodded and kept her arm around Kelsey, leading her to the door of the nursery.

"Aye. That we shall do." The motherly woman kept murmuring affirmations of Kelsey's idea as they went down the hall, through the huge kitchen, and out into the Castle yard entrance to the dungeons. "Aye, there's a good idea, lass. Aye, we shall send some guards back doon the other way from where Seamus goes."

When they finally got to the guards, it had started to rain. Kelsey couldn't wait for Isabel to get around to telling them what needed to be done. The only thing she could think to be thankful for was the fact that she was able to steel herself and speak without sobbing.

"Dubh! Luthais! Tavish is still doon thare! He hasna come up! I am sure he's doon thare bleeding somewhere. Please, let me gae doon tae find him!" Without waiting for an answer, she was already pushing her way through them.

But Isabel stopped her with a gentle but firm grab of her arm.

"Kelsey, ye must stay up here with me, lass. Ye are tae tyrit."

Suddenly Kelsey did feel tired once more, and she all but collapsed into Isabel's arms. She looked up at the guards with her pleading eyes.

"Please, please send doon tae find him."

Isabel held Kelsey and undid the brooch that fastened her thick plaid erasaid to her overdress so that she could put it over both of them to keep the rain off while she spoke to one of the guards.

"Aye, dae send some men doon, Dubh." And then the older woman turned back toward the kitchen, gently tugging Kelsey along with her under the thick plaid. "Come, lass. Let us get in oot o' the wet. The men will search. Ye hae done well seeing tae it."

Just before they went in the kitchen door, Kelsey turned around to make sure Dubh was sending a search party. Only when she was satisfied to see him speaking to a squadron of guards did she allow Seumas's mom to tug her inside.

Isabel parked Kelsey in a comfy chair by the fireplace. In a remarkable show of consideration, she turned the chair toward the kitchen door and propped the door open so that Kelsey could see through the rain to the underground castle entrance from where she sat.

"Just ye rest there nae, lass. Naught can happen but that ye shull see from here, ye ken? I wull brew us a nice pot o' tea, eh?" She dipped a copper kettle in a large vat of water and then leaned over Kelsey to place it right on top of the hot coals that had been banked to keep the fire lit overnight.

Kelsey tried to get up.

“I’m far tae worried aboot Tavish tae just sit here and watch ye work. Let me help ye.”

But Isabel put a firm hand on Kelsey’s shoulder and held her down in the chair.

“Nay, nay.” She gently raised Kelsey’s chin until their eyes met. “An honor it is tae serve ye, Kelsey. Did ye think I didna mean it when I said I owed ye a debt for getting help in time tae save my sons?”

Kelsey relaxed back in the chair and gave Isabel an embarrassed and grudging smile.

“Dinna think o' it, Isabel. If I’m tae be truthful, I did na dae it for yer sons at all. I was only thinking o' Tavish.”

Admitting this brought the tears to Kelsey’s eyes again, and she broke down into a series of sobs, with Isabel patting her shoulder and holding her hand, and finally hugging her tight until her sobs wore themselves out.

Isabel made the tea and poured it into two pretty earthenware mugs, got out a matching earthenware plate, then winked at Kelsey and revealed where the scones were hidden, probably from the children, under a bunch of folded cleaning cloths. She sat down on the hearth and put the mugs and the scones there too, then took one of Kelsey’s hands in hers and bowed her head.

“Laird God, we pray for Kelsey’s dear friend Tavish. We fear we have lost sight o' him. Howsoever, Ye dae know where he is. Wherever thon may be, please tak care o' him for us until we meet him again.” She squeezed Kelsey’s hand. “Amen.”

“Amen.”

Kelsey smiled her thanks at Isabel and resisted the urge to throw herself into the woman's arms again and hold close to the only person who was any comfort. Her mind wanted to go off into a panic about what she would do if she didn't find Tavish again—if he...

But no. She would not allow herself to think about that.

Making herself believe that the men would find Tavish only slightly injured somewhere and bring him up again to her, Kelsey took a big bite of her scone and washed it down with half her cup of tea, all while staring intently out the open door at the empty entrance where she hoped he would come out any minute.

Huddling inside their tiny guard shack out of the rain, Dubh and Luthais grimly waved at her every few minutes, and she halfheartedly waved back.

The silence became oppressive though, so Kelsey made small talk with Isabel.

"Mmmm, this is guid tea. It's no a kynd I hae tastit before. Whit is it?"

Isabel took a dainty sip of her own tea.

"Och, I hopit ye would like it. Alfred and Seumas say it tastes like soap, heh! Juist some flowers thon grow oot i the meadow. Sorcha has a name for thaim, but I can't bring it tae mind right now. Dae ye like her scones?"

Kelsey had just taken another big bite of her scone. She chewed quickly and washed it down with the rest of her tea.

“Och, aye. And I dae think I taste... Can it be dates in them?”

Isabel slumped on her perch on the hearth.

“Aye, dates they are! Och, I was gaun'ae have ye guess what they were. Wherever did ye hae dates before —and dae ye know how far they come from!”

Kelsey was starting to feel at home with this woman who was being so kind to her—in fact, sitting there by the fire all toasty, she had a warm fuzzy feeling all over —so she didn’t really think about what she said next, beyond what it took to say it in Gaelic.

“Ma maw loves dates. She puts thaim in all things. Aye, they’re a little dear, coming all the way from Arabia, but Da does na mind because they mak her sae happy.”

Isabel sat up and took notice.

“My, yer da must be well off, tae afford sae many dates. How did he make his fortune?”

Kelsey continued to watch out the door for Tavish’s return, but she felt grateful to Isabel for the company while she did so, and didn’t want the motherly woman to leave. Alfred was likely back by now from walking Eileen home. Ack, here was hoping he didn’t come in the kitchen. She felt way too tired for company right now.

“Aye, Eileen askit aboot thon earlier, and forsooth ‘tis quite a tale. My da is an excellent salesman. A merchant has attachit him, and he follows this merchant all ower the world, wheelin and dealin for him.”

Isabel looked even more impressed.

"Och, A had na idea! Sae yer da has been tae Arabia, then, and likely tae China and all!"

Kelsey nodded.

"Aye, he has."

Isabel gathered up the dishes and washed them with one of the cleaning rags and some water from the vat.

"Sae that's where ye get yer uncanny knowledge o' sums, then, aye?"

Kelsey chuckled.

"Aye, I suppose it is."

Isabel was drying the dishes and putting them back up on the board.

"I imagine yer da has telt ye some amazin stories from his travels."

Sleepiness was taking Kelsey over, and it was a pleasant feeling. The comfy chair was just large enough for her to lean to the side and draw her knees up so that she could rest in a fetal position.

"Och, aye. One time he brought home kimonos for Maw and me, from Japan..."

Kelsey giggled one note at how funny this story was, and she really wanted to share it with Isabel, but it just seemed like too much effort. She closed her eyes for a moment, and then she was vaguely aware of something soft and warm being placed over the side of her away from the fire. And then she nestled into sweet nothingness.

14

CEITHIR DEUG

Tavish woke up in a pitch black room, sore in every part of his body and with a pounding headache, lying in a strange bed. Where the hell was he? It was no place he'd been before, that was for sure.

The bed was almost too soft. And it was deep, so that he was lying on his side and only his top arm could reach out of the bed, which was more like a bowl full of blankets than a modern mattress bed. He'd had a friend in high school whose parents had a waterbed, and that was about as close to this as he'd ever heard of before.

He stretched out his top arm, looking for the edge of the bowl so that he could pull himself out. When he found the edge, he froze. The bowl was made of stone! Wanting to get out his flashlight, he reached down to where his sporran should have been—but didn't feel it. Maybe it had twisted around on his body. He maneuvered around inside the blankets, patting all around his hips and waist area, but didn't find it.

A surge of adrenaline rushed through his blood, but the only things he had to fight over the pouch and his belt were these blankets. He was wondering if it would be easier to struggle around inside the blankets to search the bowl, or if he should instead pull himself out of the bowl and dig the blankets out in his search—when he heard an unfamiliar man's voice and saw candlelight dancing on the carved rock ceiling of what could only be one of the dungeons in the underground castle.

"Are ye looking for this, lad?"

Tavish yanked himself up and out of the bowl of a bed and was on his feet in seconds, reaching over his shoulder for his sword. When it wasn't there either, he lowered his arms and studied the other man warily. Dressed in white robes and wearing his beard long, this man definitely had that evil wizard thing going on. In one hand he held up a candle, and in the other, Tavish's sporran.

Tavish reached for it.

"Aye."

His mind had nicknamed this old man Saruman, and he was surprised when he let him have it. He put it on and felt inside. So far as he could recall, all his belongings were in there. All except one.

"What about my sword. Where is that?"

Saruman put a sad look in his eyes and shook his head.

"Nay, thare wis na sword on ye whan I found ye knockit oot among the dead oot thare at the docks."

Tavish looked around for the door out of the room, but didn't see it. There had to be a door. Saruman had come through it with his candle just a moment ago.

"Och, well. I can get another sword in the castle armory. I thank ye for the... rest an all, but I must be gang back up tae the castle now. Will ye show me the way?"

But Saruman took his hand out of one of the pockets of his snowy white robes, opened it up under his mouth, and blew some kind of dust all over Tavish, who sneezed three times before collapsing into the bowl bed once more. This elderly man couldn't really be an evil wizard, could he?

Through the growing haziness of his mind, Tavish searched Saruman's face.

"Why?"

The man moved forward and covered Tavish up with some of the blankets. Tavish tried to reach out and grab the man's hand, but found that he couldn't even move. He was out before the man answered him.

But Kelsey appeared in Tavish's dreams.

Instead of Gehrig's wife's long plaid dress, she was wearing the clothes he'd seen her in the most often: her Highlands costume from his parents' Renaissance faire. Only in his dream, her long brown hair hung down, and she was wearing makeup.

"Tavish! You're alive! Oh, thank God! Where are you?"

This sure was an odd dream. Oh well. Might as well answer her.

"Uh, I'm in a weird rock bowl bed in one of the rooms in the underground castle, and there's this Saruman dude who just blew something in my face that made me go to sleep."

As he said this, he appeared in the bowl-shaped bed in his dream, too.

Kelsey came over to the side of his bed and frantically looked him all over.

"Are you okay?"

Having her this close with her eyes all over him wasn't good for his concentration. Forgetting how odd a dream this was, he pulled her into the bed with him. Suddenly, they were both naked. And the dream got really good. Who knew a bowl-shaped bed could be so useful? This allowed him to relax and really enjoy her company afterward, while they lay there in each other's arms.

"I've really missed you, Kel."

She pulled away just enough to look him in the eyes, and her eyes were full of pain, and brand-new tears.

"Then why did you drop out of my life?"

Guilt and pain assaulted his psyche on one side, anger and frustration on the other. He couldn't stand it. He pulled her close to him and held her tight—truth be told more for himself than for her. He couldn't hold her close enough.

"Please don't be mad at me, Kel. I want to tell you,

believe me I do. Believe me when I say I can't. It's not something I can choose to do. I literally can't tell you."

Hurt came into her voice, but she didn't pull away from him. If anything, she held him tighter.

"We were so close, Tavish. I mean, I thought we were. I thought I knew everything about you. And you were never like this back then. Can you tell me what happened at least?"

He stroked her hair.

"I didn't know back then, Kel. I didn't know..." He tried to tell her, but the words just would not come out of his mouth, not even in a dream. Whenever that happened, he kept trying to speak to her about it until he found words he could say. "And the moment my parents told me about it, I took myself out of your life. You deserve to find someone else and have children who won't be bound by... some promise one of my ancestors made centuries ago."

She must've found it easier to talk this way too, because she just stayed there in his arms and let him caress her, instead of pulling away and looking him in the eye again.

"Well at least I know you don't hate me. That's actually a really sweet reason for you to have left, and I'm glad I know. But Tavish, you should have had enough faith in me to let me decide if I wanted you bad enough to put up with this curse."

He laid his head against hers, willing his thoughts, his love, his very being to radiate into hers somehow so that she could feel it.

"Yeah. I should have."

Oddly, now she did break away and look him in the eye. As much as she could break away in a bowl bed, anyway.

"You know what?"

She looked so excited and enthusiastic he couldn't help teasing her a little.

"No, what?"

She scrunched her nose at him in that adorable way she had.

"It's kind of a good thing you shut me out for those seven years—but not for the reasons you think. Remember when you came back from getting me those clothes, and you thought I'd been invisible?"

He got his elbows under him and sort of sat up to face her.

"Yeah. That was even weirder than this dream."

She paused briefly, and then laughed a little.

"Well I didn't lie to you. You really were invisible to me, too—after Brian the Druid went away."

"Brian the Druid?"

"Yeah, Brian the Druid. That's probably who the Saruman dude is, the one who made you go to sleep. Anyway, he took one look at my ring and decided I was a druid too. He called me Priestess."

"O... K... I don't really see how that makes it a good thing that I had to fade out of your life seven years ago."

"Don't you see? If I'm a druid too, then maybe I can learn to remove your curse!"

She just disappeared then, as if she was a character in a video game and her player had logged out.

His dreams were unremarkable after that, boring

and forgettable, but the next thing he knew, he heard Kelsey's voice in his ear at barely a whisper, and it wasn't a dream. She was also leaning her hand on his chest, shaking him a bit. He felt her breath in his ear, warm and intimate.

"Tavish, wake up. Tavish, wake up. Wake up, Tavish."

He opened his eyes.

There she was, even sexier in reality than she'd been in his dream. The light he could see by was coming from her flashlight, which she had trained on the floor of the cave room as she knelt by his bedside. Her face was very close.

Before he remembered what had happened between them was just a dream, he reached out and pulled her to him and kissed her, putting all his need for her into it, all the longing he had felt over the past seven years.

She returned the kiss—and to his surprise, she did so without hesitation.

He deepened the kiss, inspired by the mood that had been set in his dream.

She returned the deepened kiss for a moment, but before he could pull her into the bed with him and make last night's dream a reality, she pulled away slightly and took a deep breath, then spoke softly, her warm brown eyes entreating him even as she grabbed his arm and started pulling him up.

"We have to get out of here. Please get up."

He gently took the hands that she'd put on his arm and waited for her to meet his eyes again.

"Wait. How did you find me?"

She gave him one last intense moment of intimacy from her eyes, and then she helped him get up out of the bed bowl while she answered him in her soft feminine voice.

"I was in this room yesterday while I was looking for the artifact while you distracted our friends..." She pressed her lips together and swallowed. "And then I recognized it when I saw you in your dream."

Adrenaline surged through him on hearing that, and he recognized the fear he felt. But it gradually faded. He hadn't told her, and he certainly didn't want to fight her, nor run from her. All he really wanted to do was pull her into the bed with him, but now he had woken up enough to remember it wasn't safe here. He let her help him out of bed.

She turned around and went over to a spot on the wall and messed with it until she opened one of those secret doors, then turned her head back toward him.

"Come on, before Brian the Druid catches up with us!"

He followed her through the secret door and into the stone corridor, then kept looking both ways down the corridor while she closed the secret door.

"No sign of him so far."

She got up and motioned for him to follow her, and they ran up the corridor toward the exit, speaking in hushed voices between deep breaths.

"Good. I guess he got your sword?"

"He says my sword wasn't on me when he found me."

"Do you believe him?"

"I'm not sure."

"Yeah, I'm not sure if we can trust him either."

Tavish grabbed her hand as they ran and squeezed it. She squeezed back, so he tenderly kept hold of the small part of her he could have. Not knowing was killing him though.

"So. Do you remember the rest of the dream?"

They were getting close to the exit. They could finally see the guards up there, now that they'd rounded the final corner. New guards were on duty, not Dubh and Luthais. Looking at them, she switched to Gaelic.

"Aye, I dae remember the rest o' whit did pass between us this past evening."

He felt safe from Brian the Druid now, in sight of the guards, and he slowed the two of them down to a walk while they could still speak in hushed voices without being heard. And just to make sure there'd be no misunderstanding, he switched back to English.

He knew that when the guards saw the two of them holding hands in the corridor and pausing to speak privately, word would spread throughout Laird Malcomb's Castle. It damn well better spread, because Seumas needed to know. He needed to keep his designs off her.

He brought them to a stop and turned her to face him and looked deep into her soft brown eyes.

"Something really does pass between us, Kel. It does to me. Do you feel it too, still?"

Her eyes never left his, and she nodded.

"I never stopped feeling it, Tavish."

"Oh Kelsey, I never did either. And I want to crush you to my chest right now. I want to hold you so bad."

She smiled at him then, a 'tell me about it' smile, and squeezed his hand again.

"I know. Me too. So much..."

She started drifting into him, and he almost let her. He almost said to heck with it—but he caught himself just in time and was glad, because that scenario didn't play out very well for her, here in the old time.

He held her hand between them, stopping her, and then gave her an apologetic smile, doing his best to promise things in the future with his eyes.

"Yeah, listen. While we have this chance to talk, we need to make a plan for finding the artifact and getting back home."

Slowly, she started nodding, and the pressure was off their hands from her falling into him. She righted herself, asking him a question with her eyes.

"Okay."

Oh yeah, it was definitely on once they got back. He promised that with his eyes.

"I don't think Brian the Druid will bother us if we have Seumas and Alfred along. And Alfred's more likely to come along if you bring Eileen. So we'll try to arrange more outings like the one we had last night. Let's be on the lookout for opportunities to suggest them, okay?"

She looked down at the rock floor for just a moment, as if she were searching down there for the answer to his question. She was probably just flustered because of the dream. He knew he was. But then she answered him.

"Yeah, okay. Hey, do you think we're still going to Ireland today? Or will Malcomb cancel the trip because of the raid last night?"

He took her hand again and started them walking up toward the exit and the guards. And then he made a last comment in English before he switched back to Gaelic for their audience.

"Good thinking, that's something we can be talking about when we come out in front of the guards. Aye, we wull be gang tae Ireland, despite the raid. Laird Malcomb doesna allow the MacDonalds tae spoil our plans."

15

CÒIG DEUG

As she walked hand-in-hand with Tavish down the gray rock-and-grass road to Port Patrick and Donnell's ship over to Ireland, Kelsey's mind was full of the possibility of confronting Brian the Druid in his dream tonight. She had been in Tavish's dream twice. What if she thought of Brian instead tonight? Would that work? The idea reminded her of some of the Celtic legends she'd read for class.

Tavish squeezed her hand, sending a jolt of elation straight into her heart and out to the rest of her. She squeezed his hand back.

What should she say to Brian, about keeping Tavish captive?

How much anger should she show?

On the one hand, she couldn't appear weak, or once she met the druid again outside of the dream world, he would walk all over her. On the other hand, the only strength she had was her training and her convictions—

and Tavish's sword arm. She knew that if she bluffed, Brian would call her on it.

She pointed to a vendor cart loaded with warm sausages.

"Och Tavish, will ye get us a few o' those?"

She saw another cart loaded with apples.

"Ooh, and some o' those as well?"

Seumas got himself some breakfast too, and the three of them were quiet for a while, munching on their food.

They reached the crest of a hill, and she looked down into a rocky port full of blue water and a couple dozen ships. Hundreds of men in kilts of all colors moved to and fro, loading and unloading carpets from Arabia, tea and herbs from China, cotton from India, and for all she knew, gems from Africa. Wagons and carts and their teams of horses passed her on the road, as well.

"Which ship is Donnell's?" she asked.

Tavish pointed, but he froze in place for a moment without saying anything.

Seumas pointed then, saying, "'Tis the one wi th green sail."

She gasped.

"Can we sail wi all thon stuff pylit on the deck? Will we na sink?"

Seumas laughed.

"Nay, 'tis not even an overly large load, lass. Come, let us hurry. Donnell has that look aboot him."

Tavish hung back a bit when Seumas started walking down the Hill. Aw, he wanted a moment alone. Giving him a joyful smile, Kelsey hung back with him. But he didn't look happy, and he almost painfully moved around to the other side of her and took her other hand. What was wrong? She gave him a quizzical look.

His look was stoic as he held up his other hand, calmly whispering, "Brian the Druid must have my ring."

Seumas looked back at them.

"Will ye quit nattering on and come doon here before we raise the captain's ire?"

Tavish raised his chin at Seumas in acknowledgment and started the two of them walking again, briskly.

"Aye, Seumas, we come."

Kelsey tried to control her breathing, but she was hyperventilating. They couldn't get home without Tavish's ring. Could she get Brian to give it back to them? What would he want in exchange?

She stopped walking, resisting the tug of his hand, but not letting go.

"Let's not go on this trip, Tavish," she whispered. "Let's go talk to Brian and see if we can get your ring back."

He squeezed her hand gently, but then started walking again, bringing her along in a way that brooked no resistance.

"We canna gae against Laird Malcomb's command, Kelsey, and thare is na time tae beg aff this errand before Captain Donnell wishes tae leave. Nay, we must gae."

Walking as fast as she could to keep up with him—and huffing a little because of it, darn her habit of skipping the gym—Kelsey tried to reason with Tavish under her breath in English.

"But Tavish, we aren't going to stay here, so we don't need to worry about following Malcomb's commands. We just need to get the ring back and find that artifact—"

He switched to sotto voice English too as he marched her along.

"If we go against his orders and then we can't find the ring or the artifact, then we're screwed, Kelsey. He can lock us up for the rest of our lives or even put us to death if he wants to. There is no guarantee of 'due process of law' in the old time." His voice softened, and she saw a tortured look on his face. "I'm so sorry I got you into this. It's my fault. I should have never brought you here. But please—you have to follow my lead so I can keep you safe. Promise me you will."

She sighed and quit resisting him, instead putting all her efforts into the long strides she needed to take to keep up with him.

"Yeah, okay, I will."

Donnell greeted them and gave them seats together, and then the crew got the ship underway. They left the relatively calm blue waters of the rocky cove and went out into the green sea.

Seumas offered Tavish his forearm, and Tavish clasped it. The two of them sat there for a moment. Seumas looked from Tavish over at Kelsey and back again.

"I'll be watching ye, MacGregor, and if ye don't tak care o' her, I will."

Tavish nodded, and they let go of each other's forearms and sat amicably near each other the rest of the way, chit chatting about the other guards in the lists and their families, the stool ball game last week, how many grouse Malcomb had let them take home after the last hunting trip, and finally speculating about what they might see for sale once they reached the Irish port.

It wasn't a large ship. There was no below deck, nowhere to get any privacy. So Kelsey didn't say much, just half listened to Tavish and Seumas and watched the men sail the ship, which was entertainment enough for the short voyage to Ireland.

In about two hours, they docked at Port Beannchar.

Capt. Donnell went out on the dock and loudly proclaimed to the goods that he had aboard his ship. Every so often someone would stop and talk with him about prices and quantities, until he had his first customer—a wealthy looking man. The captain brought the customer aboard and showed him the vellum they had to sell.

Meanwhile, one of the crewmen had unpacked a writing desk for Kelsey to use. She sat poised with her quill in hand and the ship's ledger open, reading the prior sums that had been done so that she would know where to put things. It was a pretty straightforward leisure, so she felt ready.

But the captain's wealthy customer didn't agree. His Irish Gaelic was more singsong than that of the Scots, but they understood each other fine—and so did she.

The customer came right over to Kelsey and made a mocking face at her.

"Och, playing at the sums, is the lass."

Tavish got up from his seat next to her, but Captain Donnell gestured for him to sit back down. Tavish obeyed the order, but Kelsey could feel that he was ready to jump back up again at any moment.

When he spoke, the captain addressed his customer.

"Let us hae a wager. Ye can check her sums after we finish here. Gin she makes any mistake, then yer purchase is on the house."

Talk about pressure. Kelsey swallowed and looked over at Tavish, who held up both of his hands palms down and move them apart slowly and smoothly. She nodded. He was right. She would be fine if she just took her time and was meticulous.

The customer threw back his head and laughed.

"A fine manner o' salesmanship ye hae found. Ha! gin she be as guid at sums as ye think, then I will have bought more than I would hae otherwise. Fine an dandy, let us begin."

The two of them walked around on the ship, discussing this pile of vellum and that pile of cow leather and how much Donnell wanted for each piece and what discount he would give for bulk and how many hides constituted bulk...

After what was probably five minutes but seemed like an hour, the customer stepped over to Kelsey and caught her eye, seeing if she was ready to take down his order. When she nodded, he began.

"I shall tak four dozen o' these hides at 18 per but wi the bulk discount for four dozen. An I shall tak three dozen o' these other hides at 19 per. Pack up for me 50 sheets o' vellum—did ye say the vellum was 35 per? or 45 per?"

Once she had added that up and checked it three times and made Tavish surreptitiously check it three times at the same time, she at last showed it to the captain and his customer. They each took her quill and did the same sums three times before Donnell gave her a big smile and a nod.

"Verra good, my dear." He turned to his customer.

But before Donnell could say anything, the customer was rattling off more things he would buy.

Kelsey added them all up and checked them three times and had Tavish check them three times.

The customer did his own calculations three times...

And this went on and on and on until the customer had bought everything on the ship. The crew carried it over to his ship and loaded it up for him, and then pretty much the same procedure was followed for all the merchants Donnell bought from. They had the ship emptied out and then filled up again in no time—and a large crowd of people cheered at the entertainment they had been given that day at the docks.

Before it was even time to eat the midday meal, they were finished—and Donnell's purse was fatter than it had ever been, judging by how it bulged and how big he smiled. He blew a kiss to Kelsey and then made an announcement to everyone.

"Seumas and Tavish and Kelsey and I are going up to the toon, and we will send a meal for ye, crew."

All the crewmen cheered.

❧ 16 ❧

SIA DEUG

Tavish did his best to enjoy the lively Irish musicians in the corner, as well as the meal Donnell generously bought them at a tavern, but he was impatient to be back at the castle, getting his ring back. He knew Seumas and Alfred would go with him, and a few more of the guards. Brian wouldn't stand a chance against half a dozen warriors. The druid's underhanded methods had caught Tavish by surprise. That wouldn't happen again.

Kelsey squeezed his hand under the table and put down her soup spoon.

"Dae ye no agree tavish, thon the underground is the most interestin part o' Laird Malcomb's castle?"

Everyone's eyes were on him. He wiped the mutton grease off his mouth and made a face, looking to Seumas for support.

"Aw, the dungeons and docks are naught but a duty

station where we dae an uncanny amount of fighting, eh Seumas?"

The large redheaded man clasped hands arm-wrestle style with Tavish on top of the table and gave him a smile so big it showed the wrinkles under his eyes.

"That be true enough of this night just past." But then Seumas dropped Tavish's hand and turned to Kelsey. "Aye, lass. And 'tis a truth that all my life I hae heard o' vast treasures lurking there in the underground beneath Laird Malcomb's Castle."

Kelsey dropped her soup spoon in the soup and sat up straight.

"I knew it. I can tell by the way the halls are sae decorated, with all those etchings."

Captain Donnell's face lit up with excitement, and he gestured with his piece of mutton.

"Aye, 'tis true, 'tis true. When I was but a lad, I did hae plans tae gae doon there and plunder all the treasure, ye ken." He took a big bite and chewed it dramatically.

Everyone at the table laughed. But it was more the laugh of people who had also considered finding the treasure and keeping it for their own.

Tavish turned his head to Kelsey and gave her a look that he hoped she understood meant "What the heck are you doing? We don't want all these people thinking about going down into the underground. And we don't want Donnell asking to go with us. The fact that you can get into the secret doors is a secret, remember?"

She caressed his hand under the table. What did that mean? She smiled at Donnell.

"Seumas and Tavish and Alfred were kindly giving Eileen and I a tour o' the underground last night when the MacDonalds sae rudely interrupted—"

Donnell dropped his piece of mutton on a plate and gazed at her with wide eyes.

"I hear tell 'twas ye who found Tavish in the underground castle last night, lass."

Great. Not only had she brought attention to the fact that she could find her way around in the underground, but now he would have to live down having been saved by a woman. Tavish looked around for something he could bring up to change the subject.

But before he could find a distraction, she went on.

"'Twas the strangest thing, Donnell. I was woken from ma sleep wi the sure conviction that gin I would only get up, I could walk tae where Tavish lay sleeping, havin been knockit i the head an laid oot."

This was even worse, of course. It sounded like the beginnings of all the Irish tales he'd ever heard. The musicians were on a break, and people from the other tables were starting to bend an ear toward theirs. He considered squeezing her hand to tell her to quit it, but the damage was done. He would just have to grab her and run out of the room if she got too close to revealing where she really came from. Her greed for the underground treasure hadn't made her that reckless, had it?

She tipped her tankard of ale back and swallowed half a dozen times.

"When I got ootside, I saw thon the clouds haed partit in the night, allowing the moon tae shine doon upon the courtyard. I took this rarity as a sign thon ma path was sure and I should continue."

Tavish and everyone else at the table drank down their ale now, and Donnell calmly put some coin on the table and beckoned over the server.

Kelsey picked up her bowl and drank down the rest of her soup, then wiped her mouth with the huge sleeve of her old time leine blouse.

"The guards wordlessly let me pass, and as I startit doon the corridor alone with juist ma torch for company, I had a vision o' where I would find Tavish. I saw the room clearly, as gin I were already thare. Sure enough, thon was where I woke him. I'm tellin ye, I was meant tae gae an get him."

With this last line, she turned to Tavish and kissed him soundly on the mouth in a way that was considered indecent during the old time. At first he resisted, but when everyone started to cheer and whistle and carry-on, he figured what the heck, and went for it.

Truth to tell, this was the first time he'd been in a bar in the old time, and not in the castle or in a battle camp or in someone's home. Maybe the rules were different in taverns. Just in case they weren't, he put his arm around her and held her close so that no one else could grab her.

The server filled up their tankards of ale, and Seumas raised his in toast toward Kelsey.

"Och, that only I could hae my own guardian angel, tae always see me home."

"Aye!"

"Aye!"

Everyone at their table and even some people from other tables joined in the clanking of tankards, and there was much more drinking and general revelry until the four of them tottered back down the hill to the ship and got aboard.

The three crewmen had been sent on ahead with the crew's meal, and they were all done eating and had sat down to play howls, a dicing game. They all stood when their captain approached.

"Thank you for the meal, Captain Donnell."

"Aye, 'twas right good of ye."

The crewman were all smiles at first, but they began to look envious when he revealed his state of drunkenness by dramatically getting up on some crates in the stern and then gesturing for quiet so he could make an announcement.

"We sail for home, lads! Take her away."

After he said that, Donnell sat down on a bench and promptly fell asleep, snoring loudly.

Tavish looked over at Seumas, who shrugged, and then sat down beside Kelsey to warily watch the crew take the ship out to sea again. Seumas sat down on the other side of Kelsey, and for once, Tavish was glad to have him near her. With their captain unconscious, who knew what ideas the crew would get? He didn't know them half as well as he did all his fellow castle guardsmen.

Kelsey took his hand, and he made his arm as firm a hold for her as he could, then turned to smile at her reassuringly.

Come to think of it, something seemed off.

He grabbed the sleeve of the next crewman who wandered by on his way to grab one of the ropes the next time they tacked.

"Why are you sailing to the north? Port Patrick is to the east."

A bit smaller than Tavish, the crewman stopped short of a physical reaction, but Tavish could tell he was affronted. The man just waited for Tavish to let go of his sleeve, and then gestured up at the sails.

"You can see up there that she's blowing hard to the south, aye?"

Tavish looked up. The sails were indeed billowing toward the Isle of Man.

"Aye, but what does that have to do with it?"

The crewman gave him a look as if to say, "Isn't it obvious?"

Tavish stood up straight to his full height and looked down on the man.

The crewman looked to the side for a moment and then back at Tavish.

"Because she's blowing sae hard to the south, we're taking her to the north so as not to blow right on by Port Patrick before we get that far east."

Tavish looked around at the other crewmen to see if they showed any signs that they were taking the castle guards for a ride. But none of them were snickering or avoiding his gaze. One even nodded at him in passing.

Kelsey held up her arm toward Tavish in an invitation for him to sit down again.

"It makes sense to me," she said reassuringly.

He looked all around one more time and then

nodded to her and sat, taking her hand in his to lend her what comfort he could. He would be fine if he was stuck here, but this had to be frightening for her.

About a mile of rocky cliff went by on their left, pounded by the foamy waves, and then the cliffs stood still while the crew were adjusting the sails to turn the ship to the right so that they could head east.

The crewman who had climbed the mast made a guttural noise and then fell to his death atop several of the many crates on deck. An arrow stuck out of his back.

Tavish grabbed Kelsey and put her on the floor, where the side of the ship would shield her from any more arrows, and then he ran to the ship's armory, grabbed a bow and a quiver, and sought out their attackers.

Good, it was just one ship, coming toward them at a fast clip with the wind in its sails while they were stalled. He only got one shot off before the other ship was beside theirs and boarding ramps came over. But he hit his mark, and the man tumbled into the sea.

Tavish drew his sword and ran over the closest ramp, swinging at every bit of flesh that got in his way, peripherally aware that Seumas was doing the same at the other ramp, and the two crews were exchanging arrow fire.

He ducked first one sword that came at him, then another, and lunged to strike yet a third man down before he reached the other side of the MacDonald ship.

Twice he crossed over the deck, and twice he dodged better than they.

Soon, they all were buried at sea.

Seumas came over and clasped forearms with Tavish.

"Ha! Those MacDonalds didn't count on finding a MacGregor aboard our ship!"

The two of them were grinning at each other when one of their crewmen shouted.

"The lass! The lass fell overboard!"

Tavish ran back over the boarding ramp to Donnell's ship and grabbed the shoulders of the crewman who had shouted.

"Where? Where did she go overboard?"

The crewman pointed, and Tavish ran over there, grabbed the side of the ship, and looked over and down into the water. But he didn't see her.

Tavish had climbed up on the side of the ship was just about to dive as deep as he could when Seumas grabbed his arm.

"Wait. The crew say we've drifted since she went over." He pointed. "They say she's back over there toward that large jagged rock that looks like a falcon, sticking up above the rest of them along the shoreline."

Finding the falcon rock and looking for any sign of her, Tavish raised his voice, calling out to any of the crewmen who would listen.

"Can we quickly take this ship over there? Or would it be faster if I swam?"

But Seumas answered for them.

"It's too dangerous to take the ship over there—both for us and for Kelsey. She may be trying to swim to us. Look, they're anchoring here until we get back. Let's go." Seumas paused to drop his kilt on the deck before he jumped in with a splash and swam toward the rocks in a style that resembled a breaststroke more than anything else.

Tavish did the same, looking every which way as he desperately clawed the water. He had to find her. She had to be alive. He couldn't live with himself otherwise. If she...

He forced himself to concentrate just on swimming and on scanning the sparkling water and the jagged black rocky coastline for any sign of her. To convert his desperate sense of loss and despair into anger at the MacDonalds and thus into strength, so that he could swim faster. That was a warrior trick, turning sorrow into strength.

The jagged rocks were sharp, which made climbing difficult. Trying not to think of what they would do to someone unconscious, born here by the waves and dashed against them, he scrambled up onto the rocky shore and all over the jagged shoreline, calling out to her.

"Kelsey!"

"Kelsey, say something if you hear us."

17

SEACHD DEUG

Kelsey clung to the rock she'd managed to swim to. Its rough and sharp edges cut at her hands and even into her arms, right through her sleeves with every wave that washed her up against it. But she didn't yet have the energy to climb up. Swimming in a long heavy woolen dress was the most difficult physical thing she had ever done. It had been a very near thing.

A shot of joy went through her. Tavish was calling for her!

She opened her mouth to answer him, but after nearly drowning three times and swallowing and inhaling a bunch of sea water, all that came out were squeaks and croaking sounds.

"I'm here. Down here. Come get me. Please."

She felt her mind getting fuzzy. Something very like sleep but not sleep exactly was coming for her.

If only she had a flare in her pocket, like the ones

her grandparents used to make sure she had when they took her out in their motorboat. "Now I don't want to frighten you, Kelsey," her grandfather had said, "but if you should ever find yourself alone, without us around, take this flare out of your life vest pocket and pull this here and aim at the sky like this!" He'd shot the purple flare high up into the night sky like a firework, and the two of them had grinned at each other while looking at it.

If only she had some way of making a noise.

The fuzziness in her mind was growing stronger. It seemed comfortable. She struggled to remember why she couldn't just to go into it. It seemed easier. She had this gnawing feeling, this nagging feeling that there was something she should be doing to draw attention to herself. But what? She didn't even have a life jacket, let alone the whistle that usually came attached.

She started to drift, both off the rock and into oblivion.

But at the last moment before she let go of the rock, she saw a cartoon in her head that she hadn't seen since she was a child. It was a whistle fight. One character had a whistle, and the other character...

Ignoring the new cuts this gave her hands and arms, she grabbed onto the rocky shore for dear life and drew a deep breath. Puckering her lips, she prayed she could still do this, and then she whistled as loud as she could, drew another breath and whistled again. And again.

She heard two splashes behind her, and then felt strong arms lifting her off the rock into the water and then swimming with her floating on her back, the gray cloudy sky drifting back toward the craggy shore. Her body was already numb from the cold, and now her mind slowly was going numb too.

Tavish's voice intruded on her comfortable numbness.

"Kel. Stay awake. We can move you across the water, but you've got to keep your lungs full so that you stay afloat."

She dutifully took in a deep breath, held it as long as she could, and then took in another deep breath. This reminded her of swimming lessons when she was a child, with all the other happy children, glad to be allowed to spend the day at the lake...

"Breathe, Kel."

She resumed her deep breathing, trying not to drift off again into memories. But it was hard to concentrate. She was so tired, and the water felt warm now. It was hard to remember just where she was. It felt just like she was luxuriating in a warm bath...

"Breathe!"

This kept happening over and over again. She had the impulse a few times to ask how far they had to swim back to the ship, but she didn't have the energy to speak, let alone the voice.

After an interminable amount of time, Tavish was calling out to the crew aboard the ship.

"Toss us down a rope."

Before long at all, there was a splash in the water, and then Tavish was putting the rope over her and then under her arms.

"She's ready. Haul her up, lads."

Her body started to shiver when she was out of the water, and once they had her on the deck she was flopping around like a fish. Tavish was there with her soon. Holding her tight with his whole body, his legs wrapped around her, he stopped the flopping. He was shouting at the crew.

"Blankets! There have got to be some blankets on this ship!"

In a minute, it felt like someone was pulling bed covers up over the two of them. Captain Donnell's voice came through the covers muffled.

"Ye can hae the use of these Persian rugs until we can get ye up to the Laird's castle."

Tavish rolled the two of them onto one of the rugs and pulled a few more over them. His hands moved over her body then, removing her soaking wet clothes, and then the two of them were together skin to skin.

And all she felt was warmth. Blessed heavenly warmth.

He whispered to her there in the darkness while he held her tight against the cold.

"I'm so sorry Kel. So, so sorry. I should never have brought you here. I'll make it right. Somehow, I'll make it right. No matter where I have to go or how long I'll be gone, I'll make this right for you."

Kelsey tried to speak again, to tell him not to go, that all she wanted was him near her and that nothing he could go get would be better than that. But her voice wouldn't cooperate, not even to whisper. She had nothing left.

So she just clung to him, trying to make him understand that she needed him near her and that was all she needed.

His next whisper was hoarse and desperate and full of despair.

"I just hope someday you'll be able to forgive me, Kel."

She clung to him and kissed him with all she had in her the whole time the boat rocked with the pounding waves and the two of them forgot all about the crewmen stomping all over the deck as they made the ship obey them and carry them into port...

Neither of them was cold anymore.

The cries of the crewmen reached a crescendo after the ship had stopped rocking. Then they made contact with the dock, and more pairs of footsteps boarded, chatting about what to lift and where to take it.

Donnell lifted up Tavish's side of their rug bed just enough to speak into it.

"Hold on to each other and I'll have you put in the wagon!"

Panic struck her, and Kelsey looked to Tavish.

"What?"

He grabbed hold of her with all of his body again and held her tight.

"Best to believe what the captain says."

And then the crew tied two ropes around their rug bed and hoisted them up in the air. They were carried quite a ways and then dumped unceremoniously into what must have been a wagon, because as soon as the ropes were untied around their rug bed, it started to jostle around to the sound of hoof beats and general laughter.

They felt some soft things landing on top of them, which must've been their clothes. Kelsey wouldn't have believed that catcalls were the same 800 years ago unless she'd heard it for herself.

"There ye are."

"You'll probably need those where you're going."

"Unlike where ye hae been!"

Kelsey was a bit relieved when the wagon outpaced the crew's laughter, but mostly she just relaxed into the bliss of Tavish's nearness and hoped he'd forget what he'd said about going away.

The sun was setting when they got to the castle. The crew carried Tavish and Kelsey's rug bed through the service door into the kitchen and then bid them farewell amid raucous laughter.

Right there in front of the kitchen fireplace, Isabel tugged Kelsey out of the rug Tavish held around the two of them and put a thick linen night dress over her head, holding it so that Kelsey could put her arms through.

"Och, ye poor dear! I won't have any argument, ye're staying with me this night. Sorcha will see to yer wet clothes and give ye some soup to eat, and then ye really must sleep, my dear."

Tavish had already donned his dry plaid, kilting one end and blousing the other. He squeezed Kelsey's hand and kissed the top of her head.

"Aye, lass. Go on with Isabel and get ye some rest."

Kelsey tried to hold onto Tavish's hand, tried to

draw him to her again so that she could whisper in his ear that she didn't want him to go anywhere, that it didn't matter if they were trapped here in the old time forever—so long as the two of them were together. But she was indeed so very tired that her grip was weak. He slipped away easily, and she still didn't have the voice to call out to him. She watched him go, hoping he would turn so that she could beckon him back to her.

But he left without looking back.

And she was not going to make a fool of herself by asking one of the women to go grab him for her. She was ashamed of herself for even thinking of that. No way was she that desperate. He would either come back, or he wouldn't.

Isabel patted Kelsey's shoulder and gave her a kind smile when she looked at the older woman.

"Tomorrow is another day, lass. Ye are plum exhausted." She nodded to the table, where Sorcha was setting down a bowl of soup and some bread, and then sat Kelsey down there.

At first, it seemed like too much work to pick up the spoon and eat the soup, but the hot liquid felt so good on her throat. The bowl was empty in no time. So was her second bowl.

Isabel came over and helped her stand up and put a supporting arm around her waist and guided her down the hall and up the stairs to the sleeping chambers. She helped her off with her boots, and before Kelsey knew it, she was tucked into the most warm, comfortable bed ever, drifting off to sweet, sweet sleep.

But she was still aware. She let herself sleep peacefully for hours, storing up her strength, and then she dressed her dream-walking self in a white Druid robe and wished her way to wherever Brian was. Who would have thought old Celtic legends were so useful?

Oh good. He was sleeping too.

She had a moment of pause. Should she bring Tavish along? She really wanted to, wanted him with her. Longed for his company, even. But he'd walked away without looking back. There was no way she would've done the same thing, and... Best not think about that.

She nudged her way into Brian's dream the same way she'd gone into Tavish's dreams.

Brian's dream was a treat. In it, the underground Celtic castle was in its glory days. Oddly dressed people who couldn't see her wandered everywhere. Every other thing she looked at was made of gold. Oh and would you look at that.

Brian sat in the grand chamber—on the throne.

When he spotted her, he raised his chin.

"Ah, Kelsey. So nice to see you again."

She didn't bow, not even her head, just advanced right in front of him and crossed her arms.

"Perhaps you won't think so when you hear what I have to say."

He raised his eyebrows and fiddled with a golden scepter that glowed with druidic magic.

"Aye?"

Kelsey gasped.

Brian's scepter was the artifact Tavish had been sent to get. She studied it and then looked all around the room as if she were admiring the place, when really she was noting where the entrances were. She would need to go out through at least one of those in order to find out how to get in here.

Change of plans.

She was so glad she had thought and looked around before speaking. She'd been about to confront him for kidnapping Tavish and stealing his ring. Now she wished she'd come in without him being able to see her either, so she could just spy on him and find out where the ring was. Heh, she'd do that later.

She gave Brian her most solicitous smile, gesturing to the room at large.

"Aye. For I wish ye to give me a tour of your lovely underground abode."

Ha. Flattery always worked on men.

He puffed up his chest and sat up straight with his shoulders back, and gave her an indulgent smile, then put the scepter down and got up off his throne and strutted toward the elaborately marked secret door in the North corner.

"Och, I suppose I can spare the time to show you around."

Biting her cheek so she wouldn't laugh, Kelsey walked extra fast to fall into stride with him. Even though this was his dream and he was obviously enjoying showing off in front of her, she wouldn't give him the satisfaction of running to catch up. That would be just too much.

She was careful to gaze admiringly at everything they passed, in keeping with just wanting a tour. She had to bite her cheeks over and over though, because all the women gazed adoringly at Brian, and he made the winks and waves at them.

Celtic guards in bronze armor decorated with elaborate interlace nodded when they neared the door in the corner.

Darn. She didn't recognize the hallway they were in, which meant she had to endure this tour a while longer. She turned around to admire the interlace carvings on the wall, taking careful note how far down the hall they were in relation to the door, so that she could hopefully find it again.

Brian stayed puffed up, watching her admire his realm.

"You should just stay here with me, Kelsey." He stopped advancing down the hall backward, and his face changed. Instead of joy at showing off, he looked determined. Uh oh. He started walking toward her. "Aye! Stay with me." His face changed again, and this time he looked lecherous.

Kelsey didn't wait around to find out what was going to happen next in Brian's dream. She wished herself back in her own body.

But it didn't work. She was still there.

Brian had a hold of her wrist and was pulling her toward him.

She screamed.

18

OCHD DEUG

Tavish was having his favorite dream. He and Kelsey were arm in arm on their couch in the suburbs watching the antics of their two small children—a boy named Dall after his da and a girl named Linda after Kel's mom. They had just gotten back from a trip to the old time to pick up some antiques for their business, with no input and no pressure from the modern-day Druids. Tavish's twin brother Tomas and his wife lived next door and had babysat for them, and they were seated on the couch across the room...

And then his favorite dream was a nightmare, because Kelsey was screaming his name in the other room.

He jumped up off the couch, and the living room disappeared, replaced by the underground castle. At the same time, his dad jeans and sweater morphed into his kilt and his claymore. He ran.

When he got to the other room, Kelsey's screams were coming from down the connected corridor. When he got to the corridor, they were coming from a room way down at the other end. He groaned and strained, pushing his legs harder, but the faster he ran, the longer the corridor became.

No way was he going to let a dream beat him. Still running, he closed his eyes and imagined himself with Kelsey, fighting whatever was making her scream, chopping it to bits.

The corridor he was in morphed into another, finer one with lighter tan stone walls decorated from top to bottom with those designs Kelsey could read. And then she was there in the corridor—being grabbed by Brian the Druid.

Tavish didn't bother saying anything, just rushed at the man and slammed him to the floor, knocking him out instantly.

Kelsey flew into his arms and held him tight.

"Thank God you're here, Tavish. He wasn't going to take no for an answer."

A rage came over Tavish such as he'd never had before. Literally seeing red, he drew his sword in one fierce yank —

But Kelsey put her hand on his sword arm.

"This is his dream, Tavish, not yours and not mine. Haven't you heard that if you die in your dream, you die in real life? We have to be careful."

Was she for real?

"Kelsey, I don't care if he dies. He needs to die, if he would do that to you."

She shook her head no and hooked her arm around his sword arm.

"It's just a dream, Tavish. People do things in dreams all the time that they wouldn't do in real life. I do. Don't you?"

She was right. He'd already forgotten this was just a dream, even while they were talking about it being a dream. He took a deep breath and relaxed a little.

"Yeah, I suppose I do." He took a new look at his surroundings, and at her. "What are you doing here anyway, scoping out the place for more treasure? A little dangerous to come alone, don't you think?"

Whoa. She looked angry.

He backed away from her a little. Huh, well he guessed she was free to do what she wanted.

She pressed her lips together and crossed her arms, looking up at the ceiling then back at him with anger in her eyes. She glanced down at Brian, and when he didn't move turned back to Tavish and whispered.

"No, I was not scoping the place out for more treasure. I came to chew Brian out for kidnapping your sorry ass the other day, but then I saw the artifact and asked him to give me a tour so I could figure out how to get into the room where it is." She pointed down the corridor.

The artifact was in here? Tavish checked Brian himself. The man wasn't going to be moving for a few minutes, anyway. He nodded and walked where she indicated, and she followed.

When they got down to the door she'd pointed at, he ducked back and pressed his back against the wall.

There were guards in the other room, and a bunch of people wandering around.

She casually walked up to the door. A little haughtily, even.

“They can’t see or hear us, only Brian can.”

He gestured at her with his palms up, asking how that was possible.

She mimicked his shrug and led the way into that room.

“I really don’t understand how it works, just that it does. I made that a condition when I entered Brian’s dream, and also when I brought you into his dream.”

She brought him over to a throne, and sure enough, there was the artifact. He reached for it, but she grabbed his hand and was pulling him back toward the door.

“I don’t know how long he’ll stay knocked out, and we need to find your ring. In fact, we should search him for it. We also need to figure out how to get to this room, and I really think we should do that while he’s still out. It surprised me when I wasn’t able to leave his dream. I’m not sure if we’ll be able to leave if... once he wakes up.”

He kept his eyes on the scepter for as long as he could, and then finally turned to follow her. When they got back to Brian, Tavish rushed to search him, holding his other hand up to stop Kelsey from coming too close. It was there. His ring was in a pouch that Brian wore under his white Druid robes.

And then Brian grabbed Tavish’s arm.

"Did ye honestly believe I could get knockit oot in ma own dream? Ha! Surprise."

Kelsey screamed again.

But Tavish asserted his superior strength against Brian the Druid and drew his arm away while at the same time making it clear that he was ready to do Brian bodily damage if he tried to stop them again.

Apparently even old time druids knew that bit about dying in your dream meant you died in real life, because Brian backed down.

It was time to get the hell out of here and wake up so they could come back with more people, overpower Brian, and get the ring and the scepter and leave. And soon, before Brian just left with those things. How much had the druid heard? Did he understand modern English? Did he know they were after the scepter? Was he aware this wasn't really just a dream? Best to assume not and hope he didn't find out.

Tavish turned to Kelsey, casually but firmly put his arm around her, and spoke as calmly as he could, under the circumstances.

"Let's go."

She nodded, but instead of dissolving Brian's dream and depositing Tavish back into his own as he had expected, she started walking down the corridor with him.

He put his mouth close to her ear and whispered.

"Get us out of this dream so we can come back in real life."

But she shook her head and whispered back to him while she scanned the walls with her eyes.

"We need to keep him in this dream as long as we can, because something tells me he'll wake up as soon as it ends."

Tavish looked back behind them, but he didn't see Brian. At least the druid wasn't following them, but not knowing where he was made Tavish uneasy.

Kelsey was still whispering.

"And anyway, we need to figure out how to get here, and this is the quickest way I can think of to do that, unless you have other ideas."

As a matter of fact, Tavish did have other ideas. Giving her a teasing look, he tested his theory by walking right up to the wall—and then through it. This network of caves have been carved out of the solid stone of the mountain, though, and so the wall he went through was very thick indeed. After about 20 feet he came into another room that he recognized, the laundry room. He looked up, which was stupid. It wasn't like he could see through the ceiling to what was above.

But he was imagining about where that other corridor that led to the scepter must be in relation to what was above this laundry room when Kelsey popped through the wall. She was in a huffy mood.

"The least you could do was tell me you were about to go walking through the wall. What if I'd been looking away? I would be back there still with no idea at all where you were."

There was no use in telling her that he'd looked to see if she was watching him. She was in that bossy lecture-y mode. Best just to keep on the task at hand.

"This system of caves over here doesn't appear to be

connected to the one we were just in. It stands to reason there's another entrance to the caves where the scepter is."

At least she caught a clue and returned to the task at hand herself. At first, she looked at the ceiling too, which made him feel better. But then she looked over toward where they'd come from, and he guessed she was doing the same as he had, imagining walking over up top from the entrance they had first used over in the direction of the scepter chamber.

She looked at him and shrugged, then turned around and *vooped* into the wall like a ghost in a horror movie. Before he could get too concerned, she *vooped* right on out, grabbed his hand, and turned around and took him with her this time.

Together, they *vooped* all over the collection of caves —finding quite a bit of treasure. It was fun for a minute, and he was laughing as much as she was. But she was getting carried away. He found out he could stop her from dragging him anymore by quite literally putting his foot down and refusing to budge.

"All right, enough of that."

She tugged at his hand.

"But we could map out the whole area in our heads —"

He refused to budge.

"We know how to get to Brian and the scepter and the ring. That's all I came for."

She clicked her tongue on the roof of her mouth, crossed her arms, and looked to the side.

"But it would only take a minute, and think how

much easier it would be to do it this way than to have to dig into all those tunnels once we get home."

Was she for real?

"Don't be stupid, Kelsey! We need to get the ring back, nothing else, and Brian's liable to leave here, or to hide it, or who knows what if we give him enough time. We need to make a plan that allows us to get here fast and then come back here with more people—as soon as possible."

She looked like she was going to argue some more, but then she finally nodded.

"Okay. As soon as I wish it, we'll wake up. I say we get dressed as fast as we can and rush on over to that other entrance, the one Alfred used."

He shook his head no.

"I want to bring at least Alfred and Seumas. Brian can trick one warrior into sleeping with his pixie dust, but if three of us surround him, he won't have a chance."

She got an odd look on her face and licked her lips and then nodded slowly.

"Okay. I'll stay here and keep him in the dream while you bring Alfred and Seumas and get the ring and scepter."

Was she nuts? He grabbed both of her arms and started tugging her toward the exit.

"No way. Remember why you brought me here? No way. You're coming with me. I'll not hear any argument."

She raised her chin, and his hands went through her as if she were a ghost.

"It's not like you can stop me from staying here, Tavish. I've learned some new tricks since then. I don't think I'm in danger. Go on. Bring them to that room where he sleeps."

And before Tavish could say anything else, he woke up on his cot in the castle barracks.

19

NAOI DEUG

Kelsey looked around on her own, learning quite a bit about the extensive network of caves that reached a good distance into the shore away from the cliffs. There was room to sleep a whole army down here, and it had probably been used for just that, she figured. It would take a year to catalog it all properly.

How much time did she have to mentally map out the place? It shouldn't take Tavish long to convince Seumas and Alfred to come with him. She maybe had half an hour. And as much fun as it was to go through the walls, it made more sense to go along the corridors the way she would have to back in her time.

Or would she?

She'd gone into Tavish's dream back in her time, so that meant she could dream walk in her time. Oh. But who was there in her time who would know all these passageways? Probably only the 'they' Tavish had been talking about. She shuddered as she counted the number of turns in this particular corridor.

And there she was, on the topic she didn't want to think about.

Tavish.

For her, it had been like old times. Being with him made her feel so good. She'd given him way more than she'd planned on. He hadn't made her, either. Hadn't been demanding or expectant or anything. It had been all her. She had based her feelings on his actions instead of his words. He'd never said they were getting back together or anything. She had just assumed.

And now it was like he didn't take her seriously. Didn't want to listen to what she had to say. Now that he knew where that precious magic scepter was, she had served her purpose and he didn't need to... He didn't need her anymore.

Was that six turns now, or seven?

Groaning, she went back to the beginning of the corridor and started over. And then she *vooped* to each storage room full of artifacts and then straight up to the surface and looked for landmarks, in case the university was even more impatient than she was and wanted to dig straight down.

Finally, she'd done all of that there was to do. How much time had passed? She reached in her backpack for her phone and was about to check it for the time when she remembered it was just a dream phone, subject to the randomness of dreams. Stupid. Was there any way to tell how much real time had passed from inside a dream?

Aw, was there really any point to mapping out dream corridors? Well, she finished doing so, on the theory that corridors never changed. They were ingrained in Brian's memories, why would they change in his dream state.

Well, now she had to face it. She was dead curious to know how Tavish was progressing in his quest to get the ring back.

So she woke up. The dawn shed just enough light through her arrow slit window that she could see everything in her castle sleeping chamber clearly.

Relieved to see her clothes and her backpack (she had long since taken her jeans off and put them in her backpack, so it was just her period clothes) but a little worried that someone might have taken a look in her backpack and seen some odd things, she quickly dressed and had a look in her bag.

Satisfied that at least nothing was missing, she threw her bag over her shoulder, rushed down to the kitchen and grabbed a roll, and quickly thanked Sorcha for it as she ran out the door toward Alfred's entrance to the underground castle.

Even with gobbling her breakfast as she ran over the bone jarringly hard paving stones, she was in front of the new guards before she realized she should've thought about what to say to them. Might as well be direct.

"Hail and well met. I'm Kelsey, o' Tavish Macgregor's clan. Did Tavish and Seumas and Alfred gae doon thare?"

The one guard was eating an apple and he turned and spat out a seed.

The other guard gave her a puzzled look as he gestured with his thumb behind him down the dark stairs.

"Aye, and they are doon speaking to some feller. They said tae expect ye and tae allow ye tae gae after them, but I dinna see how ye can without a torch, lass."

Right. A torch. She thought of just going down there anyway in the dark and then grabbing her flash-light out of her bag, but she really shouldn't let anybody see that. She made an 'oh silly me' face at the guards and then ran back to the kitchen and came back with a torch, huffing a bit for breath.

"Can I light it off yer lantern?"

The guard held out his hand and she gave him the torch, which he lit for her, moving altogether too slowly.

And then the other guard took a bite of his apple and spoke to her between chews and spitting out seeds.

"Have a care on the stairs, lass. Perhaps we should call someone to escort ye."

As if she'd wait around for that. She pushed through them with her shoulder, holding the torch with one hand and her skirts with the other in order to get down the stairs without breaking her neck.

"Nay, I thank ye. Howsoever, I'll just catch up with Tavish and them."

As soon as she was out of their sight, she grabbed two handfuls of skirt at arm's length and tucked them in through the top of her belt to make the going much easier and then ran to Brian's sleeping chamber.

She heard Alfred and Seumas and Brian's and many other voices coming from the chamber when she got near, and she paused to listen.

Alfred was saying—rather nonchalantly, "...sae yer only choices are tae leave the realm or tae stay on in Laird Malcomb's service."

Someone grabbed her hand from behind, and Kelsey gasped, half turning to do one of the self-defense moves she'd halfheartedly learned and then only feeling somewhat relieved to find that it was Tavish. Why did he have to be holding her hand? It still made her melt inside, even now that she knew he'd just been using her.

He tugged on her hand, pulling her toward the entrance and whispering.

"I've got the ring and the scepter." He showed her the ring on his hand and patted the scepter where it lay concealed inside his bloused plaid. "We need to leave before they realize you're down here or that I've gone."

For once in what seemed like a long time, she agreed with him, and they made their way down to the docks and then up the other way until they got to the special corridor.

Once inside its relative safety, to her horrified embarrassment she swooned in Tavish's arms.

"Sorry. I guess now that I'm safe, it all caught up with me."

His strong arms and firm body supported her while his voice said otherwise.

"Uh huh. Come on. We just need to get down to the

end of this corridor, and you'll be Dr. Ferguson once more."

She narrowed her eyes at him, even as he took her hand and walked her down to the end of the corridor.

"It's not like I ever stopped being Dr. Ferguson."

He didn't even look at her, just raised his eyebrows while he put his arm around her and raised his ring hand up and took hold of the ring with his other hand.

"Yeah, I guess that's true."

Kelsey knew in her mind that his arms were just around her now so that his ring would transport her along with him, back to their time. So it mostly just made her mad, the way her juices started flowing when they were near like this. Mostly. Even still, it took all of her concentration not to sink into his embrace while he was still close to her.

"Just get us home already."

His body stiffened, which should've helped her withdraw, but ironically it made that even more difficult. He was so... manly.

"As you wish."

She was rolling her eyes at his sappy response when the world started spinning really fast, making her need to hold onto him so that she wouldn't fall. Darn him and his stubbornness. Why couldn't he hold on to her so that she wouldn't fall? He had to be such a gentleman all the time, making her choose to cling to him.

The world stopped spinning, and then she knew she was back in her time. It smelled different, for one thing. Not as ... natural.

"Give me a minute. I'm so dizzy."

"A minute is exactly as much time as we have before they get here."

She had forgotten that 'they' were on their way and would get here soon. Sure enough, she heard the same voices she'd heard just before the two of them escaped to the past. Those familiar voices. Only this time, she saw 'them'.

There were five, all her parents' age or older. At first glance, they looked like anyone you would see outdoors: jeans and parka or hoodie, hiking boots or sneakers, backpack or shoulder bag, water bottle.

But then she looked into their faces as they came down the secret corridor. Wise but cunning eyes. They had never seemed creepy to her before, but she had never been the subject of their study before. These were the top echelon of professors at Celtic University. She had heard them lecture. She had looked up to them.

She was still a bit dizzy, clinging to Tavish. It was making her lean away from them.

Their leader's eyes were giving her a knowing smile even as he was clearly speaking to Tavish.

"Did you get it?"

Still keeping her firmly in his left arm, Tavish fumbled in his bloused plaid for the scepter.

Relieved to take her eyes off their leader, Kelsey turned toward the scepter and got it out.

Tavish took it in his right hand and extended it toward the professor, turning so that he stood firmly between her and them.

Their leader took the scepter and immediately

examined it, then gestured to the others, who brought equipment out of their backpacks and bags.

Kelsey knew what they were doing and followed along, half in fascination at just how powerful the magic scepter was—let alone that magic actually existed at all outside of Celtic Fairy Tales—and half in dread of whatever it was they planned to do with it.

After several minutes, they packed everything up and their leader put the scepter in his bag. He looked from Tavish to Kelsey and back again, including both of them in his upward nod.

"We'll be in touch."

All of the professors turned around and confidently headed out.

Kelsey moved as if to follow them, but Tavish held her.

"Let's give them a few minutes."

She pushed against his arm.

"Fine, but give me a little space."

He let go immediately and stepped away from her, still looking up the corridor where they were disappearing around the corner.

"Yes ma'am."

She took off her backpack and set it on the floor, squatting to dig through it. First she found her jeans and pulled them on under the voluminous skirt of her Scottish plaid dress so that she could take the darn thing off. She stood there holding it for a moment, unsure what to do with it, before she decided to stuff it into her backpack—after she grabbed her phone and her sweatshirt and put it on, stuffing her huge linen sleeves into the sweatshirt sleeves.

Once she was dressed as she had been when she came into the caves just an hour ago, Tavish's hand closed around the wrist of her hand that held her phone.

"Remember, you can't tell anyone any of this."

She pulled away from him.

He let her, but he was still looking up the corridor, not at her.

She powered up her phone, glad she hadn't used it much and had kept it off most of the time.

"I'm calling my client. You know, the guy who owns this whole place—including the artifact you just gave those creeps."

He started walking up the corridor, glancing back to tell her to follow him but not meeting her eyes.

"You just called him a few minutes ago, remember? You probably don't want to pester him. You were waiting for him to call you back."

Ug, why did he have to be so sensible? She put her backpack on but kept her phone in her hand, looking down to watch it update every few seconds as she trudged a few feet behind him up on out of the underground.

"So it's okay for you to give a golden scepter probably worth millions to those creeps, but you give me hell for wanting to upload a few photographs?"

He still didn't look back at her, didn't meet her eyes, but he took a deep breath as he kept walking up the corridor, and let it out.

"There's no way you can upload the photographs you took while we were back in the old time, Kelsey. You can't be that stupid. You know what they would do to us if you did that? You'd be accused of being a quack at best, but if anyone at all thought we were serious, they would take away any privacy we ever had a chance at having, much worse than those creeps. Yeah, they make me get them stuff, but number one, I don't have a choice, and number two, at least I do get to have a life still, unlike what would happen if you posted those photographs—"

She interrupted him, almost yelling at his back.

"I'm not talking about back in the old time, Tavish. I can't believe you think I'm that stupid. I mean the ones I took before we went, in the storage room."

They went up the stairs and out through the root cellar and across the castle way in the early morning darkness of Scotland's brooding clouds. Tavish waved to a few of the other construction workers, who were just coming out of their trailers as he and Kelsey neared Mr. Blair's trailer.

They toasted him with their tea mugs and gave her tentative smiles, which she returned.

There was a flash of lightning.

All the men glanced up at the sky casually with their eyebrows raised, sipping their morning cup of tea and visibly wondering if they were going to get a day off for rain. Poor guys. They still had no idea what a vast underground network they were going to need to buttress so that it could be catalogued safely.

Tavish turned around then to face her, but he was still looking at the guys when he spoke.

"Well you need to wait and talk to Mr. Blair first before you do anything like that."

Kelsey put her hands on her hips and squared off against Tavish.

"I know full well what I need to do, and I don't need you telling me what that is." She hit her chest with her thumb. "I'm the senior contractor here, not you, and I will be in the owner's trailer minding his and my business until he gets here."

She was just about to turn and storm up to the door of the trailer when there was a loud crack of thunder. It made her jump a little, and stumble.

Tavish caught her before she fell, but she pushed off of him—and then did everything she could not to run into the trailer or slam the door, which she nonetheless closed behind her and locked just before the rain started hammering down.

20

FICHEAD

Kelsey looked at her phone for the time. Eight on a Saturday morning. Was that too early to call Sasha? Nah.

She called, but she had to leave voicemail.

"Sorry to bug you so early. Call me when you get this, okay? Bye."

She thought about calling her mom, but she really didn't want to discuss Tavish with her. And what was she going to say when she talked to Sasha, anyway? They had just spoken last night, and so far as her friend knew, nothing much was going on.

But everything had gone on. She'd made a fool of herself with Tavish, showing him just how much she really cared. And he had rejected her. Called her stupid. He didn't appreciate all that she'd been through at Celtic University, all her hard study and her hard work. All that she knew now.

Well, he did appreciate it, but he had just used all

her knowledge to get that magic scepter for those creepy modern druids he'd given it to. Well, good. They had what they wanted from him here, so he was free to leave. She would talk to Mr. Blair about getting a different foreman. That older man Gus should probably be the foreman anyway.

She plugged her phone in and brought up the pictures she'd taken on the sly, eight hundred years ago, putting her fingers in the venetian blinds to check the current layout of the area against them—hoping she didn't see Tavish out there.

Wow, she was really glad she had the pictures. The layout had changed a lot, and all of her mental notes from the underground exploration in her dream were based on the layout in the pictures. She got her laptop out of her bag and made herself busy on the University's inter-web, mapping her dream exploration of the Alba Palace compared to the photographs and the way the land looked now out her window.

It was an engrossing job, and it should have kept her mind off painful subjects, but every picture she looked at brought up memories of Tavish and questions about Tavish and worries about Tavish. How long had he been going to Laird Malcomb's Castle? Would he be going back there? What if something awful happened to him in that time?

Her phone buzzed and she grabbed it, relieved that Sasha would be able to keep her company.

But it was Mr. Blair.

She took a deep breath to calm her nerves and hoped it made her voice sound stable and authoritative.

"Hello?"

"Hello, Dr. Ferguson. I got yer stupendous news, and I must say I'm quite surprised and o' course delighted. Can ye shew me?"

"I'm emailing you right now with the photos of the storage room we found."

"Good, good. I want tae see the storage room for myself before I decide which, if any, phootographs ye can post tae Celtic University's password protected site, ye ken?"

"Of course, Mr. Blair."

"Naught can be done i this storm, though. I'll be oot there as soon as it lets up, an we can explore yer findings."

"That sounds good, Mr. Blair. The palace is quite a bit more extensive than you thought, and I'm looking forward to showing you. To give you an idea just how much more extensive, I'm drawing up blueprints, because there's no way I could simply explain it to you."

"I've just received the phootographs, and I dinna quite see what ye mean. Sure, there are many artifacts in this room, but the room itself is rather small, is na it?"

Kelsey sighed. Tavish would know exactly what to say to Mr. Blair. It was apparent he had been here dealing with him for a long time.

But she didn't need Tavish. She had been taught how to deal with clients—although admittedly not how to explain to them how she knew something she couldn't have known unless she had traveled back in time...

She thought carefully about what she could tell him.

"When you get here, I can show you the many secret doors in that one passageway you've found. I've opened a few, and the language of the carvings tells me there are many, many more. Your construction crew will come in very useful making sure everything is structurally sound down there so that exploring can be safe..." An idea hit her, and she ran with it. "This project has grown in scope so much that I wish to bring in a colleague, Dr. Sasha Swain."

"A colleague from Celtic University?"

"Yes, we were there together and both got our doctorates at the same time. She lives here in Scotland, so it wouldn't take her long to get out here to the site, and I'm going to need her help. I just hope she's available."

Mr. Blair sounded excited on the phone, and she tried to focus on all the things that made this project exciting—except for Tavish.

"I'll have tae see the secret doors ye're talking about, o' course, and this room full of artifacts whose phootographs ye've sent me, but if that all works oot as ye say, then I see nae problem with bringing in yer colleague—and perhaps a few more colleagues, just sae this dig does na take ten years tae finish."

Now her training kicked in, and she was on more or less familiar ground, getting more confident with each sentence.

"We can make a spectacle out of the project itself, Mr. Blair. That can bring in some money for you off the tourist trade. Maybe you should build an inn nearby..."

A few minutes later, she hung up the phone, pleased

with herself and really hoping Sasha would be able to come help.

Ooh, and there was a text from her friend:

"Almost there, talk then!"

She texted Sasha back:

"In the big gray trailer out front."

Kelsey drew up one of the blinds and gawked at the pouring rain. Was Sasha even crazier than she remembered? Oh well, worrying wasn't going to help. And having her friend here was just the thing she needed to get over her disappointment about... no, to get excited about this project. It was going to be so fun! This was both of their dream project, supervising a huge dig in Scotland.

But as she continued to create the blueprints, she wondered what Alfred and Seumas were saying to Brian the Druid and how Eileen would react when she heard Kelsey had fallen into the sea and been rescued by Tavish and Seumas...

Yeah, Tavish probably would be going back to the old time, and he was good at improvisation and could explain her absence in some way. Maybe say she was moping somewhere. She could envision his face as she told Seumas that, could envision Alfred rolling his eyes at the idea and then turning to appreciate Eileen for the sweetheart she was. And then Tavish would get them all excited about some other quest they needed to go on—so that he could verify the outside location of a room they needed to dig into here in the present...

But no, he wouldn't be around to help her in that way if he chose to leave because he couldn't take her being in charge. She sighed, and her hands stopped moving on the keyboard. Her eyes drifted to her Celtic University ring. Yeah, she had book learning, and it was paying off in great ways, being able open the secret doors—and that Celtic Fairy Tale trick of sneaking into people's dreams.

But it would be so much more fun with Tavish around.

For reasons that made sense, not just sentimentally.

Tavish knew the old time just as well as the present day. He walked right in with confidence and that sexy swagger where she would always seem out of place. He had lived there. He understood history in a way that no one else she knew did. Yeah, there were sensible reasons to want Tavish around.

She didn't only want him around because he knew her better than anyone else, even Sasha. And not just because he always protected her and watched out for her, and kissed her like he meant it...

Even with all her rationalization, she concentrated hard enough to get the blueprints almost done in a few hours, but she should have been much faster at this. Too much of the time, instead of working at the computer, she played with her university ring, the symbol of her lofty educational distinction, slipping it on and off and turning it around and around.

There was a loud knock on the door.

Kelsey jumped, and then she lifted up the blinds.

Sasha smiled and waved at her through the rain, holding up a plastic bag from the Chinese restaurant in town.

Kelsey jumped up and let her friend in, giving her a big hug and taking the plastic bag from her and rushing with it to the microwave.

The food smelled wonderful. Kung Pao, if she wasn't mistaken.

Yep. And rice to go with it.

She broke the metal handles off the cartons and stuck the whole things in the microwave to heat it all up, then hurriedly dished it into two bowls and grabbed two beers out of the fridge.

"Make yourself at home. This is the client's trailer, and *he* will be here once the rain lets up. I can't believe you drove out here in that downpour, but I'm glad you did."

Sasha had sat down on the couch, and Kelsey plopped a bowl and a beer on the coffee table in front of her, keeping the other ones as she sat down next to her friend.

"Sasha, I want you to be my partner on this project. Can you spare a couple years?"

21

AON AIR FHICHEAD

Tuffy ran up to Tavish as soon as he entered his trailer, and he scooped up the little dog and petted him, then brought him back over to Gus, who was the oldest member of the construction crew in addition to being his roommate.

"He earned his name today, Tuffy did. Stood up to a mastiff over castle way."

Gus held out his arms, and Tavish placed the little dog in them, where he was tenderly held. Gus then rocked him much like one would a baby—which was always comical, Gus was so huge.

"Aye, the woman said so much when she brought him back to me." Gus nuzzled his face into Tuffy's head and spoke to the dog. "Yes she did. Yes she did."

"Sorry you had to speak to her."

The old Scot looked up at him with his bushy gray eyebrows wrinkled.

"Why do ye say that?"

Tavish wrinkled his own brow in return and reached over to pet Tuffy.

"You don't find her even a bit high and mighty?"

Gus pursed his lips and raised his eyebrows.

"Nay, far from it. She was right nice aboot bringing Tuffy back to me. She didn't have to do that." And then he spoke to the dog again, still jiggling it in his arms like a child. "Don't you be running off again now. I was so worried." Eyes back on Tavish, he said, "What makes you say she's high and mighty?"

Tavish went into their tiny little kitchenette to heat up some leftover fish and get himself a cup of tea. He held up an empty cup toward Gus, who shook his head no.

"Well you know we used to know each other when we were younger."

"Aye, it's plain to see in the way you are with each other, even if you hadn't told me."

"Yeah, well most of the time she treats me the same as always, but every once in a while now, she acts like she knows better than me—"

Gus laughed. "Bothers you, does it?"

"Well, yeah."

Gus shook his head. "Son, she *does* know better than you—"

Tavish almost dropped his teacup. Was the man serious? "She doesn't know the first thing about construction work."

"Nay, but she doesna need to. She has you for that, and us."

"Well what does she know so much about then?"

Even as he said this, Tavish knew he was being stupid. She knew all kinds of useful druidic things. But did Gus know that? And why was Gus taking her side, anyway?

Gus sighed and calmed poor Tuffy, who'd been a bit startled by Tavish's tone of voice.

"Bit rough to see when it's a woman—and a fine one at that—however, she *is* a suit, Tavish. She has a doctoral degree. She'll be second in charge of this job after the owner, and I wouldna be surprised if she brought on people who'll be third and fourth. When you've been around as long as I have, you'll be able to see these things coming. But I thought I'd better warn you. She does know better, and it'll be her job to tell you so."

Whatever. But wow, Gus really did know something. Were the druids on him, too?

"What makes you think there's a big enough job here to require a second in command, let alone a third and fourth? You do know that stuff we found in the basement was just trinkets made in the 70s by some hippies, right?"

"Aye, that it was. But you aren't from around here, Tavish. You didn't grow up with the stories about how the ancient home o' the kings of Alba resides beneath these cliffs here. You see, Mr. Blair must think there's some truth to that, or he wouldna have tried so hard and fought so long to get this land back after his drunken ancestor let it fall out of the family hundreds of years ago. This will be a big find. Depend upon it. Won't be long before news crews are out here covering it. But getting back to your friend—uh, Kelsey?"

"Yeah, her name's Kelsey, but now she seems to prefer Dr. Ferguson."

Gus nodded sideways.

"I suppose if I spent seven extra years in school to get a doctorate, I'd prefer to be called Dr. as well." He raised his eyebrows at Tavish.

"I guess." Yeah, Gus did have a point.

"I'm just saying maybe it's you who are na being a verra good friend, here."

There was a loud bang on the door, and the voices of Brody, Lyle, and Gavin could be heard outside, along with a general hubbub that said there were more guys with them.

"Are you in there, Tavish?"

"We're on to have a party because of this rain."

"Aye, and because of the boss being away."

Gus smiled at him, and Tavish went over and let the guys in. It was crowded with 10 of them in the small trailer, but they had brought whisky, so he supposed he could stand it. There were far from enough chairs, even with the small sofa, but the men who didn't get seats made do with sitting on the sofa arms or leaning on the kitchenette counters.

As they passed the bottles around, Tavish thought about what Gus had said.

22

DHÀ AIR FHICHEAD

An hour before sunset, it had still been raining, and so Mr. Blair had said he would come the next day and was eager to meet Sasha. Sure enough, the next day dawned dreary but dry, so their high-tech equipment from the university would be able to survey the land and mark out the underground castle's likely entry points. Which would all be recorded and stored away in the university's records, of course.

Kelsey and Sasha had microwaved frozen breakfast sandwiches and donned their suits—Sasha kept one in her trunk for just such emergencies—and they were getting their equipment ready to go out and start surveying while they waited for Mr. Blair to arrive.

Kelsey felt much better after a good night's sleep.

"Now don't let Tavish give you any grief," she told Sasha. "I'm not going to. He probably won't, though. He and I are having a little fight, but really he's a nice guy. I'd be surprised if he said anything mean to you at all. No, that's going to be all for me, lucky me. But yeah, if he does, just realize it's because he's mad at me. It won't be about you—"

Sasha elbowed her in the side gently.

"Quit it. I'm sure it will be just fine. You're over the fight, and he probably is too. In fact," she picked up Kelsey's purse and walked her over to the bathroom and handed it to her, "I think you should do your makeup. You never know."

Kelsey rolled her eyes at her friend, but doing her makeup did sound like a good idea. After all, she wanted to look put together when she presented her blueprints to Mr. Blair, and likely he would have her explain the project to the crew.

Half an hour later, they were immersed in their task of showing all the land to the equipment when Kelsey recognized Mr. Blair's voice.

"I like that, ye got right tae it first thing in the morning." With Tavish trailing slightly behind him, the client walked up to Sasha and offered to shake hands. "Hello, I'm Keith Blair, the new owner of these premises. And you must be Dr. Swain. Dr. Ferguson here speaks very highly of you."

Kelsey couldn't help turning her eyes toward Tavish while Sasha returned Mr. Blair's pleasantries. He gave her a tentative smile, which she returned.

Mr. Blair turned his attention toward her and gestured at all their equipment.

"So what's this all aboot, then?"

Kelsey showed him the tiny monitoring screen.

"The equipment is finding the Alba castle's likely entrance points, see?"

Mr. Blair peered into the little monitor, but then Tavish put a hand on his back, taking his attention away.

Kelsey felt her hackles rise, and she spun on her heel, preparing to get some distance between herself and Tavish—and unfortunately between herself and Mr. Blair. She was going to have to do something about Tavish. She did not want to do this job under these working conditions. It was demeaning. She felt more like an errand girl than a doctor.

But then she heard Tavish's voice.

"While this equipment is grand, and we will need its readings for all the work ahead, it's much more imperative now that you let Kelsey show you the storage room we found—isn't that right, Kel?"

Sasha gave her an 'I told you so' smile before Kelsey could answer.

She gave Tavish a 'thank you' smile and then turned to Mr. Blair with an expression she fought to keep professional, but which she knew was all excited.

"Oh yes, absolutely. In fact, let's go over there right now."

She and Sasha had been sensible enough to wear their hiking boots with their suits, so all four of them went right over to the hatch door above the root cellar. Tavish got it open and gestured for her and Sasha to go down first in their skirts, which they did, but then she heard Tavish talking to someone new up top.

"Go on down and introduce yourselves to Dr. Ferguson and Dr. Swain," she heard him say.

She looked at Sasha, who shrugged.

And then the two of them watched a third woman come down the ladder next. She was stylishly dressed, but in slacks, and her hair and makeup were Hollywood grade.

Bile rose up into Kelsey's mouth. If Tavish had a girlfriend...

But the woman no sooner made it down than two more strangers came down the ladder, men this time, with big backpacks on. They started to open their backpacks while the woman looked at all the nooks and crannies in the 10 x 10 stone root cellar with interest.

The woman finally turned toward Kelsey and Sasha and held out her hand.

"Right, sae ye're the Dr. Ferguson who will show us how tae get in the secret doors, eh?"

Kelsey made a face that hopefully showed how puzzled she was, but she shook the woman's hand.

"Do I know you?"

The woman laughed and went on to shake Sasha's hand.

"Oh, ye're American, and ye dinna have a clue who I am, dae you?"

Kelsey looked at Sasha, who shrugged again, so she looked back at the woman and shook her head no.

The woman visibly admired Kelsey and Sasha's Celtic University rings and then turned to the two men, who were unpacking equipment.

"I'm Gisa Sutherland with BBC Scotland, and we're

here tae dae a story on ye, Dr. Ferguson, complete with movie cameras documenting how ye open these secret doors."

Tavish and his kilt came next down the ladder, which thankfully was on the other side of the small room. He spoke up toward the top of the ladder, where Mr. Blair's feet could be seen.

"I can't wait for you to see this, Keith. She had it open in just a few seconds."

Once everyone was down, Mr. Blair gathered them around the secret door with the camera crew's lights blaring.

"Well nae, Dr. Ferguson, I reckon ye'd better show us yer magic."

Her eyes went to Tavish's, and the two of them shared a look which savored the excitement and the awe they had felt the first time she did this.

And then she explained to Gisa and the camera crew and the rest of Scotland and probably the world how she had read the Celtic interlace symbols and known this was a secret door.

She opened it and gave everyone a tour of the underground space you could get to without opening any more secret doors—with all of its arcane runes and ancient items. She even let Sasha explain some of it, once they got to the storage room.

BBC Scotland's camera crew were as shocked as she had been, to find that cellular connections worked down here. They'd been able to do some of the segments live.

If Kelsey was any judge, Mr. Blair was glowing

almost as much as she was from all the attention the project was getting, and he insisted that Kelsey show the camera crew her blueprints and explain just how large she thought Alba Palace was.

By the time the folks from BBC Scotland departed, the sun was setting in a trail of sea sparkles leading to the distant view of Ireland.

Mr. Blair turned to Kelsey and Sasha out in front of his trailer.

"I'll be gang back into toon where I've got a motel room for tonight, but tomorrow I'll get ye ladies yer own trailer brought oot here. I'll see that ye each hae yer own room. Any ither amenities in particular that ye'd like?"

Kelsey just shook her head no, all the while smiling at Tavish.

Sasha gave Kelsey a playful little shove and led Mr. Blair over to his car, which was parked on the other side of the trailer.

"Is it possible we could each have our own bathroom as well? And do any trailers come with full refrigerators? What about built-in espresso makers? And if this is going to be a new trailer, then I prefer blues to neutral colors..."

Alone with Tavish at long last after just stealing glances at him all day, Kelsey hurried over to him, talking before he could say anything.

"Thank you so much for today, Tavish."

He twinkled his eyes at her and raised his eyebrows as if to say, 'Whatever for?' Which let her know it was okay, and they weren't fighting anymore.

She moved closer to him, reaching out, and he opened up his arms so that they were soon holding each other close, watching together as the sky and the sea grew red.

She spoke with her head against his chest, hearing his heartbeat.

"Only you could have explained all that to the TV station ahead of time, and it was the sweetest thing you could have done for me today, making sure the world knew I had something to do with this discovery. Thank you so much."

He caressed her back.

"You're welcome, Kel. Sorry it took me so long to see how much you know, and how much you can do. I'm so proud of you, and I'm so sorry I didn't let you choose whether I'd leave or not, all those years ago. I was miserable without you, and I'm so sorry if I made you miserable by leaving. I thought I was doing the right thing, but now I see that all I did was make you lose faith in me."

She squeezed him tight.

"Apology accepted. Now it's my turn. I'm so sorry for the way I treated you in our time's yesterday, like some stupid construction worker who couldn't possibly know anything about ancient ruins."

He kissed the top of her head as he held her close and then laid his head down on top of hers, enveloping her.

"There was no way you could have known I'd been back to the old time, Kel. And for all you knew, I was just a jerk who disappeared from your life and hadn't spoken to you in seven years. Your behavior made perfect sense."

"True, but I'm still sorry. And you're at least as responsible for the discovery of Alba Palace as I am."

He started them rocking from side to side and raised his head up, then beamed a smile at her when she met his eyes. He lowered his mouth to her ear and whispered.

"But thanks to you, I got the old druids their scepter in two days instead of two years, and they'll be off my back awhile. You did me a much better favor than I did you."

She pulled away until he could see her face and know that she was sincere.

"Still, I'm going to find a way to give you credit for this discovery, too."

He studied her face, equally sincere.

"I don't need credit with the world, Kel, only with you."

Her face broke into her biggest smile.

"You have all the credit in the world with me."

He lifted her and swung her around, then settled comfortably with her still raised up so they were face-to-face, with his arms around her waist.

"Will you give me a lifetime with you to spend it?"

Lost in his eyes, all she could do was nod a vigorous yes before she was kissing him.

23

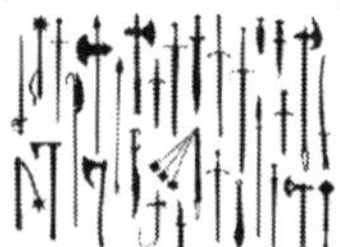

TRÌ AIR FHICHEAD

Seumas looked around for Tavish as he and Alfred and the other men escorted the druid Brian up to his audience with Laird Malcomb. That MacGregor had been here just a moment ago. Where could he have gotten to?

And then when they were almost up out of the caves, passing through the washroom, Tavish came up from behind out of nowhere and joined them, as he was wont to do in this area. Come to think of it, Seumas had been meaning to ask him about that. But not when others could hear them.

They had passed on up by the entrance guards and were in the castle town when the prisoner tried to make a break for it, lunging between him and Tavish.

He met eyes with MacGregor over the druid's head when they both threw their knees out to stop him, making the man double over and retch. They shared a grim satisfied smile, and then each took an arm and hoisted the prisoner kicking and screaming between them all the way to Laird Malcomb's office, where he ordered the druid locked into the tower, which they did with satisfaction.

The group of men paused outside the tower door while their leader spoke with another head guard.

What was it he was going to ask Tavish about again? Oh well. Must not have been important. Instead, when he turned toward Tavish, he asked the man the first thing that came to his mind.

"Is Kelsey well after her ... dunking?"

Ah, and there it was in the man's eyes. His love for the lass, aye, but also his certainty of her love for him. Seumas was happy for them.

Tavish nodded with a contented smile.

"Aye, that she is. Nae harm done."

The man's eyes had a faraway look to them. Guessing he was remembering a pleasant time he had spent with his woman, Seumas felt the urge to be elsewhere. Not because he envied the man and felt alone in the company of one so happy, no. Just because he had better things to do.

But Tavish started patting all around his waist with a bit of a stricken look on his face.

"My sporran. Must've fallen. Had it when I went down with you to go get Brian. Need to retrace my steps." He took off at a brisk pace down the hallway, looking down at the floor.

Seumas went about his duties with the squadron of guards, expecting Tavish to rejoin them at any moment, with his sporran once again around his waist by its cord.

The more time went by without that happening, the more concerned and curious he grew.

Finally, he made an excuse and ran off after that MacGregor. After descending the stairs, he encountered the man, but he wasn't alone. Kelsey was with him, and the two of them looked very happy, and again he was happy for them, but the other woman along with them distracted him.

Wrapped up in Tavish's spare plaid as if it were a cloak, she walked with as much certainty as Kelsey did—a true rarity in a woman. How remarkable for there to be two such women in his acquaintance. She spoke Gaelic with an accent like Kelsey's, but stronger. They must have come from the same glen. She spoke with confidence as well, even though she faltered for words as if Gaelic were not her true language.

And she was a beauty. Her hair was as red as his, and her skin was clear and fair between the redheaded sun dapples. She was tall and lean and strong—he could tell even through the cloak she wore.

And she was staring at him in awe.

SEUMAS

A Time Travel Romance

❦ 1 ❦

A DAY EARLIER

Sasha smiled at Kelsey as the two of them waved at the BBC Scotland news crew and watched them drive away.

"If I had told you while we were at Celtic University that we would one day be in charge of a dig worthy of worldwide news —"

Kelsey smiled back at her.

"Nope, I never would have believed that."

Sasha looked out at the tower house called Dunskey Castle and used her imaginary x-ray vision to see through it to the underground palace they were digging out beneath it. She also enjoyed the ragged sea cliffs of the Scottish coastline and finally gazed across the sea at the sunset over distant Ireland. This was exactly what she had imagined she would be doing all seven years she toiled through college to get her doctorate in Celtic archaeology to make it possible.

She was so proud of herself. Her goal in life had

been to escape the boring suburbs of Middle America, and at only twenty-five years old, she had already succeeded beyond her wildest dreams.

She turned back to her friend.

"I thought my face was going to crack, I was smiling so hard when you said I should go ahead and open one of the secret doors for the camera crew." She held up her phone for Kelsey to see. "My mom and my brother and my cousins and seventeen friends have already texted to say they saw me on TV."

Kelsey smiled, but it looked a little strained, and she kept glancing over across the dig site to the crew trailers, where her new kilted boyfriend Tavish was on the phone.

Sasha saw that all the rest of the construction workers were goofing around, now that the day was over. None of them was wearing a kilt. And they were all real Scots, while Kelsey had known her boyfriend back in the States before she went off to college. What was up with him wearing that kilt? Hardly practical for construction work.

Kelsey answered her in a soft voice while still watching Tavish.

"Yeah, my mom and everyone back home texted me, too. I gave Gisa both of our numbers, and she promised to text us a link where we can watch ourselves on a repeat of the broadcast."

"Good."

Watching the construction crew guys play gave Sasha pangs of homesickness for the seventeen friends she'd made at Celtic University in the short three months she'd been a professor there. But she was good at making friends fast. Maybe she'd go over and join the guys.

The oddness of their activity made her pause, though. They were playing this dangerous he-man game where they tried to lift up a log by the end and hold the log so that it was vertical in the air, then let it fall down in front of themselves. Guys were so weird.

Sasha flinched as one of the guys accidentally dropped the log sideways. It came crashing down to the ground, bounced off one end, bounced off the other end, and would have hit Tavish if one of the guys hadn't pushed him out of the way.

Unfortunately, Tavish was so busy on his phone, he didn't realize why the guy had pushed him, and he fell, landing on his face on a rock. He got up and shoved the guy back, but some others came over and they appeared to be sorting it out, thank goodness.

"What's so important on the phone that he almost got killed over it?"

Kelsey sighed.

"Did I ever tell you he has a twin brother?"

"He does?"

"Yeah, I thought I'd never see Tavish again — let alone be with him again — so I didn't explain his family dynamics. But among a slew of other issues that we need to explain to you once we get a chance, Tavish has a twin. His name is Tomas, and he's being stupid. Tavish is stuck here and wants his brother to come visit him, and Tomas won't come."

Sasha gave her friend a sideways hug as they stood

there watching the guys, who in no time at all had started a new game: throwing their knives into the big log the one guy had dropped, which was now wedged between two boulders ten feet away from them.

Behind her, she heard the voice of Mr. Blair, the property owner and thus her and Kelsey's client.

"Ye lasses use my trailer again this night, and I'll stay in toon again. I've texted ye the link tae the web thingy where ye can look over the trailers they have and pick the one ye want. If ye let me ken this night, maybe we can even have it oot here tomorrow, though that is Sunday, so maybe not till Monday."

He shook both of their hands as he said this, and then they walked him to his car, which was parked in front of his trailer.

He had been Kelsey's client first, so she spoke for the two of them.

"Thank you so much, Mr. Blair. We'll pick something out within the hour and let you know, so that you can call the trailer guy before it gets late."

Mr. Blair nodded and smiled at them as he got in his car, then drove off.

Sasha went on into the trailer, calling over her shoulder at Kelsey just before the door closed.

"Guess we'd better get to it. Come on, Kelsey. They won't quit goofing around until dark, and that's a good hour yet."

While she waited for Kelsey to come in, she answered her texts. The ones from her family were all gooey, even the one from her brother, but some of her friends had sent screenshots of her on TV and doctored them with an app. One made her long red hair look like it was on fire. Another made her look like a lion, about to eat the camera. They were funny, and she was laughing out loud when Kelsey came in.

"Okay Butterfly, tear yourself away from your many fans long enough to flit over here and help me pick out our trailer."

As it always did, Kelsey's nickname for her made Sasha laugh even louder.

"I'll be there in a second."

The two of them had just texted Mr. Blair their choice of a two-bedroom, two-bathroom trailer in three complementary shades of blue when there was a knock on the door and they heard Tavish's voice.

"It's me, Kel. And Gus is here too, with Tuffy."

"Come on in," Kelsey called out to them.

Gus and Tuffy turned out to be a big old Scottish construction worker and his tiny little dog, whom he cradled like a baby. Tavish had brought a case of champagne, and the five of them partied, toasting the news exposure and Mr. Blair's meeting with a publicist on Monday with the intention of bringing tourists to the area so that he could turn a handy profit— and pay them all well.

THE NEXT MORNING SASHA CAME OUT OF THE bathroom after her shower wearing the professional suit she'd put on her credit card, whose bill made her oh, so thankful to have a better-paying job.

And Kelsey was dressed in old fashioned Scottish garb: long plaid overdress in red and green, green blouse with huge billowy sleeves, worn leather belt over it all with pouches and a cup and other implements hanging from it by leather cords.

Sasha stopped in her tracks.

"What's with the outfit?"

Kelsey brought over to the table a large pitcher of suspicious-looking orange liquid.

"You'll see. Will you pour the mimosas while I finish making the omelets?"

Sasha took the pitcher and poured, secretly glad there was more champagne. She hadn't thought this place would be so far from everything. She'd need to stock the fridge better. And find out if there was going to be a problem.

"Okay, but won't Mr. Blair be upset if he smells this on our breath?"

Kelsey laughed at the stove.

"Nah, they're more relaxed over here about alcohol, especially when you don't work for a university — much more so than back home in the US. We don't usually drink with breakfast, though, but we're still in a celebrating mood, so why not use up the rest of the champagne?"

Sasha brought over two glasses and clinked with Kelsey before she chugged hers.

"I'll drink to that!"

They laughed.

Tavish joined them, and they all sat down and dug in. The food was great — and so were the mimosas.

They passed a few minutes just eating and drinking and making appreciative noises.

But Sasha couldn't keep quiet for long.

"Tavish, I know there's something going on today, because Kelsey's dressed up too, but why do you always wear a kilt? I mean, it looks great and all, but you aren't on stage. You're here to do a job. And none of the other guys wear kilts on the job. Am I right?" She ate the last bite of her omelet, eagerly awaiting his response.

"About that." Kelsey chugged the rest of her third mimosa.

Tavish had already chugged his fourth drink.

"We talked about it, and the easiest thing is if we just show you why I wear my kilt all the time."

Sasha poured her fourth mimosa while she gave them her best excitedly curious face.

"Okay. Are you going to get up and do a little dance, Tavish?"

Tavish laughed.

"The day has only just begun, so you never know. You might even do a little dance before this is over. In fact, I can't wait to see the look on your face."

Kelsey playfully hit his chest with the back of her hand and rolled her eyes.

"Sasha, there's all kinds of reasons we need to show you this — and before your dirty mind goes into full gear, all of them are professional."

Wow, they were serious. Sasha downed the rest of the pitcher and stood up, wiping her mouth with the back of her hand and then wiping the lipstick off her hand with her napkin.

"All right, so show me already."

Kelsey started to go into the other room, but Tavish grabbed her arm playfully and pulled her back.

"We'll only stay a few minutes. Don't worry about her clothes this time."

He got his long plaid cloak from the chair and held it out.

"Here, Sasha. Just throw this around yourself."

He looked at her shoes and shrugged. It was the first time a straight man had ever looked at her shoes.

She looked down at them herself, smiling at the head rush and reaching out a hand to stabilize herself on a chair. She'd known yesterday's rain would make the ground muddy, so she'd sprayed Scotch Gard on her knee-high leather boots.

She raised one eyebrow at Tavish and turned her head sideways, but she took his cloak and threw it around her shoulders dramatically. Then she gave Kelsey an incredulous look, exaggerated for effect.

"What, is there a costume party and nobody told me?"

"Even better," Kelsey said with a huge grin, heading out the door.

Sasha and Tavish went out after her, and they all headed over toward the root cellar of the old tower house.

Kelsey stumbled and laughed as she turned to walk backwards, then studied Sasha for a moment.

"Yeah, if we only go for a few minutes, you should be okay if you keep that cloak on. I can't wait for you to see this."

Mr. Blair's car pulled up then.

Kelsey wrinkled her nose in that way that meant she'd been caught being naughty. Interesting. She and Tavish looked at each other and had a silent conversation. The upshot was that they were going to stay and talk to Mr. Blair for a moment and hope it didn't ruin their plans, whatever those were.

More curious by the moment.

Sasha smiled and waved at Mr. Blair as he walked over.

After waving back, he pointed at a cut Tavish had on his face, from falling yesterday during the crew's odd game.

"I can give ye shaving lessons if ye hae that much trouble, lad."

Tavish put a hand to his cut with an odd look on his face as if he was surprised there was something there and smiled at Mr. Blair.

"Verra funny."

Mr. Blair looked at Kelsey's outfit appreciatively and then glanced at Sasha's cloak.

"Good, good, go on doon and take the photos we talked aboot, Kelsey. I'll hae the men get yer area cleared oot for when yer trailer arrives today."

Sasha felt a little disappointed at hearing they were just going to take publicity pictures, but she supposed it made sense. The prospect of getting their new trailer here today was great, though. No more sleeping in the living room, and she would have her own bathroom. Two women sharing a bathroom was a hardship. There was never enough room for her makeup.

Sasha and Kelsey spoke at the same time.

"That's great news, Mr. Blair."

"Thank you, Mr. Blair."

He smiled and nodded and moved on toward where all the construction crew were standing around drinking coffee and laughing, apparently waiting for him.

Gus waved, and Sasha waved back. Maybe later she would go over and see if she could join in on any of the gang's shenanigans.

Tavish held open the trap door to the root cellar while Sasha and Kelsey went down the ladder in their skirts.

Using her phone as a flashlight, Sasha went over to the secret door she had opened on TV.

"Should we take the pictures right here? This is one of the heavily featured places in the broadcast, so most people should recognize it, if they saw us on TV. That should be a pretty good tourist draw, don't you think?"

Tavish and Kelsey shrugged at each other for a moment, having another one of those silent conversations before Kelsey answered.

"Yeah, let's go ahead and take the pictures. Tavish, go stand with Sasha — and leave room for me. I'll set my phone up here on this ledge and use my timer app."

Sasha couldn't quite shake the feeling that something was off as they took about a dozen pictures, and then she was sure of it when Kelsey opened the secret door instead of following when Sasha started to climb the ladder again.

Kelsey called up to Sasha as she and Tavish entered the formerly secret corridor, hollowed out from solid rock. Her tone was deliberately casual, but Sasha could hear an undertone of excitement — and something else she couldn't quite identify.

"Come on, Sasha. We still need to show you something."

Sasha had been in the secret corridor with the news crew yesterday, so she wondered why her knees trembled as she went back down the ladder and followed Tavish and Kelsey down the corridor to a three-way intersection. As she had yesterday, she marveled at all the Celtic runes engraved in the walls. They were lacy and beautiful, but more so, they imparted the wisdom of the Druids — the priests of the ancient Celts. She and Kelsey had learned to read them in college.

She was about to speak up and warn Tavish and Kelsey that they were walking right into a wall when it disappeared and they walked through where it had been and turned to make sure she was following.

She did follow.

"How many mimosas did I drink?"

Kelsey sounded amused.

"I think you had five, and we all chugged our last one, remember?"

As Sasha ruminated over this, she followed the others down another corridor similar to the one off the root cellar — except this one dead ended.

Before she could ask what the heck they were doing here, Kelsey grabbed her in a hug. Good thing she had, too, because Sasha got so dizzy she almost fell down. But unlike other times she'd had a few too many and gotten dizzy, this dizziness kept getting more and more intense until it seemed like the cave was spinning around her.

The dizziness finally subsided, but Sasha was having some kind of visual problem, because the stone walls looked — cleaner. So did the floor and the ceiling.

Kelsey held her in a sideways hug and started walking her back down the corridor again.

"The dizziness will go away, I promise. I don't want to wait, though. I've just got to show you this."

Sasha imagined so, because it was turning out to be quite a lot of trouble to show her whatever this was. She hoped it was worth it. At least she didn't feel nauseated.

She figured they must be involved in live action role-playing, because Tavish walked with them on Kelsey's other side, talking nonsense.

"There's only one place you really have to be careful, and that's at the door to the tower where Brian the Druid is imprisoned. We'll show you where he is, just so you know to be careful when you go near there."

Sasha stopped walking.

"Brian the Druid?"

Tavish laughed.

"Yeah, that's what I said."

Kelsey's arm around her was shaking, she was so excited.

"Okay, once we leave this part of the corridor, we'll need to speak in Gaelic. And we won't be able to talk about certain things until we get back. No one but Tavish or a Druid can see past the illusion of the cave wall into this corridor, so this corridor is a pretty safe place to run to for refuge from anyone else. Meet here if we get separated."

Sasha laughed.

"Meet here if we get separated? You sound like my mother."

Tavish smiled.

"I'm glad you're having a good time. I can't wait to see your face once we get to the surface. We'll just go have a look around and come right back, this first time. Those mimosas will probably help you out, and you might even feel like dancing that jig."

Sasha threw her arms up in the air and gave them her best 'well come on then' look.

Kelsey turned around at the opening out of the corridor, chuckling a little at Sasha's frustration as she got out a lighter and lit three torches.

"Okay, put away your phone. Now take this torch. We're switching to Gaelic in just a second, but I'd better tell you this real quick. The only reason we came here in the first place was because the druids sent Tavish here to get a mag— ... a special artifact for them. You can't trust any of the druids, Sasha. It's not just Brian. They're all extremely dangerous."

Okay. So they wanted to play medieval dangerous druid games that involved speaking Gaelic. Fine. She played along, switching to the Gaelic she had been taught at Celtic University just as the three of them walked out of the corridor into the three-way intersection.

"Verra well. I willna fash any o' the druids. Am I

needing tae run when I see one, or are ye taking me tae a druid dress-up ball?"

But she didn't even hear their responses, because at the far end of the corridor facing her — wearing a kilt like Tavish's and at least three weapons, not to mention sporting a mane of long fiery red hair — was the most gorgeous specimen of a man Sasha had ever seen.

2

DHÀ

Sasha knew she was staring, but she couldn't help herself. The man looked like an old statue of a warrior come to life. There was not an ounce of fat on him. His muscles showed detail like those of old master statues chiseled out of marble. Unlike Tavish, who knew he looked good in a kilt and flaunted it, this man wore his kilt — as well as a coordinating linen shirt, an arisade, and heavy handmade leather boots — as if it were normal clothes. He had a huge sword strapped to his back, and the scuffs and small cuts all over it attested to the fact that he used it and didn't just wear it for show. His long red hair was tied in a loose ponytail with a leather cord, and his head was otherwise bare, his face positively glowing with health and vigor in the light of the torch he carried.

With an appreciative smile, he was looking her over from head to toe also, while absentmindedly speaking to Tavish in perfectly accented Gaelic with a deep rich voice that she would bet was great for singing.

"I see ye hae found yer sporran, as wull as a lass, whom I'm guessing is another clanswoman o' yers."

Wow, this was one elaborate role-playing game. Sasha pulled the cloak around her a little more tightly. She'd only just met him, and she felt like she had let this gorgeous hunk of a man down somehow. She didn't want to disappoint him by letting him see that she hadn't gone to any trouble to look historic.

She gave Kelsey a look that she meant to say, 'Why did you and Tavish have to be in such a hurry to get here? Didn't you mention clothes I could have put on?'

Kelsey cringed a little and shrugged at her.

Sasha couldn't see Tavish, only hear his voice responding. And Tavish sounded frustrated. She could almost hear him changing plans in his mind, because of running into this man.

But upon looking back at the man, she decided she didn't care that much.

The guy was such great eye candy. The more she looked at him, the more she was impressed by how authentic his clothing was. New details kept leaping out at her: a rip in his sleeve that had been hand mended, the hand stitching around the collar of his shirt, the way his boots were buttoned shut instead of zipped or tied.

But mostly he was just so darn good looking she couldn't tear her eyes away. And unlike how Tavish would've taken the attention, this man had the decency to pretend he didn't notice she was staring at him.

Which impressed her all the more, making her want to know more about him.

Meanwhile, Tavish was talking.

"Aye, I did find it. Thank ye for asking. Sasha, this is Seumas (Shaymus), my sparring buddy and fellow guard here at Laird Malcomb's castle, not to mention being the laird's nephew."

Seumas bowed to her in a way that made her feel honored rather than entertained. And the look in his eyes made her heart race.

And then Tavish was introducing her, and she found herself standing up straight and raising her chin in a way that would honor Seumas back.

"Seumas, this is Sasha, and aye, she is also my clanswoman. It's her foremaist time away from home, sae she wull need a bit o' understanding and looking after. Kelsey and I are sharing that responsibility, and mayhap ye will help us."

Puzzled, Sasha looked over at Tavish, and then at Kelsey. With her eyes, she tried her best to ask them why Tavish was lying and saying it was her first time away from home. And then she put her hand on her hip and raised her eyebrows, doing her best to tell them they'd better have a good reason to say she needed looking after.

But they couldn't keep her attention. Smiling tightly to keep the drool inside her mouth, Sasha turned to Seumas and held out her hand for him to shake.

"Wull met."

But Seumas didn't take her hand. No, he awkwardly looked over at Tavish, apparently waiting for permission to touch her. They were taking this game way too far, and she was about to say so when Kelsey moved in front of them all and spoke up in a take-charge way.

"Tavish, I think mayhap we'd better hurry up and show her the castle toon," she looked pointedly at Seumas, "all things considered."

But Sasha was looking mostly at Seumas and Tavish, and she saw the subtle look that passed between them just before Seumas reverently took her hand in his, saying something innocuous like she had. It could've been 'well met.' She didn't really know.

Because as soon as Seumas touched her, Sasha had a vision.

They were outside, and Seumas was lying down on the ground, his face stoically trying to hide pain. She was looking at his shoulder, which was red and blistering.

And that was it. As quickly as the vision had come, it was gone. She tried to remember all the details she could, but it was difficult because she had never seen the location before, and it was dark in the vision. Not night, just deep shade. There was some sort of structure around them — not a building, but something she couldn't define.

Seumas was still holding her hand, giving her a concerned look.

She must have been unresponsive for a moment. Pretty sure her vision wasn't part of the game, she told the first lie that came to mind, proud of herself for sticking to Gaelic as instructed, even under really odd circumstances.

"Sorry, I just had the oddest sense o' déjà vu. I'm wull now."

That seemed to placate Seumas. He nodded in understanding.

But Sasha could see that Kelsey wasn't fooled. Giving her a knowing look, her friend clapped her hands and started walking up the corridor away from whence they'd come.

"Wull, now that ye two hae met, let's go on up tae the castle toon and show Sasha aroond."

Tavish nodded sideways to Seumas, who held out his hand in a gesture that indicated Sasha should go ahead of him and follow Kelsey, so she did.

The whole way out along the corridor — which seemed a lot longer on the way out that it had on the way in — she was hyper aware of Seumas behind her. Her back and butt tingled with the awareness of his presence as if they were bidding him in like odd magical magnets.

Her attention was briefly drawn away from him when she realized they were leaving a different way than they'd come in. She almost said something, and then she wasn't sure if it would fit into the game or not, so she kept quiet — which had always been difficult for her.

And then they were outside, and everything looked, smelled, and sounded different. Really different. Too different for a mere game. A gigantic castle loomed to her left, and it wasn't the old tower house, but something truly formidable. An entire town surrounded the castle, bustling with people and animals and wagons. All the trailers were gone. There was no sign of any of the construction crew. It was like a different... century.

She walked up and got in Kelsey's face.

"What the hell's going on, Kelsey? Where did all this stuff come from, and all these people? They weren't here ten minutes ago when we went down into the dig."

Kelsey hugged her tight and stroked her back, as if soothing her. But she whispered in her ear.

"We've traveled back in time, Sasha. Near as I can tell, we're in the forteenth century. I wanted to tell you we were going to time travel, but you wouldn't have believed me. This is how we know so much about what's in the dig. Well, part of how we know, anyway. We didn't mean for Seumas to join us. Now do you see why we have to pretend like you've never been away from home before and this is your first time in the big city?"

Big city? This wasn't even a town, really, just a bunch of houses and a huge castle.

A castle.

There hadn't been a castle on this site since...

Kelsey pulled away a bit, looking at Sasha with caution in her eyes.

Sasha sat dazed, blown away by what had happened. As far-fetched as what Kelsey said was, it was the only explanation for what Sasha saw around her. Mostly the castle. It was ... huge and very real. People were going in and out of it, or she might have thought it was a movie set. But that was far from the only convincing detail. There was not a mechanical sound to be heard, nor the smell of any exhaust. And the distinct scent of manure lingered where these had been.

She'd traveled back in time! She couldn't even form words, her mind was exploding with so many implications.

But she quietly nodded her agreement to the farce.

Once she wrapped her mind around the situation, she couldn't help getting a big smile on her face. This was so cool. Already she understood a thousand times as much about the dig site as she had when she woke up this morning, and she hadn't even walked around yet.

Kelsey smiled big as well, switching back to Gaelic and speaking aloud once more, leading Sasha down the street.

"Sae this is the toon that has sprung up aroond Laird Malcomb's castle. We hae all the shops: blacksmith, fletcher, weaver, cobbler, ye name it. It's a marketplace for the surrounding area, and as ye see, folk bring their crops in tae sell, as wull as prepared food and other crafts."

Sasha could feel Seumas close behind her once more, almost burning her backside with his warm presence. Just to make sure it wasn't her imagination, she turned and looked.

He was in the middle of conversation with Tavish, but his eyes met hers, and he gave her a tentative smile. It made his face light up so that he was even more handsome.

She smiled back at him, aware that she was flirting with a man she had nothing in common with and too buzzed on mimosas to care whether it was a good idea.

Tavish and Kelsey seemed to trust him, and that was good enough for her.

Kelsey was talking still.

“And this is Captain Donnell. Captain, this is our clanswoman Sasha. 'Tis her foremaist time tae market, and we’re showing her aroond.”

This woke Sasha up from her stare at Seumas. Some part of her buzzed brain knew she’d best show her manners when being introduced to someone, especially a captain. She turned back around to see a man she could only describe as a pirate — minus the eye patch, the peg leg, and the parrot.

He had his thumbs hooked into his jerkin and he was rocking back on his heels, smiling at her even though he was addressing Tavish.

“Wull now, another braw keekin lass ye hae brought intae toon, eh Tavish?”

Sasha felt Seumas coming up close behind her.

Captain Donnell must’ve noticed that, because he addressed the man.

“Och, and it seems this one is taken as wull, eh Seumas?”

But Seumas surprised her with his smoothness, ignoring the comment and changing the subject.

“Wull met, Captain. Where are ye off tae next? Must be someplace pure special, for we are na in line tae guard ye this time.”

Captain Donnell threw back his head and laughed.

“Aye, 'tis off up and aroond tae Norway I am a few days hence, muckle tae craking a steid for the likes o' ye. Nah, for real sure, the laird telt me tae keep ye back from it this time. I dinna ken why."

He gave both Tavish and Seumas hearty pats on the back and headed off down the street past them.

They looked at each other for a moment of deep questioning, but eventually shrugged it off.

Kelsey was pointing out this shop and that vendor cart, but Sasha wasn't paying much attention. Seumas had insinuated himself alongside her somehow, and the backs of their hands brushed every now and then, thoroughly distracting her.

Kelsey's tour guide routine only intruded on Sasha's distraction when introductions were in order — but the introductions came all too often for Sasha's liking.

"Och, and there are the guards I telt ye aboot. Dubh 'n' Luthais, this is our clanswoman Sasha. It's her foremaist time tae any castle, and we're showing her aroond."

These two merely nodded and smiled as they passed by, thank goodness. Because Seumas was making small talk with her.

"Is the castle toon as grand as ye thought it would be, lass?"

She turned on her charm a little, answering as truthfully as she dared.

"I hadna given any thought tae it, in truth, but there are far more folk here than I expected."

He gave her a sympathetic smile and nodded as his sturdy legs carried him along the road, his kilt bouncing in step along with his long red hair. And then oddly, he stepped to the side of the road, pulling her along with him and bowing his head slightly.

Sasha looked up to see what the matter was, but all she saw was a rather well-dressed kilted Scot among a bunch of hangers on — looking right at her and coming their way.

Also off to the side and bowing slightly, tour guide Kelsey spoke up again right before the well-dressed man reached them.

"Laird Malcomb, may I present our clanswoman Sasha?"

The laird gave Sasha an appraising look, spending extra time looking at her Celtic University ring, and she found herself standing up as straight as she could. Should she have removed the ring when she put her phone away? She was pretty sure it would suit any period when handcrafted rings were possible.

Seumas moved in close beside her, while still leaving his sword arm free.

"Are ye wull, Uncle? Ye dinna seem at all yerself. Can Tavish get ye anything?"

The laird turned a displeased gaze on Seumas, and Sasha feared for his life. Other people had moved off to the side of the road too, also bowing their heads, and it reminded her of when cars pulled over because they heard a siren.

But then the laird gazed around at the crowd and seemed to remember himself.

"Thank ye for presenting yer ... clanswoman," he said to Kelsey. And then he turned to Sasha with a big jovial smile on his face that didn't make it to his eyes. "Well come tae Caer Uchtred."

Being American and having not watched local TV here at university, Sasha had never seen a lord before — let alone been introduced to one. She inclined her head the same way he had and then began to raise her face to his again in order to address him. She thought this was the polite thing to do. After all, her mother had always said, 'look at me when I'm talking to you.'

But Seumas put his arm around her shoulders and gently pressed her forward a bit, until her face was lowered once more.

And all hell broke loose in her body. If the mimosas were giving her a warm feeling, that was nothing compared to the fire that blazed in her at having so much body contact with him. Did he feel it, too?

She had started fanning herself with her hand when a little girl no more than six years old appeared in front of Sasha's face, looking her over with a skeptical and discerning eye. The girl had a proportionally sized marketing basket on her arm, and she was dressed in a small version of adult clothes like Kelsey's: plaid woolen overdress and solid linen blouse.

"Is this yer wife, Seumas? How come wasna she with ye afore? Dinna ye like her?"

Seumas smiled at the girl.

"I am na able tae speak tae ye just at the moment, Deirdre, seeing as how Laird Malcomb demands my attention, but I wull be with ye presently, if ye dinna mind."

Deirdre stepped back a bit and put her hands on her hips, shaking her head no.

"Nay, I dinna mind at all. Go ahead and blether tae Laird Malcomb. I shall wait."

But Laird Malcomb took one look at Deirdre and went away down the road past them, scowling at all of his sycophants. Good riddance to bad rubbish.

In the background, Sasha heard Kelsey and Tavish discussing him.

"He was sae kind when last I did see him."

"Aye, he is normally verra kind. I dinna ken what's come ower him. Mayhap a severe threat tae the castle militarily. 'Tis the only thing I ken that would make him sae... unpleasant."

But meanwhile, Sasha and Seumas were talking to Deirdre — or rather, she was talking to them.

"Ye shouldna leave yer wife oot in the land when ye come tae the castle, Seumas. Wives like it at the castle. When Da was aroond, Maw was always telling him how she liked it here at the castle and was sae glad they were na oot in the land anymore. And I ken when yer brother Alfred marries Maw, he will let her bide here at the castle, for he's the laird's nephew, and laird's nephews bide at the castle. Aw, ye are the laird's nephew tae, then. How come was he sae mean tae ye?"

Seumas stood and gave Sasha his arm to pull herself up with, which she gladly did, relishing the feel of his strong muscle under her hand just as much as the firm support he provided. Yum.

He reached out with his other hand to mess up the little girl's hair, but she ducked, making him chuckle.

"I dinna ken how come Laird Malcomb is being sae mean this day, but I'm verra glad that ye came along and made him go away."

Deirdre stood up straight and gave him a single nod.

"You're verra wull come. I can dae that anytime."

Sasha met Seumas's eyes, and they shared a smile in appreciation of how adorable the little girl was. Sasha lingered there in the smile as long as she could, admiring the set of Seumas's light blue eyes, the chisel of his cheekbones, the lustrousness of his long red hair...

Kelsey made her way back up to the front of their group and pointed out this sausage vendor and that cooper shop as she led them farther along the road through the castle town market. It made a circle around the castle, and they'd already gone halfway around, the town was so small.

All in all, it was like a carnival at home, and Sasha loved it. Every now and then, she would see a table of wares that especially attracted her, and she would stop to handle and admire them. She stopped at a table full of small handmade wooden flutes, picked out one that looked like the recorder she used to play as a child, and put it to her lips.

Without thinking, she ripped twice through "Jimmy Crack Corn and I Don't Care" while bending forward and back and dancing around the way she used to when she was a kid. She smiled and hammed it up in front of a small crowd that had gathered, stomping their feet and clapping their hands along with the music she was playing.

But then something small was behind her when she stepped backward. She lost her balance, teetered for a second, and then fell — smack in the middle of a huge mud puddle with a splash. Water soaked clear through her clothes all along her backside, and the chill autumn wind made her shiver.

Little Deirdre was jumping up and down with her hands over her ears, crying, and then she ran over and grabbed Sasha's arm and started pulling her, as if she could get her up on her feet again.

"I'm sae sorry, Seumas! Sae sorry. Maw has clothes yer wife can wear till these get cleaned. Come ower tae oor house afore she catches her death o' cauld. Och, I'm sae, sae sorry!"

3

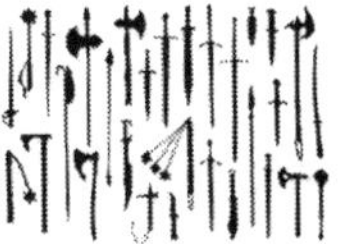

TRÌ

While he unfastened his brooch to loosen his arisade, Seumas gaped in dismay at the sight of Sasha soaked through in mud in this shivering wind. Moments earlier, she had been so lively and joyful. That had suited her much more. The sun would go down soon, and already it was cold. Still, he gave Eileen's daughter a kind look. She hadn't meant any harm, and she was just a bairn.

"Thank ye, Deirdre, but I shall help Sasha up."

Still crying, the wee lassie dropped Sasha's hand and backed up with a sniffle.

The small crowd that had gathered to hear Sasha play the flute dispersed as quickly as it had formed, with nary a word in between. The vendors were starting to close their shops and stalls.

Deirdre picked up the flute Sasha had been playing — which had flown out of her hand and landed on dry ground, but was no doubt now a used item — and gave it back to Raild, who smiled at her and then looked expectantly at Seumas.

"Give me a moment, wull ye now?" he said to Raild while grabbing first Sasha's hand and then her elbow and then her shoulder, getting her to her feet as quickly as possible while removing first her sopping wet cloak and then her strange muddy tunic so that he could wrap his arisade tightly over her wet shirt and hug her to himself to keep her as warm as could be in the whipping wind.

Once this was done, he dug a copper out of his pouch and handed it to the craftsman in exchange for the flute, which he handed to Sasha.

"Thank ye," she said, her teeth all a chatter while she put it in a small leather bag she'd been carrying under her cloak. Something blue and shiny was in there, and he made a mental note to ask her what it was, later when they were warm.

He felt a bit of guilt at the pleasure he took from the way her body felt against his while he clung to her tightly — but he only did so to keep her warm. Her friend Kelsey came over at first, visibly wanting to take over the keep-warm duty, but Tavish held her back.

"She's had a fall, Kelsey. Let Seumas hold her up." He pulled her around to face him and gave her a tender look, caressing her face. "I fear ye are na strong enough tae dae sae."

Kelsey relented, and then something passed between the two women. Seumas couldn't see Sasha's face, but Kelsey blinked one eye at her with a smile that said they were having fun.

Good. He was having fun, too.

As the five of them hurried over to Eileen's house — which thankfully wasn't far, it was getting so cold — he wondered what his chances were with Sasha, even as he held her close, gazing at her fine featured face, her shining red hair, and her tall willowy figure that made muddy clothes and a man's arisade look braw.

She was clearly a high-ranking member of Tavish's MacGregor clan. She was confident, accustomed to the respect of all, and he detected her ability to command. Her clothing was fine, and her boots finer. She knew how to play at least one musical instrument. Her hands were smooth as silk, and her face smoother still. Her laugh came readily, without a care in the world. She hadn't ever worked in the fields. No, her father was wealthy enough to keep her away from toil. And wealthy fathers wanted wealthy husbands for their daughters.

And what did he have to offer her? He was the younger son of the laird's widowed sister. His older brother Alfred was captain of the guard and had some status in the town, but Seumas was just a rank-and-file soldier. He didn't even have rooms at the castle like his brother did, let alone a house, but slept in the barracks.

Sure, he could go out in the land and build a house, but he had no men to take with him to defend it nor to work the land — and anyhow, he had already discerned that Sasha was too fine a lady to live out in the land.

Would her clan take him in? Mayhap, if Tavish vouched for him. Howsoever, after months of almost constant companionship, he didn't even know what position Tavish held in his clan. Oddly, Tavish never spoke of it, which was just one strange thing among many he had only lately noticed about the man he'd quite enjoyed being on guard duty with.

And that reminded him.

"Tavish?"

"Aye?"

"How did ye come intae the tunnel doon tae the stone docks with yer two clanswomen when ye were meant tae be searching for yer lost sporran?"

He had the man. Now it would come down to 'put up or what for.'

The MacGregor — if that was indeed his clan — was as good a fighter as they came. Up to now, there had been no one Seumas would rather have guarding his back. Howsoever, it had lately come to Seumas's attention that Tavish was always coming in and out of one particular tunnel down the dock way at the strangest times, and now twice in the past few days he'd come out with women he claimed were in his clan.

It stank the way fish do.

But the man just shrugged, not saying anything at all in his defense.

If he hadn't saved Seumas's life and livelihood more than once, the two of them would be having words. As it was, Seumas's trust in the man was wearing thin. His guard was starting to come up between them. The man had secrets, and because they involved Seumas's home, they were his business. Later. For now, he would enjoy the company of the beautiful Sasha.

Deirdre opened the door for them all and yelled into the house.

"Maw! I knockit Seumas's wife ower and she's all coverit in mud and all wet and they're all here right now and she needs some dry clothes and ye have tae help her!"

Eileen came around the center fireplace, brushing flour off her hands onto her apron.

He needed to stop this rumor before it spread.

"Eileen, this is Sasha. She isna my wife, but rather another o' Tavish's clan come tae visit. Sasha, this is Eileen, one o' our master weavers. Kelsey has apprenticed with her."

Eileen smiled in greeting at Kelsey and then spoke to Sasha while she chased her smaller three children off this side of the hearth, where they were having a grand game of storm the castle.

"Oh, ye poor thing. Here, sit doon at the fire while I find ye some dry clothes." She seated Sasha on the hearth, pulling a blanket off the chair and tucking it over Sasha's legs before she hurried into the bedroom.

Clucking just like a doting grandma, Deirdre did her best to finish tucking Sasha in, then shooed her younger brothers and sister in a fair imitation of their mother.

"Aodh! Niall! Sìle! Ye wee bairns canna be in the way, I tell ye. Sit and play ower there while ye let us grown ones have oor talk."

Sasha giggled at that — unlike Kelsey, who was too preoccupied with Tavish. Or perhaps she just didn't like children much. Frowning at Kelsey in disapproval, Seumas sat down next to Sasha, taking both of her hands in his and chafing them, just to warm them, mind.

But Kelsey walked over with Tavish close beside her and held out her hand to help Sasha up.

"Sasha, come on, let's go."

Tavish nodded.

"Aye, 'tis time we were on oor way." Inexplicably, he wiped at a sore on his face and then looked at his finger to see if blood came off, which it didn't, as the sore had scabbed recently. Nonetheless, he pointed the sore out to Sasha as if it had some deep meaning. "We hae tae speak to someone ... at the castle, ye ken?"

What in the world did they mean? Kelsey was intended to stay here with Eileen before Maw insisted she stay in the castle last night because of her fall into the sea, God bless her. Was Kelsey so attached to the castle that she wanted to hurry away from the home of the woman who had taken her in as apprentice so old as five and twenty?

And who would need to speak to Tavish? He was a guard, and he was currently in the company of himself, the brother of the captain of the guard, fool for a man. New love must have addlepated the two of them.

Thankfully, Sasha had more sense than they.

"I am na rushing off intae the cauld wind in these wet clothes, and I certainly am na rushing off withoot the clothes ye brought me in. 'Twould be different had ye allowed me tae change, as ye did, Kelsey." She and Kelsey stared at each other a moment, and Kelsey looked away first. Sasha grunted. "Ye two go on, if ye must go and speak to someone. I wull bide here till ye get back."

Seumas put his arm over Sasha's shoulders and held his arisade tighter around her while also leaning her back toward the fire.

"Aye." He looked to Tavish. "Go on and dae yer errand. I can tell it's weighing on ye, whatever secret it is. Yer clanswoman is under my protection while yer gone. Dinna fash."

Kelsey and Tavish whispered among themselves in strangely accented English, and he thought he caught something like 'no time will pass' before they reluctantly agreed to leave Sasha with him for the time it took to walk up into the castle and back. He had thought Tavish was a better friend, and hoped love had just addlepated him — even as all the man's secrets started to weigh on Seumas.

Tavish took Kelsey by the waist and escorted her to the door, turning over his shoulder to address Seumas.

"Ye must look after her, ye ken?" He sighed and gave Seumas an especially appealing look with his eyes, then moved them quickly over to Sasha and back. "She does na ken she needs looking after."

"Aye," Seumas told the man as adamantly as he could without showing the anger that had started to brew at Tavish's lack of faith in him over so trivial an amount of time. What could happen anyhow, with Eileen and all the bairns watching the two of them?

At the same time, Kelsey looked at Sasha once more.

"Dinna go anywhere. To ye, we wull be right back."

What a confusing comment. Something was going on.

But Sasha seemed to have as little patience for the two of them as he did. She made a shooing gesture with her hand.

"Go on, already."

Deirdre made the same shooing gesture at Tavish and Kelsey.

"We ken how tae dry off a wet lass. Dinna fash."

While Kelsey and Tavish shuffled uncertainly out the front door, Sasha laughed and grabbed ahold of Deirdre and hugged her, and then Aodh, Niall, and Sìle came running over for hugs too, which Sasha was giving generously when Eileen came back with an armful of clothing.

Sasha saw the clothing and let go of the children, standing up and putting the wet muddy blanket on the hearth so that she could accept the clothing from Eileen.

She held the clothes out away from her soaked body so that they wouldn't get muddy and looked around helplessly for someplace to change.

"Thank ye ever sae kindly."

Why didn't she just go into the bedroom? Houses couldn't be so different out in the MacGregor lands than they were here, could they?

The children were starting to fuss, a different one pulling at Eileen's skirts every time she turned around.

"When dae we eat, Maw?"

"I thought ye were making supper."

"Why dae we hae people over if they keep ye from cooking, Maw?"

Visibly concerned about getting supper into them, Eileen went back around to the kitchen side of the hearth and came back with a big pot of clear broth so everyone could at least have a nice hot drink while waiting for her to cook. Squab broth, if his nose served him right. She had set it down on her large round supper table before Seumas could get there to help her. Already she was off walking around to the kitchen side of the fire again — presumably to get tankards — when she spoke.

"'Tis nay trouble, Sasha. I am the one tae be sorry, sae overly sorry for Deirdre's clumsiness. I'm guessing 'tis the first time ye hae been muddy since ye were a child. Go on and get yourself cleanit up and put the clean clothes on."

And then Sasha went over to the table and started to put her hands into the pot of broth as if to wash them. It was fresh off the fire, and she cried out in pain, lifting her hands out again quickly as soon as one of them touched the surface. He had seen burns before, on the field of battle. This one on her small finger wasn't terribly bad, but probably still painful.

Just in case the lass had gone mad, he went over and restrained her from putting her hand back in the broth again.

"Eileen, the lass has burned her hand. Hae ye any butter?"

Eileen came tearing around the hearth with a very

concerned look on her face and the butter dish in her hands.

"Deirdre? Did ye touch the soup pot, lass?"

The wee lass came running up to the table from her position among the younger children, where she had been shepherding them.

"'Tis na me, Maw. Sasha put her hand in the broth." She turned to the bonnie mad lass. "Why did ye dae it? Dae ye eat broth with yer hands where ye come from?"

Sasha pulled her hand away from the butter that Eileen was trying to rub on her burn. Aye, she had verily gone mad.

"Nay, butter and other oils will only make a burn keep burning, deeper doon into the flesh. Please, just give me some cauld water tae plunge it in, and can ye hurry? Sorry tae hae ruined yer soup." She looked down at Deirdre. "I didna ken it was soup. I had thought it was hot water for washing. Where dae ye wash up?"

Deirdre pulled the wash rag out of the pile of clothing Eileen had given Sasha.

"Maw meant for ye tae rub the mud off o' yerself with this. Washing is some aught we dae tae the clothing and the dishes. Ourselves we just clean, with rags like this one. Dae ye wash yer hands where ye live?"

Eileen brought in two tankards of water from her cistern and plunked them down on the table along with a bunch of empty ones, which she began to fill with broth using a ladle.

Sure enough, Sasha plunged her hand into one of the tankards of cold water. Only this time, she sighed in relief.

"Thank ye. This is taking the burn away. Ah. It feels better already. Aye, cauld water is the best thing for burns, even better with some ice in it, but I understand 'tis not likely ye hae ice." She laughed a little, but unlike her marvelous unchained liveliness out in the market with the flute, this was an uncomfortable laugh, born of nervousness and embarrassment. It didn't suit her at all.

But at least she wasn't mad. Just verra limited in her knowledge of the world away from home. Just as Tavish had said. It was becoming clear why the man had been so reluctant to leave her here. She really was in need of looking after. A job he had volunteered for and would gladly fulfill.

"Hold on. I shall go and get ye some ice."

The look of surprise on her face as he left was priceless.

On his way back from the icehouse, he fell in beside his brother Alfred, who was also walking toward Eileen's and gave him a face of pleasant surprise.

"I didna expect tae see ye at dinner this evening. What's the ice for?"

"I didna expect tae be there. The ice is for a burn tae the hand of Sasha, another of Tavish's clanswomen, just arrived today. 'Tis her first time away from the MacGregor lands, and she tried tae wash her hands in the bairns's before-dinner broth."

Alfred puzzled over this the three dozen steps back to Eileen's, making sideways glances at Seumas — clearly in order to discern whether he was pulling his leg or not.

"Yer eyes seem awfully bright for a routine look

intae the icehouse. She must be at least as special as Kelsey."

Seumas gave his older brother a half serious stern look, holding it extra long for emphasis.

"Ye just save all yer attention for Eileen, and we wull continue tae get along fine."

At first his blond brother's face was amused, but then it turned concerned, and he stopped in the darkening street a moment, turning to him to make sure his next comment was heeded.

"Watch yer heart, Seumas. But a few days ago, ye were trying tae give it tae Kelsey."

Seumas threw his hand out toward the side as if throwing the thought away.

"Och, I am easily ower that now, believe me."

Alfred chuckled a bit.

"Even sae? How can Tavish's clan hae more than one sae lovely lass? And is this one also old enough to be wise and yet sae untouched by the ravages of time? And yet she has done something sae delightfully silly and childlike as tae wash in the broth?"

As he opened the door, Seumas nodded inside toward the table with an amused 'See what I mean?' look.

4

CEITHIR

The cold water felt heavenly on Sasha's hand while she watched in fascination as the gorgeous blonde Eileen dipped tankards of broth, cooled them a bit with cool water, and handed them to her blond children. Even the youngest child, the little girl toddler Sìle, held her uncovered tankard and sipped from it without spilling a drop, making it look easy. Sìle was dressed just like her mother in miniature, rather than in toddler clothes. This made the sight of her daintily sipping from a tankard all the cuter.

Eileen disappeared around the hearth into the kitchen area again for a while and then once the children were finished drinking their broth she came back around, once more covered in flour.

"Aodh and Niall, ye two set the table, aye?"

"Aye!"

"Aye!"

The two miniature men made a game of it, mock

sword fighting with the knives and using the wooden plates as shields.

Sasha had to dodge them twice as they came by, even though she was making her presence known with her coaching comments.

"Aodh, his left side is open. Niall, ye need to block better, lad."

She was itching to take a movie. It would be difficult with her hand in a tankard though, so it would have to wait. But she would at least get pictures of these adorable mini adults before she left.

There was a knock at the door, and Deirdre ran over and opened it, then turned her head to yell over her shoulder.

"Maw! Seumas is come with the ice! And he brought yer new man!" She turned back to Seumas. "I'm sae glad ye returned." She made a grand gesture into the house. "Will ye come in?"

Seumas gracefully bowed his head to Deirdre and came over and plopped a small chunk of ice in Sasha's water tankard before he nodded toward a door Sasha hadn't noticed before.

"Sasha, this is my brother Alfred. Now go on intae the bedroom and put on those dry clothes sae we can all eat supper."

After Sasha and Alfred exchanged pleasantries, Deirdre scampered up to Sasha and spoke solemnly.

"May I help ye? I'm verra good at putting on clothes."

Sasha breathed a sigh of relief at this and took her

tankard with her on the way to the door, speaking just as Eileen opened her mouth to reign her daughter in.

"I would be delighted tae hae ye help me, Deirdre. The clothes here are just different enough from where I come from that I dae feel the need for a bit o' help."

Understatement of the month. These clothes were riddled with little tie strings, and not a button nor a zipper in sight. Sasha hated to think how long it would've taken her to figure it all out on her own, but with Deirdre's help she was changed in a few minutes.

Eileen had told her to leave her muddy clothes in a pile on the floor and she would wash them, and Sasha hadn't known what to say. She'd always dry cleaned her wool suits, but she couldn't exactly tell Eileen that. And the woman was a weaver, so after an awkward pause she had agreed on the condition that she could help. It wouldn't hurt to find out how to wash wool by hand without it shrinking, now would it?

Eileen was shorter than her, so on Sasha, these skirts didn't quite reach the floor the way they did on Eileen and all the other women who'd been out in the market. But otherwise, the skirted shirt with huge sleeves and the plaid overdress fit well. Fortunately, her long hair hadn't gotten muddy.

Glad that it was the style in this time for women to wear their hair down and long, she got her hairbrush out of her purse, but before she could brush the second stroke, Deirdre was squealing and jumping up and down in excitement. Oops.

"That is the brawest thing I did ever see! May I try?"

With the tiniest bit of trepidation, Sasha handed

Deirdre the brush and turned her back to her so that the little girl could brush her hair.

"Sure."

The brushing she got only hurt a little bit and only snagged once. Deirdre was pretty skilled with a brush. It didn't go so well when Sasha brushed her own hair, so she didn't complain. Just closed her eyes and clenched her teeth to bear it.

When it was done and she turned around to take her brush back, Deirdre was gazing at it in awe.

Ack! No wonder. Her hairbrush was made of see-through pink plastic with little silver flecks of glitter inside.

Hm. Her impulse was to give the brush to the little girl as a gift. But something Kelsey had said lingered in the back of Sasha's mind. There was danger here from some Druid named Brian who was locked up in a tower, and maybe there were more Druids about. And they were all dangerous.

All she knew about Druids was that they used the magic of the natural realm — they thought of it as the life force that ran through all living things. And she only knew that from the occasional comments she would overhear during her brother's weekly Dungeons and Dragons games in the basement of their parents' house when she was a kid. Okay, she had hidden at the top of the stairs and cracked the door open and leaned into the crack so that she could overhear as much as possible, the games had been so entertaining. The point was, she didn't really know very much about Druids, only what some game said about them.

But she knew Druids could definitely be dangerous. And they had sent Tavish here, so they knew about time travel and would recognize this as being from the future. And time travel was a big secret, judging by the lengths Tavish and Kelsey were going to in their disguises. Who knew what the Druids might do to poor little Deirdre if they thought she knew their secret?

So Sasha decided on a different gift for Deirdre, and held out her hand to be given the hairbrush back.

"Yer turn."

With a huge pretty smile, Deirdre turned around and fluffed her long blonde hair over her shoulders so that it hung down her back.

Sasha knew that after supper, she was going to need the privy she had seen on her way in, and she was not looking forward to that. Ooh. Except that would give her the chance to get her phone situated someplace where it couldn't be seen but where she could use it to take movies of all these precocious kids.

Excited at the prospect, she finished brushing Deirdre's hair and jumped up, grabbing her hand and taking her into the other room to find Tavish and Kelsey standing just inside the front door, looking around in visible apprehension.

Kelsey relaxed and smiled when she saw Sasha enter the room.

"There ye are, Butterfly! Dinna dae that tae me ever again!"

Sasha smiled and raised her shoulder and gave Kelsey her traditional star wave.

"I willna, dinna fash."

But Tavish gestured out the door impatiently.

"Come now, Sasha —"

Oh no he didn't. Couldn't he see that everyone was just sitting down to supper and there were places set for them? She liked Eileen, and it would be rude to leave right now. She gestured toward two places together.

"Tavish, please."

But instead of moving toward their seats, Tavish agitatedly whispered in Kelsey's ear, plainly trying to get her to make Sasha leave.

Was he crazy? She didn't understand it. Rudeness certainly was not the way to avoid calling attention to yourself.

Apparently Alfred agreed, because the captain stood from his seat and called his guard Tavish on it, gesturing at the two empty seats next to each other lest Tavish overlook them one more second.

"Ye are na going anywhere till ye sit down and eat the food Eileen prepared for ye."

Tavish paused, which could not lead to anything good.

She needed to keep him from starting something ugly. In order to distract everyone's attention from the two of them, Sasha picked that moment to steer Deirdre over to the empty seat between Aodh and Niall.

"Thank ye again for the loan o' yer daughter, Eileen. She was a verra big help, even brushed my hair for me, see?" She made a show of turning around and showing off how nicely brushed her long red hair was.

Deirdre glowed with pride, and Eileen smiled at her daughter and caressed her cheek.

Sasha moved herself toward the empty seat between Seumas and Alfred.

Seumas pulled the chair out for her, and when she smiled her thanks at him, he gestured at her new outfit and smiled his approval. This pleased her way more than she thought it should, and to avoid gawking at him like a fool, she looked back over toward Tavish, truly interested in whatever he was going to choose to do.

He and Kelsey were whispering back and forth quite agitatedly, but at least they were taking their seats and no longer in danger of angering Alfred.

Sasha was embarrassed for her friends and had half resolved to distract the group once more when she noticed that no one else was paying them any mind. In fact, she caught quite a few winks and nods and eye rolls on her friends' behalf. Alfred had sat down and was being passed a dish, Eileen was busy cutting up food on Sìle's plate, the little boys were pretend sword-fighting with their forks full of food behind Deirdre's back, and Seumas ... was sipping his ale, amusedly observing her over the rim of his tankard.

"How did ye earn yer nickname, Butterfly?"

Grateful for the presence of the social lubricant, she grabbed her own ale and gulped some down. It was surprisingly light, but good.

"Hae ye na heard the saying, social butterfly?"

"I canna say I hae."

She buttered her bread, doing her best to look at him coquettishly over the top of it now and then.

"Och, wull now. Kelsey does think I am a social butterfly, which is a person who flits from one conversation tae the next, never staying quiet."

His eyes twinkled at her as he chuckled and buttered his own bread.

"Wull now, ye are a bit o' that, tae be sure. Ye hae only just met Eileen, and already Deirdre is dressing ye and the wee lads follow yer commands like those o' a queen."

Thank goodness she hadn't taken a bite of her bread yet, because this made her laugh. She made it as pretty a laugh as she could, letting the sound come out her nose in a high pitch that she had found most men enjoyed.

"Stop it. I was only playing along with their game. In truth, I thought they were gaun'ae run me ower and just was saying things sae they would notice me."

He had taken a bite of his bread while she was speaking, and he chewed it with a knowing look in his eyes. She took the opportunity to eat some of her bread as well, and it was delicious. She'd forgotten how good home-baked bread was. He noticed her enjoyment of the bread and left off talking for a while, eating and taking obvious pleasure in watching her eat.

As she basked in his glowing admiration, she heard other conversations at the table and noticed that Eileen had succeeded in getting Kelsey's attention.

"Sae dae ye and Sasha both hae rooms at the castle now, or will ye take me up on my offer tae stay with me, the two o' ye?"

Kelsey took a deep breath and turned to Tavish, and

they whispered and grunted and groaned a lot before he answered Eileen.

"Aye, the lasses will be staying with ye, at least this evening and mayhap a fortnight or more, depending on the sort o' duty I get. If that is nay trouble?"

Eileen gave Sasha and Kelsey each a friendly smile. "'Twill be my pleasure to hae the lasses stay."

Sasha wiped her mouth and kept Eileen's eye, nodding toward the bedroom and then admiring her new outfit.

"We hae tae launder my clothes sae I can give ye this back."

Eileen shook her head prettily as she sipped from her tankard.

"Nay, it suits ye. Keep it. We can work on lengthening the skirt. Yer clothing is like tae raise some eyebrows, and I want for ye tae enjoy yerself while yer with us."

Sasha had just eaten breakfast, and so she wasn't very hungry. Curiously, she saw that Tavish and Kelsey were devouring their food.

"Seumas, finish my food if ye want. I'm done."

The large red-haired man happily dug in.

Sasha got up and played some more tunes on her new flute while everyone else finished eating. Each time she finished a song or took a breath, everyone applauded and cheered. Some even whistled, very much like they would in her time. She took this as encouragement to play even livelier tunes, switching from those she'd learned in school to her favorite pop music.

Whenever she caught Kelsey's eye while she was

playing with the pop tunes, her friend burst out laughing and hid her mouth behind her napkin. By chance she caught Tavish's eye once, and he gave her a 'told you so' look. At first, she had no idea he was thinking, but then she realized she was dancing sort of jig around the table as she played the music, and it was her turn to burst into laughter.

The dishes got done in record time, with three women and young Deirdre helping. And then they all joined the men and boys around the roaring fire they had built in the center fireplace.

Alfred's smile for Eileen was like the moon and stars when she reentered the room.

"Tavish and Seumas and I will get ye more firewood tomorrow, tae make up for all that we're using this evening."

Eileen sat very close to him, and they cuddled a bit by the fire. Their closeness gave Sasha a warm fuzzy feeling, and she savored it, smiling down at them before she looked around for her own place to sit down.

Seumas gave her a more mischievous smile with an alluring twinkle in his eyes as he patted the seat next to him.

She made a show of looking around for any other place to sit down as she slowly made her way over to him, holding her skirts and moving them from side to side. And then Deirdre rushed over and grabbed her hand, and she had another vision.

Oh no.

Deirdre's lifeless body soaking wet and being pulled out of the water onto the seashore. Her face so white, not even a tinge of pink in those sweet little cheeks.

As before, Sasha tried to remember anything and everything she could from the short time she saw it. But that was it. That was all she could find in the vision. How awful.

When she came back to herself, Seumas was now standing next to her, supporting her by her elbow with his strong hand, with his other hand on her back, while Deirdre was sitting at her mother's lap, looking confused. Eileen stroked her daughter's hair and gave Sasha a worried smile.

Seumas spoke softly near her ear once Sasha met his eyes, which looked more worried about her than curious.

"Dinna tell me this time 'twas but a case of déjà vu, Butterfly."

Abashed, she gave him an apologetic smile.

"I tell ye true, this has never happened tae me afore today, and I thank ye for being here for me both times."

They stood there gazing into each other's eyes. His worry had given way to skepticism and doubt, but the majority of what she saw on his face was admiration for her, and good humor. She did her best to show the admiration she had for him, and the fun she'd been having today.

Someone cleared their throat, and Sasha looked over to see that while Eileen remained seated with her arm around yawning Aodh and holding Sìle in her lap, Alfred had stood up.

"We're keeping these bairns from bed tae late, and we men hae duty in the morning." He turned to Eileen, who smiled up at him in a way that let Sasha know the two of them had already discussed his leaving. "So we bid ye all good evening with the hope o' doing this again tomorrow."

Seumas took Sasha's hand and squeezed it once, then started walking toward Alfred. Eileen nodded at Alfred and escorted the men to the door among many more pleasantries and a very clingy goodbye between Tavish and Kelsey, with a dozen more whispers.

When the wooden plank door had closed and the men were on the other side, Eileen explained that Sasha and Kelsey would have the children's bed out here and she would take the children into the bedroom with her.

Once all the children had hugged her goodnight and the two of them were safely alone in the room, Sasha whispered to Kelsey.

"So what's the plan?"

But instead of answering her directly, Kelsey rolled over so that her back was to Sasha and said in a falling asleep voice, "It would take way too long to explain. Go to sleep, and once you're dreaming, I'll show you."

5

CÒIG

At first, Sasha found it hard to fall asleep. She was in a strange place, to say the least. But her best friend was with her, the pile of blankets on the bed was heavy and comforting, and last but not least, she'd had a very exciting day. Once she allowed herself to relax, sleep came swiftly.

Almost as soon as she succumbed, she found herself with Kelsey in what she knew was a dream, because they were sitting in Eileen's dining chairs in their twenty-first century clothes. Pants felt comforting after a whole day in long skirts with nothing under them. Even the pantyhose she hated would have been better.

Unsure how much time they had, Sasha rushed to speak to her friend.

"Kelsey, I've had the oddest visions lately. When Seumas first touched me, I saw him lying outside wounded, with terrible burns on his shoulder. It was awful. And then after dinner tonight, Deirdre grabbed me and I saw her pulled out of the water sopping wet. She was drowned, Kelsey. Both of these visions have really upset me. I don't know what to make of them, and I know it sounds crazy, but somehow I know my visions are going to come true."

Kelsey didn't seem at all surprised. Hm.

"Sasha, I'm going to tell you a bunch of stuff that seems unrelated, but bear with me, okay?"

"Uh, okay."

"When I first came here to the forteenth century, Brian the Druid looked at my uni ring and called me Priestess."

"He called you Priestess?"

"Yep."

"Are you sure he wasn't joking?"

"I'm sure. He was not joking. He's not the type who jokes, at least not with women. More like against us."

This sounded bad, especially with the sour expression on Kelsey's face. Sasha took her friend's hand.

"Kelsey, if you need to talk about anything, I'm here for you, anytime. You know that, right?"

Kelsey gently squeezed her hand and let go.

"Thanks. Maybe later, but right now there's a lot of other stuff I need you to understand."

There was more?

"Okay."

"So yeah, Brian called me Priestess, and then later, the elite crew of professors met with me and Tavish — they'd promised to be in touch, and believe me, they are. They included me in his assignment to get a sword, so I'm pretty sure they feel like they can order me around just like they can order Tavish around."

"Wait a sec. I'm confused. How come they can order Tavish around? He wasn't a student at Celtic."

Kelsey made a face that meant 'I'm an idiot.'

"Right, right, right. Okay. Generations ago, Tavish's ancestor made some kind of deal with the Druids. It's convoluted, but right now all you have to know is because of that deal, he's their slave. Well, and it's their power — their magic — that allows him to time travel. Are you with me so far?"

"Uh, I want to say that's ridiculous, but..." Sasha gestured at the dream-world version of Eileen's house and the two of them sitting in their jeans and T-shirts. "Under the circumstances, yeah, I guess I am with you so far."

"Good. So the reason they make him time travel is to get things for them."

"This is getting good. What kind of things – and why don't the druids just time travel themselves and get these things? Time traveling's fun. You'd think they'd be all over it."

"Last time, the thing we were told to get was a magic scepter. This time, it's a magic sword. And when Tavish uses their ring to time travel, he comes back to our time the instant he left it. No time passes while he's gone. So time travel makes you seem to age faster in your own time. That's why Tavish looks five years older than me. He's been here in Eileen's time for five years these past three months of our time."

"Wow."

"Yeah. So anyway, the druids don't want to age that fast in their own time, so they pop in now and then, but mostly they make others do the time traveling for them. Mostly. Oh, and when Tavish and I left for our time?"

"Yeah?"

"How long were we gone, from your point of view?"

"Half an hour?"

"Yeah, and that was the time it took us to walk to the end of the middle corridor and back. But we spent two months back in our time—"

"Two months! That's longer than I usually go without calling my mother. She'll be worried."

"Nah, I covered for you."

"What did you say?"

"That you met a guy."

They looked at each other and grinned — Sasha sheepishly and Kelsey teasingly.

"Okay, and my obvious question is why would Tavish give the Druids a magic scepter — but oh yeah, he's their slave. Hm. That kind of sucks. Was it at least a benign magic scepter?"

"I hope so. All I could tell was that it was magic. Curiously, Tavish couldn't tell that. With the sword we're looking for now, the elite crew told me it was magic ahead of time. And that brings me to the other things you need to understand." Kelsey held up her right hand, with her class ring on it. "Brian the Druid called me a priestess when he saw this ring. I'm assuming he meant I'm a Druid priestess. And the Druids Tavish reports to back home are the elite crew of professors at Celtic. They're real Druids who can use real magic – and who have slaves."

"About that last part. Tavish is really a slave? As in he has to do what they say or they whip him and stuff?"

"No. As in he magically has to do what they say. Period."

"Whoa."

"Yeah."

"Kelsey —"

But her friend held up her hand, indicating she was not going to hear Sasha's advice.

"I know it's not the brightest thing to do, being with someone who's a slave to others. But he's the one for me. End of story. Not going to discuss that."

Sasha felt like she had to try again. This was madness.

"But —"

"Sasha, it's not very smart of you to be flirting with Seumas. It can only lead to one or both of you getting your hearts broken. You'll be going back to our time and living there, right? I mean, I can't see you settling anyplace that doesn't have a hairdryer, much less no running water. I know I'm right, but I want to hear you say it."

Sasha held up her hand the exact same way Kelsey had before.

"Okay. You made your point. I don't want to hear your advice, so I can see how you don't want to hear mine."

Kelsey drew her knees up in front of her, and

suddenly her feet were on another chair that hadn't been there a moment ago.

"Yeah. So anyway, perhaps all the professors at our university are Druids, but for sure the elite crew are. And Druids do evil things like enslave people. And at least one Druid from eight hundred years ago thinks we're also Druids because we wear these rings."

"But how can we be Druids? Druids can do magic."

"But we can do magic, Sasha. I can dream walk, and you have second sight."

Kelsey sat there, quietly meeting Sasha's gaze, visibly and patiently waiting for what she had said to sink in.

Sasha's rational mind fought it for the longest time. How ridiculous. But of course finally she had to accept it for the truth, just as she had accepted time travel. At long last she spoke.

"So where's the sword you're supposed to get?"

Kelsey got up, and suddenly Sasha was standing next to her, without having moved.

"I don't know where it is, but I do know someone who probably does. Come on. Tavish and I were going to show you where the tower was anyway. Might as well do it now."

What happened next was one of the weirdest things Sasha ever experienced. She started to walk toward the door, but quick as thought, she and Kelsey were at the castle entrance that she had seen while they walked from the underground exit into the castle town.

Just a dream. Just a dream.

Once she got that settled in her mind, Sasha paused

and admired a much larger and more fortified castle than was still here in her time, before entering.

"Seems like a week ago that I saw this entrance as we walked by, but for me, it's only been a few hours."

Kelsey nodded sympathetically.

"And you've only time traveled once. I'm on my fifth time – been here and back, here and back, and now here again. Dream walking was very weird for me at first too, but two and a half months later, it's almost second nature. Don't try to move." She laughed. "And I'll try to quit suggesting you move. Just stand here with me while I move us around. Pretend you're in Willy Wonka's great glass elevator. You'll get far less disoriented."

Sasha tried it, and as long as she concentrated on just standing there and watching things go by, it worked. They went into a banquet hall first, complete with iron chandeliers. Then down several stone hallways with tapestries on the walls depicting natural scenes and finally up a long stairway that spiraled up a corner tower.

Kelsey paused before they could see the top.

"Now, the reason we were going to show you this before was so that you don't come up this way in real life. It's not very likely that you'd come here by accident, but we wanted to be sure. Do you think you can manage to not find your way up here?" Her friend smiled at how oddly she had phrased that.

Sasha nodded.

"Yeah. I think I've got it mapped out."

Kelsey looked thoughtful for a moment.

"Hm, I'm going to make you invisible, so don't say anything and he won't even know you're with me."

"O-kay."

Kelsey laughed softly.

And then Sasha looked down and saw the stairs where her long skirts should be. Panic surged through her, making her heart race and her breath catch. She gulped in several deep breaths.

Just a dream. Just a dream.

She got ahold of herself just in time to float up the last curve in the stone stairs without being able to see herself. She had to resist the urge to go 'Who-oo-oo-oo' like a ghost.

And then they were up at the top of the stone tower in a dead-end stone hallway with a stone ceiling in front of the tower-room door. It was solid oak and had a little window at face height with three iron bars going up and down.

And with his face to the window, fists holding the iron bars, was a man who could only be Brian the Druid. He wore a white robe and had long white hair.

"Priestess! Ye hae come tae see me."

Kelsey made an oddly shaped bronze sword appear in her hand.

"Brian, tell me where this sword is. Tell me now."

Brian got a look of wonder on his face as he gazed at the sword.

"Galdus?"

Kelsey leaned in toward Brian with visible eagerness.

"Who's Galdus? Is this his sword? Ye ken where it is, do ye nay. Where is it?"

Brian cackled like an old woman.

"Dae tell me what it's like in yer time, Priestess. Surely ye hae an artifact from then ye can trade me for this one oor colleagues o' the future hae sent ye back for."

That didn't sound like a good idea. Sasha prayed that Kelsey didn't fall for it.

But she appeared to be considering it.

Brian pressed his advantage.

"Aw, I am na gaun'ae show it tae anybody up here in this tower. I just want tae see it, tae know some aught o' the future." His eyes looked eager and kind of deranged. "How dae ye keep yer skin sae smooth and yer hands sae callous free? Does everyone in the future use magic, with nary a need for work? Tell me it is sae!"

Kelsey nodded slowly, and the look on her face was... apologetic. As if it were her fault that he was born in the wrong century and didn't have all our modern conveniences.

"Aye, 'tis now magic, but 'tis true. We hae machines that dae all the hard work for us. They dae the threshing and the sowing and the harvest. They bring us water and heat it for us and take away oor waste. They transport us, even fly us. And they build other machines. It truly is a wonder, and I never appreciatit it until I came back tae now and saw juist how hard life can be for the workers, especially in the fields. But na everyone has all these things. Only aboot one percent o' the world does. I'm sae blessed, and I ought tae be more grateful."

Brian's face wore a mixture of enthusiasm and puzzlement.

"How sae, lass? What is a machine?"

Sasha was puzzled too. Kelsey had said this man was dangerous, so why was she trying so hard to explain the future to him? Why did she care?

It wasn't like her friend to not notice when someone was leading her away from the subject she had come to discuss. In this case, the sword. It was very tempting to speak up and ask these questions, but maybe being hidden would turn out to be an advantage, so she remained silent.

Kelsey was uncharacteristically bland and unanimated. As she spoke, she got closer and closer to Brian, until their noses were almost touching.

"A machine is a slave that doesna live, made o' materials mined from the yard and powerit by what may and all be magic, I have sae little understanding o' how it works."

As she spoke, Brian's arms slithered out of the opening in the door through the bars like snakes, cold and slow.

Sasha's breath caught when she realized what he was going to do.

He looked right at Sasha and winked at her.

She screamed.

Kelsey startled out of whatever trance Brian had put her in. In one continuous movement, she pushed off the door, grabbed Sasha's hand, and blinked them out of the tower and clean back to their own time.

Sasha found herself sitting in a trailer she'd never

been in before, but it looked familiar. As she spoke, she offhandedly realized this was the blue on blue interior she and Kelsey had picked out. Mr. Blair had gotten it for them. It was nice.

But far from being idle, their conversation was more of the panicked variety.

"Kelsey, he put you in some kind of trance. I thought you were going to open the door and let him out, you were acting so off. How can he put you in a trance inside of a dream you control?"

Kelsey shuddered and hugged herself.

"Obviously, I'm a lot less powerful a dream walker that I imagined. I knew Brian had the power to put people under a trance. He's made Tavish sleep before. But I had no idea he could do that inside a dream. We're lucky to have gotten away."

Sasha nodded. Noticing that her hands were shaking, she sat on them.

"You also need to know you were not able to hide me from him. He looked right at me and winked before he tried to grab you. That's what made me scream, it was so creepy."

Kelsey bit her lip and looked all around.

"I hope we're safe from him here. I hope he can't follow us to our time in the dream world."

Sasha shrugged and shook her head.

"If he can do that, then we're screwed. There's no sense in worrying about it. Our bodies are back at Eileen's house asleep. I think we should send our consciousnesses there to take care of them."

Kelsey was looking at Sasha with respect now.

"You're right. I don't know why I thought he would give us an answer. You should know that the reason he's locked up is because he tried to grab me before in a dream. I'm so stupid. I keep wanting to take shortcuts instead of doing actual research and exploring. And those are the things I went to school to learn how to do." She was nearly crying by the end of this.

Sasha took both of Kelsey's hands in hers.

"Hey, hey, hey. None of that now. Very few people would remain logical in a situation such as ours."

Kelsey opened her mouth to argue and then opened her eyes wide and looked at Sasha and burst out laughing. Sasha joined her in laughter, and they squeezed hands and let go.

Kelsey stood up straight once more and spoke with humor.

"You're right. We should go back to our sleeping bodies and keep them company. Who knows what evil things could happen to us if we left them there too long."

Even though what she said was true, it struck both of them so funny that they dissolved in fits of laughter again. Which felt much better than crying.

While they laughed, another woman their age came out of one of the bedrooms, dressed for sleep in an old T-shirt and ratty old sweats. She was in the middle of redoing her long black ponytail, and she opened the fridge with her knee and bent over to sip through a sports bottle straw before she greeted Sasha. Her eyes were bleary, but they were the most beautiful shade of light brown, almost yellow.

"Hi, I'm Amber. You must be Sasha. Guess you'll be wanting your room back, huh."

Kelsey made an 'oops' face and gestured toward one of the bedrooms, and Amber was gone.

"Sorry about that. I must've walked us into her dream somehow. She was Tomas's girlfriend back when we all hung out together at the faire —"

Sasha held up her hand to stop Kelsey's story.

"Tell me later. Let's get back to Eileen's."

Although Kelsey had been right in what she told Brian about how easy life was in the modern world, Sasha thought there were charms to the old world. She couldn't wait to get back to it, finish sleeping for the night, and wake up there. And seeing Seumas again was only...

Well, let's be honest. Seeing Seumas again was nine tenths of why she was so anxious to get back. She really shouldn't dote too much on him. Kelsey was right. There was no way she could live in the past with him. She could enjoy looking at him in the meantime though, right?

6

SIA

Seumas, Tavish, and Alfred left Eileen's house together: Alfred headed toward his rooms in the castle, Seumas and Tavish to the barracks. It was dead night, but there was plenty of light from the moon. All the shops were closed except for the two taverns. Light and raucous laughter spilled out of those.

Seumas felt sure Tavish would approve of him as a mate for his clanswoman Sasha. The man had come to the castle town six months ago — a complete stranger in need of work and lodging — and Seumas had taken a chance on him when no one else would.

And come to think of it, the man's appearance had been under suspicious conditions. How could he have forgotten about that?

SEUMAS WAS WALKING OUT ALONG THE UNDERGROUND

tunnel from duty at the stone docks below when he found a stranger wandering around looking at the patterned carvings in the walls as if they were fascinating — which he supposed they were.

As soon as the man saw him, he planted a grateful look on his face.

"How blessed I am that ye came along. Can ye help me out? I'm lost, ye see."

Seumas looked up and down the tunnel. The only way in here that wasn't tightly guarded required crawling up through a narrow passageway that started under the sea, and the man was bone dry. Couldn't have been in here wandering around long enough to dry off, could he?

Best to be direct. And put a little fear in the man. He was much too carefree.

Seamus scowled at him.

"How did ye get doon here?"

The man shook his head and made a funny face that vaguely resembled bafflement but was too dramatic by far. Was he a player? Rare for one of those to be found alone without his troupe.

"I was exploring the caves ootside and I just wanderit in here. Now I canna find ma way oot."

Seumas started walking toward the nearest exit, and the man fell in alongside him. He wasn't sure yet what he was going to do with the man — take him to his uncle for questioning, most likely. If he was a player and had a troupe nearby, that would be a treat.

"I canna see any way ye could hae come in here

without us knowing. All o' the ways in are guarded. Are ye sure that's what happened?"

The man smiled at him. Smiled. And looked smug.

"Aye. Na all o' the ways in are guarded."

"Nay?"

"Nay."

They were at the guard post now, and it was the custom to introduce whoever you were walking with, if they were a stranger. Seumas turned toward the man.

"Tell Dubh and Luthais yer name."

The man bowed at them theatrically, which neither of them had probably ever seen. Seumas only knew it was a theatrical bow because he'd seen a traveling troupe of players while he was being fostered up at Turnberry Castle in Ayrshire. Aye, he was definitely a player, or at least had been, in his younger days. He was going on thirty. Bit old to be traveling alone.

"Tavish McGregor, at yer service."

Dubh and Luthais looked to Seumas, and he shook his head sternly. They moved to seize Tavish, but Seumas held his hand up.

"Tavish says he wanderit intae oor tunnels from an unguarded way in." He looked the man in the face. "Ye had best show me where that is."

Seumas expected Tavish to flinch at that demand, but he rubbed his hands together and smiled at them all as if this were some festival game.

"We wull need a hundred feet o' rope."

What? Was Tavish procrastinating in order to put off his doom? But curiosity seized Seumas. And let's face it, the man's enthusiasm was contagious.

Seumas gave Dubh and Luthais a wry grin.

"If there be a landward use for a hundrit feet o' rope, then I want tae know what it is. Call for it, Luthais."

The guard whistled, and Cormac came running from the castle with his hand on his sword, eyeing Tavish.

"Aye?"

Seumas kept his eye on Tavish while the other guards explained what they needed.

After a while, Cormac came running back with the rope, and Seumas took him along for good measure. He thought he was a match for Tavish, and the man wasn't armed, but you could never be too sure.

Tavish led them in what seemed a merry chase along the rim of the sea cliff north of the castle.

"Ye dinna guard along here, for ye dinna know. But I will show ye."

He kept looking all around as if for landmarks, both off to the right up high in the mountains and down over the cliff once he'd edged close enough to peer over without falling. At last, he settled near a large stone.

"We did secure the rope tae a ... horse when I went doon last evening. He's gone now, along with Gus the rider, sae let us secure the rope tae this stone."

Cormac looked to Seumas before doing as Tavish said.

Seumas studied Tavish for a moment. The man looked earnest — and not at all addled in the brain — so he nodded for Cormac to go ahead and secure the rope to the stone.

Once it was done, Tavish took the rope and looked to be trying to drag the stone over the cliff. When it wouldn't go, he nodded and walked backward over the edge of the cliff, with only the rope to secure his safety.

Seumas and Cormac ran to the edge of the cliff, sure that when they looked over they would see Tavish dashed on the rocks. Instead, they saw him smiling up at them, his feet against the cliff and walking down it backward, hunched over and holding the rope.

He addressed them with a challenging grin on his face.

"This is callit repelling, where I come from. My hidden way in is nay tae far doon. Here it is. I'll go in and wait for ye."

And with that, Tavish disappeared inside the cliff.

Seumas swore.

Who knew where the man would go now. Nodding to Cormac to hold the rope at the stone against Seumas's greater weight, he took hold of it and backed up over the cliff the same way Tavish had.

By the time they got to his uncle later that day, they were laughing and joking about how Seumas's face had looked when he swung into the hidden way in. Tavish had shown him an imitation of it often enough that it would never leave his mind.

Laird Malcomb had not been as amused as they were.

"The two o' ye must secure this hidden way in. Carry rocks down through the tunnels and plug it up."

SEUMAS FOUGHT THE URGE TO LAUGH, WALKING BACK

to the barracks that evening. Talk about a grueling month of labor.

But it had paid off for both of them. Tavish had turned out to be an excellent guard, even accompanying Seumas on the seaward part of his duty. And Seumas had gotten Tavish accepted by his uncle, and assigned honorable duties.

So Seumas felt sure Tavish would approve of him.

"I tell ye true, Tavish. Sasha draws me. Enough that I could be her husband and be happy all my days. Howsoever, I dinna hae ought tae offer her here, being but the younger son o' the laird's sister. Dae ye think yer clan would let me come and join them?"

Tavish looked down at the ground as they walked, rather than look Seumas in the eye. He was definitely keeping a secret. A big one. Why? He had nothing to fear from Seumas. He'd been a stalwart companion.

"I dinna think ye ought to rely on that, Seumas."

Seumas looked to Alfred for support and got a sympathetic look and a shrug.

"I would swear an oath tae yer clan chief and leave my laird behind, ye ken."

Alfred raised his eyebrows at Seumas for that, but said nothing.

Tavish kicked a small rock, and it went skittering away down the street. And then he sighed and turned toward Seumas with a look of great regret. He moved to put a hand on Seumas's shoulder but apparently thought better of it at the last moment, instead gesturing theatrically.

"Would that I could take ye home with me, Seumas.

'Tis not a question o' loyalty. That is na the trouble with joining my clan. We're ..." He blinked and turned his head abruptly toward Seumas in a manner that told Seumas he had thought of something unrelated to bring up, allowing him to evade the question. "Ye ken we MacGregors dinna yet hae our own lands, aye?"

Seumas turned to Alfred, whose look was as puzzled as Seumas felt.

"I dinna ken much aboot yer clan at all. Who was Gregor? When did he live?"

Tavish was on the verge of answering the question with pride. Seumas could tell. But the man clammed up and closed his eyes tightly, turning away from him.

They were at the castle gate, and Alfred showed his nonpartisanship in their discussion when he turned his back on them as he walked toward the castle entrance with a toss of his head and a backward wave of his hand.

"See ye in the lists tomorrow."

Seumas waved his brother off with an upward nod, then spoke to Tavish without looking at him. Direct was best.

"I can sense there is a great secret ye keep close tae yer chest. Ye can tell me."

Tavish sighed heavily and threw one of the little stones he'd picked up, knocking some fruit from a tree in the castle garden.

"I wish that I could, Seumas, but nay, I canna."

Seumas stepped up alongside Tavish and rested his forearms on the low castle wall so he could look out into the castle garden as well.

"When ye first came here, I didna trust ye. It

wouldna hae been wise for me tae. But with all we hae been through these past five years, now I dae. Dinna ye trust me? Havena I been a friend tae ye?"

Tavish nodded but didn't say anything, and they walked the rest of the way in silence.

Once they were in their racks, Tavish spoke so casually that Seumas knew this was important to him.

"Dae ye ken the story o' a sword all encircled, made by a king, wielded by a child?"

Well, two could hold things back, refusing to answer questions. Seumas rolled over on his other side and grunted noncommittally.

What could Tavish possibly feel the need to keep from him? Was the man an outlaw? Nay, he didn't seem so. And Laird Malcomb would've heard something by now, a description of the man, and a warning. Was the man a foreigner? Maybe. He spoke Gaelic very well, but his accent was a little off. He also didn't seem up on the current political climate, but not everyone was a laird's nephew. Anyway, being a foreigner wasn't a crime. It wasn't something that needed to be hidden. So that probably wasn't it.

But Tavish was hiding something. He had all but admitted it, and the man's evasiveness was deeply disturbing. Insulting, even. And worry about this secrecy kept Seumas awake a long time before he finally fell asleep.

GUARD DUTY WITH TAVISH WAS STRAINED ALL THE

next day, starting bright and early. The two of them were stationed at the stone docks at the bottom of the underground tunnels. The docks had been the site of a battle just a few days before, and tensions were high.

Seumas didn't press his questions. The man had said no, and that needed to be respected.

But the evening lists inside the castle courtyard were a perfect opportunity for Seumas to work out his frustration. They were using wooden practice swords, so the injuries wouldn't be fatal.

"Yer a madman today, Seumas!"

"Look oot, Seumas does mean business."

"Och Seumas, ye can try tae take my leg off, but I'd sooner ye did it with a metal sword."

He showed off, winning all seven of his bouts so far. But after each one, he helped the other man up and the two clasped the forearms of their sword hands in trust and friendship.

And then he and Tavish happened to be next to each other waiting in line for their next bout behind Cormac, who addressed them both.

"I did hear ye last evening, Tavish, asking about the sword all encircled, made by a King, wielded by a child."

"Aye? What can ye tell me aboot it?" Tavish asked him.

"I hae heard the story."

"Aye?" Tavish's interest was definitely piqued.

"Aye. It goes that in the time o' our great, great, great granddas, Robert the Bruce was fostered here as a child, and the smithy helped him make a toy sword."

Osgar, the man in front of Cormac in line, nodded.

"I did hear the same tale, howsoever I was told Robert the Bruce was visiting here, nay fostered."

Rob, the man in front of him, shook his head and waved his hand.

"Nay. I'm namit after Robert the Bruce, ye ken? He was fostered here, but he didna make the sword. The smithy made it for him, as a gift."

Behind them, Pòl spoke over the last half of this.

"The way I did hear it, the faeries brought the sword tae the young Bruce as a gift, in exchange for his promise o' loyalty in keeping their waurld safe later on in his life."

Warrick had just finished his bout and only heard this last version when he came over and joined the line at the end, which had bent double so as to be close to the conversation. He rushed the end of the line even closer, face red with conviction.

"Yer wrong! How can the sword be made by a king if the faeries hae brought it?"

Pòl got right up into Warrick's face.

"The king o' the faeries made it, ye bletherer!"

Seumas put his arms around Warrick and Pòl's shoulders and squeezed them both until they looked away from each other and at him.

"All o' yer stories differ a bit from the way I heard it told. Howsoever, it happened long ago, ye ken. And a good story changes each time someone does tell it."

The two backed down, but speculation on the story only ended when they had all separated into their bouts.

And then when Tavish's bout was over, instead of getting in the line again, he passed between the two carts for the practice swords, ducked low to be hidden behind them, and snuck out of the courtyard.

Seumas immediately flubbed his bout and did the same, running once he was in the street to catch up with Tavish in the failing sunlight.

No surprise really. The man was headed toward Eileen's house.

Seumas kept back far enough so as not to be noticed, stooping down below a vendor cart the one time Tavish did stop and look behind him. He remained there, where he had a good vantage of Eileen's front door if he looked through the linen the vendor had draped over everything. He noted in passing that it wasn't nearly so fine as the linen Eileen made.

Sasha was outside, playing a game of stones with Eileen's children. Tavish ran right up to her and grabbed her hand, and she swooned and she was wont to do. Tavish caught her, muttering something about having to take her back.

What could it mean? Wasn't Tavish with Kelsey? Was he greedy enough to want them both? If that was his secret, then he was going to be disappointed. Sasha wasn't interested in Tavish. It could be told by the way she didn't respond when the man held her.

She recovered from her swoon and said something too soft for Seumas to hear. The two of them looked all around suspiciously, called the children, and went inside the house.

Seumas walked up to the door and hung back a bit, looking through the window. He'd give Sasha another chance to respond to Tavish, but if she didn't this time, then he was going to continue his pursuit of her.

But their conversation was the last thing he expected.

"I had anoother vision, just now. Ye and Kelsey were in a different castle, and Kelsey was holding a sword."

Seumas was so engaged with listening to her that he didn't hear Kelsey and Eileen coming up behind him with their shopping baskets until Kelsey spoke to him.

"Dae ye want tae open the door for us, or are ye gaun'ae stay oot here looking in through the window?"

7

SEACHD

Sasha ran across the dirt street to grab the stone that had skipped over there and then threw it to hit the stone she was aiming at. She hit it! She raised her hands up in the air and went dancing all around the group of children, mostly oblivious to the smirks of neighbors looking out their glassless windows to see what the fuss was about.

"Score!"

Sìle sat there sucking her thumb as usual, but Aodh and Niall laughed from their places near the rocks they were aiming at.

Deirdre put her hands on her hips and scolded them with her index finger and a curl of her lip.

"Ye should na make fun o' her. Just because she's not from aroond here and uses funny words does na mean she has nay feelings."

Sasha hugged the little girl to her hip.

"I dinna mind their laughter. 'Tis all in fun."

Eileen's children were delightful, especially Little Deirdre. Her mother probably thought her precocious and slightly annoying sometimes, but Sasha was grateful for all the help the little girl provided. And she would add 'perceptive' to the long list of adjectives her mother doubtless used to describe the wee lass. She was pretty sure Deirdre knew just how clueless and inept Sasha felt here — though certainly not why — and the little six-year-old was such a sweetie to reach out and assist.

Deirdre had been a godsend this morning at the weaver shop, helping Sasha accept Eileen's help cleaning her suit. It was just that the suit had cost her almost a thousand dollars, and she had been cautioned to only dry clean it, lest it shrink.

SASHA CARRIED HER SUIT CLOSE TO HER CHEST ALL the way to Eileen and Kelsey's work. They all walked together in the pre-dawn light, the children too, with Eileen carrying Sìle. The door was open when they got there, and two men were already busy on looms.

"Did ye bring us anoother apprentice?"

Kelsey went over to the far right corner of the room and picked up some stuff and started working with it.

"This is my... clanswoman Sasha. These are the other master weavers in toon, Fergus and Uilleam."

The men waved at Sasha, and she waved back, giving them her friendly smile.

Eileen put the toddler down behind a row of tall

buckets on the floor and reached out toward Sasha. No, toward the suit.

Sasha heard Deirdre's voice at her elbow.

"'Tis all right. Maw won't ruin yer clothes. She's a weaver. She knows what she does."

Sasha looked down at the cute little girl.

"Why dae ye say that?"

Deirdre pointed.

"Because ye are hugging yer clothes."

She was. Walking over to Eileen, she forced herself to relax and let out a little laugh before she handed over the suit with a great deal of trepidation. And then she looked down into the buckets.

"Oh. But that's..."

Eileen turned Sasha's suit over in her hands, admiring the workmanship ... and probably the machine sewing. Too polite to say anything, she slowly pushed the muddy designer garments into one of the buckets filled with sudsy water, then turned and went over to where Kelsey was, smiling and beckoning for Sasha to join them.

Sasha sank down into a crouch, looking at her submerged suit and all the other submerged clothing in the buckets.

Deirdre hugged her and whispered in her ear.

"Ye dinna hae master weavers where ye live, I ken. Aye, those are kilts. And we make them from wool, like yer clothes. They wash oot fine if ye just sink them slowly and let them be. Go on over and talk with yer friends now. I wull watch the baby."

❧

It was Sasha's turn again, in the street with the children. She took careful aim, threw, and missed her target this time.

"Darn!"

The boys were scrunching their noses at her, visibly trying to place that word, when Tavish ran up and grabbed her hand, trying to tug her into the house.

"We hae a lead on the relic we need tae find. Let's take ye back first, and then Kelsey and I'll go. Ye hae already missed tae much time at home, on account o' not coming with us when we telt ye tae."

But Sasha wasn't paying attention to what he said. Because she was having another vision.

Tavish and Kelsey wandered a large fortified stone castle. Not the one here. This one had an obvious way to sail a boat right inside it on the water and dock there — Turnberry Castle in Ayrshire, about fifty miles north of here. Now Tavish was looking at Kelsey in wonder, and Kelsey was holding a sword.

Sasha tried to look closer and see if it was the same sword that Kelsey had made appear in front of Brian the Druid, but the vision abruptly ended.

When she came back to herself, Sasha realized she'd swooned again and Tavish had caught her, because he was still holding her. She recovered herself and gave him an awkward smile of thanks.

Still holding her by the hand, he tugged her toward

the door of the house. Just like Kelsey, he wasn't even aware of the children.

She'd been left in charge of them, and although it was probably safe to leave them alone outside here, she just couldn't bring herself to do that.

"Come on in, bairns."

Much to her surprise, there was no groaning or saying 'Do we have to?' They all picked up their favorite stones and ran right inside. She gave them her best smile in gratitude.

"Deirdre, will ye please help by supervising the bairns in setting the table for supper?"

Deirdre just about curtsied in front of her before rushing off to do just that.

Sasha was smiling when she turned to Tavish, but his face was so concerned that she rushed into her explanation of what just happened.

"I had anoother vision, just now. Ye and Kelsey were in a different castle, and Kelsey was holding a sword."

Tavish was about to answer when the door opened and Kelsey and Eileen came in with their shopping baskets, followed closely by Seumas.

Sasha didn't mean to stare, but she couldn't help it. Her gaze landed on him and she just couldn't tear her eyes away. Fortunately, he seemed to be having the same trouble. They smiled at each other in mutual amusement. She was vaguely aware of her surroundings, but mostly she smiled at Seumas and reveled in the fact that he smiled back — and not a tentative 'maybe we're attracted to each other' smile this time. Nope. This was a full blown 'Okay, we're both attracted. Now what?'

Kelsey followed Eileen into the kitchen and plunked her basket down on the counter. Tavish followed her in there and took her in his arms, dancing with her while holding her in front of him, still looking toward the counter. And doubtless whispering in her ear about the lead he had on the sword they were looking for.

Sasha froze.

He would also tell Kelsey his plan to take her home before they went looking for the sword. And she wasn't ready to go home yet.

Still smiling at Seumas, she spoke aloud to Kelsey in the kitchen from out in the front room.

"I did hae another vision, Kelsey, aboot ye and Tavish at Turnberry Castle in Ayrshire, holding a sword. I didna get a close look at the sword, sae I dinna ken if 'tis the one. Howsoever, it seems like some aught tae go on, aye?"

Seumas raised his eyebrows at her and deepened his smile while also raising his voice so loud that it summoned the children over.

"Aye? All the talk in the lists today was aboot Robert the Bruce as a wee lad, forging a sword right here where we hae the honor o' being his foster place..." He went on in detail.

The wee lads in the room were enraptured by the story. They had apparently heard it many times before — which wasn't really surprising, seeing how it had happened right here in their home town. The two of them pantomimed to match the words they spoke along with Seumas in a singsong voice, completing each other's sentences while their sisters looked on and nodded.

Niall made a big circle with his tiny arms.

"A sword all encircled."

Aodh made an imaginary crown on his head with his hands.

"Made by a king."

Niall pretended to have a Claymore in his hands as he swung it with wroth force in an arc that would've removed his brother's head.

"Wielded by a child."

Aodh ducked, and then the two of them were running around the room pretend sword-fighting again.

Seumas raised his eyebrows at Sasha. His eyes were still warm, but puzzled.

"And Robert the Bruce was born at Turnberry Castle. How dae ye ken that was the castle ye saw? Ye canna hae been there, can ye?"

Darn. She had slipped up and shown too much knowledge. How ironic that it was a structure of this time she'd said too much about, rather than an anachronism such as one of the bridges that now joined Scotland's smaller islands to the mainland. She needed to guard her tongue better, to think carefully before each time she spoke.

Tavish and Kelsey came into the room. Tavish did not look happy with Sasha for bringing up her vision in front of everyone. Kelsey looked amused. Even Eileen came in, wiping her hands on a dishtowel.

Sasha put her hands on her hips in a fair imitation of Deirdre and addressed Seumas. She vaguely sensed herself twisting from right to left and back again, making her long skirts sway around her legs. Was this how women flirted back in this day? It frightened her a bit, how easily it came to her. Women's intuition, she guessed.

"Nay, o' course I havena been there. The name was part o' the vision. 'Tis a remarkable place, Turnberry Castle, aye? Hae ye been there?"

Her flirting worked. The puzzlement left his eyes, and he was back to twinkling them at her, darn him. He was spoiling her for other men. She was going to miss his attention when she went home. None of the men there knew how to be so attentive.

Seumas nodded and pursed his lips, visibly trying to look smug that he was so important, but Sasha could tell that really he just didn't want her to leave just yet, because he assisted her in turning this into a big deal.

Gazing around at the whole crowd as if they had gathered just to hear his story, he put his foot up on the mantle, posing like an orator.

"Aye, I hae been there, tae Turnberry Castle in Ayrshire. 'Tis much closer tae the water than Laird Malcomb's castle here. Ye can sail yer boat right intae it. There are na caves like we hae here. Nay, instead, the built-up part o' the castle comes oot o' the water and encircles the docks. They must hae built it all during low tide ower several years."

He bent over to the children's height and looked in each of their faces by turn.

"Either that, or they usit the mermaids."

Aodh and Niall and Sìle all giggled at this.

But Deirdre put her hands on her hips again and shook her little finger in Seumas's face.

"There isna such thing as mermaids. Ye should na tell these children fibs like that. They'll grow up nay knowing lies from what is real."

Tavish and Kelsey laughed at that, but Deirdre didn't seem to realize they were laughing at her precociousness. She bent over at the middle and scrunched her eyebrows at them in a lecturing pose.

"I'm serious, ye ken. This is serious business. Raising children is an important task. Ye need to take it seriously."

Each time she said the word 'serious', she jerked her head and stomped her little foot in a manner that was so funny that Tavish and Kelsey burst out laughing again. Eileen was biting her knuckle to keep from laughing, and to her credit, she looked away to hopefully avoid her daughter seeing how amused she was.

Sasha felt bad for Deirdre. The poor little six-year-old had a lot of responsibility, watching her younger brothers and sister while her mother worked. Sasha looked at Seumas to see his reaction, and he looked sad for Deirdre too. This warmed her heart.

She turned to Deirdre to try and offer her some comfort.

But the little girl was already huffing off into the bedroom. She slammed the door.

Sasha started to go after Deirdre, but Eileen shook her head no. Sasha honored the mother's wishes, though it made her sad. She silently vowed never again to feel sorry for herself for having a boring childhood.

Boring was much better than no childhood. She didn't blame Eileen, though. These were tough times, and Eileen was just raising her children as best she knew how.

Now that Sasha was thinking about it, she noticed there weren't any toys in the house. The children played with stones or with the table settings or with their mother's clothes. Ordinary things and imagination gave them all the fun they were going to have. Oddly, they didn't seem deprived.

Eileen moved back into the kitchen and resumed preparing dinner.

"Aodh, Niall, and Sìle — go intae the bedroom and keep yer sister company while we grown-ups hae a talk oot here, please."

Sasha was again amazed when the children obeyed immediately and without arguing.

Once the adults were alone, Eileen turned to call the rest of them into the kitchen with her, but they'd already come. Kelsey started helping cut vegetables.

Sasha went up to Eileen's other side.

"What manner o' help dae ye need?"

Eileen filled a pot up with water from her cistern and set it on the kitchen side of the mantle.

"Ye can gather all the scraps o' meat from the larder there and put them in this pot along with the vegetables we cut up, then put the pot on the fire and stir it." She went and got a wooden spoon and handed it to Sasha.

Alfred had arrived in the middle of this and let himself in, and on their own, the men had already started adding wood to the fire and banking the coals so that Sasha could put the pot on them.

Seumas sought Sasha's eyes from across the room and spoke out loud, including Tavish and Kelsey when he did.

"Sae why all the interest in Robert the Bruce and his wee childhood sword?"

With much amusement, Sasha looked to Kelsey to explain this, however she would.

Kelsey put a fake smile on her face and shook with fake excitement, looking askance at Sasha every now and then and probably unaware she was wringing her hands.

"'Tis a favorite story in Sasha's family, and her aged grandmother askit us tae follow up on it tae see which parts are true while she was oot this way, ye ken. And now she's having visions o' it. 'Tis quite exciting, aye? I take this as a sign that we need tae go and see." She looked at Sasha to verify her story.

Sasha smiled and nodded, playing along by trying to look a little embarrassed at how much fuss was being made on her behalf.

Tavish gave a huge dramatic nod as if he had just decided they really needed to follow up on this after all. He looked to Alfred with a question in his eyes.

"We dinna hae anything planned ower the next few weeks. Can ye spare me tae go with my clanswomen on this errand, tae keep them safe? I'm thinking Donall can take us there on his way tae Norway, and we can find someone coming back this way once we arrive, so we wull only be gone two weeks at the most."

Before Alfred could answer, Seumas butted in, speaking directly to his brother.

"If Sasha and Kelsey go on this errand, then I insist on going along. I hae been tae Turnberry afore and can act as a guide."

Visibly amused, Alfred looked from one man to the other and then over at Kelsey and Sasha before he shared a wink with Eileen.

"Hoo aboot it, Eileen? Kelsey and Sasha are yer apprentices. Can ye spare them from the weaver shop for as much as two weeks?"

Eileen scrunched her nose and shrugged as she dumped the rest of the vegetables into the pot and helped Sasha put it on the coals of the fire.

"I dinna ken."

Seumas knew Eileen was teasing and meant to wait her out. Sasha could tell because of the way his eyes twinkled and his lips pursed together. Tavish on the other hand looked like he was about to lay down the law and reclaim his clanswomen from their apprenticeship.

Fortunately, Kelsey jumped in.

"How about if we bring you presents from Ayrshire, Eileen?"

Eileen smiled really big and looked around at her house.

"Ooh! What manner o' presents dae ye propose tae bring?"

Kelsey shrugged.

"I dinna ken, now having been to the place. Howsoever, we wull bring ye some ought that ye wull treasure. Ye hae my word upon it."

Eileen came over and gave Kelsey a hug, and then pulled Sasha over and hugged her as well.

"Ye are women after my own heart, sae I suppose ye can go."

They laughed and talked the rest of the evening about the legend of Robert the Bruce's childhood sword and the voyage to the castle and what manner of presents Eileen would get. Captain Donnell was scheduled to leave the next day, so they resolved to be up at dawn and head down there to ask him for passage. Eileen brought out some wine she'd been saving for a special occasion, and they all merrily toasted to a bon voyage.

Sasha and Kelsey were in good spirits as they got into bed for the night. Just as they blew out the candle, she caught sight of Deirdre looking at her intently. But when Sasha opened her mouth to say something, the little girl looked away and quickly went into the bedroom and closed the door.

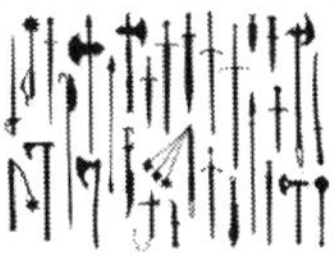

OCHD

Seumas knew that he and Tavish were getting a special favor from Alfred because he was his brother. No one else would be allowed to go on a trip just because someone's grandmother had heard a story. Normally, he would feel guilty for getting special treatment that none of the other guards got to have, but today he had a huge smile on his face as he and Tavish walked down to Eileen's from the barracks.

Tavish knocked on Eileen's door, and Kelsey let them in.

"We're ready tae go," she whispered. "Eileen and the children are still asleep. We didna hae much tae pack, but she insistit we take these provisions for the trip." She held up a knapsack.

Sasha came to the door then. She was wearing the clothes Eileen had loaned her — proper long skirts that didn't show her boots — and she clutched Tavish's plaid cloak around her tightly against the morning cold. She had braided her hair against the sea breeze, the same as he.

He got out the knife and held it out to her.

"Here. My da gave this tae me when I was a child. 'Tis now longer large enough, ye ken. But 'tis the proper size for ye. Put it in yer belt. Ye at least need tae hae a knife."

She took it from him as she and Kelsey came out the door, then intently stared at it for a few moments before giving him a huge smile that lit up her whole face and made her beauty shine like the rays of the sun rising over the distant mountains. She fell into step beside him as they walked along the cliff path to Port Patrick with the sea on their left, fiddling with the knife and her belt as if she'd never belted a knife before.

"Thank ye. 'Tis such a fine gift. I wull treasure it always."

Hm. It was fun having this effect on a woman. It had been a long time, and nothing much had come of it before. Here was hoping for this time.

He gently took the knife from her hand and secured it through her belt, conscious of the smoothness of her hand when it released the knife and the warmth of her middle when his fingers brushed against her dress in order to belt it.

He turned around and walked backward in front of her, admiring his handiwork.

"Now ye are ready for a journey."

She laughed, humoring him. When they got to the cliff side with the view down to the right into Port Patrick, she froze and stared down there in apparent awe. He followed her gaze and looked down with a mind to see it as a newcomer would. Someone who had never left their home... Oh.

She started walking again, but she was still looking down into the port.

"The ships are sae beautiful. I had heard aboot them and seen... drawings, but tae see them in front o' me? It is stunning."

He took her right hand and placed it firmly on his raised left arm, putting his right hand over hers so that she couldn't withdraw it.

"Go on and gander, lass. Howsoever, the last thing I dae need is for ye tae fall."

It might've been his imagination, but he thought for a moment she squeezed his forearm.

They amicably walked arm in arm without talking to each other for the rest of the way to Captain Donnell's ship, listening to Kelsey and Tavish speculate on whether they'd actually find Robert the Bruce's sword or just more stories.

But Captain Donnell's apologetic face told Seumas right away that he didn't have room for them.

"Sorry lads. Howsoever, ye can see I'm near the waterline already, with all o' the cargo I'm carrying for Norway. Ye might ask Captain Dowd does he hae room for the four o' ye." He gestured over toward another ship that was loading and then lowered his voice to almost a whisper. "Mind ye though, he is na verra likable."

Kelsey laughed inappropriately at this, and Seumas's breath caught in his throat.

Aye, it was true that Captain Donnell wasn't very likable himself, but you didn't laugh at a captain. Fortunately she had impressed the captain and made him a fair bit of extra money a few days ago, and he let it slide.

Seumas looked over at Sasha to see if she was aware of her clanswoman's faux pas. Good. She was more socially graceful than the other woman, though they both seemed highborn. Far be it from him to entertain snobbery about another's lack of grace, but he would only be able to kill so many men in defense of his woman before even being the nephew of the local Laird wouldn't secure his position here.

Letting out his breath and relaxing a bit, Seumas looked to Tavish, who nodded a bit grimly that yes, he still wanted to go, even if they couldn't go with Captain Donnell.

So Seumas addressed the captain.

"Aye, we wull go with Captain Dowd."

At this, Donnell waved until someone on Dowd's ship noticed and then gestured that the four of them were coming over.

Captain Dowd's ship wasn't as in good a trim as Captain Donnell's, but she looked seaworthy. Oh, it was this man. Seumas had seen him around Castleton a few times, always arguing with the local tradesmen. Well, it was a short journey to Turnberry Castle, not even half the day by ship. They could abide.

A look at Tavish told him he was thinking the same thing. How could his friend be so easygoing about most things, and yet keep some huge secret from a man whose life he had saved and who had saved his? Well, Seumas wasn't going to let it get to him.

He was holding Sasha's arm to help her aboard when the captain approached them with his nose in the air and a sneer on his freckled face.

"Oh we hae Laird Malcomb's nephew himself, eh? Not enough room for ye on yer preferred ship, sae I take it. Wull ye willna be leisurely passengers, ye ken. Ye wull have tae work." He looked Sasha and Kelsey over with just enough good manners that Seumas didn't cut him down on the spot. But it was close. "I suppose yer lasses can sit that oot." He caught the attention of one of his crewmembers and then pointed at Tavish and Seumas. "Get these two tae work loading the cargo."

Seumas found Sasha and Kelsey a seat in the bow of the boat, where they would be out of the way. He took Sasha's hand in his, but included Kelsey in what he had to say.

"I hae noticed that the two o' ye feel free tae take a lot o' liberty in yer actions. That is good for ye in yer own village and even here when amoong friends. I would na take it away from ye. Howsoever, while yer on Captain Dowd's ship, ye must dae what he says, ye ken?"

Sasha smiled at him with understanding. Kelsey at least gave a grudging nod.

Tavish was already working, and Seumas gave Sasha's hand a gentle caress before he let go and went off to join him. They loaded all manner of goods into the ship from all over the world: spices from India, tea from China, rugs from Persia... Captain Dowd worked for a wealthy man, indeed.

Finally, all the cargo was loaded and it was time to cast off — and for Seumas and Tavish to go check on the lasses. He heard Sasha's distress before he saw her, and when he did, her face was green.

Kelsey tried to chase him off.

"Seumas, why dinna ye and Tavish go talk tae the men o' the ship? Ask them if they hae ever heard the story o' Robert the Bruce's sword and if they think it's at Turnberry Castle?"

Tavish moved to Kelsey's side and held her close, making it look like affection when really Seumas knew it was protectiveness — and a determination not to let her separate herself from him and get in trouble here among men who didn't often see lasses up close and so personal.

So Seumas addressed her, but really he was talking to Tavish.

"Go on and enjoy the sights, Kelsey. I ken the way o' the sea, sae I can help Sasha with her grumbly stomach."

Kelsey looked to Sasha, who subtly nodded her head astern. Heh!

Once Tavish and Kelsey had walked away and down into the hold leaving him relatively alone with Sasha, he made it his mission to distract her. Standing behind her with them both facing the bow as the ship got unsteadily underway, he leaned in close to her cheek and whispered, pointing.

"Dae ye see off in the distance there?" He pointed off to the right where the cliffs opposite those they'd arrived on marked the opening of Port Patrick. "I did think I saw the jump o' a porpoise."

He could see her conspiratorial smile as he looked down at her face over her shoulder, but she played along, straining to see into the water over by those cliffs.

"Good, good. That's the way. I hae always had motion sickness, ever since I was a child. My da taught me how tae fend it off, and ye dae hae the way o' it. The trick is tae focus on something off in the distance, in the direction yer traveling."

It was pleasant standing behind her there. Her hair smelled like lilacs, but that wasna it. She just had an air about her that he found... comforting, like home. Well, and a bit exciting, too.

"Oh, but I dae see porpoises jumping oot there. We're closer now. Canna ye see them yet?"

"I can see them!"

Deirdre popped out of one of the crates piled up on deck. She laughed and climbed high up onto the bow, leaning forward so as to see them better.

"They're funny!"

Seumas went to grab her and pull her away from the certain peril of falling in front of the bow into the water and being run over by the ship.

Uncharacteristically, she ducked out of his grasp and was running back along the starboard side railing, stepping up on top of crates when she needed to in order to pass by, when the ship canted to starboard with the wind.

And quick as that, she went over the side and landed in the water with a splash and a scream.

"No!" Sasha yelled out as she ran over to the railing were Deirdre had gone over. Before Seumas realized what she was doing, she had climbed up on top of the same crate and dove off the side of the ship like one of the porpoises.

He yelled out to everyone around.

"The lassies went overboard!"

"The lassies went overboard!"

But no one paid him any mind. He grabbed the elbow closest to him and pulled the man attached around to face him.

"We need tae turn aroond and go back for them, ye hear?"

But the man's eyes were focused on something behind Seumas, and then Captain Dowd's voice boomed from there.

"We wull dae now such thing. If ye feel the need tae go back for them, then jump ower the side like yer fool lassie did."

If he was going to catch up with them before it was too late, then there wasn't time even to tell Tavish where he was going. Without a second thought, he was up on top of the crate and over the side himself, into the water with his own splash.

Swimming steadily toward where he could see Sasha bobbing in the water with Deirdre in tow, he felt foolish now for pointing out the porpoises jumping in the water. How had he missed Deirdre stowing herself away on board? Well, he had been rather busy loading cargo.

Sasha was making rather good progress toward the shore, and he had to veer to his left and triangulate so as not to miss her and be washed ashore too far down. She was aiming for the small beach where he and Alfred often swam as boys.

Now that he saw she wasn't in danger, he rather enjoyed watching her swim. She was strong and graceful. But then he saw that Deirdre wasn't moving, and he redoubled his efforts, hoping for he knew not what.

Sasha reached the beach before him, and she was fussing over poor Deirdre's lifeless body, turning it this way and that and patting on its back. Aw, now she was kissing the dead girl.

He swam as fast as he could, and the moment he reached the shore he ran for the stockpile of firewood he knew was there, piled up some tinder and dry leaves, and took his flint out of his sporran to spark the flame. As he worked, he called out to Sasha over his shoulder.

"I'm verra sorry for the loss o' Deirdre, Sasha. Howsoever, ye need tae take care o' yerself, ye ken? Mourn what yer gaun'ae mourn until I get this fire gang, but then come ower an warm yerself. Yer alive, and ye need tae take care o' yerself tae ensure ye stay that way, aye?"

He was working on the fire and feeling sad that he couldn't look back to console her when she said some nonsensical thing about how the little girl was going to be fine and was breathing now and wait just wait a minute and she would bring her over. Best to nip her delusion in the bud.

"Weesht. I hae the fire gang now, but it will take a

few minutes tae get warm enough tae dry yer clothes an warm ye up. We're gaun'ae have tae take oor clothes off and wring them oot sae they dry faster. I'm doing sae now while the fire gets hot. Fair warning. Cover yer eyes if ye like."

As soon as he was done with the fire and working on getting his kilt off to wring it out, he looked over to see how she was faring and froze, incredulous.

Just as she had said, Deirdre was up and walking over with her. They both had their heads bowed, and Sasha's arm was around the little girl, hugging her to her side. They were shivering with the cold.

He wrung the sea water out of his kilt and shirt as quickly as he could and put them back on, then turned with his back to them and to the fire, enjoying its warmth while he figured out what to say to her.

She was clearly...

She...

She was using sorcery.

Did he care? He was nominally Catholic, as was everyone in Castleton. The church said that sorcery was evil, but he had seen... No, he had heard tales of how... Well, never mind. The bottom line was he didn't care if she was a sorceress or not, he was falling so deeply for her.

He swallowed and cleared his throat, still looking the other way.

"How are ye, Deirdre?"

The little girl's voice sounded harsh and choky, but she responded dutifully.

"Cold."

He nodded.

"Aye, the two o' ye need tae remove yer clothing and wring oot all the moisture ye can and then put it back on and dry it ower the fire, like I am."

Sasha answered him, sparing the little girl the use of her sore voice.

"Aye, that we are doing. I know ye hae never seen a person resuscitated before. I can tell it upset ye. I'm guessing ye think it's ... I dinna ken if ye believe me when I tell ye this, but it is na. 'Tis... medicine, where I come from. Ye could dae it if I showed ye how." She was quiet for a few minutes while she and Deirdre finished putting their damp clothes back on. "Say something, sae I wull know how ye feel and what ye are thinking."

He took several deep breaths, still gazing at the trees on the far side of the fire from her, unsure he ever wanted to turn around and see the evidence of her sorcery.

He didn't blame her for not admitting it.

"Deirdre, ye canna tell anyone what happened here, ye ken?"

The little girl started to speak, but Sasha shushed her.

"Weesht. Rest yer voice, dearie." And then she spoke to Seumas. "I Dinna ken why she shouldna tell the tale o' me saving her from drowning. Anyone else would hae done the same, aye?"

"Aye," the little girl croaked out before Seumas could put two thoughts together.

Now he did turn around. If that was what the little girl thought, then it was brilliant. Ashamed at his relief in noticing the knife he had given Sasha was safely tucked in her belt and not at the bottom of the sea, he put a look of wonder on his face and crouched down so that he saw Deirdre eye to eye over the fire.

"Is that what happened? Did Sasha save ye from drowning?"

Deirdre nodded yes as she held her tiny arms out around the fire, almost like she was giving it a hug. She was still close to Sasha, and if they had dry clothes to change into, he was sure the two of them would be hugging each other for the fear of almost drowning.

He met Sasha's eyes, and they were pleading with him to just accept this about her and go back to the way they had been — was it not even an hour ago?

He couldn't think of any earthly thing to say, and he didn't trust his face to not reveal just how disturbed he was. So he did what he could to assure her that he wanted to go back to the way they had been. He walked around the fire to her side and took her hand in his and gently squeezed it. They stood there like that for an hour, making the kind of small talk Deirdre could repeat without causing alarm while they waited for their clothes to dry enough so that they wouldn't catch their deaths of cold on the walk back to Eileen's house in Castleton.

9

NAOI

Once they were dry and the awkwardness of discussing CPR with a forteenth century man had worn off, Sasha felt disappointed that they had to take Deirdre home and couldn't just continue on foot to meet Kelsey and Tavish at Turnberry Castle.

Anyway, Seumas said it was a two-day journey on foot and that she didn't have the boots for it, never mind that they would have to carry too much with them to go now, as the September nights were cold. Standing by the fire, that had sounded silly, but now walking back along the coast she felt the chill, even midday. She also felt every craggy rock through the thin souls of her dress boots.

Seumas carried Deirdre most of the way. The normally spry little girl was exhausted from her ordeal, and most of the time they could hear her snoring. This amused them and gave them a chance to talk. They spoke of everything except whether or not Sasha was a sorceress.

Seumas walked easily by her side, occasionally brushing the back of her hand with his.

"What dae ye fancy, at mealtime? Tell me the sort o' feast ye most look forward tae?"

She'd always found it awkward discussing food with men, but he looked so earnest and so curious that this time she didn't mind.

"My mama has a way o' fixing chicken I dearly love. She rubs eggs ower it and then rolls it in breadcrumbs, puts some butter in the pan, and fries it."

He hefted the sleeping girl in his arms to a more comfortable carrying position as he walked.

"Aye, that sounds good."

"What aboot ye?"

He freed one of his hands long enough to pat his stomach, then quickly caught Deirdre up close to his chest again.

"I fancy a good clam bake. What aboot games? Which games dae ye like tae play?"

She enjoyed gazing into his earnest eyes and seeing how genuinely he wanted to know.

"Dae ye mean ootside, or in the house after supper?"

He laughed.

"I did mean inside after supper, but ye have me curious. Dae ye yet play games ootside? And if sae, what are they?"

"Aye, I love tae play this game we hae where we make three places we need tae run tae before we come home again. We hold a stick, and the enemy throws at us a ball. We hit it as far as we can with the stick, and while they're running after the ball, we have tae run tae all three places and come home again."

He smiled warmly, nodding as he kicked a small stick up into the air and laughing when it landed in a tree and made several birds take flight.

"I hae playit such a game. When we were children, we playit an easy one where we put the ball on a stool and hit it off. Now, I prefer a good game o' save the castle, such as Aodh, Niall, and even little Sìle were playing when first ye saw them."

She found it surprisingly easy to talk with him.

During the times when Deirdre was awake, Sasha took her little wooden flute out of the pouch she kept it in and played some of her favorite songs for the two of them, pleasantly surprised to find that it still sounded good after the dunking it had received today. She was a little afraid Seumas and Deirdre would ask her to play some songs that were popular now, but thankfully they didn't. Whew.

If not for the severity of what had happened to Deirdre, Sasha would've considered this walk along the coastline and past the harbor a party. The sound of the ocean had always made her happy, and it was even better here. There were no other sounds to detract from it. No planes nor helicopters overhead. No automobiles with their noise and their stink. Just the birds chirping in the trees and the waves crashing on the beach.

And his voice.

Each time she met Seumas's eyes, she definitely

wanted to celebrate the closeness she felt with him, as if they had known each other years instead of days. As if they were meant to be together.

So it was with slow steps and heavy hearts that they at last arrived at the weaver shop. Eileen took one look at them and gasped, reaching her arms out for her daughter.

"Deirdre, Deirdre, ye had me worried sick, and now ye come home looking like a drowned rat." She met Sasha's eyes, and when Sasha nodded, Eileen became distraught and headed for home, holding her daughter like a baby and rocking her. Aodh and Niall followed, and Sasha scooped up and carried Sìle.

When they got home, Eileen carried Deirdre into the bedroom and laid her down to rest, cooing and fussing over her, and speaking to Sasha and Seumas over her shoulder.

"Ye wull excuse me if I dinna entertain ye, I'm sure."

"Aye," they both told her.

And then they spent a pleasant if tense afternoon playing games with Aodh, Niall, and Sìle and making a passing if messy supper.

When Alfred arrived, he took one look at Eileen and Deirdre and nodded toward Seumas, who nodded back and got up to leave. While Alfred said his good-byes to Eileen and gave her his sympathy for her daughter's illness, Seumas stood close to Sasha holding her hand and giving her hope and a promise with his eyes, but saying nothing at all except good night.

❧

In her dream that night, Sasha found herself inside Turnberry Castle with Kelsey. It was magnificent with high vaulted ceilings.

"I really think that Seumas and I should come join you. Four of us will be able to search much faster than two of you."

But Kelsey shook her head no with an odd smile on her face.

"No, Seumas is right. You need to stay put and wait for us to get back. It's too tough a journey and too risky with the cold. Besides, Eileen needs help now more than ever, with a sick daughter."

Her smile got bigger and she stood there waiting for Sasha to guess what she was smiling about. When Sasha shrugged, Kelsey held her hands out to the sides with her elbows bent.

"And anyway, I can explore much faster than all four of us put together ever could in real life—in my dreams. All I have to do is touch someone, and then I'm able to get into their dream with them..."

And that was that.

Sasha gave up any chance of meeting Kelsey at Turnberry Castle. She hung around with Kelsey in their shared dream for a while and got a tour at least, and then said she might as well go back to her body and get some good sleep.

Really, she was just jealous that Kelsey got to be in that other castle. She didn't really want to see too much of it in her dreams or she'd be too sorry she couldn't go.

Even though Kelsey had used Deirdre's illness as a reason for Sasha to stay put, Sasha was relieved when the little girl was better by morning.

She passed a normal day in the weaver shop, and then another the next day, and another the next.

Frankly, she found day-to-day life in medieval times boring. At least for the working people it was. Her evenings were pleasant, playing games with Seumas and the children and talking and laughing with Alfred and Eileen. But the days. She felt like her head would explode with boredom if she had to spend one more whole day shredding flax plant into linen threads.

And wasn't there a castle right here that she might explore? Even better, wasn't there a man here who had some answers, when all Kelsey had were hints and guesses?

On the pretext of doing a little marketing, Sasha headed out at midday toward the castle. Brian the Druid knew things. She could tell. Maybe after being alone up there for a week, he would appreciate having company.

She was almost to the castle gate when someone in the street grabbed her arm and roughly yanked her toward himself, breathing rotten alcohol breath down her throat.

"Yer a big one, aren't ye. Come shew us a little—ack!"

Seumas grabbed the man and pushed him away down the street, where he tripped over his own feet from the momentum and fell down in a heap. Seumas stood there for a long moment staring the heap down, his chest heaving and his breath coming out ragged, his fists clenched and his arms bent.

"While Tavish is away, Sasha is under my protection, ye ken?"

The man stayed down in a heap and nodded.

Seumas relaxed a bit but didn't take his eyes off her attacker. He moved around Sasha until he could see both her and the heap at the same time, looking her over with concern in his eyes.

"Are ye whole? Did he hurt ye?"

Realizing she was hugging herself, she let her arms fall to her sides naturally and took stock.

"Aye, I am whole. He didna get the chance tae hurt me, ye grabbed him sae fast."

He nodded, relaxing more but still not taking his eyes off the man — who still lay in a heap. No one was even helping the man, such was his reputation, she supposed. She resumed her walk into the castle, wondering if Seumas was going to try and stop her once he realized where she was going.

But he just looked sad as they passed through several long stone hallways and climbed six flights of spiraling tower stairs.

Brian the Druid's elderly face was looking through the bars of his thick wooden door — just like he had been in Kelsey's dream. And he remembered the dream, because he recognized her. She could tell by the look on his face.

Suddenly glad she'd brought Seumas along, she took the huge kilted warrior's hand as they walked up the last flight of steps.

He held her hand. Tensely, but he held it.

Brian threw his head back inside his tower prison and burst out laughing. He laughed from his gut for almost a minute in fits and starts, making his long white beard bounce against his white cleric's robe. He would start to speak, and then he would be laughing again. Finally, he resumed his spot with his face pressing against the bars of the door, but his mouth was scrunched up in amusement.

When he spoke, he kept shaking with pent-up laughter. If she didn't know he'd been locked up for trying to molest her friend, she might have found him fun, rather than creepy.

"Heard aboot yer little mishap on the ship. Sae sad aboot the wee lass. Och, but she didna drown, did she? Now I wonder how that could be. Someone has an uncanny skill, never heard o' before. Almost as if she had seen the future."

Sasha's heart raced, and she felt adrenaline zooming through her body.

What was the old Druid doing? Seumas couldn't be allowed to know the druids could make people travel through time.

Sasha turned around to go back down the stairs.

"I don't know why I came up here. That man is clearly daft. No way to get answers from someone who's lost his mind."

Not letting go of her hand, Seumas quietly persisted in staying with her as she started down the stairs. Any moment now, he would ask her what she was doing up here anyway.

What should she tell him? Best to keep to Kelsey's cover story about Sasha's grandmother telling Sasha to investigate the legend of the sword.

But Brian called out after her, making her an offer she couldn't refuse.

"I ken where the sword is, the one Kelsey and Tavish need."

She stopped dead in her tracks and then turned the top half of her body around to look at the white-haired druid from halfway down the staircase.

"Ye dae?"

Brian laughed some more.

"Aye, I dae. And all it will cost ye is the exchange o' yer knowledge for mine."

Her heart was still racing. She was very aware that the man was dangerous. And something about the way he had phrased that raised up the hair on her arms.

It must have alarmed Seumas too, because he let go of her hand and turned so that he could hold her by the waist—hold her back from climbing the stairs again.

She was glad. She had been about to rush back up the stairs toward Brian, and if he wanted to, he could reach through the bars. They could hear each other just fine from this distance, and they were up far enough in the tower that no one else could hear them unless they came up the stairs. She would hear anyone who came up the stairs behind her. The tower echoed.

Relaxing into Seumas's strong embrace and letting it calm and reassure her, she considered her words carefully. Many of the Celtic fairy tales she had read for her studies included battles of wits, and often some poor soul agreed to something unimagined.

At last she arrived on what she thought was the best question to ask.

"How much of my knowledge would you require in order to tell me where the sword that Tavish needs is?"

The Druid laughed again, but when he saw that it wasn't getting to her this time, he abruptly stopped.

"Clever lass. Ye need only tae answer my questions first."

Something about the way he said it calmed her and made her relax. Answering his questions wouldn't be dangerous.

But Seumas gently squeezed her to him, distracting her attention away from Brian.

Watch it, her caution screamed at her. Be careful. Druids have magic, and this one also has something up his sleeve.

She swallowed and again carefully considered her answer.

"How many of your questions would I need to answer?"

Brian backed away from the barred window a bit, smiling a knowing smile.

"Ah, now we are getting doon tae it. Ye have decidit tae answer my questions. Now 'tis only a matter o' dithering ower quantities."

She gasped, and a new shot of adrenaline rushed through her.

"I didna agree tae anything."

"Nay, not yet, but ye wull."

Seumas gave her waist a tentative tug toward the bottom of the stairs. Bless the man for respecting her enough to let her decide if they were leaving or not. She could tell he was itching to be on their way. But what danger were they in? Brian couldn't reach them this far down the stairs.

She patted Seumas's hand on her waist but stayed put, having a stare-out with Brian.

"Wull, how many questions o' yers will I need tae answer before ye tell me where the sword is that Tavish needs?"

Brian smiled huge, showing all his rotting teeth, and rubbing his hands together in odd patterns.

"Och, I say we go with the customary three, eh? Answer me three questions, and I shall tell ye where the sword is that Tavish needs."

Sasha stood there for a long moment, considering her response. She hadn't agreed to give him all of her knowledge. That could've been disastrous for her. She had a picture of him sucking all the knowledge out of her head, leaving her an idiot.

Yes, she was sure she wasn't leaving herself open to that when she replied, sneaking in a little extra knowledge for herself.

"Agreed. I wull answer three o' yer questions, and then ye wull tell me where the sword is that Tavish needs — and ye wull answer two o' my questions about the Druids."

Victory shown in Brian's eyes and his smile got huge and a little bit evil.

"Agreed. Question the first. How is it ye came tae

own that ring, the one that marks ye as a druid priestess?"

Sasha's adrenaline was all used up by now, so all she could do was gasp at the trouble the old Druid was bringing down on her head. She tried to speak, but found she couldn't. Her mouth was sealed shut and her tongue wouldn't move. She forgotten about this part of the fairytales. Only a few had this malady. Why had she forgotten? She tried to turn and go down the stairs, but felt she couldn't move either. Her feet were frozen to their place on the stairway.

To his credit, Seumas yet stayed with her, even though she had the impression that he could leave if he wanted to. But his embrace felt mechanical now, rather than warm and affectionate as it had before.

Giddily, the old Druid went on condemning her in Seumas's hearing.

"Question the second. How far intae the future are ye from, Sasha? And if ye dinna mind me asking, tell an old man aboot all the wonders yer life has seen in yer own time."

Tears welled up in Sasha's eyes, and a lump formed in her throat that she had no ability to swallow. Her throat burned, and she started sobbing. Just like that, the old man had ruined any chance she had with Seumas. Again she tried to leave, but again she was prevented by Brian's magic.

And again, Seumas stood by her. Hope bloomed in her heart afresh. Maybe he loved her. Maybe they could be together anyway. She braced herself for the one last question. As soon as he spoke it, she would answer all three questions in rapid succession and then ask him about the sword and get the hell out of there. Heck with finding out more about the Druids.

Brian was shaking with glee now, and through the bars in the wooden door, his eyes absolutely radiated victory.

"Question the third. Which type o' our druidic magic is yer specialty, Sorceress?"

⸙ 10 ⸙

DEICH

Her sobs were coming repeatedly now, racking her whole body so that she would've collapsed if Seumas hadn't been holding her. Forget never having a chance with him. Now a small kernel of fear blossomed in her heart. He would be sure she not only was a sorceress, but also was hiding it from him and had lied to him. What would he do to her?

Brian positively cackled with laughter now.

"What's the matter? Did the cat come and steal yer tongue away? An agreement is an agreement. All ye have tae dae is answer my questions, and I wull answer yers." He cackled some more.

She was in an impossible situation. She could move now. Her limbs had been freed. And she could speak now if she wanted. But what would she say? And where would she go?

After his cruelty in driving such a wedge between her and Seumas, she couldn't bear to speak to Brian again. No way would she answer his questions. They would just have to find the sword through other means. Perhaps Tavish and Kelsey would find it all on their own.

And she would certainly find another way to inquire about what it meant to be a druid. A surge of anger ran through her, directed at their professors at Celtic University. If they were going to make her and Kelsey into Druids, the least they could've done was tell them what it meant. How dare they send them off on these quests without even knowing what they were or who they could trust or what they were meant to do with their knowledge?

That small kernel of anger propelled her feet, and she started to walk down the stairs.

Seumas came with her, incredibly still holding her gently by the waist. He didn't say a word, though, and she was starting to think that was a good thing. She often let her mouth run before her brain caught up with it. Good on him for thinking before he spoke.

They went down the spiraling stone staircase of the tower. A few moments before they got to the door at the bottom, the one that led out into the hall the Castle, she figured she had better speak to him while they still had privacy. She stopped, but didn't turn her head to him. Instead she looked at the stone floor, marveling at how it was made of thousands of tiny stones fit together with barely anything between them. In the back of her mind, she wondered at the ingredients of the sealant that was used to make such a floor in medieval times. Meanwhile, her mouth was running on.

"'Tis true I'm from the future. Tavish and Kelsey are tae. We are from eight hundred years in the future, in case ye were wondering. There isna way I'm gaun'ae tell Brian any o' this, but I want ye tae know. I'm nay sorceress, na matter what it looks like or what he says. Though this ring I wear..."

She twisted the ring she wore on her right hand, the one she had been so proud of a few months ago when she was awarded it from Celtic University. Wrought from the purest silver, it looked like three pieces of thread woven together in Celtic knots of such intricacy that the eye couldn't follow all the lines of them.

"This is my ring I got for studying seven years at a Celtic place o' learning. I thought it verra prestigious at the time. Now I come tae find oot the place is run by druids and that this marks me as a druid priestess. I know ye willna believe me, but I have na idea what it means tae be a druid priestess. They didna tell me I was studying tae be a druid priestess. All they said was I would be a doctor o' Celtic archaeology. That means in my time, I find the ruins o' places like this and dig them up and find items inside which tell the story o' the people who lived long ago. Kelsey and I are digging oot the verra underground tunnels ye go intae all the time. Wull, in our time na one's been there for hundrits o' years. 'Tis verra exciting and we're getting attention from all ower the waurld for it. I guess I'd better explain. In my time, we have stuff callit technology. It's verra complicated. I dinna understand how it works. It might as wull be magic, really, as much as I understand it. Anyhow, technology allows everyone in the waurld tae speak with each other, even tae see each other across vast distances. And a great many people can see one person ... 'Tis pointless for me tae go intae what 'tis all called. 'Tis just... 'Tis an honor tae be one o' the people who speaks tae masses o' people all around the waurld. And 'tis... fun. I really enjoy being the center o' attention while I open one o' the secret doors in the underground castle in front o' all the waurld. I enjoy the admiration and awe and respect. But now 'tis all ruinit. Now ye think I'm a sorceress, and I almost wouldn't blame ye if ye felt like stoning me tae death or something."

She stood there and waited for him to say something, but he didn't. All he did was stand still with his arm still around her and nudge her a little bit on the waist, toward the door.

So she sighed deeply and headed out into the castle proper, unsure whether she was being consoled — or marched to the slaughter.

On the way through the door into the hallway, he dropped his hand from her waist. They walked the whole way back to the weaver shop in silence. She kept wanting to ask him to say something, but then fear took over and she didn't. Maybe if she pestered him about it he would explode. That was the pattern between her parents.

But the silence was maddening.

What was he thinking?

Did he hate her?

She kept her eyes on the ground in front of her the whole time, and when they arrived at the weaver shop door, she looked up to thank him for walking her back. But he was already walking away with his back to her.

Tears welled up in her eyes anew, and that choking feeling came back. She was deciding whether to go in or run back to Eileen's house to cry in private when the door opened.

All the children ran out into the street, laughing and playing a game of chase where they yelled a phrase at each other over and over.

"Galdus is gaun'ae get ye!"

The first time she heard it, she didn't understand what they were saying, they were so young and their accents were so thick and they were sing-songing it. But she heard it over and over again.

"Galdus is gaun'ae get ye!"

Hadn't Brian said something about Galdus when he saw the sword Kelsey was holding in her dream, the one that Tavish needed? Sasha went inside and picked up some of the flax that Eileen was shredding into thread so that Fergus could make linen.

"What does it mean, what the children are yelling at each oother aboot Galdus getting them?"

Eileen kept her hands on the flax and shrugged her shoulder.

"I dinna ken. It's an auld children's game we all played when we were young."

Fergus spoke up from his place at the loom.

"Galdus was an auld King. He's buried at Torhousekie, ye ken." He gestured to the east with his head, never taking his hands off his work.

Sasha's heart raced now in a good way. Brian had said

Galdus's name when he saw Kelsey with the sword. Had he thought she was the old king come to life? Maybe they would find the sword at Galdus's burial site. Maybe the Robert the Bruce story was a red herring and Tavish and Kelsey were after the wrong sword.

She went over to Fergus's loom.

"Dae ye hae a preferred way tae get tae Torhousekie?"

Fergus looked up, visibly surprised.

"Ye know it?"

You have no idea. All the vast catalogues of sites she had studied for her doctorate whooshed before her eyes. The Torhouse Standing Stones were one of the first sites she'd been taught. But she mentally chastised herself for slipping up again and letting too much knowledge show.

Putting on the air of innocence, she raised her palms up to her sides with her elbows bent.

"My grandmother knows all sorts o' stories."

Fergus went back to his work.

"The trail starts at Port Patrick. Most o' us hae been at least once. It's a favorite trip for children on All Souls' Day."

"Och, Aye" she said to him. "I can well imagine."

Fergus seemed shy about her standing there, so she nodded to Uilleam and went back to her seat, but she had a hard time settling down to work.

Eileen reached across their table and took Sasha's hand.

"Ye hae been crying, and I did see Seumas walking away. Dae ye want tae talk aboot it?"

No, she didn't want to talk about it. And what was she going to do about it? For all she knew, Seumas would come back in a few minutes with a bunch of guards and arrest her and throw her in a dungeon — or worse.

"Nah, but would ye mind a great deal if I went back tae the house and..."

Eileen put her work down and got up and helped Sasha up and gave her a warm hug.

"Go on, then. I can dae fine here." She smiled weakly at Sasha and squeezed her hands, then let go and went back to her work.

So that was it. Sasha was free to go. And she couldn't say goodbye to Eileen, nor to Deirdre — who could still be heard outside yelling and playing with her brothers and sister.

Sasha gathered her purse and cloak, resisted the urge to look longingly at her suit there in the bucket, then made her way outside and hurried down the street before the children noticed her and asked questions. She walked toward Eileen's house at first, just in case Eileen looked out the door to watch her go. As soon as she rounded the first corner though, she headed toward Port Patrick. There were food vendors there, and she had a week's wages to spend.

She would get as far as she could today, and then she'd consult with Kelsey in her dreams tonight on how to meet up with her and Tavish — and she would tell her what happened. They had to come back here to go home — and she really wanted to get her suit back —

but they'd worry about that later. For now, she would go to Torhousekie and see if she could find Galdus's sword.

And avoid death by highlander.

Oh yeah. Her boots were not good walking boots at all. She felt every rock on every step. The only things she was carrying were a thick wool blanket and a small gunnysack of cheese and apples that she'd bought. And she was exhausted after walking only six of the nine hours to Torhousekie. She hoped she had put enough distance between her and Dunskey Castle so that she could rest for the night.

For the past half-hour she'd been looking for any sort of shelter where she might spend the night and not be attacked by wild animals. What kind of wild animals did they have in Scotland in the twelve hundreds, anyway? She didn't have a clue, but she didn't want to leave her throat bare.

At long last, she found a bush the size of a car and crawled in between its branches and lay down with her back against the trunk. It was so uncomfortable that she lay there a long time before she finally fell asleep. To alleviate the boredom, she ate another portion of her cheese and apples while waiting for sleep to take her.

IN HER DREAM, SASHA ENTERED TURNBERRY CASTLE. She could tell it wasn't a normal dream. In normal dreams, she wasn't given a tour. It was a grand place full of warm fireplaces and views of the sea cliffs, and she couldn't wait to get there.

Kelsey took one look at Sasha's face and became all concerned.

"What's wrong?"

Sasha leaned out one of the arrow slit windows to feel the impossible warm sunlight and smell the fresh sea breeze.

"Seumas came with me to see Brian, and the Druid told him all about time travel."

Kelsey was suddenly right behind. Her voice sounded concerned, but not panicky. She didn't get it.

"Isn't that good? At least you don't have a secret from him anymore."

Sasha turned around so that Kelsey would see how worried she was, how afraid, how much she needed to come join her and Tavish.

"No, he thinks I'm a sorceress — and I guess I am, right?"

Kelsey vehemently shook her head.

"No."

Sasha put her hands on her hips. Feeling foolish as soon as she did so in light of Deirdre's habit, she instead gestured back and forth between the two of them, then around in include the castle.

"Well what do you call this thing we're doing right now?"

Kelsey opened her mouth to speak, closed it, grunted, and then spoke after all.

"I don't know, but we're not practicing sorcery."

Sasha turned to pace into the next room of this luxurious upstairs castle suite.

"Well he thinks I'm a sorceress, and you should've seen him, Kelsey, talking about sorcery earlier. I just barely convinced him I wasn't a witch. And now he thinks I am, and ... I left there, Kelsey. I'm six hours east on my way to Torhousekie standing stones — because the children were playing a game about how Galdus is going to get you and Fergus says Galdus is buried at Torhousekie and then I remembered what Brian said when he saw you with the sword. He said, 'Galdus?' Remember?"

Kelsey raised her eyebrows.

"Yeah, he did say Galdus."

Sasha nodded.

"So tomorrow I'll go check it out, and after that I'm coming to stay with you guys there ..."

❧

Sasha woke up in the middle of the night, shivering with cold right through her wool blanket and needing to relieve herself. The latter was easy to take care of, the former not so much. She dug through every last compartment of her purse, hoping it was still in there. All sorts of things she would normally be happy to find gave her no joy at all: chewing gum, a favorite lipstick, breath mints... Aha. Triumphantly, she wrapped her hand around a matchbook from Jack in the Green, a cool club near campus. She left it in her purse for now.

Okay, how hard could it be to build a fire?

She looked around her surprisingly easy-to-see surroundings for firewood. When she first woke up, it had seemed pitch black, but now she could see fine under just a few stars and the moon. Who knew?

She gathered all the firewood she could find and put it in a clear area a bit away from the bush where she'd slept. Carefully, she took the matchbook out of her purse, knelt down beside the firewood, lit a match ...

And the wind blew it out.

Inspiration struck. She took the blanket and put it over her head and then lowered herself over the wood... And it was pitch black.

Oh well. She lowered the matchbook down close to the wood under the blanket out of the wind and lit a match by touch. Yay! She could see, and the match didn't blow out. She held it next to the wood... And had to let go before it burned her fingers.

Okay, she needed to light something else with the match, something that would light easily and stay lit long enough to light the wood on fire. She hated to go outside of her little blanket tent into the wind, but it felt like if she didn't get a fire lit she would freeze to death.

Ooh, there were a bunch of dry leaves all over the ground. They were only slightly damp. No damper than the wood, really. She looked gratefully over at the bush's large leaves, glad her bed had been dry.

She gathered a bunch of leaves and put them in the

middle of the circle she'd made with her wood — and finally saw some flames. Not much, though. Not enough that she felt like she had to raise up her blanket tent away from the fire.

Then she coughed.

Ugh, it was getting smoky in here.

She tried something she'd seen in a movie once and blew on the smoky leaves that were close to one of the pieces of wood. That made a satisfying flare of light, so she tried that again. At least this time the fire was staying lit and wasn't going out.

But it was getting way too smoky. She was going to have to take the blanket away and let the wind in. She felt the wind mostly coming from her left, so she moved in that direction to try and block it from getting the fire. In desperation, she held out her arms under the blanket and made sort of a wall that could block the wind from getting to her tiny smoky little fire.

Blowing on it had helped. She knelt down and kept gently blowing on the smoldering leaves near the damp wood as much as she could between breaths of smoky air.

Uh oh.

Almost all the leaves were burned up, and the wood still wasn't really burning, just smoking. She made a mad dash for more leaves, having to go pretty far away this time because she had gathered all the leaves that were close by already. She ran back with an armful of leaves, wondering how she was going to put them on the burning leaves without smothering them.

And her fire had gone out.

She fished out the matchbook and counted how many matches she had left. Thirteen. And she would have to spend at least one more night out in the open before she got to Kelsey. She needed to be smarter about this.

Using the blanket as a bag, she went far and wide, foraging all around the area for as many leaves as she could carry, then stacked most of them a few steps away from where she was making her fire.

She hadn't been too careful about gathering the leaves, and a whole bunch of small sticks were in the pile. She discovered kindling wood by accident because of this, and after that it was pretty easy to keep the fire going. The big wood even caught in one place, but it was still more smoke than fire. Maybe if she—

She sat up straight.

What was that noise?

She looked all around but didn't see anything moving.

Darn, she couldn't see outside the little ring of light from her fire. Wasn't fire supposed to keep animals away? She definitely heard a twig snap. Her heart raced, and she looked over toward the bush. It would provide some protection, unlike sitting out here with her back exposed.

She hated to leave the fire, but all of her instincts were telling her to go back into the bush. She grabbed her purse and crawled in there, suddenly gasping for breath in a panic at what was coming.

11

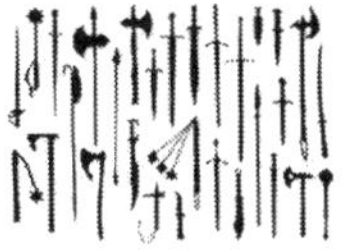

AON DEUG

The scent of smoke was getting stronger now, so he was going the right way. He hurried a little. The scent was of damp leaves burning, rather than wood. The fire couldn't be very warm, and the weather was cold this time of night. He could see his breath. Aye, he was getting quite close now. She was probably camped inside the great bush where he and Alfred had slept the summer they made their trek out here as children. It was a common campsite. Everyone knew it.

He went over the rise, and there it was, her fire — if it could be called that. But she wasn't by the fire. She was inside the bush, trembling.

His throat had become hoarse long ago from yelling out her name, and now he took a long drink from the water skin he carried before trying it again.

"Sasha, it's me, Seumas! Come oot!"

He couldn't believe his eyes. Instead of coming out,

she was crawling around to the other side of the bush. By now, he was close enough that he no longer had to yell, thank the Saints.

"Where are ye going? Ye dinna hae tae hide. 'Tis only me. Come on oot, Sasha."

It slowly dawned that it was him she feared.

His hands sank to his sides, and his lungs deflated. His anger was why she wasn't out by her fire, why she sat trembling in the bush, probably with cold as well as fear.

He approached slowly, not making any sudden moves, until he could make quick work of salvaging her fire and building it up so that it was actually warm. Once that was done and it no longer threatened to go out, he built another fire a few feet away so they might sit between the two and be warm on both sides. He sat down on the far side of the fires facing her, so that she could see him well. Then he took off all his weapons and cast them aside.

He cleared his throat, drank some more water, and tried his best to let his apology be heard in the tone of his voice.

"I ken that I went away angry. I'm sae sorry. Howsoever, never in a thousand years would I hae guessed ye'd leave the safety of oor castle town on yer own. When Eileen got home and ye weren't there, she didna worry. She figured ye and I had made peace and ye had gone oot with me. But when Alfred arrived and said he'd been with me... It was then she telt me ye had asked aboot Galdus shortly after ye and I parted. And I kenned ye had come oot here all on yer own tae seek oot Galdus's burial place for yerself. I came tae make sure ye were warm enough, and now yer hiding from my fire. Please come oot and warm yerself. I wull back away if ye like, but ye mustna get ower cauld. Ye wull catch yer death."

He got up and backed away, true to his word, and sat down again at a safe distance.

"There. Now ye can come oot with na worry."

She did crawl out then and make her way between the fires to sit down and warm herself, thank all that was holy. But she still didn't speak. She didn't even look at him, just sat between the two fires, shivering less and less.

Any moment now, she would ask him to leave. He rushed into the rest of his apology, earnest to get it out while he could — and only barely daring to hope she would accept it and agree to travel together.

"Sae glad ye are warming yerself. I've had many hours tae think, walking here alone. And the more I thought, the more I realized the ring o' truth was in yer voice when ye assured me ye were no a sorceress. Sae even though the workings o' sorcery surround ye, I dae believe ye. I mean ye na harm, I —"

At last she spoke, cutting him off.

"I believe ye as well. Now go and get yer weapons and come ower here where it's warm! Ye had me at," she imitated his voice, "'now yer hiding from my fire.'" And then she burst out laughing.

At the sound of her laughter, an overwhelming wave of relief washed over him, and he slid over to her on his bottom, so as to keep his face level with hers and eliminate any doubts that might be lingering in her mind, about whether he meant her harm. The rocks and twigs stuck to his kilt and cut into his buttocks, but he didn't care.

At last, he was by her side.

Her smile and her dancing eyes were radiant in the firelight, inviting his kiss.

His heart leapt!

Just to be sure, he moved in slowly, keeping his eyes on hers, which smiled more and more the closer he got.

And so their lips met — gently, tenderly. But they soon turned it into a wanting kiss, a promising kiss. A kiss whose fire rivaled the blazes on either side of them.

At first, he thought Sasha was giggling as she kissed him. He'd never had that effect on a woman before, but there was nothing about Sasha that didn't surprise him, so he went with it.

But then his body was close enough to hers that he should've felt it if she were giggling. And he knew it wasn't her.

With a sigh, he drew away and sat up.

"Did ye follow me here, Deirdre?"

The little girl stood across from one of the fires, leaning over and warming herself. She had a big smile on her face and a big cloak wrapped around her little body, so she seemed to be fine, but guilt racked him at not noticing she was following him before he got this far away from her mother.

Still giggling, she nodded her tiny head, bobbing her cute little blonde curls.

Seumas sighed and turned to Sasha.

"Wull, get yerself warmit up and then we can take her home. I hope ye restit enough. I havena, but I am more accustomit tae walking."

Oh no.

He knew that look. Determination was blooming inside her. This could not be good.

She lowered her forehead and raised her eyebrows.

"Yer the one she followit here, sae if anyone's takin her home, ye are. Howsoever, I'm gaun'ae Torhousekie and see aboot auld King Galdus's sword."

He raised his chin for extra authority and opened his mouth to tell her no, that it was too dangerous for her to be out alone.

But she did an odd thing and dashed her eyes over to Deirdre and back before she continued speaking. She also wrinkled her forehead at him and gave him an intense stare.

"I'm beginning tae think my grandmother was on tae something, when she telt me tae find the sword. It might be verra important, na only for me, but also for Tavish and Kelsey. I fact, I ken that tae be sae. It wouldna be..." She did that eye-dart thing over to Deirdre again, telling him she was guarding her words for the sake of not telling the wee one of her and Tavish and Kelsey's servitude to the druids. "It wouldna be healthy for us tae na find the sword. Sae I'm going, whether ye come with me or no."

He couldn't let her go alone. She would die for sure. Traits that he had thought derived from her nobility — flawless skin, filled out cheeks, bright white eyes and teeth — now made more sense to him as the traits of a person who lived in a much easier time. A time when those machines she had spoken of did all the hard physical work.

She hadn't discussed it, but he knew without a shadow of a doubt that she had never killed anything, not even for food. She had never worked at hard labor, and she certainly had never walked any great distance.

He held out his water skin to her.

"Here, ye must be thirsty."

She rolled her eyes and took it from him grudgingly, but once she had started, she drank almost all the water before she handed it back and he gave it to Deirdre, who took a sip and handed it back immediately, wrinkling her nose at how silly Sasha was. He winked at the little girl.

"Thank ye," Sasha said. And then her mouth formed a line on her face, and she looked thoughtful. "I brought food," she gestured over at the bush, "but I didna hae anything tae carry water in." She took hold of a stick that lay nearby and stirred the fire around as if it were stew.

Deirdre ran over to the bush and came back with a bag that she held open to show a few apples and a lump of cheese. She started to get out one of the apples, but he shook his head no at her. She put it back and sat down close beside Sasha, who put an arm around her and hugged her close.

He turned his water skin over and over in his hands.

"This is a cow's bladder. Howsoever, ye can use any bladder as a water skin. The kind o' animal ye can get depends upon the weapon ye have. What weapons hae ye?"

The line of her mouth deepened and her eyebrows furled again as she looked down at her waist.

"All I hae is the knife ye gave me." Inspiration must've struck her, because she raised her eyebrows and opened her mouth in a smile when she looked up at him. "But I could use it as a spearhead, couldna I?"

Heh, she wasn't entirely ignorant, but her knowledge was the kind heard around campfires and in busy pubs — or read in the pages of a rare cherished book — not the practical kind of knowledge you needed to travel on your own.

His mind whorled with the implications, trying to imagine a time when even a grown lass such as Sasha didn't know these things. He and Alfred had only been ten and twelve when the two of them traveled here on their own.

However.

He looked at Sasha's proud face.

He knew her type, albeit among men. She wouldn't listen if he tried to tell her she lacked skills. She was proud. It was one of the things he liked about her — that, and how impulsive she was. But her pride would get in the way if he tried to teach her directly. It was best to humor her.

So he nodded and gave her the closemouthed smile of someone who was impressed.

"Aye, that ye could. What wull ye use tae tie the knife ontae the long stick as a spearhead?"

She licked her lips and looked all around, as if she

would find a leather strap in one of the trees. She was adorable, and it was difficult to keep a serious face.

Her eyes finally landed on her boots, and then she looked up at him triumphantly, smiling.

"I could use one o' my shoelaces."

Ridiculous. Those laces looked to be made of some fiber that would never shrink to tighten with water the way leather would. If she were anyone else ...

But that was the point, wasn't it? She wasn't anyone else. She was Sasha the time traveler, wise in her own time and helpless in his.

But pride is a weakness that wounds deeply when pierced. No, he wouldn't do that to her. Not if he could help it. He shrugged a little, and looked around at all the materials available.

"Mayhap ye had best dae sae before we settle doon for the night, ye ken?"

On hearing him call her bluff, she bit her lip and got up, looking around rather forlornly — and adorably. She first went over to the bush and examined its long branches. She did this for quite a while, and he chuckled and sighed. This was going to be easy. Those branches were way too flexible. There would be no way to stab at your dinner.

Oh, but she tested one of them and saw this for herself. He found himself smiling, proud of her. She was a clever lass. He had never doubted that.

Deirdre scooted over toward him and curled up against his side, then whispered up at him.

"If we canna eat the apples and cheese, what can we eat? I'm sae hungry my tum is growling."

He opened the pouch that dangled at his belt, and she squealed in delight and reached in and took out some jerky and dried fruit, then munched happily.

Finally, Sasha came back to the fires and picked up the stick she'd been stirring with earlier. It wasn't so long as the bush limbs, only about the length of her leg, but it was straight and sturdy.

He nodded at her.

"Ye hae made a good choice for the shaft o' yer spear. Now let us see ye fasten the knife tae it."

She fumbled just getting her knife out of her belt, and he had to stifle a laugh by blowing his nose in his sleeve.

Deirdre had caught on to the game, and she covered her mouth to stifle her own giggles, then reached for his water skin. Once she had emptied it down her throat, she handed it back and curled up next to him between the two fires with her head resting on his leg. He undid his arisade and opened it up so that it covered both of them, and the little girl sighed and closed her eyes.

Meanwhile, Sasha had gotten the knife off her belt and was fumbling around with things in her little bag with her back turned to him. Interesting.

After a while, she turned back around again, triumphant.

"I did it. See?" She held up the spear she had made.

He reached out his hand, and she gave it to him to examine.

Much to his surprise, he had to admire her spear. The knife stayed firmly in place. It wasn't a strong enough connection to hold against deer hide, but it wasn't meant to. She could kill something small with it and have a meal.

"I hae tae admit, this is a far better spear than I imaginit ye would make. What is this material that holds the knife tae the stick sae well without having tae be shrunk on it like leather?"

Her face was glowing with his praise, making her look especially beautiful — and that was saying something, because the firelight glinting on her long red hair and the moon shimmering in her eyes were already weaving their magic on him.

She smiled, and it looked mischievous.

"I ken, it's cheating. But all's fair in love and war, aye? They are callit rubber bands. They are meant tae keep my hair up, and sae they are coverit with a layer o' silky thread. Otherwise, my hair would stick tae them and tear. They work verra well for making a spear, dinna they?"

When she looked away to swat a bug, he pulled on one of the rubber bands a bit. It sprang back to the knife with a loud snapping sound. He looked up to see if she had heard, but she was studying the spot on her wrist where the bug had been. He absentmindedly turned the spear this way and that to examine the rubber bands in the firelight.

"I dinna fancy admitting this tae ye, but I hae a strong urge tae cut these rubber bands open and see what's inside." He gave her his own sheepish smile and handed her spear back.

She laid the spear down by the rocks he had put round the fire and fished in her little bag some more. At last, she brought a tiny little thing out and handed it to him.

It was the color of snot, and about the same consistency. He could hear his mother scolding him for playing with it. That was how much it resembled the stuff. Nonetheless, he played with it for quite a while, laughing.

But when Deirdre opened her eyes for a moment, he quit and gave the rubber band back to Sasha, then stroked Deirdre's hair to encourage her to settle down again.

"Rubber. Does it come from an animal?"

Sasha gave him an understanding smile.

Which made him realize how arrogant he had been just a few moments ago, laughing at her ignorance of things he took for granted. There were just as many things she knew that he didn't — far more things, mayhap. Machines and technology. Communicating with all the world...

She was speaking.

"Nay, it comes from a tree that grows doon in the jungles near the equator."

"The equator?"

She drew with her finger in the dirt.

"An imaginit ring round the fat part o' the waurld, the warmest part — far away from here."

He laughed.

"Aye, the ships' crewmen tell stories o' lands warmer than here, saying there are far more warmer than caulder, here in Scotland. Hae ye been tae many o' them?"

She looked up at the stars, collecting her thoughts,

and he took the opportunity to admire the pleasing lines of her face, brought out by the firelight. After a moment she looked back at him and sparkled her eyes, nodding yes.

"I hae been tae a dozen o' them or more. I lived in one o' those places with my parents in my early teens."

He took her hand and guided her over on the other side of him from Deirdre, then lay down and waited for her to lie down as well.

She squeezed his hand, got up, and came back with one of Cottman Brogan's fine woolen blankets, which she wrapped around herself before lying down next to him.

"Are we gaun'ae sleep while these fires yet burn? Isna that dangerous?"

"A bit," he said. "But it would be more dangerous trying tae sleep without the fires. 'Tis quite cauld. Rest ye easy. They're doon tae coals, but the sun will be up before they go oot."

12

DÀ DHEUG

Sasha woke up cramped and uncomfortable, reaching to pull herself back up onto her bed. Must've had too much to drink last night. This always happened when she did. She couldn't reach the bed. She opened her eyes to find it — and came fully awake, gasping. Where the ...

Oh yeah.

Seumas!

Content and feeling safe now that she saw his back, she relaxed and took in the wonderful sights and scents of nature around her, covered by smoke and fire — and the aroma of roasting meat.

She swallowed. Her mouth was watering despite all the smoke from fat dripping into the fire.

When she sat up, she had to rub her eyes to believe what she saw. Seumas and Deirdre were indeed roasting meat over a fire – on her spear.

She grabbed her purse. Best to make herself

presentable before he saw that she was awake. She washed her face with a moist towelette and brushed out her hair. After she had applied the quickest version of makeup she could manage, she felt presentable. Barely.

"Couldna wait tae test my spear oot, eh Seumas? How was it?"

He gave her a goofy look that made her giggle and then walked over to offer his hand.

She let him help her up, and they embraced. It felt so good, it was making her delirious. She melted into him.

And then they heard Deirdre's giggling again.

Oh yeah. They weren't alone. Her body wasn't as willing to let go as her mind was, and their separation was slow and gradual and reluctant. Finally, though, they were only holding hands, watching Deirdre roast the meat like an expert.

The way she handled the spear really was quite amazing. It was the perfect size for her, so that it looked like it had been made for her.

And then it dawned on Sasha.

"No way."

She was so amazed, she had slipped into English by accident. Deirdre looked at her quizzically, but Seumas clearly understood what she'd said.

"Aye, the wee lass caught the rabbit, not I. She's a fine little huntress."

They had a hearty breakfast of roasted meat complemented with her apples and cheese, washed down with fresh water Seumas had walked a mile and back to fetch for them all.

The whole time, Sasha was doing her best not to feel inadequate. It was difficult, being bested by a six-year-old. No, Sasha hadn't tried and failed. That wasn't the point. Deirdre had been up at dawn and gone out and gotten them food, and Sasha had slept in.

But once the food was in her stomach and they strapped what little they had to themselves and were on their way, she gradually got over it. Walking with Deirdre and Seumas was far better than walking by herself.

Deirdre was entertaining, for one thing. She literally ran circles around Sasha and Seumas, checking out every thistle bush and oddly shaped rock until she suddenly was just too tired to walk anymore and Seumas scooped her up and carried her in his arms the rest of the way, snoring again.

They exchanged a look over the sleeping girl as they walked.

"Aye," Sasha said to him, "this is nice. It feels like we're a family."

Seumas kissed the top of Deirdre's head as he crested a hill.

"Ye took the words oot o' my mouth."

Sasha looked tenderly at Deirdre.

"Poor dear. She was up most o' the night chasing after ye, and then she was sae excited tae be underway with us this morning that she wore herself oot."

They went on in silence for a while, but it wasn't an uncomfortable silence. And for the rest of the three-hour walk, she told him about all the warm places she'd been, from Southern California to Hawaii to the Bahamas to New Mexico, Texas, Florida...

SASHA SAW THE STANDING STONES LONG BEFORE THEY reached them, of course. The sight brought on an elation so intense that she stuttered for the first time since she was a child, and immediately shut her mouth, embarrassed. It was extra awful because she was stuttering in Gaelic, so she didn't have her normal coping mechanisms to correct it — aside from closing her mouth.

"Th th th th there it is!"

Bless him, Seumas didn't show that he noticed her difficulty. He just nodded as he hoisted Deirdre into a more comfortable carrying position up over his shoulder.

Sasha ran the last hundred yards, barely noticing all the rocks she felt through her impractical boots. By the time Seumas got there, Deirdre was awake, and she ran for the last little bit to join Sasha and go exploring. Sasha pointed out every standing stone and named them for Deirdre, vaguely explaining that some old man where she was from knew a great deal about them.

And then they got to the largest standing stone, and as soon as Sasha touched it, she had another vision.

Flames springing up all around them. Streaks of lightning

scorching the earth. Laughter that she recognized but couldn't place.

When she came back to herself, Seumas had caught her once more.

She grabbed him.

"I saw this area ringed with fire and lightning. It canna hae been a natural thing, 'twas far ower weird for that. And I know it wull come tae pass. All the rest o' my visions hae. We should hurry up and find the sword and then get oot o' here."

She had the creepiest feeling she was being watched. It was raising the tiny fine hairs on the back of her neck and down her shoulders and upper arms, giving her goosebumps. She looked all around, but she couldn't see anyone. That didn't mean they weren't there.

But she had come all the way out here, so she was going to search.

Seumas searched as well.

Little Deirdre was following her all around, imitating what she was doing. Sasha wasn't sure if the wee lass was really searching, but she sure was adorable.

Sasha felt all over the rocks for places of concealment, looking carefully for runes carved into the stone like in the underground castle, telling how to open the secret doors. So far, she'd seen none of that, though. Galdus's actual grave had been dug up many times, of course. She highly doubted anything would be found in there. That would be the last place she looked.

She stood still for a moment and smiled, making herself look all around and be in the moment. She had no urge at all to take a photo. It looked the same now as it did on the Internet back in her time. But it was beautiful to her.

These rocks were so old and weather worn, yet had so obviously been placed here because of the formation they made. A clock and calendar, marking where the sun was in the sky during the day and the year. Right now it was midday, so the rocks only had tiny little shadows. The real show came at sunset and sunrise, when the sun peeked through the gaps between the standing stones.

She was reaching out to touch the second to last stone when the flames leapt up. Startled, she screamed and jumped backward into the center of the ring of stones.

Behind her, she heard Seumas scream out in pain, and she turned around to see him holding his shoulder while dodging back from the flames which had appeared around the perimeter of the stone circle.

They were trapped inside, at the mercy of whoever was causing this magical fire.

And Deirdre was nowhere to be seen.

Sasha had just started to think that fire wasn't enough to keep her in here and she could run through the flames and not get too badly burned and then roll to put the fire out if her clothes caught — when the lightning started. There was no way she would survive being hit by that.

Seumas had walked over to her and taken hold of her, probably more for their comfort than anything else. He whispered in her ear.

"Ye were on the edge o' the stone, even more ootside the ring o' stones that I was. The fire went right through ye, Sasha. Ye were no burned. I wasna in the fire as much is ye were, and look at me." He took his hand away from his shoulder for a moment and showed her where his shoulder had been burned right through his shirt. "I patted oot the flames here, and that was what made me cry oot."

She gave him a look of anguish and sympathy. It had to be excruciatingly painful to be patting flames out on top of a burn.

At long last, their attackers came near. She could hear three sets of footfalls outside the ring, and when they got close, she could sometimes see three white-robed figures through the wavering flames. They stopped only a few feet away on the other side.

And then she heard Brian the Druid's voice, and she cursed aloud.

At first, Brian was laughing. The laugh she'd heard in her vision. How had she not recognized it? The Druid's laughter was disturbing. It was the cackling normally associated with a witch, but in a male voice. It was just... Wrong.

She felt relief when at last he stopped laughing and spoke, even though he was speaking cruelly.

"Aw, Sasha. Ye hae come such a long way, all the way from a distant future. Ye left such a life o' ease and luxury. I'm verra glad ye did. And verra glad ye found love. Ah, love. A powerful, powerful force in the waurld. It is sae powerful that I will need naught else for the rest o' the year, now that I have ye. Dae ye know what I can dae with that power? Och, but ye dinna. Ye hae only the knowledge needed tae be the errand lassie for yer betters. Ye dinna ken even how tae bend time intae an instrument and have yer man use it for ye, now dae ye? Nay ye dinna."

He pointed to her ring and eyed her in a way that said she was a fool to have ever put it on, then cackled some more, and Sasha wished he would quit and start talking again.

Until she heard what he had to say.

"Ye dinna ken how much I wish I could become yer new master and keep ye tae run my own errands, lassie. Ye could make a way for me tae see the future! But ye are na suited for that. Ye are already marked for sacrifice. 'Tis such a waste, but there 'tis."

Despite her resolve, she shrank the tiniest bit at his scorn, hunching her shoulders the slightest.

It was enough. Derision poured out of the old Druid's mouth like sewer water.

"Och, and I am meant tae be locked inside the tower, ye say? Tsk, tsk, tsk. Yer friend Kelsey even knows I hae the power o' illusion, and she didna tell ye, did she? The two o' ye lasses think yer sae clever. Ha!"

Changing into the likeness of Laird Malcomb, he laughed now again, but this time it was a laugh of amusement — which was even more dreadful than his cackling laugh of mockery had been.

But right up against her ear, Seumas made a pleased sound in his chest.

At first, this puzzled her, but then she remembered Laird Malcomb was his uncle. She squeezed him tight, acknowledging his relief in realizing his uncle hadn't been displeased with him at all, that it hadn't even been his uncle they met in the marketplace. Just another of Brian the Druid's illusions.

If she hadn't been holding Seumas, she would've put her hands over her ears. Even though she was holding him, she was still tempted. Instead, she rested her head against his chest so that at least one of her ears was covered.

He must've read her mind, because he covered her other ear with the hand that wasn't holding his shoulder. She squeezed him tight again, this time in gratitude, and he caressed her cheek with his thumb.

Their mutual comforting made Brian laugh all the harder. He laughed so loud, she could swear it was echoing off the nearby mountains. And then he spoke some more, and this time she was wishing he would laugh and quit talking. She could hear him through her covered ears, but it wasn't nearly as unpleasant.

"Ha, I hae na hatred for ye, Sasha, only envy. I'm old and wise, and I can admit tae envy. It willna save ye, this realization that I dinna hate ye, but mayhap it wull be a small comfort tae ye, tae ken that yer dying now from hatred, but from greed. Aw, only greed. I want that power ye hae inside ye, the power o' creation that ye carry. I can use that power —"

He grunted. One of the other Druids must have nudged him.

He grumbled something and then went on.

"Verra wull, we can use yer power. Howsoever, it canna be harvested this day, ye ken. The moon must be at its fullest, in order for us tae take yer power. And that willna happen for a few days yet. Sae ye must stay here until then. And it would be a waste tae feed ye. Anyhow, hardship will make yer love blossom intae a greater flower than it is even now — creating all the more power for us tae harvest."

He gave his delighted laugh now, and she was starting to understand that each time he laughed, it would be even more horrible than the last time.

Well, she wasn't going to go down without a fight — or at least a negotiation. Knowing others were here who felt sure of themselves enough to nudge him gave her a little bit of confidence. It was to them she addressed herself.

"Whosoever has come here with Brian, I now speak tae ye." Remembering what Kelsey had told her, she showed them her ring. "I am one of ye."

But they all three cackled now. Aside from the fact that they were all men, it sounded just like the three witches laughing in that Shakespearean play Kelsey had dragged her to last year. And then wonder of wonders, all three were just gone, and their laughter finished echoing off the mountains and then was quiet.

If she hesitated, she would lose her nerve. After looking all around one last time for Deirdre and not finding her anywhere inside the circle of fire, Sasha grabbed Seumas's hand with her hand that had the Celtic University ring on it.

"Ye said it didna burn me. My ring is why. 'Tis touching ye now. Let's go, before they come back. This place has extra power for them. They willna be able tae keep us sae easily if we leave here."

He squeezed her hand.

"What ye say has merit. Aye, let us go."

"If ye catch on fire, duck tae the ground and roll until it goes oot. Ready?"

"Aye."

"Go!"

They took off running through the flames.

And they didn't get burned.

They kept on running, making for the cover of some nearby trees. Once they were inside the tree line, they stopped and panted for breath.

Sasha made a point of letting go of Seumas's hand.

"What aboot Deirdre?"

He looked all around.

"Wull, one thing is for certain. If they come back and catch us, then we canna help her. Sae we need tae head for home and hope that she is doing the same. We canna take the time tae look for her. For all we ken, she is..."

Tears sprang from Sasha's eyes, but she fought them back. Brushing one away with the back of her hand, she nodded.

"Let's go."

They ran deeper into the forest. The branches of all the trees hit her in the face as she ran by, but she paid them no mind. This was a different way than they had come, so she was unfamiliar with the terrain. Getting scratched up was a price to pay. Still, it seemed like a good idea to stay in the trees, to reduce the chance of their being found when the Druids came back.

Even uphill, they ran.

She stumbled over a rock and lost her balance. Felt herself falling and nearly fainted from embarrassment. But Seumas grabbed her arm and caught her before she even missed a step.

They got to the top of the hill and were relieved to be going down.

But there the three Druids were in front of them, waiting in dramatic poses. No sooner had they seen the three than the three all made gestures in their poses. It didn't make sense. They were sworn to capture and sacrifice them, not entertain them with pantomimes.

Sasha let out a 'What the heck?' chuckle, and she and Seumas shrugged at each other.

Until the trees around her and Seumas began to move.

The branches and roots moved toward her like the limbs of animals, and almost as fast. The wood crackled and popped, adding to the horror.

Sasha yanked Seumas around to run back the way they had come, but the tree roots and branches closed them in on all sides. The two of them were inside a cage the size of a small bedroom, made of living trees. The branches and leaves were so dense that the sunlight barely came in, and even now, at midday, it was almost dark inside.

Brian was laughing again, his mocking cackle. He gave them a very serious face, which she could only see in bits and pieces through the leaves.

"Sae clever ye fancy yerself, with that ring given tae ye by yer masters. Now ye wull be cauld and trapped, while ye await yer deaths."

He cackled some more, and then the three disappeared again.

Sasha sank down to the grassy ground.

"Now I dinna ken how we're gaun'ae escape."

Seumas took his sword off his back and started hacking at the nearest tree.

"I dae."

He hacked and hacked at it.

"What can I dae tae help?"

He smiled at her between swings.

"Juist stay back and give me plenty o' room. Och, aye, there is aught ye can dae. Play some music on yer flute tae give me a tune tae chop tae."

They laughed, and she did get her flute out. She had mostly played the flute when she was a child, so all the songs she knew were silly. But one came to mind that seemed appropriate: 'Whistle While You Work.' She played it a couple times and then laughed, saying the words to him.

It was wonderful watching him work, and even more so when he laughed. His laughter made his long red hair bounce and shake along with his kilt, which shuddered every time his sword hit the tree.

And then she sobered up a little.

"Won't this damage your sword?"

He laughed some more.

"That is naught tae fash aboot now, lass. Once we get home, I can hae another sword. Look." He pointed at the tree where he'd been cutting, and she bent down to look. "Once this comes free, it wull likely fall toward us, sae stand ower there."

He gestured, and she went.

But it didn't happen that way.

Instead of falling once he cut through it, the branch reattached itself and was as whole as if he'd never chopped into it at all.

Seumas sighed and sat down on the ground, leaning against the tree he'd just been chopping.

Sasha half expected the tree's branches to reach out and throttle him for trying to do it harm, but it remained still. She joined him on the ground, and he put his arm around her and leaned her against him — and then gasped when her head touched his shoulder.

She sprang away.

"Oh! Your shoulder."

She looked down at him — and recognized the sight from the vision she'd had when she first met him. There he was, lying there stoically resisting the pain. Her tears came now, and she didn't try to stop them

"I wish I had some ice to put on you."

He reached up his hand, and when she took it, he pulled her down beside him on his other side.

"I wull rest a bit, and then we wull dig oor way oot."

They spent the rest of the day trying to get out. When they dug, the roots of the trees moved into their way. When they climbed, the trees bent over so that there was a roof, impenetrable. They built a fire out of what scrap wood lay on the ground inside their cage and tried to burn the trees, but they expanded the cage out of the fire's reach until there was no more scrap wood to burn. They had a close call when Sasha tried to break off a branch to burn and the tree reached out with its other branches and pushed her away.

Nothing worked. Nothing had so far, anyway. Ever optimistic, they kept trying until after the sun went down. And then the cold came, and the only way they could escape that was to curl up together under her blanket and his arisade.

❧

KELSEY ROLLED HER EYES ONCE SASHA JOINED HER IN the dream.

"I've seen many cool swords here, but none of them are the one —"

Sasha grabbed her friend.

"Brian the Druid has me and Seumas trapped in a cage made of trees. We've tried and tried to get out ... and we don't know where Deirdre is. And they're going to sacrifice us, Kelsey, when the full moon comes in three days. This is where we are in relation to Torhouse-kie. Alfred knows how to get here."

Sasha Drew Kelsey a mind picture of their location as if she were zooming in on Google earth.

Kelsey hugged her.

"But how? Brian is locked up in the tower."

"No, he isn't. That's just an illusion."

"I'll go into Alfred's dream and tell him Brian has escaped and that Alfred needs to bring a dozen guards and rescue you, Sasha. Hang on."

13

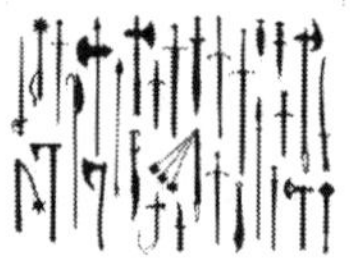

TRÌ DEUG

Seumas hadn't meant to sleep. He cursed himself when he awoke in the morning, the very early light of the morning. Carefully so as not to disturb Sasha's rest, he separated from her and crawled out from under their blankets to take a quick piss between the trees on the opposite side of their cage. He was crouching down to get back under the blanket when he heard something crashing through the forest.

He picked up his sword as quietly as he could and then stood guard over Sasha, whispering down to her while he tapped her with his booted toe.

"Sasha. Sasha, something is coming, wake up."

When she started to speak, he whispered again.

"Weesht. Something is coming."

It was probably an animal that was coming. It was too small to be a man. It was coming from the direction of Torhousekie, the direction they'd come from.

Seumas planted himself firmly between its approach and Sasha.

"Hopefully," he whispered, "the trees wull keep whatever that is oot just as they keep us in. Pray for that, will ye Sasha? I wull dae the best I can tae keep it away from ye, but just in case it gets through and we both die, I need tae tell ye something."

"Me tae," she said "there's no one I would rather spend my last few moments with than ye, Seumas. Thank ye for standing in the way and taking the attack. Most o' the men o' my time would hide behind me and hope that the animal ate me up and was full afore it got tae them."

He laughed at that, a belly laugh that was far too loud for the quiet he was aiming for. Bah, the animal could smell them anyway, what was the use of being quiet? She was so funny.

"I ken ye think I'm jesting. I wish I were. 'Tis the reality where I come from. In many ways things are better. There are more opportunities for a lass — but there's a sore lack of real men. I'm glad I knew ye Seumas."

He lowered his sword a bit though.

"An animal would hae been here by now. Animals are fast. It's taking sae long that I begin to hope..."

"Hope for what?"

"Deirdre!" he yelled. "Deirdre! We are ower here, Deirdre. Come tae the sound o' my voice." He kept calling out over and over again until sure enough, there she was — a ragged bleary-eyed little girl shivering with the cold — and holding out a strange large dagger.

"He wants tae free ye," she said. "He told me tae wait until the night had passed, because it wasna safe tae be oot by myself at night, but 'tis morning now, sae here I am." She started to pass the dagger to them through the branches.

And then the weirdest thing of all happened.

The branches moved again, but this time they were moving away from the strange dagger. In no time at all, the trees had withdrawn around the dagger to make an opening through the wall of the cage, big enough for the two of them to get out.

Seumas wasted no time in grabbing Sasha's hand and pulling her up and out through the opening. She tried to reach back and grab the blanket, but he pulled her through.

"I wull buy ye ten blankets once we make it back home. If we dinna stop verra often, we can be there by supper."

He then picked Deirdre up and hugged her to him, both to thank her and to warm her up. He himself was still pretty warm from cuddling with Sasha all night. The thought of that warmed him even more, and he had to stifle the memories, lest he become distracted and useless.

They were going west toward home through a thick forest, and it was rocky and dangerous, with branches sticking out everywhere.

He stopped and put Deirdre down, sighing and looking to the north.

"We wull need tae go back oot intae the open sae we can make better time."

Sasha followed his gaze.

"Willna they see us?"

"Mayhap, but we wull make terrible time here in the trees. Far better tae hae a chance tae make it back tae safety before nightfall. We have na chance o' that if we stay in the trees."

"Verra well."

She turned to the north with him, plainly dejected and afraid.

But Deirdre called out to them, now several paces to the west.

"He says we should go this way. He makes the trees move, ye ken."

Sasha looked just as mystified by this as he felt, but he took her hand and led her after the wee lass.

Sure enough, wherever Deirdre held out the dagger, the trees parted. Even their roots moved aside so he and Sasha and Deirdre wouldn't trip. What's more, the roots dragged all the stones and twigs with them, making the path even safer than a road to tread.

With the tree limbs drawing away into a tunnel in front of them, they walked all the way through the forest. And they kept going, on and on and on over hill and dale. Whenever there was a stream, they stopped for water. Whenever Sasha had to catch her breath — which was often — they stopped for a moment and put their hands on their knees. But mostly, they walked.

The excitement wore off for Deirdre after the first few miles. After that, it was just determination that kept her going. But she clearly hadn't slept and was drooping.

Seumas scooped Deirdre up and carried her, and soon she was snoring. The little girl wasn't very heavy. She barely caused him any pause.

After a few hours, Sasha was the one drooping — not from lack of sleep, but from pain in her muscles. She tried to explain it to him, but he already understood that life just wasn't very active in the time she came from.

"I am sae sorry I hae tae keep stopping tae stretch," she said between grunts at the pain. "Ye would think I'd be better at walking. My legs are sae long, everyone's always teasing me aboot how I should be a runner. I play tennis every weekend, and I go for a walk every day during my lunchtime. I thought those were long walks until I came here." She laughed her nervous laugh.

Cradling Deirdre with one arm, he put his finger to Sasha's lips.

"Weesht. I ken ye are trying yer hardest, and that is all ye can dae."

He started them walking again, reminding himself every few steps to slow down for her.

"I am sae grateful for yer spirit of adventure, Sasha. 'Twas different when we were children, but now that we're all grown, all the lasses here would rather stay inside the safety of the toon that venture oot this way."

What he didn't say was that he never in his wildest dreams thought he would find a companion for adventure who might also be a wife.

And there it was.

Was he thinking about marrying this woman he had just met not a seven-day ago?

Aye.

But that was foolishness.

She would go back to her time, and he was doubtless unsuited for her world. There was far too much he would be expected to know there. Fear loomed just on the edge of his thoughts. He didn't want to admit it, but the prospect of going eight hundred years into the future terrified him. He was a man. He needed to stay where he felt strong and knowledgeable.

And he would not ask her to stay here in this time with him. No. She was too soft. He was a guard who had to leave with ships and be on patrol in the caverns. He couldn't always be with her to watch over her. And no one else would understand why she needed watching over.

He chuckled a bit.

"What's sae funny?"

"Tavish's story about this being yer first time ever away from home and how it meant ye needed looking after."

She laughed her embarrassed laugh.

"Sorry about that wee white lie. Now ye ken why we had tae tell it, aye?"

He waited for her to get the jest, but she seemed not to.

"But it wasna a lie, ye ken? Ye havena ever been sae far from home — even with gang tae Florida and Hawaii and the other warm places ye spoke aboot."

There it was, her beautiful smile.

"Ye hae the right of it."

Talking on top of the unaccustomed walk was a strain for her, though, so he kept quiet awhile.

Now that they walked on easy open grasses, he held Deirdre in one arm and Sasha's hand with the other, letting himself daydream for a moment about what it would be like to go with her to her time and travel to those warm places. He let himself imagine warm sandy beaches and ocean water that wasn't so cold it hurt to swim. She had said that in Hawaii the waves rolled in and you could ride them on boards. That sounded such a marvel.

But look at her. A simple walk home — and she was not going to make it. She was limping. Her feet must be bruised because of her beautiful but thinly soled boots.

He stopped at the top of a small grassy hill where it was dry and he would see anyone coming.

"Let us take a longish rest, aye? Have us a little meal."

Sasha closed her eyes and moaned in pleasure as she collapsed onto the grass and lay down.

He set Deirdre down, and the wee lass hugged him. He hugged her back and then dug out the rest of his jerky and raisins. There were two handfuls each, washed down with the rest of the water in his skin. He wanted to be on their way again, but he saw that Sasha still needed rest.

"Deirdre, could ye keep up with me for a while?"

The lassie nodded

"Aye, if ye need tae carry Sasha."

Sasha's jaw dropped open and she looked at both of them with a wrinkled brow.

"That's ridiculous. I can walk, I just need tae rest a—"

He scooped her up and threw her over his shoulder. She weighed twice as much as Deirdre, but the weight was distributed evenly. And the feel of her against his shoulder — his uninjured shoulder — gave him a rush of energy so joyful that he wondered why he hadn't done this earlier.

They made better time this way, with him carrying Sasha and Deirdre walk-running alongside him. Both lasses had great attitudes. He couldn't ask for better traveling companions.

Unlike Sasha, Deirdre talked almost non-stop while she walked.

"Sorry I slept sae long while ye carried me, but I didna sleep at all before this. I was tae busy listening tae the dagger tell me all the things he wantit me tae dae. He talkit tae me all night long, blethering aboot all sorts o' things." She patted the dagger, which she had secured through her belt expertly, much to Sasha's chagrin.

AT LONG LAST, UNCLE'S CASTLE WAS IN SIGHT.

He put Sasha down, and the three of them hurried the rest of the way home, holding hands.

Howsoever, just as they reached the castle walls, it was as if the fires of Hell sprouted up from underground.

Seumas held fast to Deirdre's and Sasha's hands and pulled them out of the middle of the fires before a ring could form around the three of them. At the same time, he hollered out to the guards on watch, whose backs he could see in a huddle, likely lighting their pipes, the fools.

"Rob, Pòl, Warrick! 'Tis Seumas. The castle is under attack, ye ken!"

To the men's credit, they moved quickly. One sounded the horn, which would bring the archers. The other two manned the gate. But if Seumas headed that way, the Druids would get inside along with the three of them.

He sighed. If he didn't have lasses with him —

But the decision was taken from him.

One of the flames transformed and became a wild boar — and opened its snarling maw and charged at Sasha.

Seumas dropped Sasha's hand and charged straight at the boar, pulling his sword from his back as he did so.

"Sasha! Run tae the gate!"

14

CEITHIR DEUG

Deirdre fought her way free of Sasha's hand so she could turn around and run back toward the trees.

"He wull protect us if we go back tae the trees, Sasha. Come with me!"

As she ran for the trees, she turned her head over her shoulder.

With her face all twisted up in anger — or fear, mayhap both — Sasha was coming. And yelling.

"Come back here! We hae tae get inside! Come back here this instant!"

Deirdre shook her head no and turned back around to watch where she was going as she ran for the trees.

Galdus was constantly talking in her head. The way he said his words was odd — like the old folks, but even more so. It was funny. And at the same time, he was sure he knew what she should do. There was no anger nor any fear in his voice. She found his presence reassuring.

"Aye, aye, tae the trees with us, lass. Tae the trees. I can keep ye safe in the trees, ye ken. Almost there. Almost there. Good lass. Good lass."

When he was happy like this — when she was doing what he wanted — he hummed and sang to her a song she had never heard before, almost whistling rather than singing. It was catchy but odd, like everything about him.

Little did ma mother think
When ere she cradled me
What lands I was tae travel through
What death I was tae see.

At last, she was in the trees.

"Go round one o' the trees, lass. Put the trees tween ye and yer pursuers sae I hae some aught tae work with, ye ken?"

She did as he said, anxiously looking out to see what was happening with the battle and cringing to see Seumas wrestling with the boar. Oh good, Sasha was still coming.

Deirdre cupped her hands around her mouth in order to be heard over the roaring flames and all the yelling.

"Sasha! Hurry up! Get tae the trees and he can protect us, remember?"

But Sasha was still using up all her anger at Deirdre.

"Lassie, I'm gaun'ae —"

Deirdre gasped.

More of the flames had turned into boars, and two of the beasts were running after Sasha. They were getting close to her.

Deirdre screamed.

“Faster, Sasha! Run!"

At the sound of Deirdre’s screaming, Sasha did start running.

Deirdre tried to send her energy to Sasha, to make her run faster. She couldn’t help but jump up and down, she was so anguished.

Galdus laughed. He found the oddest things funny.

“Nay matter how much ye jump aroond, ye willna hasten her.”

But Deirdre loved Sasha more than she loved Galdus, so she ignored him this one time. She kept calling out to her new friend — who hopefully would soon be her auntie, if Seumas and Alfred had any sense in them.

"Faster! Run faster, Sasha!"

Galdus spoke with calm certainty.

“She isna gaun'ae make it.”

The boars were almost close enough to pounce on Sasha. They would tear her limb from limb.

Deirdre burst into tears and wailed, frantically waving the strange dagger at the boars and calling him by name, wishing and never doubting he had the power to fulfill her wish.

“Make them stop, Galdus!”

She sighed with relief.

The small bushes the boars passed over reached up

their meager little branches and stabbed into the monsters, making the boards bloody and tearing at them until they collapsed just behind were Sasha's foot had been only a moment before.

Still oblivious, Sasha ran up to Deirdre. At first her face was still angry, but it softened, probably on seeing her tears.

The relief Deirdre felt on seeing her friend still alive and having escaped those ravenous beasts was so great that she dropped all the decorum she'd been striving to have since Maw had first tasked her with watching her little sister. She wrapped her arms as tight as she could around Sasha's long skirts, clutching Galdus with both hands behind Sasha as she shook with sobs.

Sasha's arms went around Deirdre's shoulders, and her hands caressed Deirdre's hair.

"Aye, 'tis all right now. I'm here. But ye should hae come when I called ye. Grown-ups give ye orders for a reason, not just tae be bossy, ye ken? Now let us go back and get inside the castle where it's safe, and —"

All of a sudden, that terrible Brian the Druid was choking Sasha with one arm around her throat and the other over her mouth. He put his own mouth up against her neck.

"Ye need tae come along quiet like, if ye want yer death tae be painless. I canna make it quick, but I can give ye something for the pain. I dinna hae tae dae that, ye ken..."

While the nutty old Druid blethered on about his evil plans, Galdus's odd speech came into Dierdre's mind again.

"Well, what are ye waiting for? Stab me intae the man afore he notices ye. Go on." He showed her a mind picture of how to grip him so that her stab would be the most effective. "Now dae it. Ye must dae it now. In only a few moments, he wull notice ye. And he doesna need ye, ye ken? Sae go on. Ye must dae it NOW."

Just as he had shown her in the picture in her mind, she turned him so that he was facing Brian's side – and then plunged him in.

Sasha fell down on the ground, holding her throat and gasping, her pretty and normally pale face red and full of tears and her eyes wide. But she was alive. Still alive.

Deirdre knelt and put Sasha's head in her lap, stroking her pretty long red hair.

"Weesht. Weesht. 'Tis ower now. The danger's gone. Ye dinna hae tae be afraid anymore. I'm sorry he hurt ye, but ye should hae come when I called ye. Ye barely escaped the boars that were running after ye, see?"

She pointed to where the boars lay in puddles of their own blood, the snapped ends of twigs still sticking out of them.

Sasha sat up, a look of panic on her face, looking all around every which way.

"We hae tae get back tae the castle, Deirdre. Ye scared Brian off, but he wull come back." She grabbed Deirdre's hand and pulled her up, then started running toward the gate.

Deirdre ran with her, but she gave her reassurance.

"Dinna fash, Sasha. I stabbed him with Galdus," she held up the bloodied dagger for Sasha to see, "and he turned tae powder. His friends saw it happen and disappeared. I dinna think they wull be back. Not for a long time, anyhow."

Galdus laughed at her jest, even if Sasha didn't.

TWO THINGS HAPPENED AT ONCE AFTER THEY ALL made it through the gate and closed it tightly behind them. Sasha and Seumas embraced and had one of their sticky gooey kisses. And Maw found Deirdre.

Even as she hugged her and stroked her hair, Maw scolded.

"Ye evil, wicked child! I hae been sick with fashing ower ye. Dinna ever go and leave again. Na withoot telling me. Ye had the whole toon looking aboot for ye. Mayhap I wull take the strap tae ye when we get home—"

But Sasha came forward.

"I beg of ye, Eileen, dinna strap the lass. She saved my life, ye ken."

NOW DEIRDRE WAS INVITED TO HER FIRST GROWN-UP feast ever.

She twirled in the new dress Maw had made for her in the time it had taken for Alfred and the guards and Tavish and Kelsey to all return home — one full day, exactly. Everyone else was already at the feasting hall, and she was dizzy with how excited she felt.

"I love it! Thank ye sae much — for the dress and for letting me go tae the feast." She looked over where Galdus lay in the corner next to her old belt. "I wull be sae good, ye willna hae tae worry aboot me at all. I wull be just another one of the grown-ups sitting at the table with ye, I promise."

Maw smiled at her and held her hands as she knelt in front of her and then gave her a big hug.

"I ken ye wull, my sweet lassie. Ye are getting older on me faster than I can keep up with ye. I'm sae verra proud o' ye. Ye were sae brave, watching oot for Sasha's life like that. I ken Seumas is grateful tae ye as well."

Deirdre looked at Galdus some more over Maw's shoulder as they hugged again. Finally, Maw went to go fetch something she needed to bring along to the castle for the feast, and Deirdre rushed over and put on her belt and tucked Galdus neatly into it.

Now that she had him for a friend, she never wanted to be without him. She could tell she would soon love him more than anyone else.

When they arrived in the grand hall, it was just like she always imagined it would be, attending one of the big feasts for the grown-ups. Everyone was laughing and toasting and telling stories of the battle that day. At the nearest table, Rob, Pòl, and Warwick all boasted of the number of boars they had shot with their arrows. Cormac and Osgar were sour-faced at having been out with Alfred and missed the whole thing.

Her mother's friends all had their own table: Alfred, Seumas, Tavish, Kelsey, Sasha, her, and her mother. Smiles went all around the table.

Seumas looked at her very seriously and bowed his head in her direction over the table.

"I canna tell ye often enough how verra grateful I am that ye saved Sasha's life. I shall be forever in yer debt, Deirdre."

This was a little bit too much for her, and she giggled despite her attempt to put on her hard-earned decorum. Standing up so that she could reach across the table, she put her hand on Seumas's hand.

"I ken ye love Sasha. Howsoever, I love her tae. I didna save her for yer sake, but for my own. I willna accept yer service. Instead, just be my friend — and hopefully my uncle." She looked over at Alfred and giggled some more before she sat down.

Alfred smiled and nodded at her once then turned to Maw and took her hand and kissed it, and the two of them cuddled a bit in their chairs next to each other. Good. He wasn't uncomfortable with the suggestion that his brother would be her uncle. She grinned in satisfaction, knowing her mother would be happy.

Seumas stood then and extended his hand to Sasha.

"Will ye join me in the dance?"

Sasha jumped up eagerly, wiping her mouth with a cloth.

"Aye!"

The two of them walked away together hand in

hand, smiling. This made Deirdre smile too, knowing Sasha would be happy.

Simultaneously, Kelsey and Tavish jumped up and stood pointing at Deirdre, or more precisely, at Galdus.

Tavish spoke first.

"There it is. That is the sword we hae been looking for."

"Yer right. Robert the Bruce's sword was a wild goose chase. This is the one we need. It was sae close along."

Tavish came around the table and reached down toward Deirdre's lap to take Galdus away from her.

She couldn't let them take her friend!

Feeling the tears come springing from her eyes, Deirdre held on to him tightly.

"Nay! Nay nay nay! He's my friend. He talks tae me, and I'm keeping him! I found him! Ye canna make me give him away!"

But Maw took Deirdre by the arms and pulled her hands free from Galdus.

"I canna believe my eyes and ears, lass. How childish yer acting at yer foremaist adult feast. Now be quiet and let Tavish take the sword he's been searching for all this time. If ye must hae a sword, Alfred will get ye one from the practice yard."

Deirdre tried to hold on to Galdus, but Maw was stronger. She yanked him out of her belt and hands, and gave him to Tavish, who put him in his own belt. He didn't even look happy to have her friend, just determined.

Deirdre wailed.

"If he doesna even want Galdus, why should he hae him?"

Meanwhile, Isabel — Alfred and Seumas's mother — came over, smiling her sad smile.

"Deirdre, dear." She reached out her hand. "Come on. Come on up tae the nursery. Ye and me and Aodh, Niall, and Sìle wull hae more fun up there together than ye could hae doon here with the grown-ups anyhow, with all their boring talk." She smiled gently.

Deirdre wanted to be nice to the lady who had always been nice to her, so she stood up and wiped her eyes and took the lady's hand.

But she wouldn't look back at her maw, who had betrayed her.

❧ 15 ❧

CÒIG DEUG

Smiling at the people they passed by, Sasha squeezed Seumas's elbow and spoke in the lowest voice she could manage out of the side of her mouth, confident that she wouldn't be overheard in the noisy great hall full of music and dancing and revelry.

"The laird was anything but friendly tae me when we met in the marketplace. Are ye sure this is a good idea?"

He gave her a surprised look.

"That wasna my uncle ye met in the marketplace. That was Brian the Druid under illusion tae look like my uncle."

That was great news if true, but she was skeptical.

"I suppose ye ken yer uncle," was all she said.

But he nodded firmly.

"Aye, that I dae. I'm sore at myself for letting that Druid's illusion fool me."

They were almost to the dance set now, and Sasha

steeled herself. She was still shaken from the battle, and she didn't know if her psyche could take anymore battering, especially the kind the laird had given her at their first meeting.

They went around the last few people in the dance set and joined in, taking the hands of the people to their right and left — as well as taking each other's hand to complete the circle.

Seumas's hand felt warm in hers, and so reassuring. She relaxed into his touch.

And there was Laird Malcomb, directly opposite them in the set — and smiling at them jovially.

"Long time, Nephew, long time! And who is this vision of loveliness?"

Seumas gave her a knowing look and then turned back to his uncle, holding her hand up — a bit possessively, even though his uncle was dancing with a woman clearly his wife, by the way she looked at him — also possessively.

Seumas's voice was proud.

"This is Tavish's kinswoman Sasha. Sasha, meet my uncle, the one and only Laird Malcomb."

It happened to be the part of the dance where they all bowed to each other, and Sasha smiled and bowed at Laird Malcomb ironically in the course of the dance.

He returned her smile, and then they had a lively ten minutes of jumping and skipping and clapping and spinning and twirling each other by arms.

Seumas was a great dance partner. He led her with a sure hand, and she always had an indication what they would do before it came. Dancing with him was great fun, let alone dancing with a bunch of people who were all skirted — half in kilts. She had a grand old time smiling and making friends with everyone, and they all seemed happy to meet her.

When the music stopped, they smiled and bowed at everyone and moved on to the next dance set that was forming, with new people.

The musicians started playing again, a faster tune. It was still a set dance — all of them were — but this one involved lots of standing around next to each other and clapping while only one pair of dancers was active at a time.

Seumas took the opportunity to start a conversation that wouldn't be overheard, clever fellow that he was.

"Wull now that Tavish and Kelsey hae the item they came tae get, they will be going back tae yer home. And they will be taking ye with them. I sense this will be soon. And Sasha, if they take ye with them, I will lose ye forever. Nay one has telt me this, but I feel it here in my heart. Dinna go with them. Bide here with me and be my wife and an auntie tae Deirdre, Aodh, Niall, and Sìle. Be the maw o' my many bairns and yers, who will be their cousins. I am begging ye tae bide with me and share my life. I love ye, Sasha."

She had to say one thing before any time went past at all, lest there be any misunderstanding.

"I love ye too, Seumas."

Right there on the dance floor, he held her to him in a tight embrace that was not at all clinging. It was more... Triumphant.

But she had to clear up the misunderstanding she'd caused after all.

"I canna bide here with ye though, Seumas."

He froze for a moment, and then still holding her hand, he turned and walked with her through the halls of the castle in silence until they were out in the courtyard with the moonlight glinting off the practice swords in their bins, quite alone together. There, he turned to face her and took both of her hands in his, gazing intently into her eyes with yearning.

"Sasha, if we love each other, then we should be together. Marry me. Please. Make me the happiest man —"

The yearning in his eyes was so strong, she had to stop his pleading, had to make him understand before he went too far and felt the fool. Experience told her men didn't take well to that, feeling like a fool. And he was too magnificent of a man to feel that way. The sight of him made her nearly drunk, the way the shadows of his muscles flexed in the torchlight whenever he moved the slightest.

She stepped up to him and put a finger over his mouth gently, at last quieting him.

"Seumas, come with me instead. Ye said it yerself, there's naught for ye tae dae here. Howsoever, ye will be verra knowledgeable about this place in my time, more knowledgeable than anyone else on the site. Ye are an expert in this site, and in my time, that can be turned intae a livelihood — a good livelihood, better than ye can imagine. I promise. Please, let's go back tae my time together."

She watched his face, hoping against all hope that he would agree. She could see the fear in his eyes, the fear of the unknown. It ate at her, but what else could she do? Her own knowledge was wasted here. No, he had to come to her time. That was the best use of both of their knowledge.

But oh, how wonderful it had been to be here for a short time. She looked all around her at the courtyard and imagined everything she had seen stretching out for miles and smiled to herself.

And then she remembered that he hadn't said aye yet, that he would come. Her heart grew anxious, and she looked up again into his eyes with the same beseeching look that he had used on her, bless the man.

He grabbed her in his embrace roughly, taking charge once more, which made her smile — but she kept the smile to herself, hiding it by putting her head on his shoulder and putting her arms around his neck and drawing his head down for a long kiss.

The kiss was all-consuming, and it lasted much longer than she'd intended. But it might be their last kiss, and so she lived in it. She threw everything she had into it, throwing caution to the wind and even pressing the rest of her body against his in blind uninhibited passion.

This is a bit too much for his sensibilities, and he drew away from her, albeit reluctantly.

She swallowed. Was this it? Slowly, she dared to look back up in his eyes again.

They were soft and tender, and her heart leapt with hope.

When he spoke, it was resignedly, but also determined.

"I will come with ye. I dinna want tae live withoot ye, Sasha. When will we go?"

She hugged him in glee, and he hugged her back, tentatively at first, and then with strength, reclaiming her as his own. Again, she hid her smile.

"We're leaving in the morning, first thing."

"How will we go?"

"We go intae that one corridor in the underground castle, and there, Tavish can use his ring tae take us back tae my time."

He nodded.

"I did hae my suspicions about that place, but whenever I thought about it, my thoughts were redirected somewhere else. A bit o' the sorcery that protects the place, aye?"

Was he testing her? She looked into his eyes and asked him that question with her own.

Seeing only acceptance there — well, acceptance, a bitter reservation, and a huge amount of resolve along with love for her — she continued on. She'd told him this much. She might as well finish. If he was to be coming along with her, he needed to know, after all.

"Aye, it probably is sorcery. But 'tis na Tavish's nor mine nor Kelsey's. The magic belongs tae the Druids who run the institution where Kelsey and I studied. They've enslaved Tavish's family for generations, mayhap the verra same way Brian said he wished he could enslave me. They send him back in time tae collect artifacts, and this last time 'twas that sword Deirdre found and calls Galdus."

He nodded, and then he looked at her with concern.

"But we canna just go in there after we tell everyone goodbye. We need tae go north toward yer clan's land — either by foot or by ship."

This time it was her turn to nod.

"Aye, that's what we're gaun'ae dae. And then we'll sneak doon tae the corridor and go back tae my time."

He pulled back from their embrace so that he could see her face and she could see his smile.

"Tavish and I did some aught a few years ago which might make that a little easier than ye would think."

And with those cryptic words, he swung her around so they were walking together back into the great hall. This time, his arm was around her shoulders, and he was holding her close to him. Yes it was a possessive hold, but she also felt such warmth from him that it radiated through her whole body, making her a bit dizzy.

As soon as they stepped over the threshold of the great hall, he raised his voice to be heard above the musicians and all the chatter.

"Sasha and I are to be married!"

Everyone took up their tankards and raised them in the air, shouting a cheer.

"Huzzah!"

Seumas waited for the cheers to die down.

"We will be going with Tavish and Kelsey in the morning, back tae their clan's land tae start oor new life together. And sae this is goodbye this evening, but dinna make it a sad one, for I am a verra happy man indeed."

And with that, he shocked Sasha by turning and kissing her soundly in front of everyone.

The hall erupted in cheers again, and everyone came to shake their hands, even Laird Malcomb. He seemed a bit flustered and about to say something a few times before just giving them a smile and hugging both of them together.

"Wull, may ye both be verra happy. I ken ye wull live long lives and be verra good tae each other and hae many many bairns." With that last line he laughed, and everyone else laughed with him.

SASHA DIDN'T GET THE CHANCE TO SPEAK PRIVATELY with Kelsey until that night in their dreams, but then they had plenty of time. After a lot of laughing and congratulations and 'I told you so's, finally Kelsey got serious.

"Yes, it's so much safer back in our time. Can you imagine childbirth in this time? And Sasha, you want kids. It's so obvious."

EILEEN HELD OUT SASHA'S SUIT, AND SHE GINGERLY accepted it. Determined to keep a calm face, she looked the garments over, bracing herself for the damage. Not finding any, she turned toward Eileen's bedroom, eager to go change. And then remembering her manners, she turned back to thank Eileen and was overwhelmed with just how much the woman had done for her.

"I thank ye, Eileen. Na just for laundering my suit, but for allowing me tae bide here and taking me in as part o' yer family — na tae mention as yer apprentice at the weaver shop. Ye hae made my time here feel like home, and I dinna ken how I wull ever repay ye."

Eileen smiled a mischievous smile and stroked a tapestry that Tavish and Kelsey had brought her from Turnberry Castle.

"Surely ye jest. Ye are the one who convinced Kelsey tae bring me this. This is far more payment than I deserve."

They laughed together, and then they hugged.

SASHA AND SEUMAS WALKED ARM IN ARM BEHIND Tavish and Kelsey to the sendoff Laird Malcomb had prepared for them at the east gate out of the castle town. Alfred and Eileen walked arm in arm behind them. The sendoff was a nice touch. The dance band from the night before was playing.

Seumas and Alfred at first just clasped forearms, but then they hugged.

Alfred gave his younger brother a stern look.

"Take good care o' Sasha, now."

Seumas nodded upward with his chin at his brother.

"Aye, and ye take good care o' Eileen, now."

They stood hugging each other for a moment and then they both nodded and separated to put their arms around their loves, the new guardians of their hearts.

Laird Malcomb shook forearms first with Seumas, then with Tavish.

"Remember, ye can come back anytime, if there is a need. Dae not burn the bridge behind ye, aye?"

Seumas nodded.

"Aye, Uncle. We thank ye, and we will remember that. Ye never can be sure we willna take ye up on that sometime."

❧

FOR SASHA, IT WASN'T SOON ENOUGH WHEN THEY started on their way, but she knew Seumas needed time to say farewell. She could barely believe he was coming with her, and she squeezed his hand that was over her shoulder every time she remembered just how lucky she was that he cared enough to turn away from everyone else he loved and come with her.

There was no reason to speak Gaelic now, and Seumas had assured her he did understand English, thank God. At least he didn't have a language barrier to contend with when he got to the twenty first century.

Once they were out of earshot, she asked the question she'd been wondering about all morning.

"Is there another place Tavish can time travel? I thought we had to go back into the underground castle."

Tavish turned around and walked backward in front, and he and Seumas smiled huge.

"We need to go back down into the underground castle, all right, but we're going to need this rope." He held up a length of rope about 100 feet long, and he and Seumas laughed heartily.

Sasha put her hands on her hips, and as she did so, she had a pang of grief that she wouldn't see Deirdre again.

"Okay, obviously the two of you know what you're talking about. Would you please enlighten the rest of us?"

Kelsey already knew, though. She excitedly explained.

"As soon as we go around those trees and can't be seen anymore, we'll turn left and backtrack along the cliffs to where we can lower ourselves over. Tavish and Seumas know of a way in down there. They were supposed to block it, but they had a feeling they might need it one day, so they left some wiggle room."

The prospect of lowering herself over a cliff terrified Sasha, mostly because she was wearing her good suit again and didn't want to get it all scuffed up. But she didn't say anything. She was determined to be a good sport. In the light of Seumas having to leave his whole life behind, ruining her suit was more than trivial. She kept telling herself that.

When they got to the spot, Tavish tied the rope around a big rock, and then Seumas held it.

Sasha had a terrible thought.

"Who's going to hold it when the last one of us goes

down — and more importantly, are we just going to leave it there? Let Malcomb know we've gone down there, once he finds it?"

Tavish stepped forward.

"I'll go last. I'm lighter than Seumas, so the rock should hold me, but I'm still strong enough to assist you ladies after he goes first."

Seumas nodded and took position with his kilted rear hanging over the cliff and holding the rope to repel down to the hidden cave.

But before he could start, Deirdre came running out with tears streaming down her face and grabbed ahold of Sasha by the waist and held her tight.

"Take me with ye."

16

SIA DEUG

Sasha's arms automatically wrapped around Deirdre. And then Sasha was kneeling so that she could be face-to-face with the little girl whose face was red with tears because she was sobbing and gasping for breath. Tears dripped down Sasha's face too.

While she held Deirdre close and rocked her in her arms, a fierce feeling of protectiveness came over Sasha, unlike anything she had ever experienced. She opened her watery eyes and looked at her best friend, pleading for some kind of answer.

Kelsey came over and knelt beside them for a moment, clearly thinking things through.

And then she hugged Sasha.

"Stay here. You have made more of a life for yourself here in seven days than you did at Celtic in seven years. You're already an auntie to this little one, you have a future playing flute with the dance band — and besides,

Seumas shines here. His strength and fighting abilities would wither in our time. You can tell me in your dreams if you need emergency medical care or something — and I have a feeling our masters will be in touch with you. They won't let all your training go to waste."

On hearing Kelsey's permission to stay, such a feeling of relief washed over Sasha that she cried all the more, but these were happy tears. How silly she'd been. She didn't need Kelsey's permission to stay, not when Seumas had already invited her. His was the only opinion that mattered, and he wanted the two of them to stay here.

Sasha stood up, holding Deirdre's hand and seeking out her love's eyes. When she finally found them, they looked hopeful again, and all trace of fear was gone. Confident this was the right decision, she spoke, and all doubt was removed from her mind when she saw Seumas's face light up with joy.

She addressed Deirdre, but she kept looking at Seumas.

"Seumas and I are staying here, Deirdre. We are na going with Tavish and Kelsey. Na tae bide, anyhow. We may visit there someday sae I can show him a few things," Seumas beamed at her and nodded, "but we wull live here, and I'm gaun'ae be yer auntie."

Seumas hurried over, and he and Deirdre both hugged Sasha fiercely, and then he hugged Deirdre too, and they were once more like a family.

Kelsey laughed and pulled the rope back up from where Tavish had thrown it over the cliff.

"We wull go with ye back tae the weaver shop tae take Deirdre home. That way, we wull be here for ye awhile, in case ye hae need o' us."

WHEN THEY ALL ENTERED THE WEAVER SHOP, EILEEN looked puzzled — and then cross when she saw her daughter with them.

"Deirdre! Ye canna be sneaking off like this. What am I gaun'ae dae with ye?" She sighed heavily and looked at Sasha apologetically. "I'm sae sorry she ruined yer trip."

Sasha took both of Eileen's hands in hers.

"I am na sorry at all that she ruined oor trip. In fact, I'm pleased as punch. She's made me realize — we're gaun'ae bide!"

Eileen hugged her.

"Yer sure?"

Sasha hugged Eileen back and nodded against her face.

"Aye, we're sure."

Eileen backed away and held onto Sasha's hands, then looked around at everyone.

"Then I had best get ye tae Laird Malcomb straightaway."

Keeping hold of Sasha's hand, she turned and hurried toward the door, dragging Sasha behind her. Deirdre held on to Sasha's other hand and went along too, with Seumas and Tavish and Kelsey following close behind them.

"What's going on?" Sasha called out as they rushed through the castle town with everyone looking at them curiously.

But Eileen didn't answer, just laughed and hurried her.

"Quicken yer step, will ye?"

At last, they were inside the castle.

A woman who was scrubbing one of the tables in the great hall looked up and saw them all and called out to a man passing through, and he ran out of the room — and returned shortly with Laird Malcomb.

The laird looked puzzled and slightly worried.

Seumas allayed the man's fears.

"Uncle, we hae decided tae bide. I hope that is wull with ye."

Laird Malcomb broke out into a large grin and held out his arms.

Seumas took Sasha's hand away from Eileen and brought her forward into his uncle's presence. Deirdre still clung to her other hand.

Laird Malcomb embraced them all.

"Aye, 'tis more than wull with me. Much more than wull. I was utterly forlorn when ye told me ye were leaving. Ye see, I had already decided tae ask ye tae represent me oot at the surrounding castles — a different one each year – tae discuss with them what happened with Brian the Druid and what we all might dae in order tae protect ourselves. A lot o' travel, and much time away from home. Dae ye wish tae take it on?"

Did they ever!

This was exactly what she and Seumas had talked

about on their two journeys together so far. Their eyes met, and he looked just as excited as she felt about the prospect of traveling to all the surrounding castles together.

Her smile faltered when Deirdre squeezed her hand and took in a big breath to start talking. Sasha could guess what the little girl was going to say. She'd only just won her back, and now Sasha was rushing off without her again.

Sasha spoke to Eileen, but she held Seumas's eyes while she did, pleased to see that he agreed with her and would support her in this, as he had in everything.

"We will only gae if Deirdre can foster with us and come along."

Eileen looked to her daughter, who nodded yes vigorously.

"Aye!"

⁂ 17 ⁂

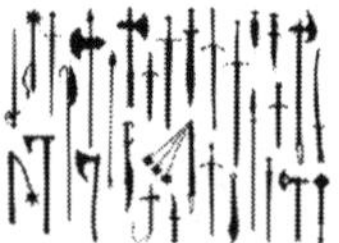

SEACHD DEUG

-After Alfred & Eileen and Seumas & Sasha's wedding at the castle-

Seumas laughed his hardest as he followed Sasha, Kelsey, and Tavish up the familiar stairs into a place that was completely unfamiliar — even though it was on the same land as his uncle's castle.

Betting he would shock them all, Seumas spoke to them in English (with his Scottish accent).

"Will ye look at that? Even though ye telt me about the trailers and the cars — and the fact that Uncle's castle is gone and the ruins o' a newer tower house stand in its place... even with the telling, ye hae the right o' it."

Speaking quite a different English, Sasha put her arms around him and leaned her chin on his shoulder.

"If it's too much for you, we don't have to visit. We can go back right now."

Quick as he could, he leaned down and looked into her eyes.

"Ye must be jesting. I canna wait tae ride a wave on a surfboard!"

She laughed and tugged him over toward one of the cars.

He went willingly, but to himself, he could admit he was a bit afraid.

Tavish shook his hand.

"Congratulations again, and I know you're going to have the most wonderful honeymoon ever."

Kelsey looked at Tavish wistfully then.

Feeling like an intruder into their private business for noticing, Seumas turned away toward the car. He was on the passenger side, of course. Sasha had offered to teach him to drive, but for this first trip into the great unknown, he figured he'd have enough to do just looking around.

She got in on the other side and reached over and pulled up a little part of the inside of the car.

"Pull on the handle and open the door and get in."

Bless the lass, she covered her laughter as he tried to find the handle. Soon, he was inside the car with her, and she put her hand on his leg while she fastened a strap over his chest.

"Are you sure you want to leave for Hawaii right away? Kelsey will let us use her trailer. We can spend the night here and..."

After she fastened a strap over her own chest, he gently took her chin and turned her face toward him.

"Ye wanted yer wedding night tae be in Hawaii, and

ye already let me hae the wedding with my family. We're gaun'ae wait till we get there."

As nonchalantly as if it was something she did every day — which he supposed it was, come to think of it — she put what she'd explained was a key inside the neck of the machine and turned it, causing a great rumble that made him try to jump out of his seat even though she had warned him it was coming. She pulled on something and pushed on something with her foot and pulled on something else, pushed on something else with her foot, and the machine took off at an unbelievable speed, making his knuckles turn white on the arms of the chair he was sitting in.

"Okay, so long as you understand my mom and my brothers will be there along with most of my extended family — and they'll throw a big party for us the first five or six hours."

It took him a few moments to find his voice, seeing as how the world was whizzing by him much faster now than it ever had on a horse or ship.

"Even sae, lass." His voice sounded shaky when it came out.

And then the car spoke to her, and he could feel his mind expanding.

18

OCHD DEUG

-A year later-

Sasha looked out the arrow-slit window of their upstairs suite at Turnberry Castle and admired her view of the sea cliffs before she laid little two-month-old Artair in the cradle that Laird Cathal had been more than happy to lend them.

She caressed their son's head and kissed him.

"Are ye full enough now tae sleep for a bit, eh?"

Seumas came up from behind her and put his arms around her waist, encouraging her to lean back into his supportive strength, which she did.

He rested his chin on her head.

"Will ye miss the view when we hae tae leave come spring?"

She turned around to face him, and as usual when they were this close and alone with the baby not crying, they kissed and caressed each other. After a bit of that, she rested her cheek on his chest and turned again so that they were both looking out at the sea.

"I dinna think sae. This has been wonderful while we were here, but new adventures await, ye ken."

She smiled up at his handsome face, deliriously happy to be his wife and to be living a life that had already surpassed her wildest dreams of adventure and was only just beginning.

The door banged open and the two of them laughed, knowing it was Deirdre.

Sure enough, their seven-year-old fosterling barged in — but she looked much more excited than usual.

"Sasha! Come on doon tae the dock! Ye hae a special surprise!"

Deirdre was already running past all the tapestries down the orange stone hallway toward the stairs, and Sasha followed, laughing and calling out after her.

"A surprise for me? What is it? I canna imagine."

But Deirdre just giggled and ran all the way down to the dock, where a ship was unloading cargo.

Sasha looked first among the crates — but she couldn't think of anything she really wanted. Besides, she and Seumas and Deirdre and little Artair had to travel light.

And then she saw her surprise.

Her jaw dropped, and tears sprang from her eyes while she ran forward with her arms out.

"Mom!"

Oops. She was so excited, she'd spoken English. But oh yeah, Mom didn't know Gaelic, so she would have to speak in English anyway. Perhaps as little speaking as possible in front of others would be the best way forward.

Things had gone excellently well this past year, but that didn't mean rumors that she was a foreigner couldn't start at any time. Comments had already been made about her accent, but those were easily dismissed among people who remained in the same place their whole lives.

Mom was beaming a smile while waiting to be escorted off the ship.

Sasha strode right up and held her hand out, steadying Mom's disembarkation.

"How did you... Who..."

Once Mom was off the ship and safely stood on the sturdy dock, she hugged Sasha tight, rocking from foot to foot as they always did when they hadn't seen each other in a while.

"Kelsey. She got me these clothes and... I'm here for two weeks. And I want to know everything about your life. Show me everything."

When they finished their hug, Seumas reached out to take Mom's hand, but she grabbed him in a bear hug as well, which he gradually relaxed into with a soft chuckle.

After hugging Mom back, he kept his arm around her and started her walking.

"I ken ye are dying tae meet Artair. Come on upstairs. He's in his cradle."

Mom was trying not to gawk, but Sasha couldn't blame her. It wasn't every day you sailed on a ship right into a castle. And then the laird and his lady happened to be passing by in the hallway, all decked out in their finest to go down and hold the weekly court.

"Laird Cathal, Lady Meg, may I present my maw, Janice, who has just arrived for a two week bide?"

Mom curtsied and bowed her head when she was presented.

"'Tis an honor, Sir. And I thank you for taking in my daughter and my grandson — and aw, this must be my foster granddaughter. Hello honey."

Sasha started to translate, but Laird Cathal and Lady Meg inclined their heads, and he answered in

English before they sedately walked down the hall.

"Wull come, and ye may stay as long as ye like."

Deirdre took to Mom right away, hugging her and even giving her a little kiss on the cheek.

"Dinna fash aboot being a stranger here who doesna ken how we dae things. I wull show ye aroond and make sure ye dinna wash yer hands in the soup."

Still being escorted by Seumas, Mom leaned back and whispered to Sasha.

"What was that she said? It sounded like she said 'soup'."

Seumas chuckled, but Sasha tapped his arm with the back of her hand. She would bet her face was beet red, she was blushing so hard.

"Nothing you need to worry about, Mom. Here we are. This is our suite. There's an extra bed in Deirdre's room. Come on in."

Artair was sleeping, but Sasha picked him up anyway and held him out proudly. "Mom, meet your grandson. Artair, this is your grandma."

Mom took him eagerly into her arms and cradled him to her, smiling the most contented smile Sasha had ever seen on her face.

Deirdre tugged on her long skirt, and Sasha turned around with a warm smile for her foster daughter.

"Aye, what is it, lass?"

The little girl looked very sincere.

"Dinna fash aboot caring for the baby. I wull watch him while ye visit."

Sasha hugged Deirdre warmly in one arm and her mother in the other, and Seumas came in and hugged them too, so that they were all hugging in a circle with the baby in the middle.

"How aboot we all take care o' each other?"

TOMAS

A Time Travel Romance

I

AON

Before she started looking for her friends, Amber went out through the terminal past the security checkpoint where everyone was waiting in line to get in. She'd never been to Scotland before, and the back of her mind was making plans just in case Kelsey and Tavish weren't there. She knew she was going out to the dig at Dunskey Castle. She could put her carry-on over her shoulder and roll both suitcases behind her out to the street, where there were always taxis waiting. The fare would be exorbitant, but she could get there okay. If she needed to.

She was looking at the overhead TV screens for which way to turn to go get her baggage when she heard Kelsey's voice.

"Amber, you made it!"

Breathing a small sigh of relief, she turned and smiled as first Kelsey and then Tavish gave her big hugs.

And then Amber pointed and laughed at Tavish as animatedly as she could.

"You aren't fooling anyone, you know. Modern day Scots wear modern kilts if they wear them at all, not old fashioned great kilts like your Renaissance Faire costume. And while our faire accent might sound authentic for a sixteenth century Scot speaking English, it doesn't sound at all like a modern-day Scot's English. I would know, because I just sat next to a whole Scottish family for six hours." She nodded to where the couple and their six and nine-year-olds were collecting their luggage.

The woman smiled and waved, and Amber waved back, making funny faces at the kids, who giggled.

Tavish flounced in his kilt as only he could, striking several manly poses and making even said modern-day Scots tsk at him playfully. Then with a teasing look on his face, he pointed at Amber's black Goth lipstick, big swinging skull earrings, lacy long black dress, pointy black shoes, and white make-up over olive skin.

"Well, you aren't fooling anyone either, you know. Modern day Goths are still in their graves, not out and about looking like The Walking Dead."

After she made a big show of rolling her eyes at Tavish, Amber told him and Kelsey about her flight while they helped her gather up her bags from the carousel and take them out to their rental car. Tavish drove them a short distance to a pub he said was a great place to have lunch, to which Kelsey gave an exaggerated shrug.

But once the waitress had seated them and taken

their orders, Amber asked her old friends the question that was on her mind.

"So how's Tomas?"

There, that was the part she really wanted to know. Well, actually, it was whether Tomas missed her. Did he ever talk about her? What did he say? Did they think the two of them would ever get back together?

But she'd settled for the tamer version. Oh, and better ask about the rest of their old gang as well. You know, so she didn't sound so desperate.

"And have you heard from your four favorite cousins or any of their girlfriends?"

Kelsey turned to Tavish and raised her eyebrow.

He smiled at Amber while he toyed with Kelsey's hand.

"I think I've finally convinced Tomas to come visit me here. You wouldn't believe how hard I've been trying, nor how long it's been since I've seen my twin."

Amber knew it was more important for Tavish to be in touch with Tomas than for her to be. Of course it was. Blood was thicker than all the spit she and Tomas used to swap. But her old boyfriend — and Tavish — had simply disappeared off the face of the earth seven years ago. And while Kelsey had explained briefly that the guys had separated from their girlfriends out of urgent necessity, Amber still didn't get it.

Ever the peacekeeper, Kelsey had warned her on the phone before she got here not to ask about the seven-year separation, though. And that was easy for her to say. Kelsey could afford to speak casually about their long time with no contact from the guys.

She had Tavish back.

Until Kelsey's call a few days ago, Amber had been almost sure Tomas was long dead. She had tried contacting his parents, but they hadn't returned any of her calls, texts, emails, or letters. She had shown up as usual at their Renaissance Faire the first two summers, but they had found a way to completely ignore her, and none of the faire people would talk about any of their gang of friends.

The whole thing was weird as a goth guy at a shopping mall.

But she wouldn't get answers by moping. And anyway, soon Tomas would be here. She would finally be able to just ask him about it—and have fun cajoling the true answer out of that cryptic rascal—so Amber smiled at Tavish as nicely as she could, under the circumstances.

"Well I hope it's true. I hope he does come see you."

But they saw right through her. At least they were nice about it.

Tavish smiled back at her and winked.

"Yeah, I'll bet you're happy he's coming to see me." He laughed a little.

Kelsey pushed her lips together in an attempt not to laugh at Amber — which saved her from being kicked under the table with one of Amber's heavy Doc Martin boots, unlike Tavish.

He took it like a man, though. Didn't even grunt.

Amber wrinkled her nose at him in congratulations, and he wrinkled his back.

"Well," said Kelsey, "it turns out not everyone was

separated these past seven years. Jaelle and John stayed together."

Amber's jaw dropped.

"No way."

Kelsey unwrapped her flatware from the napkin and put it in her lap.

"Yep, they did, but we heard from him six months ago that they broke up."

The waitress came then with their food, and as she placed it in front of them and they all nodded at her politely, Amber thought about the wonderful summers they had all spent together in their teens at the Renaissance Faire that Tavish and Tomas's parents ran with the help of Mike, Gabe, Jeff, and John's parents.

Back then, she'd been sure the guys had the coolest parents she'd ever meet. Not only had Dall & Emily and Peadar & Vange taught everyone in the Scottish guild Gaelic, but also they had let their sons' girlfriends use costumes from the costume shed instead of having to make their own when they first joined the guild — and had to change out of the English costumes they'd made when they joined the faire.

And she had spent four glorious fun-filled summers with her best boyfriend ever.

Tomas had Skyped with her every night during the school years, when they couldn't be together, and each new summer they had picked up right where they left off.

Until the day after he and Tavish turned eighteen. He hadn't been there since, and no one would talk about him. Until now. Tavish and Kelsey were saying precious little, but she got the impression that badgering them for info would make them shut down, maybe even send her away.

She raised her mug of ale in a toast.

"To reunions."

Her friends raised their mugs.

"To reunions."

After they drank up, it was Amber's turn to change the subject. She asked Kelsey logistical questions about the dig, and the two of them amicably discussed artifact cataloging methods through the rest of the meal and on the drive out to the dig.

As they talked, Amber finally understood why she had been invited to come here. She was going to be Kelsey's go-to person for practical hands-on advice.

Kelsey had a doctorate in Celtic Art History and her friend Sasha had a doctorate in Celtic Archaeology, but this was both of their first time in charge of a dig. Meanwhile, Amber had dropped out of beauty school six years ago to do grunt work on a dig — and never looked back. Her parents had known someone who got her involved in it, and she loved it.

Kelsey had lucked upon discovering a huge underground palace beneath Dunskey Castle here in Scotland. She had just been on the international news announcing her discovery, so now this was a world-famous dig that would be open to tourists and last ten years or more — and pay well.

Amber tried to sound businesslike and not show how giddy she felt.

"Yeah, Reichmann's method that we used in Mexico was my favorite. If you want, I'll help you organize it."

Kelsey turned her head toward the backseat and opened her eyes as big as she could and showed her teeth in a 'cat that ate the canary' kind of way.

"Oh that's just the beginning of what I brought you out here to help me with."

While she visited with her friend, Amber watched the city turn into green and gray mountains with deep green valleys between, punctuated by the occasional thistle bush or flock of sheep. Finally, they turned off the highway and drove out toward the sea, then parked amid twenty other cars in a field.

Kelsey looped her arm through Amber's, and the two of them marveled at the scene together as they walked from the car over toward a city of site trailers. Tavish carried all of her bags.

Well, Amber marveled while Kelsey kept agreeing with her.

"Everything's as clean as it is in a nineteen fifties sitcom."

"I know. Isn't it amazing?"

"And even though it's all cloudy and overcast, I still wanna be outside here."

"Me too."

"And we're right next to the ocean."

"Yep, and Mr. Blair has promised us a motorboat so we can go to Ireland sometimes. I mean, even now we could just go to Portpatrick and hire someone to take us, but it's not the same."

"Wow. It couldn't get any better than this, could it. Thanks for bringing me in on this, Kel."

Kelsey reached over the front seat and squeezed her hand.

"I know that was a rhetorical question, but you haven't heard yet what some think is the best part."

Amber chuckled, looking at Tavish behind his back.

"Guys in kilts bring all the women breakfast in bed?"

Kelsey laughed and held up her phone.

"No! The underground castle is well ventilated by a series of small side caves, and near some of their openings, we can get cell reception."

Amber laughed.

"I'm not going to fall for that trick. You'll have to haze your new employee some other way."

Kelsey raised her eyebrows in a 'you'll see' kind of expression and stopped in front of a two-bedroom trailer.

"This one's mine and Sasha's, but she's away for a while."

They put Amber's things in one of the bedrooms, where she chased Tavish out and hurriedly changed into black jeans and a black hoodie, then turned to Kelsey.

"Well, this is a nice trailer and all, but let's get out to the dig site."

Kelsey laughed.

Soon, they were rushing over toward the ruins of a tower house that stood just in front of a drop-off that led down to the ocean. It was overcast and misty, but as Amber looked out into the fog, she could imagine seeing Ireland in the distance. It made her smile, having something to look forward to amid the wonder of already being here and the prospect of seeing Tomas again soon.

When they got close to the tower house, Amber saw that the drop down to the sea was quite a long one.

"So the dig is inside these cliffs?"

Tavish nodded, leading her over to an open cellar door.

"Aye, and you get down to it through this hatch."

Amber made sure he noticed when she rolled her eyes at him for saying Aye instead of yes.

When they got closer to the hatch, she could see that a ladder had been installed.

"How do you suppose they got down here before the ladder? Jumped down in long skirts and kilts? Doesn't seem very practical."

Tavish pointed over to an area east of the tower house.

"Oh, this is a newer entrance. In the old time, they go... went in down the stairs over there. We don't use them, because we're trying to preserve them."

Amber pursed her lips together and tittered her head back-and-forth, imitating his serious tone and how important he looked and sounded, and then she commented to Kelsey.

"I thought you were the one who'd studied all this stuff. Why is he the one sounding like a professor of ancient Celtic architecture?"

Kelsey and Tavish shared a look, and then Kelsey burst out laughing.

"I was asking myself the same thing when I first got

here, believe me. But Tavish has been around here a lot, so on this particular site, he's at least as much of an expert as I am."

Tavish went down the ladder and stood at the bottom, holding up his hand to steady Amber in case she needed it, for which she was grateful. But not wishing to tell him so — and swell his head up bigger than it already was — she continued to tease him about how much he knew about the dig.

"Well you can't have been here that much longer than Kelsey. I mean, didn't you say Mr. Blair just took ownership of this property three months ago?"

But then she got down inside the root cellar and was watching Kelsey open a secret door using a series of ancient bricks with Celtic markings all over them, and she forgot all about teasing Tavish. If that wasn't enough, the door opened into a secret passageway full of these Celtic runes, which led to a three-way intersection full of even more of them, and then she was in a secret room with the age-old drawings all over it.

Right out of her head flew all thoughts about how long Tavish had been at the site or even how much he knew. She just stood there with her jaw hanging open and her eyes wide while Kelsey and Tavish turned on the lights they had rigged down here.

Kelsey came and stood beside her.

"I thought I'd have you start in here, dusting off these runes so we can seal them against future damage."

Refusing to take her eyes off all the ancient stone-carved symbols, Amber did the best she could to nod her head yes.

THE NEXT DAY, AMBER COULD BARELY CONTAIN HER excitement as she watched the car drive up the road toward the dig site. She hadn't seen Tomas in seven years. She was intensely curious to see how he had changed and to hear what he'd been up to. She hoped he wasn't fat. Yuck. Did he have a fun job like hers? Or did he work in an office somewhere? She really hoped the latter wasn't the case.

She was rocking forward and back from her toes to her heels by the time the car pulled up, and she had to consciously make herself stop so as not to look silly.

The car had tinted windows, so her curiosity was still unsatisfied.

Should she rush up to the car and be the one to greet him when he stepped out? Her hesitation gave the opportunity to Tavish instead. That was probably better. Tavish had been the one to invite him after all. And they were brothers. Twins. Non-identical twins, but still...

And then the car door opened.

Yum.

Tomas was still tall and lean. He had shaggy hair and wore a flowy poet's shirt. He had a tiny hint of a mustache and no beard, thank God.

The two brothers embraced, and Amber found herself smiling wistfully at them. How nice. She was glad her own brothers and sister had never lost touch with her.

Okay, Tavish and Tomas had turned around, and

Tomas was looking over the site. Now was a good time for her to go say hi.

As she rushed over there, she pulled up the long sleeves of her flowing black blouse, just in case he wanted to shake hands instead of giving her a hug. You can presume too much after seven years, after all. Even in her heavy boots, she was jogging by the time she got to him.

Oddly, he still hadn't met her eyes. When she was right in front of him, though, he didn't have a choice.

A handshake it was, then. She held out her hand to him.

"Welcome to Scotland, Tomas."

She made her smile as warm and welcoming as she could. Maybe he would stay a while and they'd get a chance to rekindle—

The most grating female voice Amber had ever heard came to her ears across the top of the car in a lilting Southern accent.

"Tomas honey, come over here and help me with this door, please."

The tone was sweet and should've been pleasing, but something about that voice just hurt her ears.

Probably the 'honey' part.

Dread sank into Amber as she looked over at the woman who was obviously Tomas's girlfriend. While Amber was dark-haired and olive skinned, this woman was honey blonde with alabaster skin. While Amber was quirky and artsy and thought of herself as fun-loving, this woman was stately and imperious. There was no way she could compete with such a woman. The two of them had absolutely nothing in common except their interest in Tomas. You could tell just by looking.

Kelsey had run up beside her. She grabbed ahold of her arm, apparently for support. Then Kelsey gasped, let go of Amber's arm, and grabbed Tavish's.

"That's Sulis!" Kelsey hissed.

Tavish's forehead wrinkled.

"Are you sure?"

"Yes!"

Amber put her hand on Kelsey's shoulder.

"What's the matter? Who's Sulis?"

Tavish rubbed his eyes and put his hand over his mouth, leaning down on it.

Kelsey swallowed, still staring at Tomas and his girlfriend over the top of their rental car.

"Sulis is friends with the druids who control Tavish."

"What?"

2

DHÀ

What Kelsey said had minorly alarmed Amber and piqued a little curiosity, but mostly she just wanted to crawl under a rock and hide. She'd left a perfectly good job at the dig in Mexico and come all the way to Scotland — pretty much just to be with Tomas. On hearing that Tavish was here, she'd just assumed Tomas would be here too, single and ready to pick up where they had left off. It had never occurred to her he might have a girlfriend. She was so stupid. She should've asked ahead of time. Should've asked Tavish for Tomas's number and called Tomas herself and asked if he was single.

Now she wished she had rented her own car and driven herself here, so she could just leave right now. But she hadn't. Fiddling with her phone in her pocket, she debated calling a cab. But it would be so expensive to take a cab to the airport. Which wouldn't be a problem if she hadn't just quit her job. Ugh! And since every dig had a waiting list of workers ten pages long, she knew her job was long gone by now.

While she debated this silently in her mind, her body moved past people of its own accord, getting them out of her line of sight so she could follow Tomas's movements. It was stupid, but she couldn't help it. Her brain knew she should go back to Kelsey's trailer and wait there until Kelsey came so she could get a ride back to the airport. But her heart kept her body right here. Watching him. If she was honest, she'd admit to herself that she was pining after him. How pathetic.

He went over to help Sulis get out of the car, then back toward the trunk.

But Sulis tossed her hand in the air cavalierly and gestured over toward Tavish as if she were the most gracious being in the world — and spoke in her sickly sweet Southern drawl.

"Oh you can get that later. Right now you should really talk to your brother. We came all the way out here just to see him, after all."

He stopped and came back to her and stood there like a little boy next to his mom. Or a dog with its mistress.

She brought his arm out and looped hers through it like some Victorian lady. "Let's go on over and you can introduce me."

Pretty much everyone had stopped what they were doing to watch the show. Amber looked around, and she and Kelsey were the only women there besides Sulis.

Kelsey was looking at Amber with an apology and a lot of guilt in her eyes.

All of the men — Mr. Blair, Tavish, and all the rest of the construction workers — were looking at Sulis as if she were something good to eat.

Tomas and Sulis walked around their car arm in arm, and Sulis smiled at Tavish indulgently with her one hand on his brother's chest and her other arm looped through his brother's arm. And then instead of waiting for an introduction, she asserted her own.

"Well you must be Tavish. I've heard so much about you. You're just as handsome as I thought you would be." Completely ignoring Kelsey — who was obviously with Tavish, having her arm through his in much the same way as Sulis was holding onto his brother — Sulis just smiled at Tavish and batted her eyelashes. Well, she didn't quite bat her eyelashes, but she might as well have.

Tavish was tongue-tied, and under ordinary circumstances, Amber would've admired anyone who could accomplish that. But this was war.

Amber straightened her back and un-hunched her shoulders. War was not the time to slouch. Besides, Sulis's posture was perfect, and Amber didn't want to give the woman any more advantage than she clearly already had.

Kelsey knew it was war, too, because without reaching out to the woman at all, in fact blatantly keeping her hands resting on Tavish, Kelsey asserted her own sarcastically sweet introduction.

"Well it's so nice to meet you, Sulis. We don't know much about you at all. Please, tell us the story of how you met Tomas — and don't forget to tell us how long ago that was." Kelsey gave the woman her own saccharin smile in perfect imitation of the other. "Please."

Admiring her friend's chutzpah, Amber winked at Kelsey.

Kelsey winked back.

But to Kelsey's obvious chagrin, Sulis took charge just by starting to walk. Like a tigress in high heels, swinging her imaginary tail back and forth with her elegant yet short skirt, she led everyone on a leisurely stroll toward the sea cliff, where the sun was just starting to set.

Even the construction workers walked with her, visibly enthralled with the way Sulis walked, the way she carried herself, how pretty she was, and whatever else men got enthralled about.

Kelsey was in charge of the dig, but Tavish was the construction foreman. Kelsey wisely didn't tell the men to get back to work, although Amber could tell she was dying to deprive Sulis of her audience.

As the statuesque blonde strolled past the other cars and the trailers toward the gorgeous view ahead — sort of dragging Tomas along with her by the arm, not that anyone but Amber and Kelsey noticed — she did tell the story of her and Tomas's meeting. However, she told it in a way that made her storytelling seem like it was her idea, rather than an answer to Kelsey's demand.

"Oh, it was so romantic. I was in the area with my... religious group. We'd had a... celebration that day, but there was nothing scheduled for that evening. So I ducked into the cutest antique shop I ever did see — you know, just to pass the time."

She smiled at all the men around her, and they nodded and smiled back at her encouragingly, eating up every word she said.

If it weren't for Kelsey's being here, Amber would've gone back to her trailer rather than hear this drivel. She met Kelsey's eye behind Sulis's back and put her finger down her throat and pretended like she was making herself vomit.

Kelsey mustered a tiny smile in response.

Now approaching the wonderful view down the cliffs of the sea crashing on the rocks below — and Ireland peeking out of the multicolored mist in the distance — Sulis gestured proudly as if this were all her creation, enjoyed the appreciative nods from the men, and then continued her story.

"Well, of course Tomas was the only one working in the antique store. His parents run it, you know — I mean, they own it." She cuddled up next to him with her cheek next to his cheek in a way that made Amber want to vomit for real. "And Tomas will own it after they're gone. Won't you, dear."

Amber gave Kelsey a "yeah right" look. Tomas and Tavish had two more brothers and a sister, and Sulis obviously didn't know that — but she was stupid not to include Tavish in her flattery about owning the antique store.

Kelsey gave Amber a worried look in return. Uh oh.

But Tavish didn't say anything, and Tomas just nodded at Sulis with a big dopey grin on his face.

And Amber's heart dropped into her stomach as Sulis reached up over her shoulder and slowly ran her fingers along Tomas's jaw, making him close his eyes in apparent ecstasy while she continued her tale.

"So, you know how it is, gentlemen. I looked at all the wonderful antiques in his parents' store, asking him to show me how this dagger works and how that sword hefts. Meanwhile, between demonstrations of his fighting prowess, he kept looking at me. Eventually he asked me out, and the rest is history."

Kelsey shrugged and put her hand out as if to say "And?" But when that didn't produce any results, she put her hands on her hips in frustration and voiced the question that was on Amber's mind too, because it didn't make sense.

"Hold on a minute. You said you were just in the area for a religious gathering. If you weren't from around there, then how did you and Tomas keep seeing each other?"

Sulis gave Tomas a very pretty smile and straightened the collar on his poet's shirt, which didn't need straightening at all.

"Well, Tomas didn't want to be without me after even that first meeting."

She looked around at all the men and received the confirmation she obviously wanted: from the look of their smiles and nods, none of them wanted to be without her after this first meeting, either.

"So, he moved to Greenwich Village with me after my week's vacation was over."

She dramatically sighed as if she'd just remembered something.

"Oh, and to answer your other question, Kelsey..."

She smiled prettily at Kelsey, but obviously it was for the benefit of the men, because Kelsey was scowling at her. So was Amber, but Sulis was plainly just ignoring her.

"That was almost exactly two months ago, when Tomas moved with me to Greenwich Village. So as you can imagine, we've been really busy."

She tilted her head just so then, and all the men grinned. Some of them actually giggled. She cupped Tavish's face with her hand.

"Otherwise, Tavish, I'm sure he would've come to see you sooner."

Surprisingly, at this, Tomas woke up from his zombielike state and said more than 'Yes, Sulis; right away, Sulis; let me be your slave, Sulis.'

"Oh, I don't know about that. My brother's been off gallivanting around on his own ever since we turned twenty five. He doesn't need me anymore."

At that, Sulis turned to him with a hard look in her eye. It was the kind of look that would make most men break up with a woman right there and then — cold and calculating and obviously uncaring. And then she whispered something unintelligible in his ear before she put on a sweet face again and spoke up for her audience.

"Tomas honey, I'm more tired from our trip over

here to Scotland than I at first thought. I'm sure these people put on a lovely spread, but I want to go eat dinner near the hotel. Be a love and go get the car, will you?"

Amber could barely control her excitement, waiting for him to explode at Sulis for ordering him around, let alone looking at him with such contempt. This was going to be good.

To her shock, he calmly nodded and started walking toward their rental car as if she'd never looked at him like he was a slave that she could whip for disobeying her. Nuh uh. This was so not the Tomas she knew and loved. No. Something was wrong with him. He must be on cold meds or something, and if so, he shouldn't be driving!

Amber went to follow him.

But she felt an arm around her waist, jerking her to a stop.

Amber turned to tell Kelsey it was fine, that she was just going to make sure Tomas was okay to drive. That she knew what she was doing.

But it was Sulis.

"Hello, doll face. I don't believe I've had the pleasure of making your acquaintance. I'm Tomas's girlfriend, and I'd really appreciate it if you didn't go with him to the car."

Amber saw red and twisted out of the woman's grasp. Who was she to say where Amber should go? This witch with a B might be his girlfriend, but...

"Listen, Sulis. I've known Tomas for eleven years.

You may be his girlfriend right now, but I am his friend-friend. If I want to talk to him, then I am going to talk to him, and you can complain all you want, but you aren't going to stop me, so just get out of my way before I—"

Of all people, Tavish came over with a take-charge attitude and put his hands between Amber and the other woman. And addressed himself to Amber.

"Now Amber, Sulis has a point. She is Tomas's current girlfriend, so I think you ought to do as she asks."

What!

Amber looked over at Kelsey and gave her a look — asking for verification that Tavish was being nuts.

Kelsey blinked a few times to show that she agreed, but then she put on a reasonable face and walked over and took Amber's hand.

"Amber, I think you and I ought to go back to my trailer and rest a bit."

Tomas drove up then and parked between Amber and Sulis, who made a pretty show of waving goodbye to Amber over the top of the car. While the look in her eyes said 'Sulis one, Amber zero,' she called out in her cloying Southern accent.

"I think that's a good idea Kelsey. You get that girl to rest up a bit and listen to Tomas's brother, who's trying to talk some sense into her." She turned and smiled and waved at all the men gathered around. "We'll see y'all tomorrow. Bye now."

All the men smiled at her and waved.

"Bye."

ONCE SHE AND KELSEY WERE IN THEIR TRAILER AND had privacy, Amber blurted out what was on her mind.

"I can't believe I came all the way out here thinking I was gonna see Tomas and not realizing he might have a girlfriend. I'm so stupid, Kelsey. Why am I out there even arguing with her when she obviously has a claim on him? He looks at her with such puppy dog eyes, I can't even stand to be around them. Maybe they won't be here very long and I can come back after they're gone, but for now, I've got to leave. I was thinking I'd fly back home, but really I can just go stay in a hotel far enough away from here that I won't see them. If you just take me into town, I can rent a car and handle everything on my own. I'm sorry to do this to you, but —"

But Kelsey was shaking her head no and had a panicked look on her face and kept trying to interrupt. Finally, Amber stopped and let Kelsey talk.

"Amber, Sulis is a druid, and she's using her magic to compel Tomas —"

What? Amber crossed her arms and raised an eyebrow at Kelsey.

"You've got to be kidding me. You know, you always had a vivid imagination, and that was fun when we were teens. But we're grown women now. You've got a PhD, Kelsey. You don't have to make stuff up anymore to get attention—"

But Kelsey was shaking her head no and holding her palms out. And laughing just a tiny bit.

"I know it sounds like something I would have made

up when we were younger, but think about it... if you remember the look in Tomas's eyes — the look in all the men's eyes — you'll know what I'm saying is the truth. Sulis has a way of bewitching men so that they see her as some sort of 'do no wrong' person."

Yeah. That was exactly what Amber had been thinking.

Despite how stupid it sounded, she found herself actually entertaining the idea that Sulis was using magic. Because really, the woman was nasty. And in Amber's experience, most men saw through that stuff. But not around this woman they didn't. There had to be a reason. Sulis was beautiful and charming, yes, but she was only human... or maybe she wasn't.

Amber gave her friend a speculative look.

"Okay, you're right about that. The men were falling all over each other trying to please her, all two dozen of them. I've never seen anything like it. I'm listening."

Kelsey nodded sharply.

"Darn straight I'm right about that. Her spell doesn't seem to work on women, but it sure is working on the men. She has them all wrapped around her little finger." Kelsey met Amber's gaze and held it with an intense look of her own. "Please don't go. Tomas needs our help, and you may be the only one who can get through to him."

Amber lowered her chin and looked up at Kelsey, making her skull earrings jiggle painfully on her ears.

"Me? Why me? He hasn't said a word to me the whole time he's been here."

Kelsey gave her a look that said, 'The whole time

he's been here? It's only been half an hour.' But when she actually spoke, her voice was sincere.

"Because you care about him so much. Tavish does too, but Tomas is angry at Tavish, so his brother may not be able to get through to him. You can't tell me you didn't notice?"

※ 3 ※

TRÌ

That night, Amber lay awake in her tiny trailer bedroom, tossing and turning. Everything Sulis had said kept running through her mind, and over and over again she saw how dead Tomas's eyes looked, and how he followed Sulis around — not even like a little puppy. Puppies were alive. He was lifeless. More like a slave. It tore her up inside.

Finally, she gave in and got up. No, there was nothing she could do to help Tomas tonight, but she knew herself well. When something was on her mind, her body needed to get good and tired, or she would never fall asleep. And then she would be useless at helping him, not to mention useless at work tomorrow.

Normally, on days when her coworkers didn't organize a basketball game — the real kind, with fruit baskets hung in trees out there near the dig site in Mexico — she did jumping jacks and then jogged in place. But that would shake the 'check' out of this trailer and wake Kelsey up. There was no need for both of them to pass a sleepless night.

Besides, after eleven years of only dreaming about being here someday, she was finally in Scotland! And the full moon was shining through the window.

Not bothering with any makeup or jewelry, she quickly dressed in black sweats, her older pair of Doc Martin boots, and her coat, then snuck outside into the damp night air. Looking up at a bazillion stars despite the full moon, she popped in her ear buds and cranked up the music, then walk-jog-danced along the cliffs over the ocean.

It was a magical clear September night even if it was freezing cold here.

Shoving her hands into her pockets, she made a mental note to get some mittens next time someone went to town. And a thick wool scarf to put over her mouth and nose. She shuddered. Bbrrr! For now, she pulled up the hood of her sweatshirt and drew the drawstring tight, tying it in a bow, then stuffed her hands in her pockets.

But it really was beautiful here.

Moonlight hit the ripples in the ocean on her left and the grey stone hills that surrounded the grassy valley on her right, yet she could still see more stars than she ever had at home — or on any other dig.

At the same time, it was rugged and untamed. But that added to Scotland's beauty.

Below the craggy cliffs, the waves sprayed up white moonlit foam when they crashed against the rocks, breaking into different intricate patterns every time that seemed to expand to the beat of her music.

"Cool," she said aloud before continuing to dance-jog along the pathway.

When it turned to the right and Port Patrick loomed down on her left, she felt tired enough to sleep. Regretting having come so far and needing to walk all that way back, she turned around.

She was as close to the edge of the cliff as she dared go, looking down to watch the waves crash against the rocks and bobbing her head to the beat of the music when out of nowhere, someone in a white hooded robe ran at her.

Her instinct was to shrink away from the running man, but her experience in basketball told her to run toward him instead. So that was what she did, knowing full well that if she hadn't been in such good shape, she would have been startled into falling off the cliff for sure.

It seemed to be the robed man's intent to make her fall off the cliff, because he kept on running toward her, not backing down and not turning aside.

She changed her course a bit so that she was running more toward the trailers and less toward the man, surging with all she had to get out of this path and run back there before he would get to her.

But he was faster than her. Even running all out, she could tell he would get to her before she could get back to the dig camp.

So she changed tactics again.

Pivoting hard to her left, she ran away from the cliffs

toward the grass, where at least he couldn't push her off the cliff. She was getting winded now, though. She wouldn't have much strength left to fight him once he caught up to her.

Fortunately, she was now within earshot of the trailers. If anyone happened to be outside.

She stopped suddenly, took in as deep a breath as she could, and screamed for all she was worth.

The man laughed just before he got to her. A harsh, cruel laugh.

And then he grunted and went down.

He must've tripped. She made herself start running again, to take advantage of this trick fate chose to play on him. But she was nearly spent. She'd been running all out for almost a mile. And besides, curiosity got the best of her.

She firmly planted her feet far enough apart that she couldn't be knocked over easily and then looked over her shoulder.

Tomas was here. He had tackled the man in white, and the two of them were wrestling on the ground.

Exhilaration swelled in her heart. Tomas had come to save her.

And at the very same time, a new fear bloomed in her head. Fear for his safety now, rather than hers.

She looked around for a rock or a stick, anything she could use to hit the robed man in the head, if given the chance.

But white-robe-man got up and ran off.

Suddenly exhausted now that she felt safe and was

sure Tomas would be safe, Amber put her hands on her thighs and gulped in the air.

Tomas stood back there where he'd wrestled with her attacker, looking past her at the trailers. He had his arms crossed, but he wasn't angry. It was more like his arms were two doors that he was closing in front of himself.

In light of that, what he said really caught her off guard. It was so familiar and informal that it made her feel like there hadn't been a seven-year separation between them. Like this was just another day the two of them were hanging out together in a long string of such days.

The way things had been between them seven plus years ago.

"You look better without all that black stuff on your mouth."

Finally, she'd caught enough breath to speak. She said the first thing that came to her mind.

"What are you doing here so late? I thought you were staying at a hotel in town."

Tomas started walking quickly back toward the dig's trailer town.

"I'm just out for a walk."

She rolled her eyes out of habit, but he was looking ahead and didn't see. She had to jog to keep up with him.

"I know that, but why are you walking here? I thought you and ... that you went back to town, to your hotel."

He kept walking on in silence.

And again, she felt foolish. Yeah, he'd been nice enough to come and save her, but he was someone else's boyfriend now. He didn't have to tell her anything about why he was here, what he was doing out at night, or anything. She had to remember that.

It was hard, though.

Walking with him like this — at night on the grass with the stars above them in the bright moonlight — well, it reminded her of many such nights they used to spend when they were together. He'd been such a romantic, inviting her to take walks in the moonlight on the grass and then gazing deep into her eyes and baring his soul to her before each kiss...

Stop it.

Yes, Tomas needed her to get through to him and get him away from Sulis. That much Kelsey had convinced her of. But that didn't mean she and Tomas would be back together again. Look at him, she told herself. He's looking off at the boring trailers. He isn't the least bit interested in you. Yeah, he cares enough to save you from some white-robed weirdo, but he would do that for anyone.

She wasn't special to him. Not anymore.

But then when they entered the dig camp, he turned to look at her finally. And rather than the studied indifference and patience — or even just the friend-zoning she had been expecting — the look on his face was ... uncertain. Puzzled, even. Like he had just woken up in a strange place and wasn't sure how he'd gotten there.

"Sulis said she wanted to walk on the grass in the moonlight, but that I couldn't come with her. I insisted on driving her here, and then I just hung out in the car — until I saw you go walking off toward the cliffs."

She raised her eyebrows at him and gave him a goofy grin.

"So if I hadn't taken a walk out toward the cliffs, you'd still be just sitting in the car all alone? Were you at least reading a book or something? Listening to your music? Do you still like Celtic rock?"

He pursed his lips and moved his eyes from side to side as if he could find the answer to her question in their surroundings. Finally, he shook his head no and gave her a sheepish grin.

"Yeah, I still like Celtic rock, but no, no I wasn't listening to music or reading or anything. Just sitting there." He rumpled his eyebrows a little bit. "Are you saying I should thank you for relieving my boredom?"

Maybe Kelsey was right. Just her being with him seemed to be working. His personality was peeking out behind the dull lifeless eyes — and maybe it was her imagination, but they seemed to be getting a little twinkly, a little less absent.

Amber laughed just a little, just enough to hopefully lighten this mood that was too somber even for a Goth girl.

"Uh huh."

He gave her a small amused smile.

"Okay. Thanks."

She gave him one back.

"You're welcome. Oh, and by the way, thanks for stopping that guy from running me off the cliff."

He nodded his head sideways once.

"You're welcome."

Amber's analytical brain was pointing out that since the mood was now light and they were joking around, it would be a good time to ask him what was going on.

And before her heart could talk her out of it — before her love for him and yearning for him could convince her to just enjoy his company for however long he wanted to share it with her, to live in the moment and cherish it for what it was — she blurted out the questions that were on her mind.

"Tomas, who was that guy? Why was he wearing a white robe? What is Sulis doing walking around in the moonlight, and why can't you go with her?"

They had reached Kelsey's trailer. Just as her heart had feared, her questions made him back away from her, from the familiarity they were beginning to enjoy again with each other. He looked out to the grassy fields where Sulis must be walking.

He said just one more thing over his shoulder as he walked away toward his rental car.

"No more walks after dark, Amber."

Amber just stood there. She watched him get in his car and close the door, but then when he just sat there waiting for some other woman and didn't look at her, she felt alone again.

Thanking the stars above that she was so tired, she snuck back into bed and fell fast asleep.

SHE DREAMED THAT SHE AND KELSEY WERE IN THE

underground castle together, the site of the dig. Only now it was new inside. All the chiseled stone pictures of snakes, dogs, birds, human anatomy, flowers, and other natural things on the walls, ceiling, and floor practically gleamed with newness. And there was furniture in the rooms. It was odd furniture, made of carved wood but in shapes she'd never seen before. There were odd niches in every room whose purpose Amber couldn't even guess at they were so foreign, and the beds were carved out of the native stone of the place in shapes like giant bowls, and full of pillows shaped like apples and pears and grapes.

Standing still yet flying up and down and sideways together as if they were on a magic painter's lift, she and Kelsey went on a whirlwind tour of the underground Celtic palace, seeing dozens of rooms in only a minute.

They stopped inside a large room with a huge golden throne. It looked heavy. How would they ever get it out without destroying the place? She looked all around for a way to get such a large object out, but saw none. How had it gotten in here? Had the ancient Celts made it down here, thousands of years ago?

Amber was imagining she saw long lines of Celtic men and women with patterns tattooed on their faces and all over their bodies bringing endless pieces of gold down here for the head druid to melt in an iron pot over a roaring fire when Kelsey spoke.

"I'm here with you for real, Amber. This is more than just a dream. No one can hear what we say when I visit you in your dreams. It's the safest way to make plans and compare notes."

What the...? To give herself time to think and analyze the situation, Amber crossed her arms and blinked a few times.

"Okay, this is weird. But what's the harm in talking to you in my dream, right? I'm ninety nine point nine, nine, nine percent sure that tomorrow you'll have no idea what's been said in this dream. But weird things are going on. So just to test it, tomorrow I'll casually say something innocuous that we've said in this dream. If this is real and you remember what we said, then wink at me. If this is just a dream, then of course you won't wink at me, and I'll know."

Kelsey pursed her lips and nodded at Amber.

"Good plan. Okay, so here's what I think we should do about Sulis —"

Amber put a hand on her friend's shoulder and shook her head no — in fact, she shook her friend's whole body, trying to get her attention.

"Oh, we've got much bigger problems than Sulis."

Kelsey lowered her chin and raised her eyebrows.

"Bigger than Sulis?"

Amber took a big breath and let it out.

"Oh yeah. Bigger than a whole pack of Sulises walking on a shoe store's worth of high heels."

She told her friend what had just happened to her, with the white robed guy chasing after her and Tomas saving her.

Kelsey's face went white.

"Are you sure he was wearing a white robe?"

What did she mean, was she sure?

"Uh, yeah. But what's the big deal about a white

robe? I was kind of more alarmed with the fact that he was trying to make me Fall. Off. The. Cliff."

Kelsey put her arm around Amber and hugged her.

"Of course that part's more disturbing. Sorry. It's just that while Sasha and I were at Celtic University, we studied druids, who were Celtic priests. They wore white linen robes during their ceremonies, which were always out in nature..." Kelsey gasped. "And it was a full moon last night."

Amber raised her eyebrows.

Kelsey took a deep breath and spoke fast.

"Druids were nature worshipers. They held their ceremonies in sacred groves of trees — which they fortified with standing stones once the Romans started coming after them. And the movements of the moon and the planets have to do with it also..."

Amber laughed and playfully nudged Kelsey's arm with the back of her hand.

"You said 'have to do with it' instead of 'had to do with it.'"

But her friend didn't laugh.

Amber tapped her with the back of her hand again.

"Come on, that's funny."

Kelsey turned around until she was staring Amber in the face, inches away from her, very intense.

"Tomas said Sulis wanted to walk on the green grass in the moonlight last night, right?"

4

CEITHIR

The next morning, Amber showered, did her long dark hair in a more romantic style, removed her black nail polish, and did her makeup normal instead of Goth. Just for variety. What Tomas said had nothing to do with it. She just had more personality than to always wear the same look, was all. She checked herself twice in the mirror, adjusting first her hair and then the lay of her clothes before she was satisfied.

When Amber came out of her bedroom dressed for work in her Doc Martin boots, jeans, and a white blouse so long it might as well have been a dress, Kelsey was busy scrambling eggs.

Amber went into the refrigerator and got out the orange juice.

"It was a full moon last night."

Kelsey paused for a moment at stirring her scrambled eggs, and when their eyes met while Amber was on her way into the cupboard to get the juice glasses — Kelsey winked at her.

A rush of adrenaline went through Amber, and she almost dropped the glasses. She managed to put them down on the counter, but her hand shook so much when she tried to pour that she gave up and set the carton down.

Kelsey handed her the spatula.

"Here, you stir the eggs. I'll pour the juice."

When they both had their food and sat facing each other, Amber opened her mouth to say something.

But Kelsey shook her head no and took a sip of her juice, staring at Amber significantly over the top of the glass.

"I hope you have sweet dreams tonight."

Oh.

They could only talk in their dreams.

Because people might be listening.

Amber nodded, and they finished their breakfast and went down inside the underground castle. Amber saw it with new eyes after that tour in her dream the night before, recognizing the odd niches in each room and seeing the barest hints of decoration behind all the layers of dust and cobwebs. Excited again about working here, she grabbed Kelsey by the arm and gestured to include the whole underground area.

"I might not have the book learning you do, but my experience tells me how this is supposed to work. You haven't gotten very far down in your dig, so you can't have turned up much of anything to base theories of origin on. How do you know what it looked like down here when it was new?"

Kelsey smiled at a construction worker passing by before turning to Amber with wide eyes.

"Are you kidding? Only in my wildest dreams would I know that!"

Slowly nodding yes, Amber let go of her friend's arm. Okay, the weird magic stuff was way more secret than she thought.

The two of them talked business for an hour — with Kelsey asking a million questions about where to keep the cataloging stuff and how to organize everything — and then Amber got her tools off a table that stood in the center of a long hallway and moved toward the room she was working on, speaking to Kelsey over her shoulder.

"I can see wc need to talk a lot more about your dreams. See you at lunch?"

Kelsey nodded matter-of-factly and waved as she walked down the hall.

Amber spent the next hour brushing dust and cobwebs out of a huge tree carved in the floor of the secret room she was working on, but all the while her mind was scheming. Tomas knew more than he let on about all this weird magic stuff. And he knew who the white robe guy was, she could tell by the way he looked at the man.

How should she go about getting Tomas alone so she could ask him about the man? She would have to get

Sulis busy doing something else. Her favorite idea there was spilling something all over blondie's designer clothes, but then she would probably just demand that Tomas drive her back to their hotel...

Before she could act on any of her ideas, however, Tomas came into her workroom.

His vacant zombielike eyes looked away from hers almost as soon as he came in, and then he turned to study the part of the tree she was done brushing free of debris and spoke offhandedly, in a barely audible voice.

"Why did you come here to Scotland?"

She sighed. She couldn't exactly tell him the truth, which would be 'I came to see you, of course. I thought we could pick right up where we left off in our relationship before you disappeared on me the day after your eighteenth birthday. I figured since Kelsey and Tavish were back together, it only made sense that you and I would be back together. Thought all I'd have to do was show up, and you'd welcome me back into your arms.'

No, she couldn't give out any hint she wanted to talk about that, or he would be stricken with the fear of his creepy girlfriend and bolt out the door. Amber knew that in her gut. And because her heart ached so for him, she knew her ache for him would show in her eyes, here under the bright work lights. So she didn't even dare look at him, but made a point of keeping her eyes on the carved-out tree as well, while she formulated her answer.

She did come up with something truthful she could tell him.

"Kelsey called and begged me to come help her. She

just got her doctorate in Celtic Art History, you know, but she doesn't have much experience at dig sites. Well, I've spent the last six years working at them, so I'm helping her in lots of little ways only a real friend can."

She kept working while he slowly wandered around the large room, aimlessly looking at the wall carvings that were still barely legible beneath all the dirt and grime. When he was back near the doorway a quarter hour later, he spoke again.

He kept asking her pretty much the same thing: why was she here. Each time he asked, he would be near the door, looking like he was going to leave as soon as she answered.

Leave and go report back to Sulis.

For all Amber knew, Sulis had sent Tomas in here to ask her that very question. The thought enraged her, made her want to get up and go find that woman and tell her to mind her own business — and to admit that Tomas had friends and family who deserved to spend time with him.

But all of Amber's instincts told her to keep Tomas here in this room with her as long as she could.

So each time he asked why she'd come here, she scrambled her brains for a more interesting way to answer. Her aim was to keep adding more layers of meaning and connection and common history to her answer, yet to always be truthful. And she always emphasized that she was Kelsey's true friend — and by extension, she hoped she was reminding Tomas that she was his true friend.

She cared about him, and this was the hardest thing

she'd ever done: telling him she cared about him without appearing to be doing so. Because again, her gut told her that the slightest appearance of her reaching out to him would trigger some sort of fear his faker of a girlfriend had implanted in him. Because Kelsey was clearly right: this was not the real Tomas. That woman had used magic or hypnosis or threats or something in order to charm him into submission to her.

And Amber had to keep telling herself his distance was a product of whatever spell Sulis had put on him, that it wasn't his decision to be like that. But his coldness hurt nonetheless.

By the fourth time he asked, he had been there in the secret room alone with Amber an hour — and she was blinking back tears when she answered his 'why are you here' question.

"A bunch of memories came back to me when Kelsey called, and I couldn't wait to see her and Tavish and you and everybody else again."

He wandered around some more. Was it her imagination, or was he staying closer and closer to her the longer he was here?

He asked it again, but this time he was definitely closer to her. And looking her in the eye. And rather than cold and distant, he looked ... lost. Confused. His voice sounded that way, too.

"Why are you here?"

She longed to stand up and give him a hug, to remind him who she was and how much she had missed him. To ask why he had disappeared from her life. To tell him she still loved him and ask didn't he love her? But what did she dare do but answer his question?

Well, she could drag as much connection to him into her answer as possible, that was what.

"I've had a great time working at digs in Mexico and South America these past six years, but remember how all of us wanted to come to Scotland together — you & me, Tavish & Kelsey, John & Jaelle, Jeff & Ashley, Gabe & Lauren, and Mike & Sarah — how we would plan it out together, dreaming of some day when we'd all be here?"

He froze there, after she said that. It happened so abruptly that it broke her resolve not to look at him. There he was, still healthy and hale and handsome as ever, but shut down inside. It was as if someone had put opaque contact lenses on his eyes. He just wasn't all there.

But right this second, something different was happening. He had stopped and he was looking at her, right into her eyes. And she was looking into his, desperate to see him recognize her the way he had last night. She imagined she could see the wheels turning behind his eyes.

She imagined she was watching his very psyche battling the spell that held it captive.

After a long time as thinking goes — a minute or more — he nodded his head.

And now that she had drawn Tomas out a bit in the direction she truly wanted to, she didn't dare ask him about the white robed guy last night — whether he was a druid or not, and especially whether Sulis was a druid or not.

No. That would trigger some defensive part of the spell and undo all she had done over the last hour. She just knew it would. She had to keep things light, easy, unchallenging — or he would leave. She could get through to him if he would only stay awhile. She knew it. Just knew it.

There was one question she felt she could ask.

"What have you been doing with yourself these past seven years? Anything new?"

He paused, and the look on his face was heartbreaking. He looked like he couldn't remember the past seven years. But he kept quiet for a few moments, just looking into her eyes. Ever so gradually, his own eyes grew softer with recognition after a while.

When he spoke, his voice sounded almost normal. It reached deep inside of her and drew her to him, made her want to hug him and hold him close and love this blockage out of him.

But she knew she couldn't. Or else.

And it was so hard to see him like this. His face was not as animated as it normally was. Not nearly. He looked her in the eye though. That counted for a lot and relieved some of her hurt feelings.

"I've been taking some business classes," he said, "now that Mom and Dad and Vange and Peadar are talking about leaving me, Mike, Gabe, and Jeff in charge of the fair. They want to get Tavish and John more involved in the antique business."

She smiled at this.

Ha! So Sulis didn't know what she was talking about when it came to the antique store after all. It would be Tavish and John, not Tomas, who inherited the antiques business. Amber stopped working on the runes and settled back, leaning against the wall and really looking at Tomas.

"You get to be in charge of the fair? That's so cool."

He smiled. Actually smiled. It reached his eyes and everything.

She kept her smile up, careful to keep it friendly, though that was tough when his sudden joyous smile made her body want to tackle him like she would have seven years ago and...

She made herself focus on drawing his personality out, as if he were a stranger she was just getting to know.

"Have you and Mike and Gabe and Jeff worked out who will be in charge of what?"

He smiled again and nodded yes.

"I'm the only one taking business classes, so I'll be in charge of the money."

They laughed together, and it was the most wonderful feeling Amber'd had in years.

But never mind what her body wanted. That was tough enough, but her own psyche was begging her to reach out to him and hug him and tell him how much she'd missed him — and to demand that he tell her why he had left her — why he'd disappeared from her life seven years ago.

Seeing how vulnerable he was, how hard he had to

struggle just to remember his own life these past seven years, she told her psyche to shut up. This had to be about him. First. She promised the little abandoned girl inside of her that they two of them would get their turn. That once Tomas was himself again, she would insist on getting the answers they needed.

When he finished his brief laugh, Tomas continued talking.

"It's more complicated than that, of course. I'll be the business guy, which will include marketing the fair as well as the accounting and making sure vendors are licensed..."

She nodded.

"That's a lot of responsibility."

He let out a sigh.

"I know. It's much more responsibility than running an antique store." He looked at her with an 'oh yeah' look on his face, and then gestured toward her inclusively. "Well you know."

She smiled a goofy smile at him and nodded yes. Good. He remembered at least that she'd worked at the fair with him. Did he remember the rest? She was dying to ask him, but he still wasn't himself. Not by half.

"Yep, I know."

He relaxed a little and smiled, and she could have sworn he kicked some imaginary dust on the floor.

"Yeah, that's right, you did the fair with me for four years, so you know there's thousands of people involved who work there and hundreds of thousands of people all over the world who look forward to attending the fair every year..."

To draw his attention away from his embarrassment at forgetting she'd been there, she stood up. It worked. He watched her.

She smiled at him kindly.

"Yeah, that's a lot of responsibility you'll have. What are Mike, Gabe, and Jeff going to do?"

He chuckled at her joke about him doing everything.

"Well, seriously, there's still scheduling all the shows, and outreach to all the participants, getting the insurance — well I guess that's a business thing, so it's mine, too..."

She chuckled at his joke and then used one of the gestures they had used at the fair in their shows together, hoping the familiarity would draw him out more.

"Back up a minute. Did you say there were people all over the world looking forward to attending the fair every year?"

He had stayed by her side without wandering away for a good ten minutes now. This was working. Hope blossomed in her heart. And her body told her to grab him and kiss him and make him hers again. But her mind warned her that would be disastrous.

He stayed with her and nodded.

"Yeah."

She gently shook her head no, smiling at him incredulously.

"I didn't know that. I thought your fair was just in our town."

He scratched his head.

"Well, no. We have three different locations in the US while it's warm up there, and then when it's winter there, it's summer in Australia, so we have three locations down under, too." He wrinkled his nose up and twinkled his eyes at her. "Okay, I guess two countries isn't really all over the world."

She opened her mouth as wide as she could and let her jaw hang, bending her head forward a bit to show how shocked she was.

"And so you're going to be managing this whole thing? I guess you'll have business licenses to renew in six different locations — not to mention all the different taxes you'll have to file..."

He pushed his lips together and raised one eyebrow while nodding just a little in acknowledgment of a good summation of the scope of his duties.

"Mmhmm. But we have a good accountant and a good manager who will help train me before they retire — oh, you know them. Remember Edgar? Not Edgar the pickle monger, but Rowena's cousin Edgar?"

Her heart pounded in her chest with renewed hope. He was remembering!

She smiled and whirled her eyes around.

"Oh my gosh, don't tell me he's an accountant now? He could barely sit down, he was so hyper. But it was good for the show when he walked on stilts all the time!"

They laughed together.

He closed his eyes tight and lowered his head and stomped his foot, he was laughing so hard.

"Ha! No. No. No. He's our business manager, and he's really good at it. He gets us good deals from the vendors and even from the insurance company, with being so entertaining and how personable he is — and the way he never sits down, he gets more done in a day than the rest of us would in a week, it seems like."

Ever so gently, ever so slowly, she continued to draw out his personality by encouraging him to talk about his work.

Ever so gradually, he participated more and more in the conversation.

After a few hours, he seemed almost normal. Almost warm. Almost alive.

Hope blossomed in Amber's heart. Here alone with her, he was himself again and not that sycophantic zombie following after Sulis. Maybe he would see his way out of her influence. Maybe Amber would get her second chance with him after all, despite the difficulty and all the weirdness. She nourished the hope. She let it convince her things would be okay, that everything would work out.

Until Sulis barged in.

The perfectly coiffed blonde stormed over and grabbed Tomas's hand, pulling him to her and whispering in his ear, the whole time staring daggers at Amber.

Immediately, Tomas zombied up again.

The twinkle left his eyes.

The sense of camaraderie they'd been sharing disappeared — worse, all signs of intelligence or even autonomy left his whole countenance. He was like a walking rag doll. Blank. Empty.

Without saying anything, Sulis dragged him away, casting a furious glance at Amber behind her.

Cursing, Amber threw her tools down and left the room to follow them.

☙ 5 ❧

CÒIG

Amber ran quite a ways down the carven stone corridors lit by strings of white Christmas lights, thinking to at least hear Tomas and Sulis if not see them after rounding each corner. But it was as if the living rock walls of the ancient underground castle had swallowed them up.

She finally had to admit that Sulis had won this round. She couldn't find them.

So she sought out Kelsey instead, and joined her and Tavish for lunch at the crew's lunch truck. Amber was dying to tell them she had connected with Tomas again and Sulis had ruined it, but with all the people around, they could only talk shop. They did so for several hours, with Amber supplying mostly answers and Kelsey asking a thousand questions. And then Kelsey excused herself and Tavish to do some errand or other, and Amber went back to her room with the tree carved in the floor and worked, alone.

Just after sunset as everyone was headed back to their trailers, Amber was still alone when she saw Sulis walking out in the grassy field in a white robe, singing.

Amber headed off into the grass to follow the druidess.

Sulis headed toward the cliffs.

Amber followed, growing more and more curious what the woman would do when she got there. Did she know Amber was following? Did she hope to make Amber fall off the cliff the way her fellow druid had failed to?

Yeah, Sulis knew Amber was following, because she waited at the edge of the cliff. She had no other reason to do that. But Amber wasn't sure how Sulis knew she was coming. She was hiding under a bushy tree, peering through some branches, so she should have been invisible from over there on the cliff. Oh well.

Wait, what!

Amber rubbed her eyes.

Sulis was going over the edge of the cliff.

Amber took off running as fast as she could.

"Wait! I don't mean to hurt you. I just want to tell you to release whatever unnatural hold you have on Tomas. Don't jump. We can work this out. It's not too late!"

But Sulis only laughed and slowly lowered herself over the cliff on a rope that must've been hidden from Amber's view.

Sure enough, when Amber got to the cliff, she noticed a rope ladder that was tied to a tree stump. Taking a deep breath and letting it out slowly, she took hold of the top rung and tugged on it, unsure if it was sturdy even after watching Sulis go down it.

Don't be a coward, she told herself. However else the two of you are different — which is pretty much in everything down to the smallest detail — you look like you weigh about the same.

Before she could lose her nerve, she planted her foot on a lower rung and swung her butt over the edge of the cliff. Whoa, looking down was a mistake. There were the waves crashing violently against the rocks.

Heart beating rapidly, Amber made herself put one foot down, then the other, then both hands — until she saw a cave there in the side of the sea cliff.

Wow.

She stepped off the rope ladder into a tunnel. This one was down deeper than those she and Kelsey had been working on, but the failing sunlight penetrated the cave somehow up ahead, so it wasn't dark.

Taking confidence from this, she entered the cave, keeping on guard in case Sulis jumped out at her. This was a natural cave, rough and dirty, not a carved out corridor — though her mind told her it would connect to the network of those eventually, or why would there be a ladder to it.

After a few seconds, it was tempting to call out Sulis's name, it seemed so desolate down here. At least it didn't stink like some of the ruins where she'd worked. These cliffs under Dunskey Castle were open to the ocean air, so there was a pleasant nautical scent.

Oh, she could hear footsteps up ahead, now that she

was deeper into the tunnel and out of earshot of the waves.

Speeding up to a run, Amber followed the sound of Sulis's footsteps through ancient rooms full of secrets. She longed to linger down here, exploring. Nothing was as she expected it to be in a castle. This was old. A relic from a much different time. The Iron Age, Kelsey had said.

Sulis led her on a merry chase up one level and down the next, around this bend and over that set of stairs. Amber ran down a hallway where she'd thought she heard Sulis's footsteps only to hit a dead-end.

When she stopped to turn around, Amber reasoned that she must've run really fast down that particular hallway, because she felt so dizzy she had to stop and put her hands on her knees and wait for the vertigo to pass.

It took an unusually long time.

It took so long that once she had recovered, she could no longer hear Sulis's footsteps.

Amber crept down to the beginning of that dead-end corridor and looked around, listening. Still no sound of Sulis, but at least she was pretty sure she knew where she was now. Checking on her theory, she walked toward her and Kelsey's work area.

Well that was strange. She was sure this was the area where the big table should be with all the artifacts they were cataloguing and everybody's pouches of tools, but someone had turned out the lights. She got out her phone to use as a flashlight. Maybe this wasn't it after all. But it sure seemed to be. There was the crevice which looked like a dog. And that was the spot she was always having to duck sideways to miss as she made the last turn into the room.

Well, maybe everybody had moved their things out while she was chasing Sulis?

Including the lights?

What the heck was going on? Kelsey would know. Amber went over near one of the small drafty side caves where she had used her phone this morning successfully.

But now there was no signal.

Kelsey had better have a good reason why all their stuff had been moved — and where was it? Had Mr. Blair brought in yet more trailers?

Suddenly needing to know if her tools were still on the floor where she had thrown them, Amber headed over that way. But she stopped abruptly. The secret door to the room she had been working in two hours ago was closed. And there were cobwebs in front of it.

Goosebumps rose on the back of her neck and trailed down the backs of her arms.

She kept looking for the signal to re-connect as she walked toward the root cellar with the ladder that went up out the trap door. But the secret door at the end of that hallway was closed. It had never been closed before.

She had no idea how to open that door.

Panic rose in her chest. She hadn't had a panic attack since she was thirteen.

There had to be a logical explanation for why these doors were closed and why all their stuff was missing—

Tavish.

Tavish must be playing a practical joke on her.

It wasn't funny.

The anger she felt at him gave her the strength to turn around and retrace her steps back to the rope ladder. Only, it wasn't there.

Panic tried to take hold of her again, and fortunately, her therapist's advice for fighting panic twelve years ago came back to her. Slow, deep breaths. Think logically. Work on the trouble.

The deep breaths were the easiest part. She had them down. Thinking logically about all this, though? Maybe she'd better just skip to working on the trouble. But doing what?

Looking for a way out, that's what.

Maybe the rope ladder was there and had just drifted outside of the cave a bit. Maybe if she went to the opening and felt around outside, she would find it.

She got to the cave opening — high up over the crashing waves — and held on to a rock which jutted out of the cave wall while she reached out and felt around.

Puzzled at what she felt, she nonetheless pulled it inside to have a look.

It wasn't a rope ladder at all, but it was a rope. A single strand of rope that looked handmade.

She'd had enough, and she yelled up out of the cave mouth.

"Tavish! There's no way I'm climbing up with just this stupid flimsy old rope! Throw down the rope ladder. Right now! Do you hear me? I said throw down the rope ladder right now."

❧

AFTER YELLING UP THE CLIFF FOR HALF AN HOUR, Amber was seeing red. Tavish still hadn't come.

And maybe he expected her to repel up the side of the cliff with only the handmade rope as a safeguard against falling down onto the rocks, but she didn't feel up to that. She had barely made herself climb down the rope ladder. Climb up with just this rope? Nuh uh.

Tavish had told her on her first day that there was another entrance down a stairway that wasn't in use now because they were trying to preserve it. She hadn't seen that staircase in her wanderings today, but she had mostly been deeper than the first level, where a staircase would be. In most of the underground palace, the halls just slanted downward.

But in Kelsey's whirlwind tour in their dream, there had been a staircase up. Amber turned around to go back down the cave again.

As soon as she did, she saw Tomas coming toward her — wearing a kilt like Tavish's. A pleat-it-each-time-you-put-it-on 'great kilt' like the ones they had worn to the Renaissance Faire. He looked wonderfully familiar in it. And sexy.

She felt so confused in the moment that her tongue was tied, a rarity for Amber. Usually she talked way more than was good for her. But right now, Tavish was playing this trick on her, and she felt inadequate to climb up a rope, and Sulis had led her down here and then abandoned her, and now Tomas seemed to be playing along with this part of the joke.

How stupid could she be?

Somehow, Tomas had been the one person she thought she could trust, even more than Kelsey. But now he had proven otherwise by showing up in this kilt and being part of this stupid joke. She was angry and frustrated and sad and lonely.

Considering he'd been a zombie most of the time she'd seen him lately, Amber was surprised when Tomas had no qualms at all about how he felt.

He yelled at her, making her jump.

"What are you doing here in modern clothing?"

Finally settling on feeling defeated, Amber slumped down and sat on the cold stone cave floor.

"Tomas, I don't know what game this is, but I'm not playing."

Surprising her again, he took her by the arm and pulled her up, then tugged her down the hallway.

"I can't believe you're doing this, Amber. You don't even know how serious this is, do you? Of course not. You just got here. Why did you have to do this? Sulis is so pissed, I think she might even... I don't know what she's going to do, but it's not going to be good. Just let me get you out of here, okay?"

It had felt wonderful when he first took her arm, and it wasn't half bad even now, with him tugging her along as if she were a child. He seemed oblivious to the effect it was having on her, however. Didn't chemistry work both ways? If she was feeling chemistry, wasn't he feeling it too?

She took a deep breath and let it out, surprised to find that she really didn't need to. Her anxiety had disappeared as soon as he showed up — even though he had yelled at her.

Resigned to being tugged by the arm, Amber just followed along. At least Tomas seemed to know where he was going. She just stayed quiet, hoping he really would get her out of here.

But no such luck.

Tomas continued this weird game they were playing, although at least his yelling had gradually wound down, and now he was just talking.

"I'm going to take you to the travel spot. You need to stay there while I go get Tavish, okay?"

Just play along. Get the game over with.

"Okay."

He took her back to that room where the table should have been with all their stuff, and planted her against the wall at a T intersection of the corridors.

"Okay, I'm going to get Tavish so he can take you home. Wait right here."

He looked her in the eyes when he said to wait right here — and took her breath away.

She saw deep concern for her in his eyes.

"Yeah, okay, I'll wait right here."

She watched him run back toward the staircase, his kilt swishing in a pleasing way. And she did wait there. But while she was waiting, a strange song came to her ears. It was barely audible, but pleasing. Just when she was starting to wonder again what was going on and where everything had gone, the music changed.

It was singing, she realized. Soft, beautiful singing in a woman's voice. She couldn't understand the words, but the song called out to her nonetheless in feelings that her mind translated for her.

"Follow me. Follow me to beauty. Follow me to happiness. Follow me to the answer to all of your dreams."

The song just hinted of this at first, but the longer she listened, the louder it got — and the more insistent. She found herself getting up and taking a few steps forward, the song was so compelling.

"The worries of your heart will be answered. An end to all your yearning is near. Come, taste the freedom."

But it was more than just these promises. The song somehow made her see visions of green fields with butterflies fluttering above them, and glittering waterfalls with fairies dancing in the mist. Vaguely, she was aware that she was wandering through the underground castle, but she was going a way she hadn't gone before. She didn't worry about it. She was following the promise of the song, and it kept getting brighter and more hopeful by the minute.

"Come dance with your love up in the sunlight. Come out of these caves in this darkness into the glorious day."

In the back of her mind, her logical reasoning protested that the sun had just set and it was night time now, but she ignored this still soft voice. Because the promise was so strong, so alluring.

"You can have everything you desire if you only follow. Come with me on a journey into the best places you'll ever see."

Already she was seeing things she'd never seen before. Oh, she passed through the grand throne room Kelsey had told her about, with the golden throne. It did look heavy. Vaguely, she wondered how Kelsey and Tavish and all the crew would ever get it out of there. And she passed through several secret doors that hadn't been open before — and again she wondered who had done the secret combination of movements of bricks to open them. She knew she hadn't.

But it really didn't matter. Nothing mattered except following the song that was going to bring her back to Tomas. It was going to join the two of them in all the ways that she was dreaming of. It was going to make them happy together for the rest of their lives.

Her feet moved faster now. She was running through the decorated stone corridors. She had put her phone in her pocket when she was looking for the rope ladder, but a twinkly fairy light guided her steps and didn't let her trip.

Way back in the background of her mind, she noticed that the wall and floor carvings here weren't so debris-filled as the ones she'd been clearing. The tiniest part of her mind wondered why that was — but the greater part dismissed it.

She could see the stairs now, the stairs Tavish and told her about, that she had been wondering about. There was nothing fancy about them, so why weren't they being used? They didn't appear to need preserving.

This also was dismissed. The song was full blast now. The source of the song was at the top of the stairs, waiting for her along with all the promises of the song — everything she ever wanted.

She ran up the stairs two at a time, impatient to get to where the promises waited. Bursting out into the cloudy light of a typical dreary Scottish day, she smiled and looked around for Tomas.

She didn't see him, but the song told her where she would find him.

"Come over here to the edge of the cliff."

She couldn't get there fast enough. Even though it was difficult to run in her Doc Martens, she did run. Over the grass and stones. Across the path she had taken toward Port Patrick the night before. Right up to the edge of the cliff she ran, and stayed there, gazing at the waves as they dashed against the jagged sharp rocks far below.

"Are not the waves gallant?" asked the song which still hummed in her ear with a melodious beauty surpassed by nothing she ever imagined. "Are they not strong and beautiful, the way they dash with such purpose — and that magnificent sound?"

In Amber's imagination, the song was now a beautiful fairy who had come to grant all of her secret wishes. So Amber nodded yes in response to the fairy's question. For the waves were indeed majestic and noble, deserving a great strong purpose. It was nearly impossible to tear her gaze away from them.

When she had been there a minute or so, watching the waves, she began to yearn for them. To want them to embrace her. For their strength to carry her with their purpose.

At that point, the song changed again. It became even more beautiful, with lovely notes that carried on the wind and reminded her of the ocean, the way they drifted up and down so predictably and so comfortingly.

"The gallant waves wait to take you to your own personal paradise. All you need do is go to them. Now."

Realizing this was her cue, that she was meant to do this and it would be the answer to all of her wishes, Amber raised her foot to step off the cliff.

6

SIA

Before Amber fell off the cliff into the welcoming waves, a hand snatched her arm and pulled her back. Irritated, she turned, ready to chew the person out, whoever it was.

But it was Kelsey. Since lunch, she had changed into a floor-length plaid overdress in blues and browns with a bit of yellow. Under that was an extra floor-length skirt in plain brown. The big billowing sleeves of her linen blouse were light blue.

Her stricken brown eyes searched Amber, and when Kelsey spoke, it was in Gaelic.

"Whatever are ye doing, Amber, trying tae give us the vapors? How did ye get here, and why didn't ye change clothes first?"

Even as she listened to Kelsey, Amber could still hear the song, but it was fading. Desperate to get what she wanted, Amber fought against Kelsey's hold, fought to go over the cliff after all. She could still see the waves down there, waiting to welcome her. Just a few more inches, and she would join them.

But another hand took hold of her other arm and yanked her away from the cliff. Oddly, this second person stopped and fell, but Kelsey caught the second person.

This new person — also a woman, it turned out — spoke to Kelsey, also in Gaelic. What was up with these people and their costumes and their old-fashioned language? What kind of game was this?

"Naught much. She will be at oor wedding. Nevertheless, we need tae get her inside."

"Aye, howsoever for now, just put yer cloak aroond her."

The other woman laughed. Laughed. At a time like this. Kelsey and her friend must still be playing Tavish and Tomas's game. Great. For a moment, Amber regretted ever leaving the Mexican dig site. Her old friends were strange to her, and she felt more alone than ever. But...

Now that she was away from the cliff and these women were talking...

What was she doing here?

Oh yeah. There had been that song... It was gone now.

She stopped fighting against them and relaxed. Kelsey was her friend. She wasn't going to hurt her. Why was she fighting against her? The idea of walking off the cliff now filled her with horror instead of... Why she been walking off the cliff, again?

Meanwhile, Kelsey's friend had removed her cloak

and was arranging it over Amber's shoulders, where she fastened it with her brooch. She looked at Kelsey and grinned.

"We will take ye inside and find ye some aught tae wear, but in the meantime ye will be fine sae long as ye keep this cloak about ye."

Amber looked at the woman. Also dressed in a long plaid dress and a bell-sleeved linen blouse, she was tall and red haired and smiling with joy.

"Ah, ye must be Sasha."

Sasha nodded and smiled.

Amber studied her. She seemed to be a modern woman, but did she only understand Gaelic? Amber spoke to her in that language, which Tavish's parents had taught her at the fair.

"Hae I seen ye afore? Because ye look familiar."

Sasha laughed again.

"Wull if ye were a man and I wasna about tae be marrit — in the middle o' planning my wedding ceremony right at this moment, as a matter o' fact — I would tease ye and say some aught like 'only in yer dreams.'" She gave Amber a weird significant look, giving her the impression she should know something but didn't, and then shrugged and went on. "Howsoever, syne ye are na a man and I dinna feel like teasing ye, I shall just say nay, na really. 'Tis nice tae meet ye, Amber. I hae heard a little about ye and all yer other faire friends ower the years. I lived with Kelsey during her studies. Did she tell ye?"

Amber didn't answer, because she couldn't get enough breath.

She was coming out of a daze and had only just noticed the huge very solid stone-on-stone castle that loomed next to them. In no way shape or form had that been there three hours ago when she followed Sulis over the cliff. There had only been the old tower house, which was much smaller than this... fortress.

Sasha and Kelsey turned to follow Amber's gaze at the castle, and then turned back to her.

Kelsey nodded.

"'Tis magnificent, aye?"

Still struggling to get enough breath because of the anxiety that now gripped her again, Amber wrinkled her brow at Kelsey and managed to squeak out a question.

"Magnificent? More like impossible! Where the 'check' did it come from?"

But Kelsey and Sasha weren't looking at Amber anymore. She followed the direction they were looking in.

Half a dozen kilted guards outfitted in leather armor, heavy handmade boots, and hundreds of pounds of weapons were headed their way. And Sasha and Kelsey were smiling at them.

The guards halted when they got to Amber and her friends. Their leader looked Amber over appreciatively but politely as he spoke to Kelsey.

"Wull now am I tae be supposing this is another o' yer clanswomen come tae market, Kelsey?"

Kelsey smiled at him and put her arm through Amber's arm.

"Aye, she is. Cormac, this is Amber. And afore ye ask, I dinna ken how long she will be staying. Amber, these are some o' Laird Malcomb's brawest castle guards."

Amber tried to be polite and play along. She really did.

But this was all too much. What the heck?

First she almost stepped off the cliff — had seen the dashing waves beneath her with their foam coming up and known she was going to fall to her death — and now here was a whole castle that hadn't been there before — and guards straight out of Braveheart. The only thing missing was the blue face paint. The rational part of her mind said she would have to ask Kelsey about that later.

But most of her struggled to say something, anything, that would make sense in the situation.

But her lungs constricted until she was gasping for air. Black spots appeared before her eyes, and the next thing she knew, she was collapsing.

AMBER WOKE UP IN A BED. IT WAS VERY comfortable, and the covers were heavy and luxurious — handmade quilts, going by the stitches she felt with her fingers. She pulled the covers up over her head to go back to sleep. For some reason, she was stressed out. Yeah, best to go back to sleep before she remembered why.

But no such luck.

Kelsey's voice grabbed her attention and wouldn't let go, and Kelsey's hand pulled the covers down.

"Oh good, you're okay. It's safe to talk now. It's just us women. You can trust Sasha. The guys are waiting outside. We're all dying to know how you got here by yourself, and why didn't you change clothes first?"

Huh? This must be another persistent dream. Maybe if she sat up, she'd wake up more and things would be less confusing. Instead, she pulled the covers back over her head again.

"This has got to be a nightmare. Just let me go back to sleep so I can wake up again and have all this be over."

Kelsey pulled the covers down to Amber's waist.

"I wish this were a dream, because then I could manipulate things the way I wanted them, but it's not. We're really here in the fourteenth century, and you're really with us. I found some clothes you can change into, so that's less of a problem. But Amber, how did you get here? The only way the rest of us are able to time travel is with Tavish's ring. We're super curious to know how you managed it."

Amber put her elbows behind her and used them to help her sit up. As she did so, she noticed the stone block construction of the small but nicely appointed bedroom they were in. Its windows were skinny and tall, barely letting in any light, but it did have a warmly burning fireplace. More light came from candles in holders on the walls. Aside from the bed, there was just an armchair and a dresser with a pitcher and bowl on top of it.

Sasha was sitting in the armchair. She waved.

With a heavy sigh, Amber sat up in the bed and

threw her legs over the side, waved back, then turned to Kelsey.

"I didn't get here by myself. Are you kidding? I had no idea. Sulis must have brought me here. She was wearing a white druid robe like you described, and she was singing out in the grass. I followed her down a rope ladder over the cliff into a cave that led to the underground castle, and she led me on a merry chase. She must have taken me back in time while she did so—"

"Did you get dizzy?"

"Yeah, really dizzy. But Kelsey, that's not the scariest part. Her song hypnotized me. It made me want to jump off the cliff."

Kelsey sat down on the bed next to Amber and hugged her, then jumped up and went and got a parcel Amber hadn't noticed before.

"Fortunately, we're apprenticed to a weaver here, and she likes to sew. There's lots of extra clothes lying around. They don't have sizes, but I think these will fit."

Amber got up and put the outfit on. It was much like Kelsey and Sasha's, only more green and yellow, less brown. While she changed, Kelsey and Sasha exchanged worried looks.

When she had finished dressing and adjusting, Amber put her hands on both of their shoulders.

"Please, tell me what's going on. I always thought it would be fun if I could go back in time. Why are druids making me jump off cliffs?"

Kelsey furtively glanced at the door.

"How about if we let the guys come in so that Tavish can explain?"

Amber looked at the door too.

"Is Tomas out there?"

Kelsey nodded yes.

There wasn't a mirror in the room, or Amber would've been in front of it checking herself out. Not having that way to stall, she simply ran her fingers through her bed hair and then nodded yes in return.

Tomas was scowling at her when he came in, but it wasn't a strong scowl. His face looked more worried than angry.

"Why did you have to go and wander away from that spot? I got Tavish as quickly as I could, and we went back there and you were gone."

Kelsey appealed to Tavish with her eyes, and her boyfriend put his hand on his twin's arm.

"Let it go, okay? She's had a shock, and she fainted after nearly falling off a cliff."

Tomas opened his mouth to argue, but then he nodded up once and turned aside and crossed his arms.

Amber went over into his line of sight.

"What's going on, Tomas?"

And just like that, all the animation left his face. He got a glazed look in his eyes and didn't answer.

Kelsey gave Amber a significant look that said 'I told you Sulis put a spell on him.'

Tavish stepped forward and took Amber's arm, walking her away from Tomas.

"To make a long story short, our ancestor made a pledge to a druid a long time ago — well actually, it's in the future right now. Anyway, every fourth born son in our family has to serve the druids if he lives to be twenty-five. I'm the fourth born son, and I've been serving them for nearly six years—"

Amber cut in, gesturing back and forth between Tavish and Tomas.

"But your twenty-fifth birthday was only six months ago."

Tavish nodded.

"Yes, but I've been here — in the past — for six years on-and-off during those six months. No time passes back home while I'm here. This magic ring they gave me on my birthday is set that way." He held up his right hand and showed her a silver ring that looked uncannily like the rings Sasha and Kelsey wore on their right hands.

Now Tomas scowled at his brother.

"Would you quit bragging about your time traveling ring?"

Fortunately, Tavish didn't get in an argument with his brother, just swallowed and looked back at Amber, still holding his right hand up and showing her the ring.

"Ironically, the young druid known as Lachlan the Dark — the one who tried to run you off the cliff the other night — thinks he can hide here in the past. He's working on enslaving humans in our time, and we're trying to catch him. With this ring, I can take you back to our time if you want. But I think it's safer if we all stay here together."

Amber gasped.

"Uh, yeah. If he can go back and forth in time at will — and he's trying to enslave people in our time — and all of you are here? Yeah, I'm staying here with you."

Tomas spoke up again, with his eyebrows wrinkled at Amber.

"It appears that you can go back and forth in time at will by yourself too. What's up with that? And you never explained why you came here without changing into period clothing, putting us all in danger."

He had to be kidding.

Now it was Amber's turn to scowl at Tomas, and she did so with a dropped jaw.

"I didn't bring myself here. I had no idea anyone could. It was Sulis. She sang some sort of song and it hypnotized me and almost made me jump off the cliff."

At the mention of Sulis's name, something snapped in Tomas. All the anger drained out of him, and he slowly turned on his heel and left the room without saying a word.

Tavish went after his brother.

"I'm sorry," he said over his shoulder.

Amber stood there just taking one breath after the other, trying to calm down. What were they going to do about Tomas? Any mention of Sulis, and his brain went to mush. He had seemed almost normal up until she mentioned the druidess. Why had she done that?

Kelsey put a hand on Amber's shoulder.

"Don't."

"Don't what?"

"Don't blame yourself. I can tell that's what you're doing. Remember this is Sulis's fault, not yours. Stay strong and positive. Remember, when all is said and done, you're probably the only one who can get through to him. He needs you, Amber."

Amber looked around the room.

"I want to go to bed. Is this where we're all staying while we're here? Because it seems pretty small for the four of us, and that's not including the witch with a B."

Kelsey gave Amber a minor smile at her little joke.

"No. In fact, Sulis has charmed Laird Malcomb into giving Tomas this castle room. Her magical powers are mighty, I can tell you — so long as she renews them out in nature daily. That's where she is right now. The laird's own nephew Seumas sleeps in the barracks along with Tavish and the other guards, while Tomas — a complete stranger to the laird — gets a room in the castle. But not only has she convinced the laird to give Tomas this room, she has also convinced him to put Tomas in charge of the underground castle guards, usurping part of the command of Laird Malcomb's elder nephew, Eileen's fiance Alfred, Seumas's older brother."

Amber made a face at Kelsey.

"Yeah, I didn't follow all that. I was with you so far as Tomas has this room in the castle when he really shouldn't, and Tomas is in charge of the guards of the underground palace when he shouldn't be. The rest of it was just a bunch of names I don't know."

Kelsey pursed her lips.

"Understandable. But you need to understand—"

Amber stretched her arms out and yawned.

"Can't we just go to our room at the inn and take a nap before I have to digest anything more today?"

Kelsey scrunched up her mouth.

"'Fraid not. This castle has spawned a town, but not

a big enough town to support an inn. Nope. We're staying with Eileen, the weaver I'm apprenticed to, the one whose fiance Alfred is the rightful captain of the guard. And we're helping Eileen and Sasha plan their double wedding to Alfred and his brother Seumas."

7

SEACHD

That evening at the front of the great hall of the castle, Tomas set his pewter goblet down on the long wooden plank table and sighed with satisfaction, then turned to smile at his beautiful Sulis, who was seated in the highest place next to Laird Malcomb. For this feast was in her honor, as every feast rightfully should be.

Gazing into her sapphire eyes, he almost forgot what he was going to say. Oh yeah.

"I didna ken they had such good wine here, or I should hae come sooner."

She turned to the laird.

"Did ye hear that, Laird Malcomb? Tomas gives his compliments on the wine. He's sae thoughtful, on top o' being such a capable captain for yer dock guards."

The laird of the castle smiled the smile of a man truly pleased to have a lovely woman ministering to his needs. He was suitably grateful that she was arranging things so advantageously for him. Good on him, because she was saving him the trouble of finding a good dock guard captain such as himself.

But the laird's wife, seated on his other side, stared daggers at Sulis. Silly woman. Sulis was with Tomas. There was no need to defend her territory.

Heat rose in his body, from his shoulders up into his head.

No one should look at Sulis disrespectfully.

Not and get away with it.

As it was his duty to see that this didn't happen again, Tomas calmly put his hands on his chair arms in preparation to get up and go strangle the lady of the castle.

But beautiful Sulis put a hand on his shoulder, staying him. She put her mouth up against his ear and breathed into it, and calm washed through him. She stood up instead, addressing not only the laird, but the whole room of a hundred revelers whom the laird had gathered to do her honor, as was proper and only her due.

She raised her pewter goblet to them.

"Tae happy company!"

They all raised their tankards to her, for they were drinking ale at the lower tables.

"Tae happy company!"

They started to turn away, but she raised her hands up prettily and kept their attention with her lovely voice.

"I dae believe 'tis time the dancing began. I wish tae

stretch my legs. Laird Malcomb, will ye tell the musicians tae start?"

Eager to please her — as he well should be — Laird Malcomb nodded at Sulis and then at the musicians, who were already assembling on their stage, brushing off food crumbs and still chewing. They knew they had better hop to it, or face her temper. Sulis had this place whipped into shape after only a week, she was so good at what she did.

Tomas turned to his goddess and smiled his congratulations for a successful feast in her honor.

She petted the back of his neck, and warm pleasure shot through him with the promise of what was to come later on that evening. And then she turned away from him, forcing him to focus on the room again.

He saw that Tavish and Kelsey's red-haired woman friend was one of the musicians, and she smiled with extra pleasure at being up on stage before she put her flute to her lips and played, dancing about to the beat. Her man Seumas stood in front of her clapping, and admiring her beauty, no doubt.

And then Sulis grabbed Tomas's hand and pulled him up and paraded with him proudly over to the dance area in the center of this great hall.

Tavish and Kelsey smiled and made as if to join their dance set, but Sulis turned her back on them. They should have known better. Tavish might be his brother, but he was only a common soldier, while he, Tomas, was captain of the dock guards.

The thought made him stand up straighter and swagger a little.

Instead of Tavish and Kelsey, all the most prominent people in the hall joined Tomas and Sulis's dance set. Well, the laird himself stayed at the table, presiding over the event, but his sons and their wives joined, along with his nephew Alfred — Tomas's fellow captain of the guard — and the nephew's fiancé, Eileen, the weaver who Kelsey was apprenticed to in this time.

And all of this honoring was only Sulis's due, to have the admiration and respect and homage of everyone.

She was so beautiful, his Sulis. So, so, so beautiful standing opposite him in the dance set clapping her hands prettily and smiling at everyone and nodding in time to the hammered dulcimer while the laird's eldest son and his wife swung down the line.

How nice it had been of the laird to give Sulis and him a room in his castle.

No, not nice, only what Sulis deserved.

Tomas smiled back at her, willing all of his gratitude to shine through.

She cozied up to him while the dance set allowed it and breathed her lovely warm juniper-scented breath on him while speaking softly to him.

"I see how ye look tae yer brother. Look again. Mayhap he's been coming here for years, but ye hae it better after only a week. He and his friend Seumas are just guards here. Their lasses are just a weaver's apprentice and a flute player. Ye, Tomas, hae a room here in the castle. Ye are a captain o' the guard. Ye are important."

It all made him shiver in delight.

He danced proudly by her side the rest of the

evening while his brother and his brother's friends watched enviously.

❧

SHE WAS WITH HIM THAT NIGHT AGAIN IN HIS CASTLE room, and it was glorious.

He woke from a joyous sleep to see her dressing in her white linen robes. It was nearly sunrise, but they didn't have to get up yet. Breakfast wasn't for another hour.

Quite groggy, he fought with his lazy tongue in order to speak.

"Don't go."

"Aw, I must, my angel, but I'll come back."

"Take me with you."

She finished dressing and sat down on the bed, then leaned down and breathed in his ear again, making him tingle all over.

"I can't. Stay near the castle, in this time, until I return. Obey Laird Malcomb."

"I will."

She left, but he was no longer worried. Quite the opposite. She had something important to do out there in the woods in her white robe. What she needed to do was the priority. She would return and be with him again, and only that mattered.

He thought of her pretty face and lovely body as he gave himself a sponge bath with water from the pitcher on top of the dresser. He thought of her silky spun-gold hair as he dressed for the day in his kilt and humongous-sleeved linen shirt, plaid blanket wrap, and heavy boots. Her birdsong voice was on his mind while he went down the stairs toward the great hall to break his night's fast.

He sat down and was served a plate full of fried eggs, ham, and baked beans. There was a sturdy mug of ale to go with it. He was happily tucking in when someone sat next to him and plunked down a plate of self-serve food. Not a resident of the castle, then.

He looked up with the amount of condescension in his face that Sulis had encouraged. She'd said he mustn't allow his inferiors any room to question him or doubt him — that he must be superior at all times around those he was in charge of — namely, the underground castle guards.

He didn't know them all yet, and so he had to be that way with all the guards. And since he didn't know who was a guard and who was just a craftsman at the castle on an errand, he had to be that way with everyone.

Logic.

Sulis was teaching him, and he was grateful.

But he turned his head and saw not a stranger, but his brother Tavish. Well, Tavish was one of the guards. And he'd done his duty in the underground castle before. So...

"What are ye doing here at the castle, Tavish? Should na ye be eating wherever it is the barracks guards eat?"

Tavish raised his eyebrows.

"Ye hae na been paying attention. This is where we lowly barracks guards eat, Captain."

He said 'Captain' as if it were a dirty word, but he said it. Tomas would let that go. For now.

"Well, ye should na be sitting next tae me, ye ken? I've got tae keep up appearances. Make sure the men ken my station." He looked over at another table where some men were gathered together. "Ye should go sit with them."

Tavish pursed his lips and made an angry face and shook his head. And lowered his voice to a hiss.

"If ye were na my brother... But ye are. Still and all, I care about ye. Ye hae been acting sae different syne this Sulis came intae yer life. It isna flattering for ye, Tomas. Dae ye na see that? Should ye na be in charge o' yerself?"

His brother's words made Tomas's jaw and fists clench.

"And if ye were na my brother... but ye are, and sae ye shall live. But dinna sit at my table again. And ye are na tae speak with me till I hae spoken tae ye. And dinna speak o' Sulis in that manner. Is that clear?"

Tavish didn't answer. He just got up, grabbed his food, and stomped over to the other table. Once there, however, he smiled and laughed with his fellow guards while they ate together.

The base of Tomas's pewter tankard made a dent in the wooden table when he put it down, causing it to spill his ale all over. Some splashed on him.

Cursing and brushing himself off, he jumped up to go back to his room.

"Ye there! Coome and clean up this mess at once."

Tavish could be civil and even jovial with these strangers from another time, but he couldn't give his own brother the respect due his station? Who needed him. Kelsey would probably see how much trouble he was soon and leave him. It wasn't like they were married or anything. Why had his brother even let her get close to him?

And there it was.

A vision of Amber swam before Tomas, the way she had been in that room inside his new domain: the underground palace. Her amber eyes were soft and affectionate whenever she looked at him, and her face appealed to him every time their eyes met.

What was she doing here at this site, let alone here in the past? Didn't she remember they couldn't be together?

Wait.

Tavish and Kelsey weren't supposed to be a couple anymore, either. Every time he saw them together, something inside him shuddered in fear. He and Tavish had a good reason for staying away from Kelsey and Amber.

He didn't want Amber in his life anymore. For her own good. He... He'd had a good reason for leaving her. He couldn't put his finger on it right now, but it was a really good reason. He knew that. Why couldn't he remember?

Anyway, he had walked away from her. He had left her seven years ago without even saying goodbye. It had hurt him, but he had known it was the right thing to do.

It had been the right thing, hadn't it? Yes. Yes, he felt assured it had. And now she was aware that he had a new girlfriend.

Why was she always coming into his thoughts like this? She didn't have to walk in front of him while he was dancing with Sulis and come up for wine at the same time as he did. She really shouldn't look into his eyes as if she were searching for a lost part of herself.

Well, she wasn't doing that last thing right now anywhere but in his imagination.

But she shouldn't be here.

Even though nothing else she was doing was wrong.

Her being here distracted him, and he had important things to do here at the castle for Laird Malcomb. He was the captain of the underground guard now, and he shouldn't be distracted. Not even by a dark-haired beauty who sometimes brought back memories of a love so strong, he had been willing to give her up for her own good.

Tomas had just finished changing into fresh clothes when Sulis came in, smelling of the woods.

He was so glad to see her, he ran over and hugged her tight.

"Why did you have to go out to the woods alone? Something might have happened to you. You should let me go along to protect you. You—"

But Sulis kissed him then, a breathy wet kiss that started at his ear and worked its way around to his mouth. Fireworks went off in his mind, and the world narrowed down to just her lips on his, she was that good a kisser. As soon as she was done kissing him, he would ask her…

What had he been wondering about?

Oh, who cared? Being with Sulis was bliss. He should enjoy her.

8

OCHD

Amber woke up in the throne room of the underground palace and gasped when she felt the huge golden throne beneath her and looked down to see that she was wearing a crimson gown made entirely out of handmade linen lace. There was weight on top of her head. She reached up and grabbed something, then lowered it down so she could see. It was an ornate golden crown made from many strands of gold woven into Celtic knot shapes.

A woman giggled from the other side of the hall.

"Don't look so shocked. Just pinch yourself, hint hint."

Pinch herself?

Oh yeah.

She looked up to see Kelsey and Sasha dressed equally as beautifully in handmade lace gowns, only theirs were blue and green.

"So this is a dream." Amber smiled appreciatively

and nodded. "It's a good one. Do you plan on wearing a gown like that at your wedding?"

Sasha moved gracefully in her green dress as if she were dancing with Seumas the way she had the night before.

"Nah, they just get married in their regular clothes in this time period, so unfortunately I won't have a special wedding dress. We come here often in our dreams. It's a much easier way for her to show us around. You could have danced last night too, Amber. That one guard Cormac was really anxious to dance with you. All you would have had to do was smile at him, and he would have asked you."

Amber gave Kelsey a look that said 'Tell her what's going on, because I haven't the patience to and will end up being rude about it. You know me.'

Kelsey nodded then turned to her new friend.

"Amber's Tomas's ex-girlfriend, and we think if anyone can get Tomas away from Sulis, it'll be her—"

Impatient now with Kelsey's explanation, Amber threw her head back to look at the carvings in the ceiling—and get the other two women's attention.

"It's maddening, this assignment you've given me, Kelsey. It's really hard not being with him and yet hoping that I can be, you know? Especially since making him jealous is out of the question. I don't have a clue how else to get a guy back."

Sasha gave her a puzzled look.

"Why not make him jealous?"

Amber closed her eyes to try and escape from some of the pain of thinking about Tomas with that blank look on his face — or even worse, looking at Sulis as if she were a goddess — but that just made it all the more vivid in her memory.

"Because he's too broken already, by Sulis's machinations. I'm going to have to draw him out little by little until he remembers me again, and I don't even know if I get to keep him once I do that, she has him so messed up. This is the hardest thing I've ever done."

Kelsey gave her a determined face.

"He's worth it though , isn't he."

Sighing, Amber shook her head yes slowly.

"Of course he is."

This was getting too heavy. Time to think about superficial things for a while. Amber stood from the huge throne and found that she was wearing strange sandals made of rope. They were not the most comfortable things, but they were interesting.

She looked quizzically at Sasha.

"If there aren't any special clothes to prepare, then why is it taking so long to plan this wedding?"

Sasha and Kelsey shared a conspiratorial look, but kept their mouths shut.

Amber threw her hands up.

"Out with it."

Sasha put her palms forward.

"Okay. Remember how I fell when I first touched you, out there on the cliffs?"

"How could I ever forget?"

"Well, I had a vision of you at my wedding, and you were fine, not a scratch on you. Tomas, too. My visions always come true, so we know that as long as we keep putting the wedding off, this Lachlan character won't be able to catch you, or at least he won't hurt you."

Amber looked at Kelsey for confirmation, and her friend gave her a playfully guilty look.

Sasha ran her hand down her long flowing red hair while she continued explaining the plan she and Kelsey had apparently made without Amber.

"Everyone who knows about time travel except Tomas—me, Seumas, Kelsey, and Tavish—knows you're safe. And Kelsey thinks we can use that to help snap Tomas out of the funk Sulis has him in. His urge to protect you is really strong. I was skeptical, but now I think it'll work."

Amber didn't want to think about that right now. It was too much on top of all this time travel stuff, so she gestured around at the throne room.

"Sulis lured me through here on her wild goose chase. But it didn't seem this new — well, I guess it did happen eight hundred years from now, but—"

Kelsey nodded quickly and waved off Amber's puzzlement in a promise to explain.

"Yeah, no, you're right. This lower part of the underground palace is thousands of years old. The dream memories I have of it are from when it was new. Tavish and I came down here into this throne room after finding it through the dreams of an evil old druid named Brian. He must have time traveled back here during the Iron Age, when the Celts reigned here and raided the blue-painted Picts, whose kingdom was the eastern half of what is now Scotland."

The Celts! They were all anyone had talked of at

faire. Celtic knots. Celtic warfare. Celtic culture. How exciting to actually go back to their age and see how they lived. She would be the envy of all her old friends. They would hang on her every word.

"I've heard all about the Celts, of course, but you said something about blue painted Picts? I meant to ask you about that when I saw those guards straight out of Braveheart earlier. They had everything except the blue face paint Mel Gibson wore in the movie."

Kelsey laughed. So did Sasha.

"Just because it's in a movie doesn't mean it's authentic. It was the Picts who painted themselves blue with woad, not the Celts."

And then Amber jumped, because Kelsey gestured, and for a moment they were out in a field of battle watching Roman soldiers get jumped by naked people painted blue with odd blue designs all over their bodies. And then they were back inside the underground palace.

Amber gave Kelsey a huge grin.

"Does this Brian still know how to get there? Can he take us?"

Kelsey shivered.

"Ew, no. The man was evil, Amber. He's dead now."

Amber's face fell.

Kelsey snickered at her.

"But I still have all of his dreams in my memory, so I can show you some more sometime."

Amber nodded vigorously, still with that huge grin on her face.

Kelsey laughed at her.

"Tonight I'm going to show you the entire Celtic underground palace, so that you won't get lost again. That B-witch may be able to humiliate us at grand feasts held in her honor, but never again is she going to make any of us get lost inside our own dig site."

Amber jumped up off the stone counter she was leaning on and followed Kelsey and Sasha down the corridor. But as they walked, she just couldn't help hashing over last night's feast.

"Maybe it's sour grapes on my part because Sulis is with Tomas now, but I thought she was the biggest B-witch ever last night."

Sasha made a cutting gesture with her hand.

"She was unconscionable, no sour grapes about it. I could see everything from up on the stage. It's the custom to form new sets for each new dance, but whenever others tried to form up with Malcomb's sons, Sulis stepped on their toes or stared daggers at them so they would back off. She even shoved this one couple out of her way so she could continue monopolizing the spotlight."

Kelsey put her arm over Sasha's shoulders.

"I saw how rude she was to Seumas."

Sasha looked at something down at the end of the large hollowed-out stone hallway while she sighed deeply.

"It broke my heart, seeing his brother shun him like that. It was all her doing, of course. I think I'll refrain from playing at any more feasts while she's here. I could have warned him if I hadn't been playing. But Kelsey, if she's here during our wedding..."

Kelsey gave Sasha a quick sideways hug.

"No way. We are not going to let Sulis ruin your wedding. She puts on those white linen robes and goes out in the woods every chance she gets, have you noticed?"

Sasha nodded.

"We'll just stall until she feels her powers fading and needs to go out there, is all. You'll play the flute, and you can get the other musicians to play. Maybe even have dancing. Let her dance awhile. She seems to like that. It'll be worth it in order to get her out of the picture for the actual wedding ceremony."

Sasha laughed a little, but she also brushed a tear away.

"I think that may actually work. Thanks. I feel better."

With that, all three women linked arms — and then Kelsey slowly floated them around the entire underground palace until Amber knew every inch of it. She still didn't know how to open the secret doors, though. Kelsey just made them float right through those.

"We would teach you how to open these doors if it were simple, Amber. But it isn't. It took us years of study not really aimed at this — or so we thought — in order to open them, so you'll just have to take one of us along whenever you explore down here."

Amber scoffed.

"Wish I could have had you down here when B-witch brought me through the cave off the cliff down the rope ladder."

Kelsey dropped their linked arms and side hugged Amber.

"She brought you in that way? I'm so sorry — but I'm impressed you were able to make it."

Amber hugged her friend back.

"That's how pissed off I was. It made me stronger. Thinking about it now makes me feel strong enough to chew rocks."

Kelsey patted Amber's shoulder.

"Here in the dream, you could chew rocks, but let's not and say we did."

At that, Amber laughed the tiniest bit.

"Deal." But then her anger took over again. "Sulis has some nerve, showing up here at our dig site and taking over — and using Tomas against us."

Kelsey growled a little.

"I know. She's gotten him installed here so that she can recruit more of her zombie slaves out of his guards and then have them loot everything out of here before we even get a chance. But you know that's not the worst of it. What she's doing to Tomas is. It isn't really him doting over her like that. She has him charmed but good. His real personality comes out every once in a while. I know you've seen it. Tavish has too, but for some reason the sight of his brother makes Tomas so furious that Tavish can't get through to him."

Amber took a deep breath and let it out as the three of them floated down the corridor past rooms that nearly sparkled in their cleanliness under the light of many torches.

"Aren't there ever any people in here in this Brian the Druid's dreams? It's really eerie without people."

Kelsey gave Amber a 'let's be frank' look.

"At first, I used to have the people in the dream with me. They are interesting, and maybe some time when one of us isn't in urgent need of knowing where everything is, I'll let you see the people too. But they're so distracting. We'd spend our whole time watching all of their fascinating rituals."

Sasha gave Kelsey a hopeful look at that.

Kelsey nodded at her, and the two of them might as well have been rubbing their hands together, they looked so eager to study the Celts.

Amber took Kelsey's hand and squeezed it.

"This was a good idea. I'm glad to know my way around. You're right, we shouldn't let her have any advantage on our own turf. And I hereby declare this underground Celtic palace ours."

The place was magnificent, and quite a bit larger than Amber had first guessed, going down four levels before it reached the sea. She lost count of how many secret doors they passed through in order to get that far down, and then they went up by a different route, passing through even more and taking several flights of stairs. But she thought that as long as it didn't involve opening any secret doors, she could now find her way out no matter where she was in the underground castle.

And the night's adventure had to end sometime.

Sasha was especially pale in the light of all the torches, and her face looked especially mournful.

"Well, we'd better get home and go to bed."

Amber jumped in before Kelsey could say anything.

“Aw, can't we stay a little longer? This is fun, and you have to admit, life in the waking world is trying right now, dealing with Sulis.”

Gently shaking her head no, Kelsey took Amber and Sasha's hands, and then all three of them became ghost-like and floated straight up through four layers of rock corridors until they were on the surface, standing on the wet grass in their bare feet under a sky that held so many stars, it was almost solid light.

Kelsey gave it a moment before she spoke and broke the peacefulness.

“No, we don't really get rest while I'm manipulating our dreams. Sasha's right, we have to go back to our bodies and allow them to rest.”

Amber squeezed Kelsey's hand.

“Well at least tomorrow you can show me the upper castle in the real daylight.”

But Sasha put a hand on Amber's arm.

“We were going to do that, but Seumas thinks it's too dangerous for us to let Lachlan run around without watching where he's going... Amber, we want Tomas to think Lachlan is after you in particular, so that his protectiveness is aroused. He'll see otherwise if you come with us, so you're going to stay and help Eileen in the weaver shop tomorrow while we're out.”

Amber opened her mouth to speak, but what could she say really?

Kelsey put a hand on Amber's back.

“I'm sorry. I know that's not too exciting. You can

have a tour of the castle and the town the next day, okay?"

Sasha gave a little laugh.

"It won't be all bad. Wait until you meet Eileen's daughter Deirdre. Heh! She's six years old going on sixty. She'll keep you entertained."

❧

AMBER WOKE UP WITH A TINY PAIR OF BLUE EYES A foot from her face, staring at her unblinking.

"A good morning tae ye. My name is Amber, and some aught tells me ye are Deirdre."

The blue eyes widened.

"What is it that tells ye?"

Amber smiled at the little cherub of a girl.

"I would say a little birdie telt me, but ye ken that would be a lie, dae ye na?"

Deirdre's nose scrunched up, and she backed away and put her hands on her hips.

"Dinna be silly. Little birds dinna talk. I thought... wull, never mind what I thought. If ye are gaun'ae come help us in the weaver shop today, then ye had better get up and eat yer parritch. Maw has already left with the bairns. She left me tae look after ye." Deirdre gave Amber a quick once-over. "I daresay ye dinna ken any better than Sasha how we live here, dae ye?"

Wow, Sasha wasn't kidding.

"I reckon I ken how tae eat parritch."

❧

EILEEN SMILED WHEN HER DAUGHTER DRAGGED Amber into the weaver shop.

"Thank ye for watching ower my new apprentice, Deirdre. Sìle needs ye tae look after her now, please."

Amber expected Deirdre to put up a fuss, but to her amazement, the little girl went right over to where her baby sister was playing with some fist-sized wooden spools and took over supervising her, modulating her voice to sound somewhat like their mother's.

"There's a good lass. Are ye playing nice, now?"

Eileen beckoned Amber over into the far corner of the shop, where piles of burlap bags were stacked up against the wall.

"Ye are in luck. Kelsey has been helping me pound flax intae thread, and 'tis a tedious task." She gestured over at the man who was weaving on a huge loom between them and Deirdre. "Howsoever, Fergus just traded for all o' this raw wool, sae we get tae spin it intae yarn instead. Much easier."

Amber looked at the spinning wheel dubiously.

Eileen bit her thumb and smiled around it for a moment before saying anything.

"'Tis na sae daunting as all that. I shall feed the wool intae the groove here. All ye need dae is keep the wheel spinning."

It took a few minutes, but Amber got the hang of spinning the wheel. Because it was tedious, repetitive, boring work, and Sasha and Kelsey had spoken of Eileen like she was one of them, soon Amber found herself sharing what was on her mind.

She spoke in hushed tones so that the men across the room wouldn't hear.

"Hae ye noticed aught strange about Tomas?"

"Plenty, and Alfred has noticed as wull. I hear about it daily. Alfred is having tae train Tomas in how tae captain the guards. A man that inexperienced should na be in command, says Alfred."

"But Laird Malcomb would be the one tae dae some aught about that, aye?"

"Aye, howsoever, if ye ask me, the strangeness is in Sulis. She has that Tomas bewitched, and mayhap Laird Malcomb as wull."

They worked for a while in silence, and then Eileen made a noise and put her finger in her mouth.

Amber jumped up.

"Dinna ye hae a thimble I can get for ye?"

Eileen laughed.

"I ken ye are na ower enchanted by the work we dae here."

Amber laughed too.

"Daes it show that much?"

"Aye. But I hae good news for ye. I hae lost my thimble, and I dae think ye should go and get me another."

Amber knew her face had brightened an obvious amount because Eileen's smile grew larger as she dug in her pouch for some money and handed it to her.

"I buy whatsoever I can from Joanna the Tinker, a widow who needs all the help we can give tae her. The booth is just doon the way there—"

Dierdre came running over.

"Canna I show her please Maw?"

Amber shrugged when Eileen looked for her opinion on this idea.

Eileen gave Dierdre a serious look.

"Verra wull, howsoever, ye must dae as Amber tells ye."

Dierdre nodded somberly and then looked up at Amber.

"I will." And then she grabbed Amber's hand and tugged her toward the door. "Let's go!"

Dierdre tugged Amber to a small market table in a group of other small tables, where a bunch of older women — could they all be widows? That was so sad. — sat in a haphazard circle mending shirts or darning socks while they talked and waited for customers who needed something mended or washed.

Amber had just bought the thimble and was thanking Joanna when Sulis turned the corner and stopped almost on top of her.

Tomas followed close behind Sulis, holding everything she had bought. He had a bolt of cloth in one arm and a bunch of do-dads in his other arm and wore three of her hats on his head as he walked along the street like a zombie with his eyes not showing any life.

Feeling horrible for him, Amber rounded on Sulis.

"How dare ye turn such a smart and vibrant man intae such a drone and call it love?"

Sulis took a haughty stance and crossed her arms over her ample chest and raised her chin up high before she spoke in a loud voice so that everyone nearby could hear her and didn't have a choice but to listen.

"Move on tae some poor shop where ye can trade for what ye need, Amber, because I ken for a clean fact ye don't hae any money tae pay for anything. Ye are just wasting the time o' these craftsmen, hanging about and staring at everything with longing. Move aside and let those o' us who can afford the goods shop here."

Amber made a show of looking about.

"There are nay craftsmen tae be seen anywhere close by, only widows. Who are beneath yer notice, I see."

Sulis just stood there looking down her nose at Amber, plainly expecting her to cower before her magnificence and clear away.

But Joanna stood from her comfortable chair and turned to Sulis.

"I dinna ken about what ye say."

And then the tinker widow turned to Amber and Dierdre.

"Ye are welcome tae stay as long as ye like. Ye hae been nought but helpful and kind tae me. Na everyone is like that in this world, and I truly appreciate ye."

Joanna sat down again, and Amber pressed her lips together to avoid laughing at Sulis, but only because that might have made things worse for Tomas.

Joanna hadn't really said anything about Sulis at all, but there was a general tittering in this area of the market. Apparently, all the widows nearby were amused by Sulis's having been subtly put down by Joanna.

Of course, Sulis couldn't just leave it well enough alone. She had to make a scene even bigger than the one she had already made. She had to have the last word. That was the kind of person she was.

Sulis stood up even taller and moved her head from side to side in a mocking way and raised her finger at Joanna and shook it at her as if she were a small child and not an elderly widow who deserved respect. When Sulis next spoke, it was as if she were making a speech to everyone in the whole town, it carried so well.

"Upon closer examination, the goods at this booth are na up tae my standards, and I will take my business and my ample money tae spend doon the way, where people are more respectful o' their betters."

Sulis flounced off in what she plainly intended to be an imperious way.

But all the women in the area tittered again, putting the lie to the druidess's assumption that she had this whole town sewn up in the palm of her hand.

☙ 9 ❧

NAOI

Amber helped Eileen walk all her children home that night, and the two of them had supper ready before Kelsey and Sasha got home. Amber could tell by the looks on their faces that they had been unsuccessful in their search for Lachlan the Dark. They nonetheless passed a pleasant evening playing with the children. The men were drilling at the castle and weren't present this evening but said they'd have dinner with the lasses the next night.

Sasha and Kelsey met Amber in her dreams briefly to reassure her that she would be touring the castle and the town.

The next morning, Tomas was there at the castle gate when Amber arrived. He was leaning listlessly against the fence, and he stayed that way even when she got there.

She stopped next to him and defiantly decided to look him in the eye — but with raised eyebrows.

"Good morning. I did na expect tae see ye here."

He didn't look at her, just kept staring at a hole in the road.

"Aye, I would na hae been, howsoever, Tavish just asked me tae escort ye aroond, right after Sulis left on one o' her jaunts intae the forest."

Amber clapped a few times, ostensibly because she was happy to have him as a guide — but really to try and awaken Tomas from his stupor. It sort of worked.

He pushed off the fence with his elbow and — turning his back on her and leaving her to follow if she would — started walking through the gate into the castle courtyard.

She hurried to catch up, and walked by his side.

He walked through the castle courtyard and was opening a door to go inside when she grabbed his elbow to stop him. She knew the answer to the question she asked, but this wouldn't be any sort of tour if all he did was walk around and ignore her. She figured it was up to her to get them talking.

"What are those bins full o' wood for?"

He slowly turned to look at them and then back at her.

"They're practice swords."

He tried to pull away and open the door again, but she held onto his elbow.

"Sae dae ye guards practice in this courtyard? When? I would like tae watch that."

He wrinkled his brow at her.

"The guards practice every afternoon, and sometimes intae the evening, like yesterday. But 'tis naught tae watch, just ordinary men keeping their skills braw sae they can dae their duty."

On a hunch, she pushed for more details, giving him a soft smile.

"Sae where and when dae the extraordinary men practice?"

Aha. He stood up a bit straighter at that. He did consider himself extraordinary. Unfortunately, in this context it meant he thought he was better than everyone else. He hadn't been like that before Sulis. If Amber ever got that woman alone when her powers were low, she would shove her face in the mud. What a B witch she was, corrupting someone as honorable as Tomas once had been.

He still was, she reminded herself. This wasn't really him, just a spell that Sulis had over him. And Amber needed to break him loose from it.

He was responding.

"We officers practice in a room Laird Malcomb designed for it, directly after breakfast."

She thought about it for moment.

"But that's now. Are ye missing practice on my account? Won't ye get in trouble?"

Until she'd mentioned trouble, he had been not quite smiling but at least not scowling. That changed. He sounded almost like a child, he was so cranky.

"Nay, I'm na gaun'ae get in trouble. I'm fifth in command o' this whole place, Amber. All the men look up tae me, and Laird Malcomb and his nephew Alfred look tae me tae help them run things. I get a certain number o' favors tae go along with that, and I spent one o' those precious favors getting out o' practice tae show ye aroond today. Least ye could dae is act appreciative o' it instead o' suggesting I'm gaun'ae get in trouble."

Before she could say anything else, he pushed through the door into the castle, once more leaving her to follow if she would.

She ran inside after him.

Not taking any notice whether she did or not, he stomped down the cold stone-on-stone hallway toward the corner, where there was another door.

Again she ran, so as not to allow him the satisfaction of losing her in the huge above-ground castle and thus shirking his duty as her escort for the day.

He looked resigned when she caught up to him at the door in the corner, and he sighed deeply before pushing it open and revealing a spiral staircase that went up into a tower. He started climbing up the stairs.

At least he wasn't running now, so it was easy for her to keep up. She could even talk while they climbed the stairs.

"Is this the tower where they kept that prisoner, Brian the Druid? Kelsey telt me aboot him."

He answered without looking back down the stairs at her.

"Aye. Howsoever, he was gone before I arrived. This is where they keep any prisoner. The underground palace is hardly a dungeon."

Amber knew better. She had seen dungeons in the underground palace — but her gut told her not to give this voodoo-doll version of Tomas any idea she knew better than him about what he considered his domain.

So she just slightly changed the subject.

"Is there a tower prison up at the top o' each o' the four corners o' the above-ground castle, then?"

They had reached the top of the stairs now, and he proudly took out some keys and unlocked the prison room door, pushing it open so that she could see how small the turret room was.

"Nay. This corner faces the underground palace entrance and the cliffs that go doon tae land. No one would be able tae attack from that direction. The other three corners face the sea and land approaches. Those towers are reserved for archers when the need arises."

He had moved inside the room.

So she did also, surprised to see a bed in here. It really wasn't such a bad prison, albeit small.

"There are arrow-slit windows in this room, tae."

He moved over to one and looked out.

"Aye. There aren't always prisoners in here, such as now. And anyway, the prisoner needs tae be able tae look oot and see what he's missing."

She looked out one of the windows for a moment.

"I see what ye mean. Let us move on. This room creeps upon me."

He nodded the slightest bit as he locked up the room and started down the stairs. Was he showing agreement?

They left the stairwell on the third floor of the castle, where he opened the doors to several apartments so that she could look inside, but they didn't go in. Each time, he would tell her whose apartment it was. He didn't use names, just said 'Laird Malcomb's eldest son and his family' or 'younger son and his family' or 'Laird Malcomb's elder nephew.'

At this last apartment, Amber got curious.

"After their wedding, will Eileen and her children move in here with Alfred?"

He nodded again.

"Aye. Even though Alfred's marrying a commoner and her bairns are common, Laird Malcomb and his wife — and especially his maw — are fond o' them. Next, we can see the nursery where his maw takes care o' them when they're here at the castle for feasts. I suppose she will always take care o' them once they live here."

This made Amber smile, the thought of Eileen's lovely children being taken care of by someone here in the castle who was fond of them.

"Aye, I should like tae see that."

Was it her imagination, or was he walking more slowly now, even waiting for her to catch up with him if he did leave her behind?

They went back inside the stairwell and down a flight of stairs. But before they could leave on the second floor, a squadron of kilted soldiers with big swords strapped to their backs entered the stairwell through the same door they wished to exit, one at a time in single file.

The last man stopped and stared at Amber for a moment, then smiled and bowed his head slightly.

"Hello again, Amber. D'ye remember me? Cormac.

We met on the cliffs the other day, and I saw ye at the feast the other night. I wonder if the next time there is a feast, ye might want tae—"

Tomas cut between the two of them.

"Get on yer way back tae yer squadron."

Cormac looked confused for a moment, and then he stood up straight and took the steps two at a time on his way up.

"Aye aye, Captain."

Shocked, Amber just stood there gazing at Tomas. He sure had broken out of his zombie stupor. His eyes looked a lot less glazed over, and his face was even flushed a bit.

He cleared his throat and opened the door for her, waiting for her to precede him through it.

"What? He canna be shirking his duty. We let a wee bit o' that take hold, and there would be chaos."

Amber's natural inclination was to tease him, but intuition told her that would be disastrous in his current state, so instead she simply smiled and went through the door he was holding into an older part of Laird Malcomb's above-ground castle, where the halls were wider and the stone building blocks darker.

She paused, unsure which door would lead into the nursery.

Tomas smiled slightly at her as he passed by. It was a friendly smile, and she almost didn't notice, it was so normal for him. Had been normal for him seven plus years ago, anyway.

He stopped at a set of double doors and opened them wide.

"Here we are, the nursery. There is na anyone here now."

Amber smiled as she went in.

"I can imagine Aodh and Niall playing in here, and little Deirdre supervising them."

Tomas went over to a hand carved rocking horse and stroked his hand over it.

"'Tis someaught of a spectacle, aye?"

Amber felt drawn to him then, as if some sort of tractor beam from his eyes had attached to her and was actively reeling her in. She went over and used the rocking horse as an excuse to get close, touching its sanded and painted smoothness with her own hands — and letting her shoulder nearly touch Tomas's shoulder.

"Mmmhmm, all that is in here is beautiful."

Their eyes met then, and his looked aware, but confused and unsure. His brow wrinkled then — in concentration, she thought — and he swallowed, making his Adam's apple go up and down pronouncedly before he spoke.

"Amber?"

Not breaking eye contact, she nodded at him slowly.

"Aye, 'tis me."

He reached for her. She knew that was what he was doing, reaching out to take her into an embrace that would heal the worry in both of them. It would feel like home, and she welcomed it with a triumphant smile. He was hers. They hadn't ever broken up. He'd simply disappeared from her life. He was hers, and she was going to reclaim him now with a wonderful warm embrace.

But as his hands slid over the rocking horse toward her, its smooth painted surface distracted him, and he looked down, away from her eyes. Once their eye contact was broken, his brow wrinkled in confusion once more, and he looked around the room as if seeing it for the first time.

And then he grabbed her hand and started walking briskly toward the double doors into the hallway.

"I hae tae get ye out o' here."

He pushed through the double doors, then turned the opposite direction from where they'd come and hustled her down the dark stone hallway into another spiral stone stairwell. The door at the bottom opened out into a huge room with a bunch of plank wood counters and herbs hanging from the ceiling and a huge fireplace in the center. Amber gradually realized this was the castle kitchen. A bunch of women paused from kneading dough and cutting vegetables to look at them with surprised faces as Tomas hurried Amber through an open door and outside.

They were near the spot where she had first become aware of her surroundings when the song stopped making her want to jump off the cliff, which she could now see again.

He was walking her toward the stairway into the underground castle.

Her breath caught. Getting her out of here meant sending her home. She couldn't leave him, or he would fall right back under Sulis's spell again and she wouldn't be any closer to saving him then she had been when she first arrived.

But then she remembered that Tomas would need Tavish to send her home, and Tavish had agreed it was safer if they all stayed here in the past together. So she relaxed and just enjoyed being with Tomas. Enjoyed having his hand in hers once again.

Enjoyed it that is until they got to the bottom of the stairs and ran smack into Sulis.

Still in her white linen robes — now stained green and brown from the woods — the druidess grabbed Tomas away from Amber and whispered something in his ear.

Amber tried to get him away from her.

"Tomas, ye dinna hae tae go with her. Just tell her tae—"

But it was too late. As soon as Sulis whispered in his ear, Tomas's eyes clouded up again. His posture became listless — he became a zombie again.

Amber tried to talk to him, to snap him out of it.

"Tomas? Tomas!"

But Sulis was standing right there. Her close proximity to him must have made the spell stronger. He just stood there by his mistress's side, staring into space.

Not so with Sulis. She tossed her blonde hair back and then stood there regally with her pretty nose in the air, subtly but effectively snarling at Amber.

"Ye had yer try at getting him back, and ye failed. He wants me, na ye. Stay away from him, or I will see that ye dae, permanently."

Sulis went up the stairs as she said this, just about dragging Tomas behind her by the hand.

Amber followed them, even as they reached the top

of the stairs and went walking toward the main castle entrance. Sulis's legs were longer than hers, though. She wouldn't be able to catch up without running after them, and that was far too undignified for what Amber had in mind.

Only slightly aware of the guards at the top of the stairs looking at her curiously, she called after Sulis.

"Ye better na harm him, or I will see that ye never harm anyone again — permanently."

The druidess merely threw up her other hand in a dramatic flair in response, just before she reached the castle gate and made Tomas open it for her. And then the two of them disappeared together into the great hall where the feast in Sulis's honor had been the night before.

Amber's stomach growled.

The guard behind her snickered at that.

She turned around and looked at him. He was eating an apple.

"Are they serving the midday meal in the great hall nae?"

He nodded.

"Aye, howsoever, 'tis only for them as live in the castle, and the guards."

She gave him her most mischievous grin and glanced sideways at the kitchen door she and Tomas had come out of a few minutes before.

"Thank ye."

Before he had time to say you're welcome, she scrunched her nose at him and ran toward the kitchen door. She needed to break the spell Sulis had over Tomas. While he and Sulis were busy eating, maybe she could find something in Tomas's room that would help.

10

DEICH

Shocking the same women she had a few minutes ago when she and Tomas ran through the castle kitchen, Amber ran right through there again, not stopping when she got into the cold stone hallway but running all the way down to Tomas's pointy-topped bedroom door, opening it, and hastening to close it behind her.

She paused with her back against it. Breathing heavily. Expecting any moment to hear a castle resident ask what business she had in this room. And toss her out on her ear.

After a few minutes, she caught her breath. She was lucky today. She didn't hear anyone coming.

Nodding with pride in the instinct which had told her to run through the castle, thus giving people the least chance of seeing her, she turned to the room at hand.

Maybe Sulis had made some sort of voodoo doll of

Tomas and hidden it here in this room, controlling him. Amber itched to find it — or anything that would help her break the spell.

First, she searched the chest of drawers. Five clean linen shirts, two clean kilts, two clean plaid overdresses, and five clean pairs of socks later, she moved on to the bed. It had been made, but she turned down the covers and searched between the blankets and even between the handmade mattress and the wooden platform it sat on before making the bed up again, having found nothing.

Finally, she lay down on the cold stone floor and looked under the bed. Ah, there were Tomas's weapons — his large claymore and his bow & quiver. She had drawn out the quiver and was searching among the arrows when she heard the door open.

Ready for a fight with Sulis, Amber got up with defiance in her eyes.

But it was Tomas. His glazed-over eyes traveled the room, then finally zeroed in on his quiver in her hand. The faintest hint of half a dozen different emotions passed over his face one by one in the next few moments: shock, unbelief, anger, fear, cunning — and was that last one ... hope?

When he spoke, his voice was low and breathy, almost a whisper — like he was just as afraid as she was, of being overheard by people outside the room in the rest of the castle.

Like the two of them were in this together.

But his words were contrary.

"What are ye doing in here going through my stuff?"

He pointed to the quiver. "Put that back where ye found it."

Not taking her eyes off his, she squatted and did as she was told. There hadn't been anything in the quiver but arrows, anyway. And then, seeing how this might be the last time she saw him, the last chance she got, she stood again and just laid it all out on the line for him. Quietly.

"I was trying tae find some aught that will get rid o' this horrible influence she has ower ye, Tomas. Ye are na the same when she's aroond. Ye were weird and grumpy this morning, but the longer we bided together today, the more normal ye got. Ye were almost yer usual self — right afore she showed up. There has tae be some sort o... some aught she's using tae keep this hold on ye, and I was looking for it. I did na find it, though."

He stood still for a moment, and again she could almost see the wheels turning behind his eyes in his mind, processing what she had said. Even though his eyes were glazed over in that infernal zombiehood, she thought she detected the barest glimpses of a dozen emotions running through his eyes quickly, like the spinning wheels of a mechanical slot machine.

Unfortunately, this time they landed on anger.

He leaned into her face and pointed at the door. At odds with his angry mood, however, he still kept his voice down.

"I was ready tae just accept that ye were a nosy person in here poking intae my business as some-aught o' an auld friend. I was gaun'ae just let ye go and na think any more o' it — excepting tae say dinna dae it again. But now ye hae gone and dragged Sulis intae this. Ye shouldna be badmouthing her. 'Tis unattractive. It makes me want tae tell ye tae leave and never come back."

Amber growled the tiniest bit.

In an attempt to let off the steam his little speech had built up inside her, she stomped her feet and brought her arms down with force to her sides.

"I shouldna be badmouthing Sulis? Tomas, that woman tried tae make me jump off a cliff! She has ye doing a job ye are na fit tae do, just tae satisfy her drive for material things. She has ye fighting with yer brother, whom I know ye love more than ye could ever love a woman ye hae only known a few months. That woman is evil, Tomas, evil and conniving and ruthless! And she's manipulating ye. Canna ye see that?"

Oh, it was on, now.

He got in her face.

His own face looked angry, but his body was still slumped and zombielike. His hand that had been pointing to the door dropped to his side. Contrary to his posture, his voice came out like an angry hiss, and he lapsed into English.

"She didn't make you go to that cliff, Amber. Do you know how stupid that sounds? She is not manipulating me. She's my girlfriend, and I'm with her now. We've been together three months."

Amber put her hands on her hips and stood up straight. His zombified brain was denying reality, but his body seemed to remember her. Maybe if she appealed to his body, his brain would snap out of it. And if it did, then heck with this long-time-ago place.

Once Tomas snapped out of his zombie coma, she was going to go find Tavish and have him take them back to their time. She would get Tomas on a plane far away from here. Just keep running and never let Sulis near him again — or take him to his parents' faire. They would help her protect him.

She didn't dare touch him yet, though. She needed to soften him up a little more, like she had this morning. Gazing into his eyes with all the emotion she felt — all the love bottled up inside her — she lapsed into English as well and made her voice as soft and loving as she could, considering her frustration.

"Tomas, I care about you, or I would've gone home as soon as I saw..."

No, don't continue along those lines. Better not to mention the B witch. She tried again.

"Don't you remember half an hour ago, Tomas? When you and I were talking like old times? You showed me around the castle and we both really liked the rocking horse in the nursery?"

His face bunched up in grumpiness like when they had met out in front of the castle this morning, and one side of his mouth rose in an ironic smile, as if what she said couldn't possibly be true.

But his body turned away from the door and toward her.

And his eyes stayed on her. They weren't nearly as glazed over as they had been this morning. Was she imagining it, was there a glimmer of recognition in them?

He evaded her question, but when he spoke, he didn't sound angry anymore, just determined.

"I don't know what you're doing here, Amber, but in this time, do you realize how dangerous it is to barge into a man's room uninvited? This castle is a fortress full of guards who mean business and train with swords every day to keep in shape for fending off the Raiders — who are other Scots. These people fight against each other all the time. This isn't some game. This is a real castle and there are real guards outside and they have real weapons, Amber."

The earnestness in his voice was at such odds with the way his body stood limp that for a moment she was at a loss for what to say. But she decided it was good that he was still talking to her, and that she should encourage him to keep on doing so.

Almost like he was programmed, he seemed to shy away from some subjects, while other subjects were fine. She guessed at which subjects might be fine.

"But I should be safe now that you're here. I mean, you're the captain of the guards, so they'll do as you say."

He stood stock still again, and then he nodded the tiniest little bit, while at the same time moving closer to her so that they were standing side by side, both facing the door. What he said didn't make sense at first.

"Yes, I am the captain of the guards who work in the underground castle. They do as I say most of the time, but there have been times when I didn't feel like I was in charge."

He sounded so puzzled and confused and lost. She longed to hug him and tell him he didn't need to be in charge of these guards, that the two of them would go back to the future and have a life together with nothing to do with all this. He had the business aspects of the Renaissance Faire to run, and when he was himself, he was really keen on running them.

Soon.

Soon she would be able to hold him and say these things. He was coming out of the funk, just as he had this morning. Each moment, he was less zombified and more like the Tomas she knew and loved.

She just had to keep him talking a while longer.

"Well it makes sense that they wouldn't completely think of you as their captain. I mean, you've only been here a week, but the other captain — Alfred is it?"

He nodded once.

She shrugged and gave him a sympathetic smile.

"Well, Alfred is someone they've known their whole lives, so of course they're going to follow his orders more readily than they follow those of a relative stranger—"

His body was stock still and slumped, but his head was shaking 'no,' vigorously— and then he touched the back of her hand, and she stopped speaking out of shock more than anything. His touch felt so wonderful, like coming home after a hard day at work to a surprise party with all your favorite friends and family — and a homemade cake. A simple touch from him sent that kind of warmth through her.

With a mind of its own, her hand turned to hold his, palm to palm, and they stood there like that quietly for several moments. She was dying to ask him if this meant they were getting back together, but something weird was going on. The real Tomas seemed to have control of his body, the Tomas who was going home to see to the business side of the faire.

But his speech and his thoughts? Amber hadn't snapped those away from the zombie Sulis had recreated inside Tomas's head half an hour ago, undoing all the progress Amber had made this morning. Not just yet. Amber would have to give it a little while. But in the meantime, holding hands with him was comforting.

But he had interrupted her for a reason, and soon he spoke again, his face so confused it made her heart ache.

"It isn't because I'm not Alfred. That's not why they sometimes don't listen to me. They do it to him too. We've talked about it. We don't really know what it is, but something's going on. I think it has to do with that Lachlan the Dark. Tavish and I have a plan to catch the man, and then we'll question him and find out."

A pang of guilt hit Amber, for keeping the secret of Sasha's wedding vision from Tomas. Still holding his hand, she longed to sit down with him on the bed and get comfortable, but it seemed like anything that hinted at being more than friends set off some sort of trigger that brought back Sulis's zombie full force. Amber had to keep reminding herself that it had taken a couple hours to bring him out of the zombie state this morning.

And it had taken Sulis just one whisper in his ear to put him right back there.

But where was the B witch now?

Ha. Apparently, it had taken Sulis so much magic to zombify Tomas again that she was back out in the woods now, sinking her teeth into trees. Or whatever she did to soak up more of that druid magic.

Amber gently squeezed Tomas's hand.

"You're probably right. It probably does have something to do with Lachlan. You'll fix that soon. I know you will."

There was a lull in their conversation then. Still clinging to his hand, Amber fished around in her mind for another innocuous thing to talk about. But maybe it was better if they didn't talk. Maybe now was the time to see if her body could bring his out of the stupor. As friends, so that she didn't set off the zombie alarm.

She looked up into his eyes.

They were doing that slot machine thing again.

Better make her move before they settled on any one emotion. She slowly moved in for a hug, raising her arms up over his shoulders so that she could clasp them around the back of his neck. This was going to work, she could feel it in her bones. Especially once they were hugging.

Ah. Peace at last.

Settling down for a deep rest in his embrace, she laid her head against his chest and held him close. They stood there for the longest time, and it was heaven when his arms moved around her waist to hug her too. They started to rock back and forth slowly, slow dancing with no music.

She had him back. Tears came to her eyes, and then whispered into his ear the question that had been on her mind for seven years.

“What happened on your eighteenth birthday, Tomas? Why did you disappear out of my life?

He trembled as soon as she started whispering.

Elation went through her body, making her tingle all over. She clung to him in return and spoke the thoughts of her heart.

“Can we get back together again?”

But he was no longer returning her embrace.

And he didn’t answer, just stumbled away from her and hurried out the door.

✠ 11 ✠

AON DEUG

Tomas had to find Sulis. If he didn't go look for her right this minute, something horrible would happen. It could not be allowed to happen. He had to find Sulis. Right now. Or he would be sorry.

What would happen, anyway?

Pain shot into his head from his eyes.

He had to find Sulis...

She wasn't in the great hall anymore.

How about if he asked this man—

As soon as he had that thought, he heard her Southern accent in his head.

"Tomas honey, in these times you cannot let anyone think you don't know where everything is and where you need to be."

He had to find Sulis by himself.

He went toward the stairway down into the underground palace. She was often down there. It was sort of a long way though. And he had to find her soon, her terrible consequences would ensue. Better hurry.

But as soon as he thought of running, he heard her words again.

"Tomas honey, you know you really must set a stately example for the men under your command."

Walking, it was.

And all the while he looked for her, the story his dad had told him and Tavish on their eighteenth birthday played over and over again in Tomas's mind.

OOR ANCESTOR SEAN MACGREGOR WAS BETWEEN A rock and a hard place. You see, Sean liked gambling. It didna matter what he gambled on. Oh sure, he would play games o' dice, but even the little things in life were subject tae gambling for him. How soon were the lambs gaun'ae come? How soon was the snow gaun'ae fall? How many kittens would be in the next litter?

The will tae gamble put Sean intae a fever, it did. And as is always the case with men who hae a weakness such as gambling, there were those who took advantage o' him. They baited him tae gamble, knowing he couldna always win and that they would hae his money.

Because o' his gambling, Sean owed more money than he would ever make in his lifetime, and no one would give him loans anymore.

Now Sean had three sons and two daughters tae feed, as wull as his wife and his maw and his wife's maw.

The clan would help, aye, but as all MacGregors are, he was a proud man who didna want the charity o' others.

One gloomy Scottish day on the moor, Sean was out gathering peat for the family fire. He had gone farther than he normally would, because 'twas an exceptionally cauld winter, and all the fuel nearby had already been burned. He was all by himself, and verra far out o' earshot from anyone he knew.

He was getting close tae the mountain when he noticed there were some wee lights up there. With naught left tae lose, he slung his large sack with a few clumps o' peat ower his shoulder and climbed up tae see what they were.

When he got close enough for his eyes tae show him the goings-on, he could na believe them. A large hole had been dug intae the side o' the mountain, and men were going in with picks and coming out with chunks o' gauld.

He knew 'twas gauld, for he had seen raw nuggets in their dirt-covered form afore. Ye see, back in those days, they used tae trade in nuggets o' gauld, na sae much in coins as we dae now.

Sean felt the drool dribbling doon his chin and doon his neck as he watched the men come oot with all this wealth while he hid in the brush and heather. Why should those men hae all that gauld? He could go in and dig some oot for himself. That would solve all o' his problems, said the devil on Sean's left shoulder.

The angel on his right shoulder argued that he wasna likely tae go home with nary being tarnished by the experience.

Sean sat there quite a while, stroking his beard and thinking this through afore he ran ower and fell in line with the men going in with their picks.

Only he didna hae a pick.

Just when Sean had this thought, a man stepped oot from between two boulders and held oot a pick tae Sean. The man was auld, and he wore a long white robe o' a cut Sean had never seen afore. 'Twas made o' the brawest white linen, with patterns embroidered intae the collar. Only 'twas stained green and brown from life in the wild.

"Here," said this grizzled auld one, holding oot the pick tae Sean.

Sean wasna one tae look a gift horse in the mouth, sae he took the pick and was on his way, na even pausing when he called ower his shoulder, "Thank ye."

Sean fell back in line with the men just as they entered the cave. 'Twas dank and dark, but Sean could almost smell the gauld up ahead, sae he didna mind.

Digging oot the gauld took longer than Sean thought it would — all day and all night for three days, just tae dig oot enough that he thought he could repay his debts. Food would coome in, and the men would lie doon on the grass tae sleep, but otherwise, they were digging and picking and pounding tae get oot the gauld.

And Sean thought tae himself, "Why should I stop with just enough gauld tae repay my debts? Let me work another three days, and I shall have enough to last the rest o' my life, and even be able tae gamble some o' it."

Sae Sean dug and ate and slept and dug some moore for another three days and three nights, until he had na only enough gauld tae repay all o' his debts, but enough tae set himself up comfortable fer life and still hae some for gambling.

When he had all o' this, he hoarded it up intae his sporran and his other pouches and made his way oot with some men who are heading oot, picks ower their shoulders.

Howsoever, when Sean got out o' the cave, who should be lingering there but the auld man who had given him the pick?

At foremaist, Sean thought the auld man only wanted his pick back, for his hand was oot as if waiting for it. This Sean gladly gave him.

But the pick wasna what the auld man was after. His beady eyes studied Sean with a malevolent intelligence, and his voice came oot harsh next he spake.

"Let us hae what ye got oot o' the cave, aye?"

Now, giving the man back the gauld that Sean had worked sae hard for six days and six nights tae get was the last thing on his mind. Nay, he was looking aboot for some aught tae use as a weapon in order tae beat the man doon sae that he could flee with the gauld.

Not all o' oor ancestors were honest, sorry tae say.

While Sean was thinking this, the auld man called out tae several men aroond him, who came ower and seized Sean and tied him up. Once he was helpless, the auld man's beady eyes were on him again.

"Well nae," says he. "I can take the gauld by force, ye ken. Howsoever, 'tis curious I am, what ye will give me for it."

Sean opened his mouth tae suggest what he might give.

But the auld man gestured, and his cronies gagged Sean as wull as they had tied him up.

Sean couldna speak if his life depended on it, and fair tae likely it did.

The auld man was speaking, puffing on a pipe he had lit while Sean was being gagged.

"I will tell ye what ye will give me in exchange for the gauld. It willna be all bad, ye ken. I will get rid o' this reckless abandon ye hae at gambling yer wages away — and then some. Sae ye hae that gift as wull as the gauld tae pay back what ye hae squandered. In fact, I will dae this now. Tae show my good faith."

Sean felt his mind scramble when the auld man put his hand on Sean's forehead. Visions o' all the wages he'd held and lost went spinning aroond in his mind, followed by a whirlpool that spun aroond faster and faster till it drained out the bottom o' his nose in a bunch o' snot that he blew intae his sleeve.

"There nae," said the auld man. "Yer urge tae gamble is gone forever. Nay need tae thank me, for now yer debt is greater than afore, when all ye did was steal my gauld."

Sean fought against his bindings and his gag, thinking, "Where did the auld man get the idea this all was his gauld?" Ye see, this was Sean's clan's territory — oor territory. Sae the gauld was rightfully the clan's, didna the auld man ken?

Sean could hae sworn up and doon he hadna said a word o' these thoughts.

Even so, the auld man threw back his head and laughed. "The land doesna belong tae yer clan. Nay one owns the land. 'Tis older than all the rest o' us put together. Nay, the land isna owned. And what is in the land isna owned either, till it is brought oot with the work o' one's hands." He looked askance at the men who obeyed his every word. "Or the hands o' those one owns."

Hearing the auld man say that he owned these other men greatly disturbed Sean — as ye can wull imagine. On hearing this, he looked intae the eyes o' the men who had bound him.

They were glazed ower, na quite clear. But there was nay sign o' fear in these men. They were resigned tae their lot. They didna look at all unhappy... just na sae delighted as they might hae been tae be digging up gauld.

The auld man brought his beady eyes right up in front o' Sean's.

"Aye, they are na unhappy. And what I hae in mind for ye, 'tis na sae bad even as they hae it. Ye wouldna need tae serve me and my line yerself. Only the fourth son born tae ye would need tae — and every fourth son barn intae yer line after that — and only once they've reached the age o' five and twenty. Only tell me ye agree tae that, and I will tell my men tae let ye go with yer gauld back tae yer clan and live yer happy life."

Now Sean was still trussed up, and he couldna give his aye or nay till they removed the gag from his mouth. He took the opportunity tae think the offer ower.

On the one hand, there was slavery for his fourth

born son — who had na in fact been born yet, and might never be — and neither had the fourth born sons o' any in his line. That last bit was verra distant for him, ye ken. On the other hand, he was already trussed up, sae these men would hae little difficulty at all in beating him senseless and taking the gauld from him.

He nodded tae show he was ready tae give his answer.

The auld man cackled in a frightening though somehow still humorous way and gestured that the men should undo Sean's gag, which they did — still leaving the trusses.

Sean took a deep breath in order tae give out the speech he had prepared in his moments o' contemplation.

But the white-robed auld man interrupted him.

"We will na hae a speech. Just tell me aye or nay. Will ye be gang home with enough gauld tae pay off yer debts — and then some, I daresay — or nay?"

It seemed tae Sean that even the glassy eyed slaves o' the auld man leaned forward tae hear his answer. There really wasna a choice, howsoever.

"Aye."

The auld man leaned forward and put his hand tae his ear.

"What's that?"

Sean spoke up loudly.

"Aye."

The auld man turned aroond and looked smugly at all o' his servants, nodding mostly tae himself.

"Ye all are witness tae that. He took this on willingly, ye ken?"

They all nodded, and then the auld man gestured, and one o' them took off Sean's right boot.

Sean looked at him quizzically.

The auld man hollered, and yet another man came running up the hill from doon below wth some aught glowing in his hand. Sean couldn't make out what 'twas for the longest time, but then he gasped.

Soon as he did, the men ganged up and forced the gag back in his mouth and then held doon his body by sitting on it all ower, leaving his right ankle exposed.

Sean tried tae scream when the brand hit his ankle, but he couldna get wind with all the men sitting on him, let alone get the wind oot o' him with the gag in his mouth.

And then the auld man touched the branded place, and the pain disappeared — but in its place came the oddest sensation through his whole body. Visions o' all his descendants flashed afore his eyes, and each fourth born son was born with this mark aroond his right ankle.

In the vision, Sean saw that the mark was a ring o' standing stones.

After the story, they had all looked at the standing stones birthmark which Tavish clearly had on his right ankle. It had been so disturbing at the time, and sometimes, like now, Tomas thought of Sulis's white robes and compared them to the robes in the story. His mind was going a million miles an hour with fear and worry and even guilt.

But then he found Sulis. He didn't even know what she whispered in his ear, only that all the turmoil in his mind went away.

12

DÀ DHEUG

Beset by a sudden drench of tears and choking sobs, Amber ran out of the castle and through the town to the weaver shop, where she flung herself on the floor in front of Eileen's spinning wheel, laid her head in the woman's lap, and wept.

Eileen stopped working and stroked Amber's hair.

"Ye must get hold of yerself." She projected her voice across the room to her children. "Gae on ootside and play, ye bairns." She waited a minute while they complied, then spoke in the same soothing voice as before. "What is it?"

Amber was sobbing so hard, she could barely breathe, let alone talk.

"I... He... Sulis..."

Eileen handed her a handkerchief.

"Here ye are. Try yer best tae pull yerself together now."

Amber gratefully blew her nose. Doing so helped

her gain her composure a bit, so she got up and sat on her stool and began carding wool after she wiped her tears as well, taking several deep breaths in order to calm her breathing and stop the choking effect.

"I thank ye. Oh, 'tis Tomas. Ye wouldna ken from how he behaves now, but he is a good man, Eileen. A good man who is trapped under Sulis's thumb."

Eileen watched Amber card for a moment, as if she expected her to break down again, but when she didn't, Eileen went back to spinning the wool into yarn.

"'Twouldn't be the first time a pretty lass brought a good man doon. Nay, 'twouldn't."

Thankful for the affirmation, Amber gave Eileen a grateful look.

"I did spend the day with him yesterday, ye ken. At first, he was grumbling, but toward the end o' it he seemed wull. Howsoever, then she showed up and whispered in his ear — and he transformed once again tae this zombie—"

Eileen put a hand on Amber's elbow.

"Pray tell, what be a zombie?"

Amber cast about the room for an answer that would be suitable.

"'Tis a creature in a story I heard once. A mindless slave."

Eileen nodded.

"'Tis a suitable name for him, aye."

Eileen studied Amber's face a moment, appearing to be making a decision. And then she lowered her voice to barely a whisper, darting glances over at the male weavers at their looms across the room.

"There is a good enchantress nearby tae the south. Elsbeth may be able tae help him. Mayhap she is powerful enough tae break the spell. Howsoever, ye mustna go alone. 'Tis tae dangerous. Seumas knows the way — everyone roond here does — and if ye ask him tae go with ye — and perhaps Tavish as wull — I'm certain they will."

Amber wiped the last of her tears away with a small smile for Eileen, then held up the handkerchief with a questioning look in her eyes.

Smirking, Eileen pointed to the wash buckets on the other side of the looms.

Amber put the handkerchief in with the white clothes and then helped Eileen spin some more.

But the first chance she got, she excused herself to go to the privy, asked someone how to get to Elsbeth's, and set off on her own to the south.

❧

AMBER EXPECTED THE WOODS TO BE SCARY, GOING BY Eileen's warning. So she was pleasantly surprised that the birds were singing and even the sun was shining and the flowers blooming as she made her way to the witch's little cottage by a stream, deep in the woods.

Only two things kept it from being a pleasant stroll.

One, she had the uneasy feeling someone was following her.

Every once in a while she would pause at what she thought a random point and whip her head around in the direction she thought she felt the pursuit from. But she didn't see anything. She thought she heard something a few times, but with all the birds singing, it was hard to be sure.

Two, she was going to visit a witch.

Three days ago, Amber would've laughed if you told her someone was a witch. She hadn't believed in such things. But with the evidence that magic actually did exist all around her because of this trip into the past, a healthy amount of fear loomed in her mind. Would she herself fall into some sort of spell as soon as she saw the woman?

But when she got there, she laughed.

The enchantress's cottage was adorable. Different-colored river rocks piled up on top of each other to make walls. The roof was made from a million handfuls of straw. Amber walked up the stone pathway through the grass and flowers and knocked on the cute little maple-wood door.

"Aye, be with ye in a moment," called out a sweet woman's voice from within.

While she waited, Amber took stock of the cottage. There was smoke coming out of the little stone chimney, and little maple-wood shutters covered the tiny windows. The whole cottage could fit in her parents' living room. She wanted one just like it.

The little door opened, and inside was a woman as pretty as Eileen, only thirty years older. Her smile was tentative, but welcoming.

"Hello, I suspect ye know I'm Elsbeth."

Amber found herself stumbling over her words, the woman had such a presence.

"Aye. Eileen told me o' ye. She says ye might be able tae help me — or rather, tae help my friend Tomas. I'm Amber."

After briefly looking over Amber's shoulder for a moment for some strange reason perhaps only a witch would understand, Elsbeth stepped to the side and opened the door wider.

"Come in."

The cottage looked cozy from outside the door, with a fire in the grate of the little stone fireplace and a handwoven rag rug on the hardwood floor.

But something in her gut made Amber hesitate. The decision to cross the threshold of this house seemed monumental. But she'd walked all the way out here just to see this woman, so it would be silly to turn around and walk all the way back without even talking to her.

Amber went in and paused, looking about while her eyes adjusted to the firelight.

There were drawings of people mounted on the wattle and daub that sealed the river rock walls, and the only furnishings were a bed, two chairs, and a tiny kitchen table.

But the fourth wall grabbed Amber's attention, once she could see. It was full of little cubbyholes that held the most random collection of things: feathers, tiny little sticks of different varieties, stones, mushrooms, whole leaves, tiny glass jars with different colored liquids...

Elsbeth gestured to one of the chairs and sat down on the other side of the tiny table.

"Sae Amber, I will save ye the trouble o' making

small talk and just ask ye now — why hae ye come tae see me?"

Amber searched Elsbeth's eyes for any sign of mocking, but they looked sweet and kind. She decided she was going to trust Elsbeth. After all, Tavish and Kelsey trusted Eileen, and Eileen had said Elsbeth was a good enchantress.

"'Tis a long story."

Elsbeth rested her head in her hands, which she had propped on the table by her elbows.

"I hae naught tae do all the day. Dae tell."

Somehow, looking at the witch was tiring. So while she talked, Amber slouched in her chair and studied the slats of the ceiling that held up the straw of the roof. She had to concentrate in order to pick out only the details in her story which would make sense to a woman of this time.

"When I was fourteen, my parents finally let me volunteer at the Ren... at the market fair for the summer. 'Twas far enough away from oor haime that I had tae camp there overnight two days a week. I'd never stayed away from haime afore, and it gave me a lot o' freedom. I met Tomas there, and we had sae much in common. We were inseparable whenever I was at the fair. I fell in love with Tomas, and I am certain he fell in love with me tae. For four summers this went on. I thought we would be together forever — that once we were grown, we would be marrit. But the day after his eighteenth birthday, Tomas disappeared from my life. Went away withoot saying where. All his kin went, tae."

Elsbeth's face looked sorry for her to the extent

Amber hadn't expected. It was almost as if Elsbeth were living through what Amber described, the sorrow in the enchantress's eyes was that deep.

"Such a loss is hard to bear. It strengthens us, but the pain... Most believe the pain is not worth the gain in strength of character."

What an odd thing to say.

Amber had to think about it for a minute before she even realized what it meant. Deciding she had been paid a complement — albeit a weird one — she smiled the tiniest bit and gave the enchantress a little nod before continuing her tale.

"That happened seven years ago. I tried tae forget him, tae fall in love and marry anoother, but 'twas a losing cause. I despaired o' ever being marrit."

Elsbeth closed her eyes and wrinkled her forehead, as if she were experiencing the despair that Amber had gone through.

It freaked Amber out a little. Before going on with her story, she waited patiently for Elsbeth to relax and slough off the despair and open her eyes to listen again.

"But seven days ago, a mutual friend called me — invited me here tae come work with her and Tomas's twin brother Tavish. I came right away, sure that Tomas would be here tae."

Elsbeth was smiling now, and it looked just like she was hopeful that she would see Tomas once she arrived at Kelsey's worksite.

Amber shook her head a little, to clear her mind of such a fanciful idea.

"Wull, Tomas is here all right, but with his ... intended, Sulis."

Elsbeth's shoulders slumped.

Forgetting for a moment how strange this was, to have the woman living through the emotions Amber had, she gave her a sympathetic nod before she realized how silly that looked and put on a serious face, appealing to Elsbeth for whatever power she had to change the situation.

"This lass Sulis isna normal, Elsbeth. She has him under a spell o' some sort. He isna himself when he's aroond her. His eyes glaze ower and his body is unanimated. He's what we call a zombie where we come from: a mindless slave. Howsoever, Sulis goes intae the woods often. Kelsey says it's tae renew her powers, that a whole lot o' her magic is used up keeping the spell on Tomas. Mayhap ye would understand that?"

Elsbeth shook her head no the tiniest bit.

"I ken the druids. Doesna everyone? But nay, I am na one o' them. If it please ye, go on with the tale."

Amber sighed, then continued.

"Wull, when Sulis is gone off tae the woods tae soak in their sap or some aught—"

Elsbeth laughed at Amber's joke, and Amber gave her a small smile.

"When she goes off into the woods and I can be aroond Tomas by oorselves, he comes out o' his daze. It takes a few hours, but he does return just about tae normal. But as soon as she returns — and she whispers in his ear, I hae noticed — then he's a zombie again.

Elsbeth, ye hae tae help me break the spell of hopeless zombie-ism she has ower him. Please say ye will."

But Elsbeth's welcoming smile was now a resigned smile, and as she spoke, she slowly got up and showed Amber to the door of her tiny cottage.

"I canna help ye. Only true love can break the curse o' false love. If there is one who Tomas truly loves, then his love for her can overcome this curse. 'Tis the only thing which can."

Amber's heart sank.

Once upon a time, Tomas had loved her, but he sure didn't today. If only it were her love for him that mattered, she felt sure that she could save him from a life of servitude. How would they ever rescue him from Sulis now?

Still, none of this was Elsbeth's fault. The woman had been nothing but kind and sympathetic. So Amber gave the enchantress the most grateful smile she could manage.

"Wull, thank ye for yer time."

Elsbeth said a farewell before closing the door softly.

"Ye were well tae come."

Amber slumped as she was left to look at the charming little maplewood door. What a disappointment.

However, all thoughts of Tomas's plight fled Amber's mind as soon as she turned around. The forest, once warm, was now getting dark, and it was shadowy and spooky. An owl hooted nearby, making her jump up a foot as she swiftly walked through the creepy trees.

She was hitting her stride when something came at her from the shadows. Scooping up her long plaid skirts, she broke into a run. But she couldn't see the ground very well with all that fabric in her arms.

A tree root got in her way, and she tripped and fell hard.

And then the eerie laughter of the man who had tried to run her off the cliffs back in her own time came toward her swiftly. The laughter of Lachlan the Dark.

13

TRÌ DEUG

Pushing herself up off the damp leafy forest floor, Amber willed herself to be angry instead of afraid. Looking around for a branch that she could use as a weapon, she took a deep breath so that there would be force behind her voice when she spoke, instead of it coming out as a squeak from her fear-constricted throat. She spotted a good branch and grabbed it. She used English, since there was no one else around and no need to put on her Gaelic and try to fit in.

"Why are you following me, Lachlan?"

She couldn't see him, but she turned around when his voice gave away his location.

"The better to catch you with, my dear."

The menace in his voice made the hair on her neck stand up, but she was not going to cower in fear. Her self-defense coach had told her that was what predators wanted, so in all cases she should go down fighting, even if it was just biting and scratching. He had also told her to scream bloody murder, but that was hardly going to do any good out here in the middle of the forest. She was far enough away from Elsbeth's now to be out of earshot.

She felt strongest when she was being snarky, so she poured it on.

"Very funny. You're hardly a wolf, though. More like an uppity little puppy."

A twig snapped, giving away his new location and making her turn again. He was getting closer, but he was moving very slowly and circling around, trying to be stealthy.

Yeah, stealthy.

She had barely any warning when he launched himself at her, only the movement of some branches at the corner of her eye to the left. Determined to go down fighting, she raised the branch up to defend herself.

But before Lachan could touch her, Tomas swept in again. He shoved the other man so hard, the man's head hit a tree and he slumped down onto the ground.

Amber opened her mouth to ask Tomas what he was doing here, but before she could, he turned around and leaned down, motioning for her to get on his back.

"I don't know how long he'll be out," Tomas said, "but I want to get you as far away from here as possible while he is."

Seeing the sense in that – and feeling so much relief she almost collapsed — she did as he asked, thankful that the long skirts of the day were full enough to allow it.

He started running as soon as she had locked her ankles around the front of him and grabbed his shoulders. She'd ridden on his back like this many times during a game they used to play at the faire, and this brought it all back to her as the trees went whooshing by. More owls hooted, but they were just lending atmosphere to an adventure she was having with her favorite person in the world.

And it was so nice, being close to him like this. Breathing in the warm woodsy scent of him. Feeling his muscles tense and his heart beating. Her body wanted to hug him close while she clung to him, to put her head against his shoulder and soak in the closeness of him...

And why shouldn't she?

The woman who claimed him did so under false pretenses. She didn't love him, and he didn't love her. It was just her artifice that kept him following her around like a lost puppy.

He'd been Amber's for four whole years, and he'd never broken up with her, just disappeared. And they'd been so good together. Even now, riding on his back, she already felt like she'd come home.

But she didn't dare say so.

She didn't dare mention any of these thoughts to him.

When it came to love between a man and woman, the language of the body was a lot more reliable than the language people spoke – so long as you didn't bring lust into it too soon. She'd made that mistake a few times and lived to regret it.

Talking would have been awkward anyway. Nothing she wanted to say was appropriate for his supposed social situation as the cherished intended of the B witch. Blech. Amber threw up a little in her mouth just thinking about what that woman really intended to do with Tomas according to Kelsey: leave him here as her slave in order to supervise his other slaves and loot the underground castle before Kelsey's client Mr. Blair ever came to possess it.

That was no kind of life for Tomas! He was bright and competent. He deserved to do as he wished and go home to manage his parents' business at the Renaissance Faire. That was his real life. All this was just playing pretend. No, worse, it was a trap the B witch had snared him in.

So the whole time Tomas was running with her on his back toward Laird Malcomb's castle, Amber did just what she wanted to. She hugged him and put her head against his shoulder and soaked in the nearness of him without saying a word. She caressed his back and kissed his neck and gave him all the love she had despaired of ever giving him.

She might've squeezed him with her legs, too. She wasn't sure.

And then they got back to his room in the castle.

When he put her down, the separation was almost unbearable for her.

But he spoke as if unaffected.

"We need to wait for Tavish and Kelsey and their

friends Sasha and Seumas. They're chasing Lachlan, and hopefully they'll find him while he's knocked out. I was with them, trying to help, but then I needed to get you to safety."

What a roller coaster ride. She'd been riding high only a moment ago, and now she was crashing down. He didn't seem at all affected by her closeness, the way she was by his. He must've moved on to someone else even before he met the B witch. He...

She did a double take on Tomas.

His eyes were clear, and he was talking sense. He wasn't a zombie at all right now. And the only person he was with was her. She was affecting him, even if he didn't acknowledge it. Maybe he did have feelings for her, but he didn't want to admit it. What had Elsbeth said? Did he have to show his feelings, or admit them?

She narrowed her eyes at him.

"Why were you so intent on rescuing me, then? If catching Lachlan was the bigger priority, why didn't you do that instead of grabbing me and taking me here?"

He looked down and away, fussing with the hair on the back of his head.

"Everybody knows women and children come first in a rescue situation."

He was in denial! His body language screamed it: avoiding her gaze and fidgeting with something else.

The spark of hope that had bloomed in her when Kelsey called, the hope she had nurtured during her journey to Scotland — and that she thought had died when she realized Sulis was Tomas's girlfriend — that spark of hope bloomed again in Amber's heart.

But she didn't dare touch him right now.

Call it feminine intuition, but somehow she just knew she had to let him make every first move.

Even though she had just ridden on his back in a very intimate way for the past half hour, she knew beyond a shadow of a doubt that she didn't dare reach out and touch him now, or he would withdraw, and she might never have a chance to try and get him to admit his feelings for her.

Instead, she needled him with her words. This wasn't unusual. She'd always teased him.

"But you'd already rescued me when you knocked him out. He was right there, incapacitated. You could've just as easily grabbed him and brought him here as me, and then you could have locked him up in the dungeons everyone says are downstairs, when we know full well they're ancient palace rooms, not dungeons."

He went from playing with the hair on the back of his head to sitting down on the bed and playing with the bedspread, and then quickly got up off the bed. Was that the hint of a blush she saw on his face?

Unfortunately, before she could get an answer out of him, everyone else came in the room.

Amber made a sour face at Kelsey. She couldn't help it. Here she and Tomas were — so close, and yet so far — and in come two happy couples, hands casually resting on each other.

Tomas, on the other hand, brightened up. Was he relieved to not be alone with her anymore?

"Did you get him?"

Tavish looked at Amber for a moment as if she

might have developed a wasting sickness while he was away and he was checking to see if she still lived.

"No, and it's much worse."

Tomas's brow wrinkled.

"How it could be any worse?"

Kelsey came over and hugged Amber.

"Lachlan's after Amber. Specifically. He had plenty of opportunities to take other people easily, and he ignored them to follow her. He's been following her ever since she got here — and even before she came here, remember? We don't know why, but it doesn't matter. All that matters is keeping Amber safe. And the best way to do that is to catch him and keep him locked up."

Tomas briefly looked around at everyone else's faces, but when he saw that they were all nodding in agreement with Kelsey's assertion that Amber was the target, he flew into full-on protection mode, stuffing the arrow-slit windows with extra blankets — presumably to block the sound of their voices from getting to anyone outside. The castle walls were certainly thick enough to prevent it otherwise.

"Okay, that's it. Amber, don't go to Eileen's anymore to sleep. You're staying here with me—"

"But you share this room with Sulis —"

He made a dismissive gesture — dismissive of the woman he usually followed around like a dog on a leash.

"Sulis left this morning on some overnight errand, something about not being able to function with walls around her. So it's fine, and until we catch Lachlan — which we will, soon — Amber's going to stay in here.

It's the safest place, a virtual stronghold. He won't be able to get in here. Seumas, tell the guards to be on the lookout for him."

The redheaded highlander nodded, kissed his redheaded woman — Sasha — and ducked out of the room.

Tomas went under the bed for his sword and his bow and arrows, then turned toward Amber.

"Stay in this room. There's a chamber pot over there in the corner, and I'll have someone bring you something to eat for dinner. The man can't be far away. We'll use Laird Malcomb's dogs, and we'll have him tonight, but until we do, promise you'll stay here."

Amber had barely nodded yes when everyone rushed out of the room and she was alone.

How long would it take to catch the man so that Tomas would come back here to this room where she would be waiting?

14

CEITHIR DEUG

Tomas was exhausted. It was still dark, but morning wasn't far away. He took the spiral stone stairs two at a time, thinking that perhaps he could get a little bit of sleep before he had to wake up and be on duty supervising the guards down at the docks inside the underground palace.

One of the guards on the floor of the castle where his bedroom was nodded at him in passing, and Tomas nodded back. Was that an amused smile on the man's face? What was that about?

Finally at the door to his room, he pushed it open, dropping his kilt to the floor as he did...

And there was Amber in his bed.

He sighed.

Careful not to rock the bed and wake her up, he crawled in beside her, dreading what it would be like if she woke up and pulled away from him. He didn't care, of course. He had a girlfriend. But it would be, you know, awkward if Amber were to wake up with a horrified face at seeing him in the bed with her and pull away. That was all.

Except she did wake up. And she didn't pull away.

She reached over and pulled his arm around her, pulling him close behind her like a cloak of safety against the evil cruel world.

And it was just reflex that made him hold her close. A protective reflex. Because she was probably afraid, being here all alone in this strange room not knowing what was happening with... her friends.

They cuddled, and a peace came over him such as he hadn't known in seven years. Not only peace. Something else was lurking under the surface of it. Something he tamped down so that it wouldn't catch flame. He was with Sulis. Amber was just a friend who needed his protection, and he was only doing what any friend would do.

But her voice was throaty and sexy with sleep when she spoke.

"Did you get him?"

He sighed, which pressed him closer to her. She caressed his arm in response, and it felt good. His mouth went to kiss the back of her head, but he stopped it in time. Just an old habit, you know, from when they used to be together.

He cleared his throat

"No. And we searched the whole town. The dogs only just caught Lachlan's scent an hour ago. They followed him all the way out to Port Patrick. We had to turn back or else their barking would've woken everyone there. The good news is it looks like he's taking ship and going somewhere else. Good riddance."

She squeezed his arm and shook it a little in victory.

"That is good news."

He nodded his head, and because her head was so close in front of his on the pillow, it was as if he were nuzzling her, but he hadn't meant to.

"Yeah, so you don't have to be afraid."

She drew his arm more tightly around her.

"I'm not afraid, not now that you're here."

His heart swelled when she said that. Just because, you know, it was good to feel he had helped her.

It was quiet for so long that he thought she'd gone back to sleep. Fat chance of him getting to sleep with his front pressed against her back like this. It didn't mean anything except that he was a healthy male and she was an attractive...

Never mind. He was with Sulis. He couldn't be thinking that way.

As gently as he could, he put some of the covers between their middles. He didn't want to wake Amber. But then after a while, she spoke again, so softly he could have pretended he was asleep and didn't hear.

"Tomas?"

But what was the fun in that?

"Yeah?"

"What happened on your eighteenth birthday? Why did you leave me? I worried about you, and I've missed you something awful. Tell me you had a good reason."

Her words hurt. He had tried to put out of his mind how he must've hurt her.

"I was trying to protect you, Amber. I was sworn to secrecy about all this, the time travel stuff. I guess it's kind of pointless to be silent on it now. But the answer to your question is a long story."

"I'm not going anywhere."

Good, because I like having you here.

Keep talking though, or you'll lose control of yourself, Tomas.

His hand started combing through her long dark hair while he thought on how to introduce his dad's story about Sean MacGregor. It didn't seem anything but friendly, though, so he let it keep smoothing through her silky tresses.

"You know how authentic everyone always says my dad is, his Gaelic accent and his skill at sword-fighting and even the expressions on his face?"

"Yeah. Yeah, it's like he's from..." She raised up and turned her head to look him in the eye, and she had a 'Eureka!' look on her face. "Oh my... He is from back in the past, isn't he."

He gathered her close again so that she would lie down. Looking into her eyes felt just as wrong as kissing her would have felt. No, that wasn't quite true. Looking into her eyes made him want to kiss her, and he mustn't do that. He was with Sulis.

"Yep. My dad was born in the 1520s on the MacGregor lands in Glen Strae, Scotland, near Kilchurn Castle... It's so strange. The MacGregor name doesn't even exist yet in this time we're in now, you know."

"It doesn't?"

"No. The name comes from Viking Lord Donnchadh Beag's son Griogair, and he's just a boy right now."

"That is weird. No wonder Seumas looks at Tavish and you so oddly sometimes."

"Well, Seumas knows everything."

Her muscles flexed.

"He does? Who else knows, Eileen?"

"No one else."

She relaxed again.

"Anyway, so your dad is from the 1500s in the Highlands. And he's a time traveler. So why did that make you leave me without saying a word, and without your parents telling me anything? I looked up to your parents, you know. I thought they were my friends. Losing them hurt almost as much as losing you."

He stroked her hair some more, but this time tenderly, trying to soothe her.

"They still are your friends, Amber. In their own way, they were protecting all of us by keeping this time travel stuff from us until we were old enough to see the sense in keeping it a secret, but I do think they should have told us about the curse earlier."

"What curse?"

"Well, Dad wasn't a time traveler by choice. Neither is Tavish."

"Sort of like I didn't travel here by choice."

"You didn't?"

"No. No, I was... wandering around in the underground castle that same night after you stopped Lachlan from running me off the cliff, and suddenly I just got dizzy. I didn't know what was happening to me, Tomas."

He squeezed her tight, remembering with shame how impatient he'd been with her when he found her in this time in her modern clothes.

"I'm so sorry for how I acted when you got here to this time."

"You're forgiven."

He relaxed his hold on her until they were just cuddling again.

"Anyway, Dad — and now Tavish has taken his place — they are servants of the druid family whose ancestor enslaved one of our ancestors, a certain Sean MacGregor, who was stupid enough to have insurmountable gambling debts." He told her the whole story.

She pounded the bed with her fist.

"What an idiot."

Tomas laughed in spite of himself. She had always said exactly what was on her mind. It was one of the things he... one of the reasons she was his friend.

"Yeah, he was an idiot. Sean chose enslavement voluntarily, and for that reason we've been told there is very little chance of our family ever escaping the curse that druid put on us through Sean."

He stopped there and was quiet for a while, letting that sink in. That was the part that he and his brothers and his nephews had argued the hardest against when their parents had told them the story. 'Can't we just break this curse?' they had insisted when told their girlfriends might have children who would be enslaved, if they married them. 'There has to be a way.'

Amber didn't argue, though.

"I see," was all she said. It made him feel like a child,

compared to her. Had she always been more mature than him?

Probably.

He resumed combing her long dark hair with his fingers.

"That was what my parents told us on our eighteenth birthday, me and Tavish. That, and the fact that with two others among the faire people, Dad was sent to our time by the druids he serves in order to make the faire authentic and a crowd pleaser and a moneymaker for the druids—"

She sat up and looked down at him.

"Wait, so your parents don't get to keep any of the money the faire makes? It all goes to the druids? Why don't they just quit? And why would you want to be a part of that, running the business end of it for the benefit of a bunch of druids? That's stupid, Tomas!"

He sat up in bed as well and took her hand, wiggling it to negate what she was thinking.

"No, it isn't like that anymore. I would never want to be a part of it if it were. No, now, our clan does get to keep most of the money. Dad and Mom and Peadar and Vange, they bargained with the druids. They think they got a good deal, but the curse is still intact, so not really. Every fourth-born son in our line still has to serve the druids if he lives to be twenty-five years old. In our immediate family, that's Tavish. He's the younger of us two. I came out first."

She laughed a little at that.

"I know. Do you realize how often you used to say

that? Every time you wanted to win an argument with him, you'd bring that up, 'I came out first.'"

Her laughter did awkward things to the front of him. He turned around and pulled her close to his own back. She fit there like a glove. She always had. And the connection he felt with her now was just as strong as it had ever been.

He felt a pang of guilt. What about Sulis?

What about her.

She's pushy and arrogant and loud and obnoxious.

Has no manners whatsoever.

Worse, she belittles all the women and manipulates all the men. It's a wonder none of the women have punched her, she's so awful. Why on God's green earth am I with that... Just what is she, anyway? And what am I doing here playing Captain of the Guard when all I've ever wanted to do is help run the Renaissance Faire that Mom & Dad built up to such a wonderful event and such a financial success?

Memories of Amber trying to tell him Sulis was a druid who had charmed him with magic came to him. He pondered them in the back of his mind while he enjoyed being here with Amber in the moment.

But he also decisively resolved some things.

When Sulis came back, he would break up with her. And he would leave this ruse of a life she had stuck him in and return to his own time and his real life. And once he was free of Sulis, he would ask Amber to join him.

But for now, we would enjoy this moment.

"Yeah, well... So anyway, that was why Tavish and I

left you and Kelsey. We didn't want you to have to see your children enslaved to the druids."

She took a deep breath and let it out slowly.

"But in the modern world, there are ways to avoid having more than three kids."

"Vange tried that, but even in the modern world there are druids, and they have life magic, Amber. Vange was only going to have three kids, and look. She had two sets of twin boys."

"I'd like to see druidic magic work on someone who's had a hysterectomy. That would foil them for sure. But even if we did have a fourth son, this time travel thing's kind of fun."

He chuckled.

"Yeah, it kind of is, but now that I see it with clarity, being here in the past feels like playing at life rather than living life, even though I know for the people here, this is real life."

She smirked mockingly at him in a playful way.

"Wow, that was deep."

He raised his hands up like claws and put a crazed look in his eyes.

"Yeah? I'll show you deep. My fingers are going to go so deep into your sides that your laugh will wake up all the guards in the whole hallway."

She lay back and raised her knees up in front of her and lowered her hands to her sides in order to prevent him from tickling her, but he was familiar with these defenses. Every time she moved, he moved the opposite way and went in for the tickle.

Her giggles melted him though, and he stopped

abruptly, sitting up above her and looking down at her long chocolate brown hair splayed on the pillow and her cheeks rosy with exertion and her soft brown eyes dancing with laughter.

"Amber, I was a fool to ever leave you."

With that, she stilled, and the look in her eyes turned from playfulness to an adoration so deep, it made him yearn to live up to it.

15

CÒIG DEUG

Tomas was snoring when Amber woke up.

She used the chamber pot, washed her face and hands, and went out in the hall and waved to the first guard she saw.

"Tomas was oot late last night with the dogs, hunting Lachlan the Dark. I ken he's supposed tae hae duty now, but can ye let him sleep? He truly does need the rest."

The guard must have been a dullard, because he just kind of stood there gaping at her, not answering.

She would just have to assume he'd pass on her message. She needed to get out of this castle and talk to Kelsey. It was late enough in the morning that she knew her friend would already be at the weaver shop.

Amber passed through the great hall on her way out in the hopes that someone would feed her. Sure enough, a serving woman handed her a plate of eggs and ham and beans, which she ate up quickly, she was so hungry from staying up late and sleeping in.

All the way to the weaver shop, she rehearsed what she was going to say to Kelsey. It was hard, because she had felt so close to Tomas last night. It had been as if they never parted and were still together.

But they weren't together. He was still with Sulis.

Kelsey took one look at Amber's face as she entered the weaver shop and handed her work to Sasha, who set it down next to her own and gave Amber a sympathetic look.

Kelsey walked over and gave Amber a hug, then turned to Eileen and Sasha.

"Amber and I have an errand to run."

The pretty blonde weaver looked from Amber to Kelsey and back again with a smirk on her face and opened her mouth to say something.

But before she could, Deirdre came running over to Amber and stopped with her hands on her hips.

"I want tae go with ye. Ye are na gaun'ae run errands. Ye are just gaun'ae go walking aroond and talking, aren't ye. Probably even buy one o' Maureen's sticky buns and eat it all by yerself. I want tae go."

Amber was feeling guilty for not wanting to take the little girl. She was so darn cute, and she had helped Amber find the tinker's booth...

But the girl's mother put an end to her demands.

"Deirdre Anne, ye go right back tae yer washing and close yer mouth this instant. Ye dinna speak tae grown ones that way." Eileen turned to Kelsey. "I am sae sorry. I dinna ken what got intae her. Go on with ye." She made shooing gestures with her hands as she sat back down at her spinning wheel.

To Amber's amazement, Deirdre went and did exactly what she was told without any complaints. Her brothers were helping her, and their little baby sister sat watching with her thumb in her mouth.

As Kelsey walked Amber toward the door, she made a face that said, 'Yikes. I'm glad we're getting out of here for a little while, aren't you?'

Amber nodded, and together they waved goodbye to the others.

Instead of walking around town as Deirdre assumed they would, Amber walked Kelsey straight past the castle and out toward the cliffs, where the noisy ocean would prevent their voices from carrying to anyone.

And then she looked Kelsey in the eye and bared her soul, as tears came and showed just how upset she was.

"Yesterday Eileen told me about a local enchantress named Elsbeth, and I went to see her. That's what I was doing out in the woods when Lachlan found me and Tomas found Lachlan. Kelsey, Elsbeth says the only thing that can break the curse of false love is true love. Last night after Tomas came back to his room, I thought we had true love. But when I woke up this morning, I realized he's still with Sulis. Nothing has changed. Soon as she comes back, he'll be that zombie again. I can't take it."

Kelsey caught her up in a hug.

"Whoa, whoa, whoa. What happened?"

Amber brushed her tears away with one of her huge voluminous linen sleeves.

"Nothing and everything. We spent most of this morning spooning."

Kelsey tried to hide a gasp.

"Did you..."

Amber shook her head violently no while she fought the choking sobs that wanted to prevent her from talking.

"We just cuddled and talked and got caught up, Kelsey. And it was like we'd never been apart. And that's even worse than if... I feel so close to him, but he's still with Sulis. Nothing happened at all — and everything happened. I mean I'm feeling so close to him, but I shouldn't be. I almost wish I had never come here to Scotland. Having him so close to me again just brings home how much it hurts that he doesn't want to be with me, not in the way I want. I'm trying, Kelsey. I really am trying to save him from that B witch. But if he doesn't come around soon, I'm going to ask Tavish to take me back to the modern world so I can move on without Tomas. It kills me to do it, but I won't have my heartstrings pulled by someone who isn't sure how to feel."

She dissolved into sobs then, grateful that her friend was there.

Kelsey gently patted her back.

"He'll come around soon. I know he will. He loves you, even if he doesn't know it right now. Don't give up yet. Stay just a little bit longer, because I think all he needs is just a little more time. We can't let that B witch win without a fight. Remind him that he loves you. Give him a fighting chance to choose you."

Amber wanted to believe Kelsey, wanted to with every fiber of her being. Her heart begged her to believe. It was everything she had ever hoped for. But her head kept telling her to guard her heart and withdraw before her heart broke beyond repair.

The two of them walked slowly back toward the weaver shop. All that awaited them there was boring work. Or so she thought. Right up until she found Tomas standing outside the weaver shop holding the bridle of a horse and grinning at her in invitation to go for a ride with him.

Filled with elation, she ran to him without even looking back at Kelsey, whom she vaguely heard laughing behind her.

Amber had ridden horseback with Tomas many times, and before she knew it, she was on the horse behind him and they were galloping away from the town with her laughing with delight.

Once more, she had her arms around him and her head pressed against his back, soaking in the closeness of him — albeit through far more clothing than there had been between them last night.

This was what life was meant to be like! Galloping through the Highlands — green grass, gray rocky hills, soaring cloudy skies — while holding on tight to the man she loved. It was so wonderful, she didn't even dare ask him where they were going.

This probably wasn't a date. He probably had someplace he needed to take her for her safety. And she was glad he was concerned. That was a good sign, right? It meant he cared. He had even admitted that. She sure as heck didn't want to ask and find out for sure this wasn't a date. Sometimes, silence really was golden.

Live in the moment. Wasn't that what they always said?

It would be difficult to talk on a galloping horse anyway. Best to just enjoy the feeling of closeness, the thudding of their bodies together as the horse bounced off the rocks and dirt and rocks again. To count the trees in the forest they rode through, or the different kinds of bird chirps that could be heard amongst the branches.

But mostly just to feel him against her and be happy.

They rode close together like this for half an hour or so.

But all things must pass, and she felt the pang of sadness when he slowed down.

Their halt wasn't all bad, though. He had stopped the horse at the top of a long gradual hill that sloped down to the ocean. It was sandy down there. He climbed down, tied the horse to a tree, and then handed her down.

"We'll leave him here where he can graze."

Tomas was still holding her hand, and it felt so right — but a beach awaited them. With one accord, they ran down to the sea. The weather here in Scotland was much too cold for swimming, but this was nice. Far away from everyone else, with only the waves and the wind looking on or listening.

Their eyes met, and they smiled together as they shared a sense of wonder at their surroundings.

But a dark question took hold of her, and she

searched his face for the answer, a bit worried about what she would find.

"Have you been here before?"

But his eyes reassured her.

"Yeah, but only with fellow guards. This isn't the type of place she likes, but I know you like the beach. And Amber, I broke up with Sulis this morning."

"Say that again?" She knocked imaginary sand out of her ear. "I think I'm hearing things."

He laughed.

"I broke up with Sulis this morning."

"Really?"

"Really."

"How did she take it? Was anyone else around? Does everyone know?"

He laughed again and smiled his handsome smile at her.

"Oh, yeah. Everyone knows. They all know I'm out with you now, too."

She smiled at him in genuine enjoyment then.

She was on a date with Tomas. He was making an effort to spend time with her outside the fortress where he had the excuse of keeping her safe. Hope swelled in her heart. And she almost grabbed him and kissed him until the sun was setting and it was too cold to stay outdoors.

But she would still wait for him to make the first move. He would want to. That was the sort of man he was: a manly one. She wouldn't have him any other way.

He took her hand in his and led her along the line where the sand met the cliff.

"See that little cranny in the rocks that looks like a clown?"

She tried her best to enjoy taking this slow and have a good time and appreciate the small things. She really did.

"It does!"

They walked along the cliff line some more, commenting on this little nook and that little cranny, this flower or that fern. And still all she could think about was grabbing him and sticking her tongue in his mouth, dueling tongues with him, then going home and telling her parents they were back together.

It was a sunny day, and they pointed out where they could see buildings sticking up on the shoreline of distant Ireland across the sea. And she imagined what it would be like to move to Australia with him and help run the faire. So exciting! The life she had always wanted but never dared to dream about...

They picked up seashells.

Combed designs in the sand with sticks for the waves to wash away.

Watched sand crabs burrow.

Built a sandcastle.

And midway through their date, she was able to stop dreaming of their future and just live in the moment. She had a wonderful time. All the while they also played a game of tag, where one would run and the other would chase. It was how they were accustomed to being together, having last dated when they were teens.

A few hours later when they had completed their circle around their private oasis, Tomas hugged her close with the sea breeze whistling through their hair and the seagulls calling out as they soared in circles through the air overhead and Ireland gradually disappearing into the mist across the sea.

And then his lips were on hers.

It was a spontaneous kiss, born out of delight at the scenery and how fun it was to be exploring this together, playing together.

Wanting more, Amber grabbed ahold of him with a reckless abandon born from wanting him so much this past week and not being able to act on it. She poured her heart into kissing him back, opening her mouth to deepen the kiss and holding him close to show him just how much she'd missed him, just how much she loved him.

But he didn't respond in kind.

No, his arms dropped to his sides and the look on his face was...

Well, it was a look of bafflement, really.

Amber's blood boiled.

The stupid spell was still getting in the way!

She kicked sand onto Tomas's legs to try and snap him out of his stupor.

"Tell me right now, do you want to be with me, or Sulis?"

He didn't even answer her, just stood there with his forehead wrinkled, not saying anything.

That was it. She was so pissed off, she was back up the hill in no time and on top of the horse and galloping away without him.

16

SIA DEUG

Well, this was awkward. She was riding up to the stable on the horse before she remembered that guard she'd told that Tomas needed his sleep. And this was the smallest of small towns she had ever been to. Everyone and their mother likely knew now that she had slept in Tomas's room with him — before he broke up with Sulis.

So now on top of everything else, her face was beet red when she approached the stable hand, an older man who vaguely resembled her uncle. Great.

Quick as she could, she dismounted and handed the man the reins, then turned to leave.

But of course she didn't get away that easily.

"Hey now, lass. This is the horse Tomas took oot. Where is he?"

TOMAS WAS BOTH RELIEVED AND EMBARRASSED WHEN one of his guards showed up on the trail back to Laird Malcomb's castle from Maidenhead Bay — leading an extra horse. Mostly, he was glad to get back in the saddle after walking for an hour. No, mostly he was angry at Amber for leaving him in that embarrassing situation.

Maybe he was a little angry at himself. One moment he'd been kissing Amber — and loving it. The next moment, he'd been standing there like a simpleton, unable to decide what to do or say, just simply stupefied.

What the blazes had come over him? Why had he let himself hurt yet again the woman who had left her whole life behind to fly to him?

As the horses' hooves clopped over the mossy roots of the forest, this question kept running through his mind. He found that he suspected Sulis had something to do with it — but he couldn't say why. It was just there, the thought that she would do something if she found out he was kissing Amber. He certainly didn't have any love in his heart for Sulis.

Quite the opposite, really.

He had ridden up to the stable and dismounted and was handing the stable hand his reins when the older man spoke to him.

"The lass what stole yer horse is being held in yer chamber."

Hearing this, Tomas's body went rigid, ready to run to her and fight for her freedom. And then terrible visions came to his mind.

"They didna hurt her, did they?"

To Tomas's relief, the stable hand shook his head no, although he did have a teasing look in his eyes, as if he were bursting to ask Tomas how Amber had gotten his horse from him. Thankfully, the man had more sense than to ask.

"They await yer orders."

Tomas breathed a sigh of relief. He had to try and remember how brutal this place could be. He didn't like it at all. He should have gone after Amber and not let her return here alone. What was wrong with him?

"I thank ye."

The gray stone hallways and stairways of the castle whizzed by along with several people he merely nodded at on his quest to get to Amber before they did hurt her. What was the punishment for horse thievery in these times? He ran harder. It might be death.

Heaving for breath, he pushed into his chamber, ready to throw out anyone who had lifted a finger against her.

But he found Amber sitting in the one chair in the room, laughing and talking with the two guards who stood on either side of the door.

"Och, I dae wish ye could hae seen him. Head tae toe in mud he was, and chasing the rest o' us aboot like a moor monster! Och, there ye are, Tomas. Ye got here faster than I thought ye would. I was just telling these guards about the fun times we used tae hae together in oor village."

At first, the guards smiled at him in appreciation of her story, but then they seemed to remember themselves, and they stood up to attention, looking like they were afraid of reprimand.

Why were they afraid of him?

Doing his best to put them at ease, Tomas smiled back and rolled his eyes to show them that yes, Amber's tale was true, and he didn't like to think about it.

"Ye are dismissed. Leave us."

At this, the guards definitely smirked at him as if to say they knew exactly why he wanted to be alone with this pretty lass.

He put the air of command on his face and raised his chin at them.

They got the message and beat it out of there quickly, closing the door behind them.

Tomas turned to Amber.

"I can't believe you left me there to walk home."

Amber shrugged, not looking at all sheepish. No, she looked more like the wolf. She even gave him a few notes of sharp derisive laughter. She got up while she spoke, and paced the room, alternately making wild gestures and giving him heated stares.

"Are you kidding? You deserved it. You kissed me, Tomas. All I did was respond to you — and then you looked at me like I was nuts. That's no way to treat a stranger, let alone an old friend who cares about you, unlike... the people you choose to spend your time with. I really don't get it, Tomas. You're so hot and cold. I want to believe you care about me, and sometimes I do believe it. And then you go and do something like pull away when I'm kissing you. Your embarrassment at having to be picked up by the guards is nothing compared to how that felt for me."

Her ferocity amazed and attracted him like nothing else ever had, and her determination to get what she wanted, because that was him. A warm spot heated up in his heart at that thought.

But she was trying to push past him and get to the door.

"I can't stand to be here in this room with you one more second, Tomas. You need to make up your mind who you're going to be with and quit playing with me like I'm some toy you keep to the side until your woman comes back to you."

What?

He put his arms around her.

"Amber, I already told you. I broke up with Sulis. She is out of my life once and for all. Don't go."

She squeezed him tight then.

"Oh Tomas, really?"

He deepened their embrace.

"Really."

And then he gave her the loving kiss he should've returned earlier.

❧

Amber awoke with a start. What the heck was she doing here? This room still smelled like Sulis. Sure, he had broken up with her, but he hadn't said that she and he were together. He had simply kissed her and expected her to stay with him, with no assurance it meant anything beyond warming his bed for the night. There wasn't even the excuse that she was here for her safety, now that Lachlan had sailed away.

How could she have been so stupid?

Glancing over to make sure he was deep asleep — which he was — she pulled herself together and hightailed it to Eileen's house, not looking at any of the guards or the few townsfolk who were out and about at the crack of dawn. She didn't want to see the pity on their faces. Pity for the woman who was the plaything and not the wife or even the girlfriend.

She would wake Kelsey up and make her go get Tavish so he could take her back to her own time. If Tomas really did want to be with her, then he would come back to her. And right now, all she could think was fat chance of that happening.

He had admitted that life here in the past seemed like playing pretend. Well, she wasn't going to pretend with him. She was either his partner in real life, or just a memory. And he had better come back soon and say so. Seven years was all the time she had to waste, and that time had already been wasted.

Not about to knock and wake everyone up, she opened Eileen's door as quietly as she could — and saw that the place had been ransacked, torn to bits. Heart thudding in her chest with worry, she searched all the rooms, but not a soul was to be found, dead or alive. She needed to go tell the guards! But a hand came from behind her to cover her mouth, and a sudden spell washed over her, knocking Amber out cold.

17

SEACHD DEUG

Amber was dreaming. Kelsey's face kept appearing in the shadows of the woods. Her friend was talking, but no sound came out. Amber cupped her hand around her ear and shook her head, trying to tell Kelsey she couldn't hear her. But her friend just kept talking. She had an urgent look on her face, as if what she was saying was critically important. Amber strained to hear, but she couldn't.

Gradually, the dream faded away until Amber was aware of a cold hard stone surface pressing up against her back and head. Her arms were stretched back around the slender cold stone and tightly secured at her wrists. She could move them up and down a little, and when she did, she felt the leather cord that tied them together scraping against the stone she leaned against.

Admitting she was awake meant she could listen to the voices a few dozen feet away in front of her. At first, she just heard a man's voice asking questions, in modern-day English. But then a woman started answering, and she had a Southern accent. Sulis.

"I'm truly glad you want to help me with the ritual, but remember, it is far more important for you to keep an eye out in case someone comes."

"What should I do if someone does happen along?"

"Don't you say a thing. Just kill them before they know what hit them."

"Yes, Mistress."

Amber gasped and cautiously cracked her eyes open the tiniest bit.

She was in a church graveyard, tied to a gravestone. It was early evening, just about dark but not too cold yet. She saw a little church, a bunch of gravestones, and a forest all around them with trees so thick she felt walled-in. Owls hooted in the trees, lending that spooky atmosphere she had felt near Elsbeth's without the good enchantress nearby to allay her fears.

Spread all over her clothes were flowers, and at her feet, brambles were heaped up. Something prickly rested on top of her head. She tried to shake it off, but it was snug.

And not thirty feet away, Sulis and Lachlan tended a big fire in their white robes.

Amber wanted to scream and have someone come help her, but the druids were the only two people near enough to hear her. And she sure enough didn't want their attention. Instead, she kept working the leather cord up and down on the other side of the gravestone.

Lachlan sounded whiney as he went on.

"You know I would do anything for you, Sulis, unlike some people."

Sulis stopped tending the fire and turned her deceptively pretty face to the other druid. She took his hand in hers and softened her tone when she next spoke.

"Oh sugar, you know I was just dating Tomas in order to put him under the spell."

She tooted a derisive laugh.

"It was so cute of him to break up with me, like that would make any difference. He'll still be a wonderful slave once the ritual is complete and the spell takes hold completely. I have him set up as Captain of the guard, you know. I'll be able to loot all the relics in this time, before that busybody Kelsey and her modern-day client can ever get ahold of them."

The big sleeve of Sulis's white linen robe billowed as she gestured over toward Amber.

"Only recently did I realize someone was preventing all that."

Lachlan laughed that evil laugh he had. It gave Amber the shivers before he even spoke.

"Glad I was able to help in capturing that someone for you."

Sulis raised her chin and stuck a pose.

"I really don't get what he sees in her. I'm much prettier."

Apparently emboldened by her obvious fish for compliments, Lachlan dropped his voice lower to something that was supposed to sound sexy, but it just made Amber roll her eyes.

"Of course you are. You are perfection."

Sulis laughed at that in her sickeningly sweet false modest way that made Amber throw up a little in her mouth. And then the two of them kissed.

Amber scraped the cord against the back of the headstone as hard as she could.

But Sulis made quick work of kissing Lachlan back into submission mode.

"All right, let's get on with the ritual. Once this is done, nothing will stand in the way of Tomas's complete obedience to me. Hand me that rag to catch the blood, will you?"

Blood?

At that, Amber's eyes popped open wide.

Sulis was coming toward her with evil in her eyes, holding a dagger.

Wait... was that...? It was!

Sulis was brandishing the very same dagger that had been tucked in Tavish's belt after he had left with a different dagger that day in modern times in the underground palace. How had Sulis gotten the dagger?

Oh.

Kelsey had mentioned something about giving it to... The druids.

Amber started trembling.

Because behind Sulis, Tomas was rushing out of a hiding place to stop the druidess. He was close enough that he was going to catch her. He was also close enough that he had heard everything — and seen Sulis and Lachlan kissing.

Tomas's arms came out. Two more seconds and he would grab hold of Sulis's waist and tackle her.

But Lachlan was running toward Tomas, and he tackled Tomas before Tomas reached Sulis.

18

OCHD DEUG

Amber feared for Tomas's life as he wrestled with Lachlan on the graveyard grass. Because the druids didn't fight fair. Someone had used magic to knock Amber out at Eileen's house, and it must've been Lachlan, kidnapping her for his slave-mistress.

But Amber had to tear her eyes away from Tomas and Lachlan's fight.

Because Sulis was still running toward her with that nasty dagger sticking out in front of her. The druidess's white robes billowed out behind her like flags waving in the wind, and there was a crown of leaves and brambles and flowers on her head. Her hair was down, wild and frizzy. She held the dagger in her right hand and a rag to collect Amber's blood in her left.

Amber furiously dragged the leather cord up against the back of the gravestone as hard as she could — and it snapped. Just in time, too. Sulis was lunging at her with the dagger. Purely by instinct, Amber brought her arms forward just in time to tear the dagger out of the witch's hands. The impact threw Sulis off balance, and she went tumbling through the grass and fall leaves.

But Amber's attention was riveted on the dagger.

For as soon as she touched it, the dagger began speaking in her mind.

"Wull met, sweet lass. I am Galdus, king o' auld, now residing inside this dagger. Sae long as ye possess me, ye will hae my undying loyalty. I am sae glad ye rescued me from that evil druidess. I dinna want tae serve the likes o' her. Howsoever, I will gladly serve ye. And tae that end, I dae tell ye now: in but a moment she will get up and come throttle ye with her hands — unless ye stab her in the heart with me. Dae it! Dae it now!"

Glancing over at Sulis, Amber saw the truth in what the dagger had told her. The druidess was getting up. She seemed none the worse for her fall, and she had threatened to drain Amber's blood in order to safeguard her false-love spell on Tomas.

Galdus spoke up again.

"'Tis tae late tae go after her. Lie here in wait with me prepared, and as soon as ye see the whites o' her eyes, raise me up and she will land right on me and impale herself. Ye dinna hae tae fash about having her blood on yer hands, for twill be her own intent that does her in. Aye, 'tis a good way tae go aboot it. Good on ye for waiting till the evil lass came toward ye. Bide a bit. Bide a bit. She's a coming. Now!"

Amber raised Galdus up just as Sulis dove on her.

The weight of the woman pushed the dagger down toward the ground, and Amber's arm was against the grass when she felt the dagger go in. And then the weight was gone.

Amber opened her eyes to find that Sulis had dissolved into a pile of ashes: white robe, garland of flowers, and all. Relief washed over Amber, allowing all of her limbs to relax and her heart to calm. A deep breath filled her lungs.

But her relief was short-lived.

Looking for Tomas, she saw that Lachlan had indeed knocked her love out with one of his evil spells. And the druid was holding up another dagger over Tomas's heart, chanting an evil incantation.

Galdus didn't waste any time.

"Get up, lass! Get up and go stab me intae his back from behind. He is na worth the wee bit o' fashing I sense in ye at the thought o' backstabbing anyone. He is na deserving o' yer fashing, lass. Just dae it. Dae it now!"

Amber wasn't a fighter by any stretch of the imagination. Oh sure, she dished out snark whenever she could find a receptacle for it. But those were words. The thought of a physical fight? Yeah, that usually had her crawling away to hide like the coward she knew she was.

But that was Tomas over there in peril.

Adrenaline pumped through her veins, giving her just the burst of energy she needed to jump up, run over, and stab the white-robed druid in the back before he plunged his dagger into Tomas's heart.

As soon as Amber stabbed Lachlan, he too dissolved into a pile of ashes: white robes, garland of brambles, and all. Only this time it happened right before Amber's eyes. It wasn't a gradual thing. No. One second she was plunging Galdus into a man's back, and the next second the man's ashes were falling to the ground in a heap.

Amber didn't care about that.

Eyes blurry with sudden tears and throat choked up with sobbing, she cast Galdus aside and threw herself to the ground next to Tomas, despairing that he would never wake up from Lachlan's evil spell, now that the druid was gone.

In the firelight, Amber saw Tomas lying stock still on his back in his billowy sleeved linen shirt and his scratchy wool kilt on top of the green, green grass with his gorgeous face upward toward the gray Scottish sky. He looked so peaceful lying there among the gravestones — too peaceful.

Amber leaned over her love's face, trying to feel any breath coming out of him.

She felt none.

Grabbing him by the shoulders, she shook him.

When that produced nothing, she dropped down and hugged him to her.

"Tomas? Tomas, wake up. The evil B witch is gone, and so is her minion. I'm here free and whole, and I love you, Tomas. I love you with all my heart. I always have."

He didn't stir.

She felt no heartbeat in his chest.

She waited there holding her breath, with her tears falling on his face.

Nothing happened.

Amber couldn't blame the next impulse on Galdus, for she had cast him aside, and now that she wasn't touching the dagger, her mind was free of its urgings.

Tenderly, lovingly, she kissed those lips that were cold with the promise of death, pouring into the kiss all the love she had.

❧

CERTAIN SHE WAS DELUSIONAL, AMBER FELT TOMAS respond to her kiss. Her desperate imagination had him holding her tight with his arms and turning his head so that their mouths locked together and dueling her tongue with his. She didn't care if it was just her imagination. She was going to enjoy this last moment of warmth and joy and pleasure with the man she loved.

So she did. She held him close and soaked in the nearness of him one last time.

And then she knew she needed to let go of this dream and embrace reality. It wasn't healthy for her to stay in this fantasy for too long. With despair in her heart, she withdrew from Tomas.

But the fantasy clung.

She heard his voice, soft and caring and loving — the way she had been longing to hear it for seven years.

"Can't you bear to look at me? I guess I can't blame you after my idiocy with Sulis. But I want you to know that I love you, Amber. I've always loved you. Please tell me you came to rescue me because you love me too. Tell me we're going to spend the rest of our lives together. I'm so sorry I was deluded by Sulis. I was there the whole time inside my head, and once you showed up, I wanted to break free. But I couldn't fight my way out of it. You did that for me, Amber. You broke through the prison I was in, deep inside my own mind. I loved you even before, but the love I have for you now knows no bounds. I should have known it would be you who would save me from that prison. Will you ever forgive me? I know it must have hurt, you seeing me with her. I wouldn't blame you if you didn't forgive me, but I'm begging. Please forgive me, Amber."

She must have been holding on to the fantasy in order for his voice to come to her so clearly and so realistically. But with a heavy sigh she opened her eyes.

And gasped.

He was right there, sitting on the grass. Her face must have shown her confusion and doubt.

Because he laughed.

"That is so not the look I expected to see on your face when I declared my undying love."

She felt herself laughing, but inside she was still not willing to believe this was real.

"Any moment, I'll wake up and this will have been the most wonderful dream ever — well, except for the part where we both almost got killed by crazed druids."

It was at that point she realized this was real, because his face turned to a look of anguish.

"Amber I'm so sorry — just so, so sorry about everything... Leaving you when I found out about the

MacGregor curse, and letting Sulis take control of me, and being so rude to you when you got here to Laird Malcomb's castle, and—"

She grabbed him and shut him up with a kiss. She made it the best one she had ever given him. They made out for all they were worth.

❧

WHEN AMBER WOKE UP ON A BED OF GRASS IN Tomas's arms, he kissed her tenderly and then smiled in reluctance and gestured at the sun coming up over the church.

"We should be getting back."

She scrunched up her nose at him.

"Yeah, we probably should."

"Are you ready?"

"I guess so."

He got up and pulled her up, then brushed the grass off her long skirts and turned around so she could brush the grass off his kilt.

"We'll have plenty more opportunities to do this."

"You had better stick to that promise," she said in a teasing way, because experience with men told her they didn't like being scolded by their women.

But he gave her a sincere look.

"I will."

He threw his arm around her and started to walk her away from the almost-gruesome scene.

But on impulse, she went and snatched up the bag

of Sulis and Lachlan's things — and found a rag inside to grab up Galdus with, then threw him in the bag as well.

Tomas reached to take the bag from her, but she smiled her best 'I can manage' smile, so he threw his arm over her shoulders and started them down the road with the birds chirping to greet the new day.

19

NAOI DEUG

It took two hours to walk back to Laird Malcolm's castle. Amber was relieved to find that Tomas knew the way, so they had two hours in which to plan their future together. They would stay on at the dig with Tavish and Kelsey for a month so that Amber could get Kelsey on her feet with the cataloging and such, and then Amber and Tomas would be off to Australia to learn how to run the business side of the Renaissance Faire. It was going to be an even better future than Amber had ever dreamed it could be.

When they got close to the castle along the cliff path from Port Patrick, they heard music playing and people talking and laughing. Amber looked over at Tomas with a question in her eyes. He looked back at her and shrugged.

To Amber's shock, the first person to greet them was Tomas and Tavish's mom, Emily. Wearing her Renaissance Faire costume — which Amber now realized must have been made in 1540 — she ran out from the castle town to grab them both together in a big hug.

"I knew ye were all right. And afore ye ask, aye, everyone here is all right as wull. Kelsey and her friends had already left for the weaver shop afore Eileen's house was ransacked—"

But even though Amber had come to Scotland to meet up with the woman's son, she couldn't wrap her mind around seeing her old guild-mistress from the faire again after seven years of being shunned by her. She stood off, pleased that Tomas stood off with her.

"Emily? What are ye doing here?"

Emily smiled at her in a knowing way, looking at Tomas's arm around her waist with a motherly gleam in her eye. It was an accepting look. In fact it was a little teasing.

"Why, I'm here for the big occasion. Tavish and Kelsey decided tae join in on Seumas & Sasha and Albert & Eileen's double wedding and make it a triple. And 'tis na just me who's here. Look."

Amber looked over toward the music to see that tables had been set up outside between the castle and the cliff. A small outdoor chapel had also been set up nearby, and a monk was standing ready with a glass of wine in his hand, smiling and tapping his feet to the music.

Half of her and Tomas's gang of friends from the fair sat around a table together, joking and laughing: Tavish and Kelsey, of course, and also Tavish and Tomas's aunt and uncle Vange and Peadar with their sons, who were Tomas and Tavish's cousins: Mike, Gabe, Jeff, and John

—the John who hadn't deserted his girlfriend like all the others had, but who had broken up with Jaelle six months ago, back in their own time.

Emily caught Amber's eye and gave her and Tomas a mischievous grin. "Maybe the two of you would like to join in and get married too?"

That did it.

Amber was on the defensive again.

But she was guarding her heart.

Marrying Tomas was what she wanted more than anything in the world. Not daring to say anything and chase him away again, she just looked at him and tried her best to show in her eyes what she was feeling inside.

He raised his eyebrows at her.

"I'm game if ye are."

How dare he be teasing in a time like this? She went to pull away from him.

But he must have caught on to what she was thinking, and she melted into him when he took her in his arms and hugged her tight.

"I'm serious. Seven years was a long enough time tae wait tae be with ye. I want tae stop waiting. I want the rest o' oor lives tae start now — and what better time tae get marrit then when my whole family is already here?"

Wait, that wasn't fair. She playfully shoved him.

"Easy for ye tae say. Yer family is all here. But what aboot my family?"

He gave her a big smile and rocked back and forth with her in his arms, from foot to foot.

She sighed and relaxed into him. He knew her so

well that he had seen right through her snark and realized she was saying yes.

Soft and rational though they were, his next words made her heart soar.

"We need tae make this legal, sae we'll dae it all again back at home where both o' oor families can attend."

They stood there grinning at each other — him in a know-it-all way and her in a you-really-are-serious way — until she grabbed him and hugged him tight.

"I'm guessing I canna get oot o' it that easily, eh?"

He held her close, getting several scandalized looks from the people passing by them on the path from Port Patrick.

In sotto voice, he said, "What's their problem?"

In kind, she said, "Ye know full wull the laws against public displays o' affection. Tae them, we're criminals."

For some reason, this struck them as hilariously funny, and they broke out in laughter just as Tomas's dad, Dall, came over and put his arm around Emily.

Dall gathered the two of them into his hug as well, smiling with the same gleam in his eye as Emily had shown them. It said he had known all along they would get back together — and it welcomed Amber into their family. Amber's in-laws were going to be people she knew well. That should make everything a lot smoother.

Dall had caught most of what was going on with just a glance at Tomas's arm around Amber's waist, but he was at a loss as to what they were laughing about.

"What's sae funny?"

Emily winked at Amber.

"Tomas and Amber are gaun'ae make it a quadruple wedding."

Meanwhile, over at the tables, Tomas's family were calling his and Amber's names and making noises in a blatant attempt to get them to come join in on the revelry.

Dall smiled and gestured toward the party.

"Shall we?"

Amber beamed her biggest smile at him and grabbed Tomas's hand.

"Aye!"

They hadn't gone far when Kelsey ran out to join them, flapping her hands like the nervous wreck she obviously was, having known this was going to be her wedding day twelve hours longer than Amber had. She crashed into Amber and hugged her, then hugged Tomas too.

"Ye live! Thank all that's holy! What happened?"

Clutching the bag of druid stuff to her side, Amber squinted at Kelsey as she dug through the bag with one hand, looking for Galdus.

"To make a long story short, Lachlan kidnapped me, Tomas followed him, and I turned Sulis and Lachlan into ash with this dagger —"

Kelsey gasped and lunged into Amber, closing the bag tight around her hand and stopping her search. When she spoke, it was to Dall and Emily as she grabbed Amber's hand and started dragging her toward the castle.

"We hae some aught urgent tae dae. Dinna begin the wedding withoot us."

Amber walked along quietly until they were out of earshot from everyone.

"What is it, Kelsey?"

"You can't keep that dagger. Someone else has an earlier claim to it, and I believe she'll know how to keep it safe — and secret."

At this, Amber felt rebellious. She hadn't given a thought to keeping the dagger until now, when someone was telling her she had to give it up. Suddenly, she wanted to insist on keeping it. It was special. It spoke in her mind!

Kelsey squeezed her hand and spoke softly.

"I know it's a special dagger, and you're probably getting really fond of it, but it's dangerous and distracting, and it will be much safer back here in the past, where no one knows where it is. There are those who will guess that you might have it and come after you. And if they find you with the dagger... Look, just trust me, okay? You're better off not keeping it." She took the bag off Amber's shoulder and put it on her own shoulder. "You can go back to the party. I'll be out in just a minute."

Amber was caught between the urge to be outraged that Kelsey had grabbed the bag off her shoulder and her common sense telling her that Kelsey was right and she should run far away from any druids wanting to come after her looking for the dagger.

"Uh, no. I'll stay with you, thank you very much."

As she followed Kelsey and the druid bag up the

spiral stairs she had climbed with Tomas only a few days ago, Amber wondered who this person was that Kelsey was so sure would be careful to guard the secret of the dagger. Was it Laird Malcolm? He was a very responsible person of course, being the laird of a castle. Or maybe it would be the laird's wife. She wouldn't be nearly as busy as Laird Malcolm, not having to run a castle. What did the lady of a castle do, anyway? Amber had seen very little of Lady Malcolm.

She and Kelsey had finished climbing the stairs and were going down the stone hallway covered in tapestries toward the... nursery?

An older lady came out to greet them. Oh, maybe she was the one. Amber studied her.

The older lady smiled.

"Kelsey! Tae what dae I owe this pleasure on yer happiest o' days?"

Kelsey smiled back.

"Hello, Isabel. This is my clanswoman Amber, who will also be getting marrit today. How about that? Might we borrow Deirdre? 'Tis the custom where we coome from tae hae a young lass carry flowers in the wedding ceremony, and she would be perfect."

Isabel turned around toward where Eileen's children were playing what looked like a game of King of the Hill.

"Deirdre! Come on ower, sweeting." She turned back to Kelsey and Amber. "What a lovely tradition. I would coome doon and watch, but these monkeys are much better off up here, and sae ye are as wull, ye ken?"

The children heard that and started making monkey noises and movements.

Kelsey laughed, and Amber joined in.

"Where on Earth did they ever see a monkey?"

Isabel looked at Amber as if she were daft.

"In the traveling menageries, o' course. There hae been two coome round here since they were old enough tae remember — ah, perhaps yer clan lands are away from the sea, then, eh? I forget how much more o' life we see here in a port town."

Soon, they had taken Deirdre back down the spiral staircase and through the bottom of the castle and out the door, where they had a brief time alone before they got to the wedding party.

Kelsey stopped and turned Deirdre round and fished Galdus out of the bag still inside the rag and covertly gave him to the little girl.

"Deirdre, Galdus is yers tae keep."

The excitement in the six-year-old's face was palpable, and Kelsey had to put her hand over Dierdre's mouth to keep her from screaming out in joy and excitement.

"He's yers tae keep, but ye must keep him in secret. Ye must na show him tae anybody, nor even let anybody see him. Ye ken?"

Deirdre nodded, and Kelsey helped her hide Galdus under her clothes before the three of them walked back to the wedding party tables and joined their friends.

But that little Deirdre was so clever. As soon as they sat down, she had something to say.

"How am I gaun'ae be a flower lass if I dinna hae any flowers tae bring?"

Kelsey gave Amber an amazed look and then turned to Sasha.

"Will ye help Deirdre pick some flowers tae carry during the wedding ceremony?"

Deirdre got up and ran over to Sasha, who held out her arms and then hugged the little girl, and the two of them ran off together where some flowers were growing near the cliffs.

The actual wedding ceremony was over in a whirl of activity before Amber could quite get a hold of what was going on, and when they were feasting afterwards, it was all fun and laughs because the pressure was off and they could just enjoy themselves and their friends' company.

Once all the food was eaten and quite a bit of wine had been drunk, and the men were relaxing with their pipes while the women turned toward each other and traded memories, Tomas squeezed Amber's arm as a sort of goodbye for a moment and got up and went over to Tavish's side of Kelsey.

Interesting. What was Tomas going to say to his brother?

To top it off, Tomas's face was all scrunched up with worry, and he didn't ask for his twin brother's attention, but rather just stood there quietly until Tavish noticed him and turned to him.

Tomas gestured, and with one accord, Tomas, Amber, Tavish, and Kelsey walked to the cliff, where the sound of the sea hitting the rocks would keep their voices from carrying back to the tables.

When Tomas finally spoke, a hush had come upon their group.

"Tavish, I've been under a terrible sense of envy for you ever since I found out about the curse and that you would be the one who got to time travel. I wanted to be the one. All I thought about was the fun of it and the adventure of it and what might be gained from it. I never once considered how awful it must be to have to answer to the druids as their slave. These past few months I've gotten a small taste of what you must be living with, and brother I've got to say I'm so, so sorry. You have it worse than I ever imagined or gave you credit for, and I'm here now to ask your forgiveness. If I hadn't felt so envious of you, I never would have fallen under Sulis's spell. She was able to get me because of my envy. It was my strongest motivation, and she used it to trap me. Again, Tavish, will you forgive me?"

Tavish embraced his brother, and the two of them hugged and slapped each other's backs, but Amber could see that Tomas was crying silently as Tavish spoke his pardon.

"Of course I forgive you. You're my brother, and I'll always be there for you. I'm so, so glad to have you back!"

Amber and Kelsey laughed and clapped and cheered at that. And then the musicians got up and played, and they all joined in on the set dances, even Deirdre, who laughed when the men picked her up to twirl her around instead of linking elbows with her.

Once the dancing was well underway, Tomas took Amber by the hand and led her back to the edge of the cliff, where they stood hand-in-hand watching the sea. It was cloudy as usual, but they could just make out Ireland in the distance over the water, and Amber wondered how soon Mr. Blair would get that motorboat so they could go explore. What a great honeymoon that would make.

Tomas startled her out of her reverie.

"What's on your mind, Mrs. MacGregor?"

For a moment, Amber looked around to see who he was talking to. And then she saw the teasing look on his face and laughed.

"I'm eager to get on with being married, Mr. McGregor."

He kissed her then, a warm loving kiss full of promise, and then turned them back toward the wedding party area.

"It looks like you're not the only one."

Sure enough, Kelsey & Tavish and Sasha & Seumas were all headed toward the stairs that went down into the underground palace.

Tomas put his arm around Amber's waist and turned them toward the stairs too.

"I think we'd better catch up with them, because I'm not sure they'll wait for us."

Laughing, Amber hustled off arm-in-arm with her husband, toward their future.

20

FICHEAD

Amber sat awkwardly on the bed in the room she now shared with Tomas in the trailer, resting her bare foot on a folded pillow so she could paint her toenails dark blue. On her cell speaker she was also talking with Jaelle, their faire friend who had still been with John until six months ago.

"Yeah, the Scottish skies were sunny for once, and we had a beautiful old time wedding on the cliff overlooking the Irish Sea—and then we all high-tailed it back here to the present."

"But no one in the present knew you were married, and no time had passed in order for you to get married in. How did you deal with that?"

Forgetting she was talking on the phone and not in person —or perhaps just accustomed to being flamboyant when she spoke—Amber gestured wildly, and a blob of blue nail polish fell off the brush. Good thing she had put a paper towel down on the pillow. Wait, what was she thinking?

Amber laughed.

Jaelle sounded amused.

"Must be a good story."

Amber grabbed up the paper towel, wadded it, and made a basket into the trashcan. She just barely remembered she still had the brush in her hand before she raised her arms up high and declared a score— and got nail polish who knew where.

"No, no. I was laughing because I splattered some nail polish."

"Huh?"

"It could've gotten on the pillowcase if it weren't for this paper towel, but with the amount Mr. Blair is paying me for helping Kelsey out with her cataloging system for the dig, I could buy a thousand pillowcases, so what am I worried about?"

They laughed together for a moment, and then Jaelle cleared her throat.

Amber snorted to let her old friend know she'd received the subtle hint to get on with her story.

"Okay, I know you don't want to hear about that. We made our marriage legal two days after we got back to the present. We just flew back home and saw a justice of the peace."

"Aw, that's too bad—"

"No, I wanted it that way. Over and done with as quickly as possible so we could get on with married life, already—"

Jaelle burst into a loud peal of laughter.

Amber growled at her playfully.

"Oh, would you get your mind out of the gutter for once. My family were all there to witness my happiness, and getting married to Tomas was all that really mattered to me. It wasn't about the dress, or the ring, or having to dance to a certain song at a reception, cutting the cake, throwing the bouquet, riding in a limousine, or picking out bridesmaids' dresses. It was about declaring in front of witnesses our intention to spend the rest of our lives together as husband and wife."

To Amber's puzzlement, Jaelle's voice sounded clipped when she spoke next.

"Did you at least get a honeymoon?"

Huh. Where was that coming from?

"Tavish & Kelsey and Seumas & Sasha had plane tickets to Hawaii already, so they were all gone for two weeks. Me and Tomas were bummed we couldn't go along — until Mr. Blair showed up with the motorboat he'd been promising everyone."

Jaelle blew her nose. Maybe she was getting sick. That would explain her tone. A runny nose would make anyone impatient. Yeah, that must be it. She sounded stuffed up when she spoke.

"Wow, cool."

Amber brought the pillow forward a little bit so it was easier to reach her toes, and then she put down a fresh paper towel and repositioned her foot on it. This time when she dipped the brush back in, she was much more careful to wipe off the glob at the end of it against the bottleneck.

"You can say that again. It has a cabin and everything, and when he heard we just got married, he let us take it over to Ireland for a week, all by ourselves. We docked at a different port every night and went sight-seeing every day, not to mention all the pub crawling we did. Couldn't have planned a better honeymoon if I tried. —And like I said before, on Tuesday we're headed 'down unda' to Australia to learn the business-end of the faire. When I hear myself say that, I just can't believe it. I get Tomas in the fair in Australia and Dall and Emily back as my friends... All my dreams are coming true!"

Jaelle had been quiet longer than usual.

Guilt grabbed Amber's heart and yanked on it till it hurt.

"Listen to me, going on about how happy Tomas and I are. How are you doing? I can't believe you and John defied his parents, let alone broke up after seven years of defiance together. Really, how are you doing?"

Jaelle sniffled.

"Thanks for shutting up about you and Tomas. Now shut up about me and John." She laughed a little.

Amber laughed a little, too.

"Sorry. That was really stupid of me. All of it. What kind of friend am I?"

"No, I get it. And I'm really happy for you. You and Tomas are both great people, and I know how in love you are. And I'm one of the few who know why you were apart these past seven years. I know you never really broke up, how Dall and Emily dropped a bomb on him and Tavish on their eighteenth birthday and he disappeared from your life to protect you. Dall and Emily thought they were doing the right thing, you know, not telling him until then. You do know that, right? Because I don't hate them, and you shouldn't either."

"I don't hate them. I know it's not their fault. He told me the story about their ancestor with a gambling problem — uh oh, I hope I'm not saying something you don't already know." She laughed her exaggerated nervous laugh.

"Yeah, that story. I bet it was a lot easier for you to believe than it was for me, after what you just went through. I'm having trouble believing your story, and I've known the gambling story for seven years now." Jaelle laughed again, and this time there was actually joy in it.

"Heh," said Amber, "I wouldn't believe my story if I hadn't lived it, so I know what you mean. But here we are talking about me again. I really want to know if you're okay, and if there's anything I can do to help you. I'm not even above going over and giving John a piece of my mind, if that will help."

Jaelle cleared her throat.

"About that."

"What?"

"Well, has Tomas told you how he's related to John?"

"Huh? We've always known."

"Okay, we always thought we knew, but Amber, John's dad isn't just some random part of Dall's fifteenth century MacGregor clan. He's Tomas and Tavish's brother."

"Nuh uh! He can't be. He's Dall's same age."

"Right, but now you know this is a time-traveling family."

"So?"

"So Dall was born in the early 1500s. He got married when he was young and had three children: Peadar, Peigi, and Dombnall. His wife died when they were twenty three. Then Dall turned twenty five and started his servitude with the druids. They picked Emily out for him among some others and brought her and the others back to his time for him to bond with her. When she got back to her own time, she didn't remember that. They had cursed her so that she wouldn't remember time travel unless she joined with him—"

Amber cut in.

"Get to the point already. What does that have to do with John's dad Peadar?"

"I'm getting to that. Just listen."

"Okay, but get to it faster."

"Very funny. So anyway, Dall and Emily got together, right, and then they started experimenting with time travel. They had a lot more freedom to time travel than John and Tavish do, because they had an app on their cell phone that enabled them to go to any time and any place where a loved one was—"

Amber gasped.

"You're kidding."

Jaelle laughed.

"You and Tomas sure haven't been doing very much talking."

Amber laughed too.

"Shut up. Yeah, we're a married couple who should

know all these things about each other, but we only just now got back together. There hasn't been time to talk about everything."

"Uh huh. So anyway, Dall and Emily could go to any time or place where one of their loved ones was. The druids had Tavish living mostly in our time, but Emily told Dall about how the MacGregor name would soon be outlawed back in his time. So they sought out his son Peadar when he was twenty-five, to make sure he was okay. Vange went with them, and as soon as she met Peadar — well, you know how in love those two are."

There was a scraping noise on Jaelle's end of the line.

"What was that?"

"Oh sorry. I told you John let me keep his house after he broke off our engagement, right?"

"Yeah, you did. And I have to admit, that was really nice of him. Most guys wouldn't even let you keep the ring."

Jaelle snorted a laugh.

"It's not like he's still paying the rent. Anyway, I'm going through the boxes of junk he left in the basement, and some of this stuff is really cool. Here, I'll take a picture of this helmet I just found so you can see."

Amber waited, and then she got a text with a picture. The helmet was really dark, like an iron skillet.

"Wow, that is cool."

"Isn't it? Here, I'm going into video chat to try it on so you can see."

Amber laughed.

"Okay."

There was a pause as Jaelle set the phone down and ran around in front of the camera holding the helmet.

"Are you watching? I can't tell."

"Yeah, I can see you."

Jaelle held the helmet over her head.

"Here goes."

Amber thought this whole idea of trying on the helmet was silly, but Jaelle was hurting inside from losing John, even though she tried to play it off like she wasn't. So Amber humored her. She felt terrible about going on and on about herself and Tomas.

But she soon forgot all about those worries.

And then some.

Because as soon as Jaelle put the helmet on...

She disappeared.

Amber screamed.

Kelsey came running in.

"What's the matter? You look like you've seen a ghost — and I certainly hope you haven't discovered that ghosts are real. Please tell me they aren't." Her friend had been smiling up to that point, but now her face grew serious. "Wow, something's really spooked you. What is it?"

Too shocked to even speak, Amber pushed play on the video of the call and handed her phone to Kelsey.

Kelsey gasped.

"Well, at least we'll be able to see it in her dreams."

"Huh? See what?"

"That was a Roman helmet Jaelle put on, from the period when they were building Hadrian's Wall."

Amber made a sour face.

"I'm not excited about the Romans."

Kelsey's face had cracked into a huge grin.

"Me neither, but the Romans built that wall to keep out of England the people they called savages."

"And?"

"And Jaelle just went back to the time of the Celts."

AFTERWORD 1

The next box set in the Druids Bidding Series is RenFaire Druids. It is a prequel about how Tavish and Tomas's parents met, Dall and Emily.

If you would rather skip to Jaelle's story, then go on ahead to Time of the Celts.

There are links on the next page. If Amazon throws you out of this book, then you can page back to get to the links.

See you there!

Jane

AFTERWORD 2

RenFaire Druids (the next box set in this series)

Time of the Celts (Jaelle's story)

Or see many more books in the Druids Bidding world on Jane Stain's Amazon Page

Sign up for new release alerts at www.janestain.com

Made in the USA
Middletown, DE
20 July 2019